MIND GAMES

Also by Nora Roberts

Series

Irish Born Trilogy
Born in Fire • Born in Ice • Born in Shame

Dream Trilogy
Daring to Dream • Holding the Dream • Finding the Dream

Chesapeake Bay Saga
Sea Swept • Rising Tides • Inner Harbor • Chesapeake Blue

Gallaghers of Ardmore Trilogy
Jewels of the Sun • Tears of the Moon • Heart of the Sea

Three Sisters Island Trilogy
Dance Upon the Air • Heaven and Earth • Face the Fire

Key Trilogy
Key of Light • Key of Knowledge • Key of Valor

In the Garden Trilogy
Blue Dahlia • Black Rose • Red Lily

Circle Trilogy
Morrigan's Cross • Dance of the Gods • Valley of Silence

Sign of Seven Trilogy
Blood Brothers • The Hollow • The Pagan Stone

Bride Quartet
Vision in White • Bed of Roses • Savor the Moment • Happy Ever After

The Inn Boonsboro Trilogy
The Next Always • The Last Boyfriend • The Perfect Hope

The Cousins O'Dwyer Trilogy
Dark Witch • Shadow Spell • Blood Magick

The Guardians Trilogy
Stars of Fortune • Bay of Sighs • Island of Glass

Chronicles of The One
Year One • Of Blood and Bone • The Rise of Magicks

The Dragon Heart Legacy
The Awakening • The Becoming • The Choice

The Lost Bride Trilogy
Inheritance

eBooks by Nora Roberts

Cordina's Royal Family
Affaire Royale • *Command Performance* • *The Playboy Prince* • *Cordina's Crown Jewel*

The Donovan Legacy
Captivated • *Entranced* • *Charmed* • *Enchanted*

The O'Hurleys
The Last Honest Woman • *Dance to the Piper* • *Skin Deep* • *Without a Trace*

Night Tales
Night Shift • *Night Shadow* • *Nightshade* • *Night Smoke* • *Night Shield*

The MacGregors
The Winning Hand • *The Perfect Neighbor* • *All the Possibilities* • *One Man's Art* • *Tempting Fate* • *Playing the Odds* • *The MacGregor Brides* • *The MacGregor Grooms* • *Rebellion/In from the Cold* • *For Now, Forever*

The Calhouns
Suzanna's Surrender • *Megan's Mate* • *Courting Catherine* • *A Man for Amanda* • *For the Love of Lilah*

Irish Legacy
Irish Rose • *Irish Rebel* • *Irish Thoroughbred*

Jack's Stories
Best Laid Plans • *Loving Jack* • *Lawless*

Summer Love • *Boundary Lines* • *Dual Image* • *First Impressions* • *The Law Is a Lady* • *Local Hero* • *This Magic Moment* • *The Name of the Game* • *Partners* • *Temptation* • *The Welcoming* • *Opposites Attract* • *Time Was* • *Times Change* • *Gabriel's Angel* • *Holiday Wishes* • *The Heart's Victory* • *The Right Path* • *Rules of the Game* • *Search for Love* • *Blithe Images* • *From This Day* • *Song of the West* • *Island of Flowers* • *Her Mother's Keeper* • *Untamed* • *Sullivan's Woman* • *Less of a Stranger* • *Reflections* • *Dance of Dreams* • *Storm Warning* • *Once More with Feeling* • *Endings and Beginnings* • *A Matter of Choice*

Nora Roberts & J. D. Robb

Remember When

J. D. Robb

Anthologies

From the Heart • *A Little Magic* • *A Little Fate*

Moon Shadows
(with Jill Gregory, Ruth Ryan Langan, and Marianne Willman)

The Once Upon Series
(with Jill Gregory, Ruth Ryan Langan, and Marianne Willman)

Once Upon a Castle • *Once Upon a Star* • *Once Upon a Dream* •
Once Upon a Rose • *Once Upon a Kiss* • *Once Upon a Midnight*

Silent Night
(with Susan Plunkett, Dee Holmes, and Claire Cross)

Out of This World
(with Laurell K. Hamilton, Susan Krinard, and Maggie Shayne)

Bump in the Night
(with Mary Blayney, Ruth Ryan Langan, and Mary Kay McComas)

Dead of Night
(with Mary Blayney, Ruth Ryan Langan, and Mary Kay McComas)

Three in Death

Suite 606
(with Mary Blayney, Ruth Ryan Langan, and Mary Kay McComas)

In Death

The Lost
(with Patricia Gaffney, Ruth Ryan Langan, and Mary Blayney)

The Other Side
(with Mary Blayney, Patricia Gaffney, Ruth Ryan Langan,
and Mary Kay McComas)

Time of Death

The Unquiet
(with Mary Blayney, Patricia Gaffney, Ruth Ryan Langan,
and Mary Kay McComas)

Mirror, Mirror
(with Mary Blayney, Elaine Fox, Mary Kay McComas, and R. C. Ryan)

Down the Rabbit Hole
(with Mary Blayney, Elaine Fox, Mary Kay McComas, and R. C. Ryan)

Also Available . . .
The Official Nora Roberts Companion
(edited by Denise Little and Laura Hayden)

MIND GAMES

NORA ROBERTS

ST. MARTIN'S PRESS
NEW YORK

First published in the United States by St. Martin's Press, an imprint of St. Martin's Publishing Group

MIND GAMES. Copyright © 2024 by Nora Roberts. All rights reserved. Printed in the United States of America. For information, address St. Martin's Publishing Group, 120 Broadway, New York, NY 10271.

www.stmartins.com

Design by James Sinclair

Library of Congress Cataloging-in-Publication Data is available upon request.

ISBN 978-1-250-28969-8 (hardcover)
ISBN 978-1-250-28970-4 (ebook)

Our books may be purchased in bulk for promotional, educational, or business use. Please contact your local bookseller or the Macmillan Corporate and Premium Sales Department at 1-800-221-7945, extension 5442, or by email at MacmillanSpecialMarkets@macmillan.com.

First Edition: 2024

10 9 8 7 6 5 4 3 2 1

In memory of my grandmother,
who was a force of nature, and knew things

PART I
Tragedy

Wrath is cruel, and anger is outrageous,
but who is able to stand before envy?
—Proverbs 27:4

Give sorrow words: the grief that does not speak
Whispers the o'er-fraught heart and bids it break.
—William Shakespeare

Chapter One

For Thea, the very best part of summer started the second week of June. The last day of school earned a big red heart, and meant she could start swimming and splashing around in the backyard pool, which she loved. She could ride her bike and play with her friends every day. Though they didn't call it playing anymore. Now they hung out.

She was twelve, after all.

She liked cookouts, and long summer days, and she especially liked no homework.

But every year, just about a week after that big red heart day, she piled in the car with her mom; her dad; her little brother, Rem; and their dog, Cocoa. They started the long drive from Fredericksburg, Virginia, to Redbud Hollow, Kentucky.

Her mom grew up there but had gone off to Virginia to college, where she met John Fox on the very first day in the very first class.

And the rest, like they said—or like her dad said—was history.

They married the summer after their sophomore year, and ten months, two weeks, and three days after, she'd come along. Not quite two years later, Rem popped out.

Now her dad designed houses and her mom decorated them. Their company, Fox and Fox Homes, did just fine.

She knew stuff. Grown-ups didn't think kids knew much of anything important, but she did. She knew her grandparents, her dad's parents, were rich and snooty, and didn't think much of her mom—the girl from eastern Kentucky.

But her dad's parents lived out in San Diego, so they didn't have to see them much. Which was more than fine with Thea. She didn't have to hear Grandmother—that was the snooty name they had to call her—think her thoughts about how her mom laughed too loud or would never shake the Appalachian dust off her shoes.

She could hear those thoughts if she tried hard enough, and when she had to visit Grandmother, she couldn't seem to help it.

She thought so *loud*.

Grandmother and Grandfather didn't seem to care that John and Cora Fox were happy, and even successful. That they all lived in a pretty house in a nice neighborhood. That Thea and Rem (or as they insisted, Althea and Remington) did even better than okay in school.

But Grammie cared. They all talked on the phone every week on Sunday, and at Christmastime, Grammie drove up with her truck full of presents she'd made. Most of the time her uncles Waylon and Caleb came, too, so they had a big family party, and the house was all full of music and lights and the smells of baking.

That was her second favorite time of the year.

But the best time, even though they had to drive for seven whole hours, and sometimes more, came in June.

They always left bright and early, and passed the time with Road Trip Bingo. Rem usually fell asleep, and sometimes she did, too, but they always gave a hoot and holler when they crossed the line into Kentucky.

They stopped for barbecue and hush puppies—that was tradition. She'd be hungry when they did, but always wished they could just keep going, keep going and get there.

Keep going over roads that started to twist and climb, over bridges that spanned rushing rivers.

She loved watching the mountains happen, those rolls and peaks of deep green that were somehow sort of blue, too. The plateaus and ridges, the forests and streams.

And when she was in it, deep in those rolls and peaks where the road wound and wound, she knew her pretty house and really nice neighborhood in Virginia could never compare.

She wondered how her mother could leave it all, and whenever she asked, Mom always said: "I had to meet your daddy, didn't I? Or else you wouldn't be here asking me."

She knew it was more. She knew her mother had wanted that pretty house and nice neighborhood. Knew, in her heart, her mother had wanted to shake that Appalachian dust off her shoes.

She didn't say so, or else Mom would get that look in her eye. She didn't want Thea to know things, like when Dad said: "Where the hell did I put my keys this time?"

And she knew he'd tossed them on the kitchen counter, then laid some of his paperwork over them, even though she'd been outside when he did it.

So she knew regardless of the fact that her mother loved Grammie, she wanted something more than the house in the hollow and wanted less than what she'd left behind.

She didn't think about that now, as they skirted around the mountain town of Redbud Hollow with its climbing streets and shops like Appalachian Crafts, where Grammie sold her soaps and candles and such.

Because at last, at last, they were almost there. The sun still shined bright. Through the sunroof she watched a hawk circle. Deer walked through the woods here. Sometimes she saw deer in the neighborhood yards back home, but it wasn't the same!

Her mom always drove the last leg of the trip, along the roads she'd once walked as a girl. And when they rounded the last curve, Thea saw the house.

Painted blue as the sky, with shutters—real ones—and the posts of the long front porch green as the hills, it sat back from the skinny, snaking road. Azaleas and mountain laurel flowed along the front. Dozens of colorful bottles hung from the branches of a redbud tree.

Thea had never seen it blooming, except in pictures, because school, but she could imagine it.

In the back there would be gardens—flowers and vegetables and herbs—and the chicken coop where Grammie's ladies clucked and pecked. The goat named Molly had a pen, the cow called Aster had two small fields where Grammie moved her from one to the other every few months.

There was a little barn and a garden shed. A stream meandered through and slid right into the woods.

And the hills rose up, all around.

Duck and Goose, Grammie's two coonhounds, raced around the house toward the car.

In the car, Cocoa rose up to wag and whine.

The minute Thea opened the door, Cocoa leaped over and out. The three dogs began to sniff butts to reacquaint themselves.

The door of the house opened, and Lucy Lannigan stepped out on the wide front porch.

Her hair, the true black she'd passed to her daughter and grand-daughter, had a thick white streak, like a wave, from the center down to the tip on the right side. She'd passed on the lapis-blue eyes as well with their long lids.

Her height, five-ten with a willow-stem frame, had missed Cora, but from the length of Thea's and Rem's legs, it wouldn't miss her grand-children.

In her faded jeans and simple white shirt, she threw open her arms.

"How many can I hug at once? Let's find out."

Like Cocoa, Thea and Rem jumped out, and they ran into the open arms of the woman who smelled like bread fresh from the oven.

Lucy said, "Mmm-mmm-mmm!" as she hugged and squeezed, then managed to gather in Cora and John. "Now my heart's full to brim-ming. I've got all the love in the world and more right here on my front porch. I hope you're hungry, 'cause I've fried up enough chicken for an army after a hard battle."

"I'm starving," Rem told her, and brought on her rolling laugh.

"I can always count on you for that. There's fresh lemonade for some, and some damn good apple wine for others. Your rooms are all ready if you want to stow your bags away."

"Let's do that." John kissed both Lucy's cheeks. "Then I could sure go for that apple wine."

The house always smelled so good. To Thea it smelled of the moun-tains and good cooking, of herbs and flowers.

She'd only been to Grammie's house in the summer, so she'd never seen a fire crackling away in the living room with its big old blue couch and armchairs covered in what her grandmother called cabbage roses.

And there were flowers from the garden, and wildflowers from the hills, the candles Gram made herself, and always the latest school pictures of her and Rem in frames.

Her dad helped carry the bags up while her mom went into the kitchen with Grammie. Because, her dad always said, they liked a little mom-and-daughter time.

Thea didn't mind because she'd have two whole weeks.

She loved her room here with its view of the mountains. Though it was smaller than her room at home, she didn't mind that either.

She liked the old iron bed, painted white as snow, and the quilt covered with violets her grandmother's grandmother had made. White daisies stood happy in a little glass pitcher on the dresser. Though the room had a tiny closet, it also had what Grammie called a chifforobe.

Thea liked it better than any closet.

And she liked knowing her mother had slept in that room as a girl.

Rem had the room right across—Uncle Waylon's childhood bedroom—and then her parents would take Uncle Caleb's old room for the night. One more bedroom Gram had set up for sewing and things, then she had the biggest room with the four-poster bed that had come down to her.

A bed she'd been born in.

Thea couldn't quite imagine that one.

Because she wanted to feel like she was really *here*, she unpacked even when she heard Rem run back downstairs.

After she put her clothes away, the room became hers.

Downstairs, she took her time. The living room, then the parlor with its old TV and its much, much older big radio. The easy chair and divan, the books on shelves, the basket of yarn, the cuckoo clock on the wall.

Then the room with the upright piano, the banjo, the guitar, the mandolin, the dulcimer.

Grammie could pick up any of those if she had the mood and play. She knew Waylon could do the same, not only because Grammie said so, but he always brought a banjo or guitar to play at Christmastime.

Plus, he made his living playing them in Nashville, where he lived. Caleb could play, too, but he'd gone to college to study theater and acting and stuff, so he did that.

Her mom played sometimes, but Gram said Cora's instrument was her voice. And Thea knew that for truth, as her mom—especially when she was happy—sang like an angel.

But in the whole house, the kitchen was her favorite.

It was massive—one of her current favorite words. Big enough for the kitchen table Gram's grandpappy had built out of solid oak. It had a six-burner stove Gram bought when she'd made some changes, but she wouldn't part with the table.

She called it the heart of her kitchen, and her kitchen the heart of her home. She had lots of cupboards and long, long counters, a whole wall of shelves holding pots and cookbooks of family recipes and glass jars of rice and oats and pasta and grits, beans, colorful jars of pickled beets and chowchow and peppers and apple butter and more.

Open to it, the craft kitchen with its big stove had sturdy work counters and shelves holding bottles and jars and tools. Grammie grew herbs in pots in the sunny windows and had more hanging to dry.

There she made her candles, her soaps, her lotions and medicinals for her business.

In what had been a pantry, Grammie kept a supply of what she'd made, in case she wanted to give a gift, or somebody came down from the hills to barter.

Always curious, Thea opened the door and breathed it all in as she looked at the shelves.

To her, it smelled like a garden planted in heaven.

Roses and lavender, rosemary and sage, heliotrope and pine, lemon and orange and fresh mown grass.

Grammie called her business Mountain Magic, and that's how Thea thought of it.

She saw the apple stack cake still wrapped on the counter, so she'd keep room for dessert after fried chicken.

Outside, Rem already ran around with the dogs, while her parents and Grammie sat on the back porch with their apple wine.

Through the open windows she could hear the dogs barking, the chickens clucking, her grandmother's laugh.

She made a picture of it in her head, one she could take out sometime when she felt lonely or sad about something.

"There's that girl," Lucy said when Thea came out. "Get yourself some lemonade before Rem sucks that pitcher dry. Being a boy of ten's thirsty work."

"Needs to run off being cooped up in the car." Smiling, Cora reached over, brushed a hand down Thea's arm. "All settled in?"

"Uh-huh. Can I go see the animals?"

"Sure you can."

"A little later, you and Rem can give them their evening meal. Go on." Lucy gave her a little pat on the butt. "Stretch those long legs. We'll call when it's time for supper.

"Growing like weeds," Lucy murmured when Thea raced off. "Both of them. I'm so grateful you give them over to me for this time every summer."

"They love you." John reached for the jug, topped off their wine. "They love it here. And, I can't lie, two weeks alone with my bride?" He winked at Cora. "That's a gift."

"And they'll come home with half a million stories." Cora leaned back in her rocking chair, relaxed as the travel fatigue, and the faint headache that came with it, drained away. "The fox the dogs chased away from the chicken coop, the fish they caught or almost caught, milking the cow, milking the goat, the old man leaning on his walking stick who came by for some ointment for his arthritis."

"And," John added, "they'll bring home soap you helped them make, and ask why we never have buckwheat cakes for breakfast."

"I love them to pieces and back again. One of these days, Waylon and Caleb are going to settle down and give me more grandbabies— since the two of you seem to be finished there."

"We hit the grand prize with two." John toasted her.

"Well, from where I sit you surely did. I'm hoping my boys and their ladies-to-come will be as generous as you, and give me the time to watch those babies grow. Means the world to me."

"We're never going to talk you into moving to Virginia, are we, Mama?"

Lucy just smiled out at the mountains.

"I'm an Appalachian woman, darling. I'd wither away if you planted me somewhere else. Now, I'm going to go make some buttermilk biscuits. No, you sit right there," she ordered. "You've had a long drive, and I haven't. Tonight I get to spoil my grown-up babies, too."

"You spoil us all, Lucy, and we're grateful you do, you will."

When Lucy went inside, John reached over to squeeze Cora's hand. "Go on in and talk to her about our compromise. See what she thinks while the kids are occupied."

With a nod, Cora rose and went inside.

She sat at the island while Lucy grated butter she'd frozen into a bowl of flour.

"You got your something-to-talk-about face on."

"I do, and we think it's a good thing. I hope you will."

"I've got my I'm-listening ears on, baby mine."

"I miss you, Mama."

Lucy's hands stilled a moment, and her heart swam into her eyes. "Oh, my darling girl."

"I know your home's here, and you know I made mine in Virginia. But it's not so big a distance, not really. I miss my brothers, too. Never thought that'd happen," she added, and made Lucy laugh.

"They surely did dog their big sister. But they loved you, just like those two outside love each other. Brothers and sisters, they gotta squabble. It's a job of work."

"Well, we did our job of work, that's for certain. Caleb's moving to New York City."

"He told me." After tossing the butter and flour, Lucy set it in the refrigerator to chill a few minutes. "Just like he told me there was this newfangled invention called an airplane, and he could use it to come back to the homeplace and see me. And how I could do the same to go up there so he could take me to see a Broadway show."

"It's a chance for him to do what he loves, and what he wants, but we won't see as much of him as we did when he lived in DC. And Waylon's mostly in Nashville or traveling."

"My minstrel man."

"Mama, you know John's family . . ." She trailed off, glanced out toward the back porch. "They don't think much of us. Me anyway. And they've got no interest in the kids."

"That's their very great loss." Lucy's mouth tightened before she said something she shouldn't. "I feel sorry for them and their closed-off hearts."

Or she tried to.

"That man out there—the one running around with his children after driving all this way? If I could've imagined just the right husband for my girl, just the right daddy for my grandbabies, I couldn't have imagined better than John Fox. He's as dear a son to me as the ones I birthed."

"I know it. More, John knows it. And you're more a mama to him than his own."

"Another blessing for me. Another reason to feel sorry for the one who can't see the gifts laid in front of her."

Cora rose to make sure John was out of earshot. "You know what they did for Thea's twelfth birthday? Sent her a card with twelve dollars inside. One for each year. It came a week late on top of that. It's not the money, Mama," she said quickly. "We don't care they've got piles of it. We're all doing fine. It was . . . The card said 'Happy Birthday, Althea. Your Grandparents.' That's all it said."

Lucy picked up her wine, took a small sip. "Did you have Thea write them a thank-you?"

"I didn't have to. She sat down and wrote one: 'Dear Grandparents, Thank you very much for the birthday wishes and the twelve dollars. I hope you both are well. Your granddaughter, Thea.'"

Lucy gave a nod of approval. "You're raising her right."

"As I was. It burned me inside, Mama, and it hurt John. He tries to not let it hurt, but it does. I don't want our family to ever grow apart and careless like that."

"We never could, darling."

"But people get busy. You're busy, Mama, with your home, your business. Caleb and Waylon are busy, and like you said, they'll likely start families of their own and get busier yet. John and I, we're busy raising the kids, with our business. And, Mama, twice a year, it's not enough."

She wandered as she spoke while Lucy watched and thought: my clever, restless girl.

"You made an apple stack cake," Cora murmured.

"Of course I did. It's John's favorite."

"I don't know why things like an apple stack cake and flowers on the table mean more to me now than they did when I was a girl in this house, or why this house is more special to me now than it was when I was living in it."

"You were looking ahead, and away, Cora."

"And you let me. One day, Thea's going to look away, so I understand what I didn't, how much it costs to let a child live their own."

"It costs," Lucy agreed as she got the bowl and the buttermilk out of the refrigerator. "But it pays off so in pride of what you see that child become. And I'm so proud, Cora, of the life you've made, of the person you are. So proud."

"I didn't appreciate you enough when I was a child."

"Oh, stop that."

"I didn't," Cora insisted as she watched, as she had countless times before, her mother make a well in the flour and grated butter before pouring the buttermilk into it.

It made her smile, so she asked what she'd asked countless times before. "Why do you stir it with that wooden spoon fifteen times? Exactly."

Their eyes met as Lucy smiled back, and answered as she had countless times before. "Because fourteen's not enough, and sixteen's too many."

"I didn't appreciate, Mama, how hard it was for you, especially after Daddy died. How hard you worked to keep it all going, to keep a roof over our heads, food in our bellies, to push your business on so you could. I didn't appreciate it enough because you made it look—"

Cora shook her head as she wandered the big kitchen again.

"Not easy, not really easy—but natural. Like loving us was natural, and keeping the music playing, making sure we got our homework done, brushed our damn teeth, all of it, just natural, just life. Saving, like you and Daddy started, so we could go to college, just part of the whole."

"Your daddy didn't want his boys in the mines. He went down so they never would. He wanted—we wanted—our children to get a good education and have choices."

Lucy dusted the counter with flour, turned the dough on it, dusted the top, then rubbed more on her old wooden rolling pin.

"Your choices, the lives you're making with them, honor your daddy, and his sacrifices."

"And yours, because you clearly made sacrifices, too. I see that, now. So twice a year isn't enough, not for family."

Lucy rolled the dough into a rectangle, then folded the short ends together and rolled once more. With a glance at her daughter, she did the same again.

"You've got a plan in there somewhere."

"We do, John and I. We'd like to come down more. The Easter break at school, and Thanksgiving."

Once again, Lucy's hands stilled. "Cora, I'd be thrilled. And oh so grateful."

"But that's not all. We know it's harder for you to travel. You have to have someone tend the animals, but if you could pick just one time to come up, even for a few days, or with Caleb in New York, maybe we could all go up there for a few days, or to Nashville to Waylon. And the kids, they love it here and those two weeks you give them means the world because that's the start of the summer. We like to take them for a week at the beach before school starts again."

"They love that week. I get lots of pictures and stories."

After the last fold and roll, Lucy dipped her round cutter in flour and made her dough rounds.

"We want you to come. We want everybody to come if they can. So we've rented a great big house on the beach in North Carolina. A week in August. We're going to fly you there in that newfangled airplane."

"Fly? But—"

"Please don't say no. Waylon says he'll talk Granny into it, and you know he can talk a man dying of thirst to hand over his last drop of water. We hardly ever see her since she married Stretch and moved down to Atlanta. We'd have a real Riley-Lannigan-Fox family reunion. And if Uncle Buck, Aunt Mae, and the cousins want to come, well, we'll just get a second house to hold us all."

Lucy had never been on a plane in her life—though she'd seen that coming in her future with a son living in New York City.

And she saw, very clearly, how much this meant to her girl. The girl who'd always looked forward and away had looked back some. And looked toward family.

"Well, I guess I'd better get these biscuits in the oven, get this meal on the table so I can think about buying myself a bathing suit."

"Mama!" With a hoot of delight, Cora threw her arms around Lucy. "Oh, the kids are going to go crazy when we tell them. I want them to have what I had growing up, and damn it, I want John to have what he didn't."

"Then let's get the table set. We'll call them in to wash up, and lower the boom."

They feasted on fried chicken and potato salad, snap beans and buttermilk biscuits. And Cora had it right, the kids went crazy.

It filled Lucy's heart to have them filling her home and saturating it with the happiness they generated.

Her restless girl had found her center, and reached a point in her life where she wanted to open it to the people and places of her origin.

She'd had a part of that, Lucy thought, and now an invitation to take a bigger part.

In later years, she'd look back on this simple family meal at summer's beginning and remember the sound of children's voices, so high and bright. She'd remember the laughter in her daughter's eyes, and the utter contentment in the eyes of the man who was a son to her.

She'd think of the breeze fluttering through the open windows, and the screen door where the dogs lay just outside hoping for scraps.

She'd remember how the evening sun had slanted its light over the mountains and how blue the sky held above them.

She'd remember all of it, and hold on tight.

Chapter Two

In the morning, Lucy mixed up batter for buckwheat pancakes, another favorite of her son-in-law's. She already had bacon and sausage keeping warm in the oven, and coffee done when John came in.

"Thought I heard some stirring up there."

He raked a hand through his curling mop of brown hair. "I haven't managed to shave, and you've already fed the chickens, gathered eggs, milked the cow and the goat, fed the dogs."

"Why's a man need to shave on a quick little holiday?"

"I'll bet you haven't had a holiday, little, quick, or otherwise, since Christmas." He shook his head as he went for coffee. "You work too hard, Lucy."

"I love what I do."

She'd twined her hair into a braid today, and he ran a hand down it in one of his easy gestures of affection. "It shows. You know, I look at you and I can see how Cora's only going to get more beautiful. Reminds me how lucky I am we happened to sit next to each other in that lecture hall the first day of college."

"And I say luck had nothing to do with it. If I've ever seen two people meant to be, it's you and Cora. Now sit down there and tell me what's on your mind. I can see it without looking."

"I wanted to tell you how much it means you're willing to travel, and to have us come down when I know you're going to do just what you're doing now, and more. Making big, amazing meals. She's been pining the last couple of months."

Sitting, he sighed a little. "It was that stupid birthday card, the ten and two ones inside that snapped it. It didn't bother Thea, but she doesn't expect anything from them. I don't expect anything from them, but Cora? She kept hoping they'd warm up."

"Some don't have the warm in them."

"Ain't that the truth." His words carried simple resignation. "Still, they're warm enough to their other grandchildren, and generous, reasonably attentive. They expected me to marry . . ."

"As befits your station, or theirs."

He shrugged. "It doesn't matter how much we love each other, what a wonderful mother she is, what a solid partner in business she is. She tried so hard, Lucy, and none of it mattered to them. I married too young and to someone they disapprove of, so I'll always be a disappointment. It doesn't matter to me."

"It mattered to her."

"Too much, if you ask me. My sister's daughter is Rem's age. For her birthday, they bought her a horse."

"A horse. An actual horse?"

"That's right. She's been taking equestrian lessons for about a year now. So they bought her a horse. They forgot Rem's tenth altogether, but for some reason that didn't snap it. It was that card, the ten and two ones that did it. The imbalance of it, the fact that she finally realized our kids would never matter to them."

"All it makes me wonder, John"—she turned away to heat up her big cast-iron skillet—"is how they managed to help make someone like you."

"And I wonder sometimes if I'd be who I am if Cora Lannigan hadn't sat down beside me and smiled."

"Meant to be," Lucy reminded him.

"Meant to be." He toasted her with his coffee, and drank. "She stopped letting what they thought or felt matter, which is a relief to me. And she started pining for you, her brothers, for what she knew she had with all of you and tried too hard to make with them. Family time, closer ties."

"She needed to make her own before she really wanted what was always there. I'd say we're giving each other a gift. Now, I hear more stirring up there. You call them down, and I'll get these pancakes going."

He came around the counter first to hug her. "I love you, Lucy."

"John." She pressed a kiss to his cheek. "You're one of the bright lights in my life."

They had breakfast at the kitchen table as they had dinner the night before. The kids helped with the dishes, as that would be a daily chore during their stay, as would making their beds in the morning, helping with the laundry, and tending the animals.

They would help, as their mother and uncles had before them, weed the gardens, mow the grass, keep the house clean, and learn to cook some simple dishes.

Lucy pressed a container with a generous slice of apple stack cake on John.

"You take a taste of Kentucky with you."

"You know I will. Okay, Foxy Loxies, bring it in, and pretend you'll miss us."

"I'll miss you, Dad." Giggling, Thea snuggled in. "A little bit."

He laughed, hauled her up for a kiss, then did the same with Rem.

"I don't have to tell you to mind Grammie." Cora squeezed them hard enough to make them squeal. "I know you will. Y'all have fun now."

"Call when you get home," Lucy said, "so we know you got there safe."

When she hugged them, she felt a clutch in her belly. When it fisted over her heart, she hugged harder. "I'll miss you both, more than a little. Drive careful now, and look after each other."

She made herself let go. "I've got these two hooligans in hand, don't you worry."

With waves and blown kisses, they got in the car. Cora looked back as they drove away, then turned, looked forward.

"You and me, babe." John flicked a glance in the rearview, then smiled at her. "What should we do when we get home to a quiet, empty house?"

"I think we should open a bottle of wine and have really loud sex."

The smile turned into a grin. "Great minds."

With a kid on either side, and three dogs panting, Lucy watched the car until it drove out of sight.

She willed the pressure on her heart to release, then looked down at the kids. And quoted from a favorite book of hers, and theirs.

"Let the wild rumpus start!"

With a cheer, Thea executed a very solid cartwheel. Rem settled on making monkey noises.

Since she'd write in her journal that night, Thea paid attention to everything they did during the day.

They weeded the garden first because the mountain air held cooler than it would after noontime. If they forgot some of the names of the plants, Lucy helped them remember using rhymes.

"I had a friend named Hazel."

So that was basil.

"I try to imagine what will be."

And that was astilbe.

It made it all fun, and they all wore floppy hats.

Then they made butter, better than anything in the store, from the cream from Aster's milk. And Thea got to pour off the buttermilk to save it.

They both got to wash it in cold, cold water, then knead it—Rem said *Oooey-gooey* a lot.

And Grammie took some of it and added honey for what she called a sweet spread.

For lunch they had leftover chicken, and biscuits with the sweet spread they made themselves.

They took a walk in the woods and the hills with the dogs. Lucy carried spray she made to chase bears away if they needed to. But they didn't.

They stopped at a house that was really a kind of cabin even Thea knew had seen better days. A scrawny gray cat raced up a tree and hissed at the dogs from a branch but they didn't pay him any mind.

A boy younger than Rem sat on the saggy front porch playing with a little car. He was what she'd heard Grammie call a towhead because his hair was so blond it was nearly white.

"Hi there, Sammy. Is your mama home?"

"Yes'm, Miss Lucy." He yelled out, "Ma! Miss Lucy's come around."

A woman came to the door with a baby on her hip and a toddler clinging to her pants leg. The toddler had red, scaly rings on both arms.

"Afternoon, Miss Lucy." She shoved at her hair—a darker blond than the boy's. "These are your grandbabies? Lordy, the girl looks just like you."

"My pride and joy. Thea, Rem, say afternoon to Miss Katie."

"Afternoon," they said in unison while Thea tried not to stare at those weird red circles.

"I heard Sharona there had a problem."

"Picked up the ringworm. I've been trying to keep it clean. Got it on her scalp, too."

"I brought you some special soap. You want to use this." Lucy took a wrapped bar from her pack. "You wash her arms, her scalp with this, and dry it good. It's the moisture helps it spread, so dry it good with a clean cloth. Then take this."

She produced a small bottle. "And mix it with just a little water. You want to make a paste of it, and spread it on until it dries. It's turmeric," she added, "and won't do her any harm. It should help."

"I sure will. I thank you, Miss Lucy. I don't have—"

"You don't worry about payment. Next time Billy makes up a batch of his special, you send me some. And if what I brought you doesn't fix this pretty girl up, you send word to me."

"I'll do that. I'll do all that. I've got some catnip tea brewing in the sun out the back if y'all want to come in, have a cup."

"Oh, that sounds good, but we've got other calls to make. You go on, wash that sweet baby up. Let me know how she does."

"Bless you, Miss Lucy."

When they'd walked on, Lucy said, "Katie lost her daddy to the black lung some years back, and her mama this past winter to pneumonia. It's hard when you don't have people to lean on."

"What's the special?" Thea wanted to know.

"Oh, that's moonshine, honeypot. Billy does make some fine moonshine. He works hard, Billy does. Drinks a little too much of his own special, from time to time, but he works hard. He's a good husband and a good daddy."

They made more calls, a bar of soap here, a candle there. She took payment when the item had been requested, or a barter if payment wasn't ready.

By the time they got back, the dogs were ready for a snooze. Thea sat with her brother and Lucy on the back porch with cold lemonade and some sugar cookies.

"Do you know everybody in the mountains, Grammie?"

"Most hereabouts I do. Some want to keep to themselves, so I leave them be unless they come down for something or other. If somebody needs help, like Katie or old Carl with his bursitis, I help as I can. If I were to need help, help would come.

"I've got half a cord of wood over there for when the cold comes. And somebody'll bring more when I need it. That's how it works, and should."

Every day brought its own adventure. The chores remained the chores, but they were fun. Only at Grammie's could Thea milk a cow or watch Rem milk a goat. They fed the chickens and gathered eggs. Lucy taught them how to make redeye gravy to go with ham and eggs and grits.

Every night they could stay up past even their no-school bedtime and sit outside. Lucy knew all about the constellations, and Rem got really good at pointing them out by name.

One night they even saw a shooting star, and Rem decided he'd be an astronaut. And every night they took turns reading out loud from the book they chose at the start of the two weeks.

Any book they wanted, and Lucy never said: *No, not that book.*

Stories, she told them, held the world together. The best part was acting them out, using different voices. Thea had to admit Rem had a talent for it, the way his voice would change from growly to high and shaky or all prissy, depending. And he could make his face to match it, all wide-eyed or slitty-eyed, curled lips or big grins.

He hardly ever stumbled over the words, even the big ones.

Lucy said he was a natural-born actor, like his uncle Caleb, and since he'd be an astronaut, maybe he'd make movies on Mars.

Lucy always tucked Rem in first, and Thea could lie in bed and listen to their voices. Rem always had a million questions, especially at bedtime.

Then Lucy would come in, sit on the side of the bed.

"What's tonight's dream?"

"A magic forest."

"That sounds promising." Lucy stroked Thea's hair back. "Is it full of fairies and elves?"

"It has to be, and there's an evil sorceress and she's got evil dogs she conjured, with sharp wings and sharper teeth. She wants to rule the forest and everything else, so there has to be a big battle. And there's a young witch, elf, and fairy who have to, ah, band together and use their powers and like their wits to defeat the sorceress. And a quest, I think. I need to dream it out."

"I bet you will." Leaning down, Lucy kissed her cheek. "Maybe one day you'll write down the dreams and Rem can act them out. Go to dreaming now, my treasure. It's a whole new day tomorrow."

As she did almost every night, Thea closed her eyes and began to build the dream.

On mornings when she woke early enough, as she did on this last morning of innocence, she wrote down the dream. The forest with its thick trees, the blue leaves, the golden apples and purple pears. The evil sorceress, Mog, in her long, hooded black robes with strange symbols.

She added some illustrations even though she wasn't as good as she wanted to be at drawing. Her heroes—Gwyn, the witch; Twink, the fairy; and Zed, the elf—the evil winged dogs she called Wens.

She'd write down more later, as her story-dreams always stayed clear in her head.

She made her bed, because Grammie's rules, then brushed her teeth. Before she dressed, she checked to see if she'd sprouted breasts overnight.

No luck there, even though she'd started her period two days after her twelfth birthday in April.

She had a training bra, just in case, but felt stupid wearing it when nothing went in it. Plus, stupid name, she thought as she did her hair in a single braid like her grandmother's.

If she could've trained her breasts to come out, she would have!

She took a moment to study her face in the mirror and wondered how she'd look if she had a white streak in her hair like Grammie. It always struck her as kind of magical.

Then again, that white streak had appeared overnight, according to family lore, when the grandpa Thea never knew except in pictures and stories died in the mine.

When she got married, Thea didn't want her husband to die. She wanted the happy ever after, the way she made sure her dreams worked out.

Because she thought of Zachariah Lannigan, she walked to Lucy's room. A made-up bed because her grandmother always woke up first, the scent of the hills from the flowers on the dresser, and the breeze fluttering the sheers at the open windows. And the photo in a brown leather frame of a fair-haired man with eyes the color her mom called seafoam green when decorating.

He was handsome, not like her current dream boy, Nick Jonas, but handsome even though he was a lot older.

Lucy said she'd taken the picture herself on his thirtieth birthday.

He'd died, crushed in a cave-in, less than a year later.

"I'm sorry that happened." As she spoke to the picture, she touched the frame. "Grammie—Lucy—still misses you. I can feel it. My mom—that's Cora—thinks of you on Father's Day, and at Christmas, on your birthday, the day you died, and sometimes between. She thinks Rem, my brother, has your chin and your mouth, and I guess he sort of does. Anyway . . ."

She couldn't think of anything else to say to a photo in a frame, so she went out and downstairs.

Lucy sat on the back porch drinking her coffee.

"Morning, honeypot. Did you dream good?"

"Uh-huh. Mog's the evil sorceress. She has a pointy black beard and eyes that are almost black, too."

"Gracious, she even looks evil!"

"If she finds the Jewel of the Ancients before Gwyn and Twink and Zed do, she'll make slaves out of everybody and rule the forest and the hills and the valleys and river lands beyond it."

"They better get to work! I do admire your imagination, my own Thea, and like to wonder what you'll do with it. Rem's still sleeping."

She nodded, bent down to rub the heads on the two hounds sprawled at Gram's feet. "Cocoa's in the bed with him."

"They're tuckered, so we'll leave them be. We had a late night, didn't we? Why don't you take Aster into the barn for milking. We'll get the ladies fed, see what they've got for us. Molly's milk's going into soaps we'll make today."

"Rem's supposed to help with the chores."

With a quiet look, Lucy rose. "If you were tuckered, I'd ask him to do the same for you."

"Okay."

"And we'll have him wash the poop off the eggs."

"He actually likes doing that."

"A task enjoyed doesn't make it less done. When the milking's done, we'll put Aster in the next field for the day. After supper, we'll put her in the barn for the night. We've got a storm coming. A boomer."

Thea looked up, saw the blue sky with a few puffy white clouds. But she didn't question Lucy's weather forecasting.

"Okay."

"A storm's coming," she said again, and rubbed at her heart.

Thea led Aster to the barn. She actually liked doing that, but like Lucy said, it didn't make the chore less done.

She liked squirting Aster's milk in the pail, too. Some of her friends back home thought that was gross, but she liked it.

While Aster munched away on her grain, Thea washed her udder and teats, then dried them. She washed her hands, too, then used Lucy's udder cream.

Next came the stripping, to make sure the milk was clear of any dirt before she placed the bucket.

But then came the fun part, the way the milk pinged in the clean, empty bucket at first. Then it sort of plopped when the bucket started to fill.

She liked to sing along with the rhythm of the pings and plops, and thought Aster liked it, too. When the first quarter went soft, saggy, she moved onto the next, still firm to the touch.

She imagined outside her magic forest, in a green valley, another girl milked a cow. She wouldn't know about the struggles inside the forest, the quest, the battles that could make her a slave until good defeated evil.

As she milked, Thea added the girl to the dream. Then the milking was done. Or that part was.

When she carried the pail, now lidded, into the house to strain and pour into a glass jar, Rem stood at the sink washing today's eggs.

His hair stood up in spikes, and he had a sleep crease in one cheek.

"Did you feed Cocoa?"

"Yes, yeah, yep. She was *starving*. I'm starving."

"You're always starving."

"Grammie said we could have scrambled eggs and ham, cheesy grits, and toast with blackberry jam. We've still got eggs from yesterday, but I gotta wash the poop off these. Lots of poopy poop! Chicken shitty poop!"

Thea just rolled her eyes at him.

By the time they all sat down for breakfast—and now she was starving—the animals had been tended, the milk pails ran in the dishwasher for sanitizing, and the dogs barked away squirrels trying to get into the bird feeder.

The rest of the morning meant making soap.

Lucy had an order sheet from the shop in town, and some special requests, so they came first.

Lucy called it cold process making, but it was hot work!

She had special pots just for soap making, and all the oils and the colors, Molly's milk and lye water, the dried herbs and flowers.

Everybody had to wear long sleeves and gloves and goggles. And even though Thea was almost a teenager, Lucy said another year before she could handle the lye or pour the piping hot, raw soap into the molds.

But she got to weigh the oils and melt them, and after Lucy added the lye water, and it looked like batter, Rem got to add the colors, and she got to add Molly's milk.

They made a batch with dried lavender, another with rosemary, more with oatmeal, and Thea's favorite, one with mixed flower petals.

Lucy tapped the mold pans on the counter to get out air bubbles, then set them aside to cure, and that took a whole day before Lucy could cut it into bars. And she always waited two weeks before she put her rope tie and label on it.

It seemed like an awfully long time and a whole lot of work for soap, but Thea knew people bought Mountain Magic soap, and candles and lotions and bath salts and all the rest.

People from all over who came to Redbud Hollow to hike in the mountains or just stop off on their way someplace else went into Appalachian Crafts and bought things her grandmother made right in the craft kitchen.

It felt good knowing somebody would buy and use something she'd helped make.

"Now, that job of work's done." After stripping off her gloves, Lucy swiped a hand over her forehead. "I think we'll have a little bite of lunch, then we're going to box up some already made stock and take it into town, so that's another job of work."

"Can we get Popsicles?" Rem wanted to know.

"Now, that seems like a fine idea, as the day's sure heated up. And I've got another fine idea seeing as I've got two such hardworking helpers. What do you say if I made us a pizza for dinner, and followed that up with hot fudge sundaes with homemade vanilla bean ice cream?"

Rem's opinion was a cheer as he threw his arms around his grandmother. "With a cherry on top?"

"Can't be otherwise."

They bumped their way to town with the windows open and the radio on bluegrass. It seemed just the right way to drive to the hilly little town with its Front Street lined with shops and restaurants with names like Taste of Appalachia and Down Home Eats all hoping to snag some tourist dollars.

They helped carry the boxes to the back porch of the shop. A woman came out, clapped her hands. Thea remembered her from other visits, and knew the woman with the blond hair all curled up and the glasses hanging from a gold chain owned the shop.

"I swear, Lucy, we were just saying we hoped you'd bring us some

Mountain Magic today. Didn't we sell out of your lavender soap this morning. Sold the last bar, and the lavender candle and lotion, to a woman from Chicago, Illinois. And we're down to your last orange peel candle, and the one you call Forest Walk."

"Just in time then. Y'all remember Miss Abby, don't you?"

"These can't be your grandbabies!" She slapped a hand to her heart in what Thea knew was fake surprise, but it made her smile anyway. "Why, I swear they've both grown a foot since last summer."

"My precious weeds. Thea, you go on and carry the soap into the storeroom right in there. Rem, you can handle that box of the liquid soap. People sure do seem to like that nowadays."

Lucy lifted the first box of candles.

"I've got the door for you. And we've got some sugar-stick candy for you kids, if that's all right with your grandmama."

"They've earned it today."

"Y'all go on out there and tell Miss Louisa that Miss Abby said you're to get two sticks each, one for now, one for later."

"Thank you, Miss Abby."

Thea didn't really like the sugar-sticks, but she knew she could bribe Rem with hers later. Plus, she could poke around the shop. It would take time for Lucy and Miss Abby to settle accounts, to gossip some and ask about each other's families.

Her mom said it was the southern way, how everything took twice as long or more than it might because you had to pass the time and converse.

She didn't mind waiting, since she could look at the crafts, the ones out of wood, or out of glass or metal, or some of each. She could look at the paintings, and she could feel pride looking at the shelves holding her grandmother's work.

And when Lucy came out, she had to pass the time with Miss Louisa, and somebody named Jimmy who'd started working there before Christmas.

He had big, wide eyes and a long neck. Thea imagined him with pointy ears and decided he could be one of her dream elves.

Devouring his sugar-stick didn't stop Rem from devouring a grape Popsicle. She ate hers more slowly as they took a little walk down Front Street.

Lucy passed the time some more because she knew mostly everybody and mostly everybody knew her. They walked clear down to the bank, where Lucy made what she called a night deposit, since the bank closed at two.

"How do they know it's your money?"

Lucy looked down at Rem as they walked up the hill. "Well, the check's made out to me, and endorsed by me, and my name and account number's on the deposit slip."

"How do you know they won't just steal it and say they never got it at all?"

"You got a cynical mind in there, boy. One good reason is I've known the man who runs the bank since he was your age. He used to run around with my brother, Buck. I even went to a dance with him once because your grandpa was too slow to ask me. It was the last time he was slow."

"Did you kiss him on the mouth?"

"I did not, because I had my sights set on Zachariah Lannigan."

"Maybe he'll steal your money because you didn't kiss him on the mouth."

Tousling Rem's hair, Gram let out her rolling laugh. "I don't think he'd carry that one so long, especially seeing as he married my good friend Abigail Barns—that's Miss Abby? And they had three daughters together, and have five grandbabies."

"Men can hold a torch," Rem said wisely.

"Remington Fox, you never fail to entertain me."

"Do I have a purple tongue?" He stuck it out for examination.

"You surely do."

"It'd be fun if it always was."

"See that?" Gram slung an arm around his shoulder, then the other around Thea's. "You never fail."

Thea ranked it as the best day yet, and even wrote that in her journal. She'd milked Aster *all* by herself! And made an extra note to try to make the ham and gravy—with Rem's help (and maybe Dad's) for Mom for her birthday breakfast. She'd helped make soap, and though she wouldn't be there when it was ready to wrap all pretty, Gram would send pictures.

They'd gone into town and passed the time. When they got back, the dogs got treats for guarding the homeplace. They got to make ice cream, and stick it in the freezer to ripen for later.

She and Rem made their own pizzas from Grammie's dough and sauce while Grammie grated cheese. Thea made hers almost perfectly round. Rem said he made a hexagon pizza. Grammie added mushrooms and olives to hers so Rem made an *ick* face behind her back.

After the evening chores, after the stars came out, they had their sundaes on the back porch.

So many stars, Thea thought maybe her grandmother was wrong this time about a storm coming.

When Lucy came in for her good-night tuck, Thea set the journal aside.

"Tomorrow, a whole week's gone already."

Lucy sat on the side of the bed. "That means you got another whole week left. And aren't we all going to the beach together in a couple months? I'm going to stay with my family in a house on the beach for the first time in my life! Your mama and daddy? It sure is a loving thing they're giving us.

"And then, just a few months later, y'all are coming down here. I'm going to fix a Thanksgiving dinner even you can't imagine."

She tapped the side of Thea's head. "You wait and see."

"Everything'll look different then. I want to see it all looking different. Then you'll come for Christmas."

"I surely will. And you'll come for Easter."

"I'll see the redbuds bloom."

"You should, and the wild dogwoods. They do make a picture. You dreaming that dream tonight, or are you starting up a new one?"

"I haven't finished the other yet. The one in the magic forest of Endon."

"Endon."

"That's the name of the world. And I thought of a couple new characters. I have to see what happens."

"Then you dream good." Lucy leaned down for a kiss. "I want to know what happens, too."

Content, Thea snuggled in, closed her eyes. She drifted into the dream, so full of color and adventure and magic. While she dreamed, clouds began to smother the stars. In the distance, thunder grumbled.

When the storm came, as predicted, the magic dream became the nightmare.

Chapter Three

About the time Lucy put the ice cream in the freezer to ripen, Cora came out of a meeting. A very successful meeting, so she mentally patted herself on the back.

With the rest of her day clear, she decided to run some errands, and treat herself and John to a little celebration.

She could pick up the dry cleaning, stop by the printers for their newest flyers, hit her favorite wine store, swing by the market for a couple of steaks John could grill, then the farmer's market for salad makings, a couple of potatoes.

John loved her twice-baked potatoes.

She'd never be the cook her mother was, but she thought between them, she and John did just fine in that area.

Since she'd come from that successful meeting with a very fussy, very high-end client, she wore what she thought of as her Professional Woman look.

She'd rolled her hair back in a smooth twist and wore a sleeveless sheath in deep rosy pink paired with heeled sandals.

Instead of her Working Mother watch, she'd put on the Bulgari John gave her on their tenth anniversary. A ridiculous indulgence, she thought.

He'd had it engraved on the back, with *For All Time* inside a heart.

She loved it.

She drove from errand to errand with the radio on and a smile on her face.

The market made her think of the kids, and how whenever she or John made the mistake of letting them come along, they always, always ended up with two kinds of chips, two kinds of ice cream, two kinds of breakfast cereal, and God knew what else.

She missed them like crazy.

Not that this time as a couple wasn't lovely. And restorative. And, oh boy, sexy. But she missed their faces, their energy, even their squabbling.

Still, they talked at least every other day, and when they did, Thea and Rem's joy and excitement just poured out and filled her right up to the brim.

They loved the little farm, and her mother made sure they had a wonderful two weeks every summer. She paid attention; she showed them love in countless ways.

They'd have more of that love and attention now with the beach and Thanksgiving and Easter wrapped into it.

Those little breaks with family would pay off, for all of them.

With her mind on selecting the right steaks and her heart with her children, she didn't notice the man with a six-pack of Coke, a bag of Cheetos, and a package of Chips Ahoy! cookies in his basket.

But Ray Riggs noticed her.

He knew a rich bitch when he saw one, and he saw one now.

The snooty hairdo, the square-cut diamond on her wedding ring set, and that way-high-dollar watch.

To his eye, the watch just screamed: *I'm better than you, Ray.*

He hated her for it.

Dressed up like that to go to the grocery? Probably some rich bastard's trophy wife. The kind who looked down her nose at people like him.

And that just burned him.

The kind who had a lot of fancy cars and a fancy house. With a lot of high-dollar things, like that watch, inside. Cash in the safe for sure.

And that interested him.

Interested him enough he left his basket where it was and sauntered out of the store and to his car.

His car now, he thought, since he'd had it painted. The attention-grabbing cherry red its previous rich bastard owner had chosen now gleamed a discreet black. He'd switched out the license plate straight off, ditching the Maryland plate for one from Pennsylvania.

You could always find an out-of-state plate at a crap motel along the interstate.

At eighteen, with two solid years on the road, Ray knew about crap motels and disguising a stolen ride.

Now he sat in the black Mercedes sedan, registered to one Phillip Allen Clarke, who, along with his hag of a wife, Barbara Ann Clarke, lay moldering in some grave in some cemetery in fancy-ass Potomac, Maryland.

He'd scored four fancy watches from the Clarkes, and had pawned the man's Rolex in DC two weeks after he'd acquired it. The old hag had some solid jewelry, but he'd wait, wait a good long while, before he turned all that and the other watches.

Ray Riggs was nobody's fool.

Add he'd gotten the combination to the safe from the old bitch before he'd killed her, he'd scored seven thousand in cash. And twenty-three hundred more from their wallets and the little stash in the old hag's underwear drawer.

So, flush, he'd rented himself a beach house in Myrtle Beach.

Get himself a tan, case the rich tourists.

He'd stopped in this grocery for some road food because gas stations ripped you off there.

One day he might blow one up just to prove his point.

But now he figured the stop ordained. He felt damn sure of it when the rich bitch came out and put her single bag in a BMW—didn't anybody buy fucking American?

Time to change his ride anyway, and hadn't he lifted some West Virginia plates as backup?

Ordained.

He followed her out of the parking lot, followed her to a farmer's market. As if people like her gave one hard shit about farmers.

She came back to her car with another small, single bag.

No kids, he decided. Not enough food.

Maybe a yappy dog, and he'd have to take care of that.

She looked like the type for a yappy little dog, with a name like Fluffy or Chauncy.

Well, he'd kick Fluffy's yappy head in.

She drove to a neighborhood with big, important houses. MFMs, he called them. Mc-fucking-mansions.

He pulled over, knowing the Mercedes would give him enough cover, at least for a few minutes. People who lived in fancy houses didn't expect trouble from people who drove high-dollar cars.

Their mistake.

The garage door opened, she pulled in, it closed.

He sat another few minutes, thinking, planning, and didn't she come out the front door again?

She watered the flowers in pots on the front porch, the ones hanging from the posts. No yappy little dog came out with her, so maybe not.

As she set down the can, an SUV pulled into the drive. Another BMW.

It wasn't an old bastard that got out, but a younger one than he'd figured. A tall one, looked fit, so that changed things a little bit.

She walked down, he walked over.

They put their arms around each other, kissed each other.

He didn't hear any dog barking, didn't see any kids come out yelling: *Daddy's home.*

Most likely they lived just the two of them in that big-ass house. A house that should've been his. It all should've been his.

After tonight, some of it would be.

As they started inside, he drove down the street—at the precise speed limit—and circled around to see what he could see of the back.

Damned if he didn't spot a big back yard and a goddamn pool.

Too many people had too damn much as far as he was concerned. It seemed only right and fair he get a part of that, that he get what he wanted and what he deserved.

After all, where he'd send them, they couldn't take it with them.

Inside, Cora handed John the watering can. "Do you mind filling this up and putting it back on the porch? I want to go up and change."

"You sure look good."

"I do, don't I? Adele admired my shoes, and like every time I wear it around her, I could feel her envy for my wonderful watch. I'll tell you about the meeting—all good news—after I change out of these admirable shoes my feet are starting to complain about."

"You do that. I've got mostly good news on the Barnaby project. Or you could stay like that, let me take you out to dinner. Maybe a movie after?"

She paused on the steps, shot a flirty look over her shoulder. "Why, John Fox, are you asking me out on a date?"

"I'd be crazy not to."

"I absolutely accept, but I'd like to rain check that until tomorrow. I have plans tonight."

He angled his head, gave her a mock rough-guy look. "What plans?"

"Well, I'll tell you." Maintaining the flirty smile, she slipped off her shoes. "The plans include you grilling the steaks I picked up on the way home. Me making my famous twice-baked potatoes."

"World-renowned."

"A nice salad with makings from the farmer's market. Then there's the bottle of cab you especially like I picked up on my travels."

"That sounds like an excellent plan. What's for dessert?"

"I was thinking about the kids, and what a good time they're having. And here we are, just the two of us in the big, empty house." She swung the shoes by their straps. "So I thought I should have a lot of crazy sex with my husband."

"Best dessert ever."

"Does it beat Mama's apple stack cake?"

"Even that."

"Smart answer. Why don't you open that bottle, and I'll get the potatoes going when I come down? We can take a nice breather out back before you start the grill."

"I love you, Cora."

She kept walking but looked back again. Tapped her watch. "For all time."

He started back to the kitchen through the wide-open space, and paused at their gallery wall. The family wall, as he thought of it. Pictures of the two of them, then the three, then the four. Of the kids together. Of her mother, her brothers. Group shots, solo shots, they filled the wall.

They made him the luckiest son of a bitch in the world.

For all time.

He walked back to open the wine and fill the watering can.

Ray took the Mercedes to the car wash, and paid to have it detailed inside and out.

Clean as a whistle.

He found a place for a pulled pork sandwich with damn good slaw and fries. He sat outside, enjoying the heat, and while he ate, worked on a drawing of the house.

He figured he could've been an architect if he wanted, but why the hell would he want to draw up houses for somebody else to live in?

The way he saw it, the bedrooms would be upstairs, most likely with a fancy-ass master suite. If they had a safe, it'd be up there, too, or in a home office deal or some look-how-smart-we-are library.

His take? Cash, jewelry, and one of the cars.

Then he'd drive it on down to North Carolina, have a night in a crap motel. Hit the road in the morning and be well on his way to Myrtle Beach before anybody knew the rich bitch and bastard were dead.

Solid plan, he decided, and gulped down some Coke. Now he just had to find something to do for a few hours.

He went to the mall, wandered around, hit the arcade, then went to the movies. *Transformers: Revenge of the Fallen.*

It wasn't half bad.

About eleven, he took an easy cruise down that quiet, high-class street.

Too many lights on in the neighborhood yet. So he drove around awhile, noting the best routes to take to 95 heading south after his work was done.

By one, the street held quiet. Some porch lights, some security lights, a light here and there people left on in a house thinking it would scare a burglar off.

He'd worked out his plan of approach, so drove around to the back. Cutting the headlights, he pulled into a driveway, switched off the engine.

He waited, watching for a light to come on, a dog to bark, but the silence held. After pulling on his gloves, he gave the front seat, the steering wheel, the dash, another good wipe down. Then took the 9mm Smith & Wesson from under the driver's seat.

He'd scored that after his third kill—the slick lawyer and his bitch with the big fake tits.

He'd slit their throats like he had the couple before them, and Jesus! That was a fucking mess. Not that he didn't like seeing all that blood, but he didn't much care for having it all over him.

But along with the cash, the jewelry, he scored the gun.

Plenty of ammo, too. And he could buy more when he needed.

He didn't claim to be much of a shot, but at close range, it didn't matter.

He'd proven that his next time out.

He put the gun in the leather clip-on holster he'd scored from the same slick lawyer, then got his bags out of the trunk.

He traveled light, so he hitched on the backpack, shouldered the duffle.

He closed the trunk—quietly—wiped it down, then headed off.

His route took him across the yard of another rich man's house, over an easily scalable fence, and straight into the one he wanted with its sparkling pool and wide patio. And that second-story deck? Oh yeah, inside those doors, that's where the rich bitch with her fancy watch slept.

He skirted the pool, crossed the patio, where he noted the grill, one so big, so shiny, that it probably cost two or three grand.

Just seeing it standing there, shining, made his resentment build. He wished he had a bat or a pipe. If he'd had a bat or a pipe, he'd have beat the shit out of that grill.

Instead, he pulled in the rage. He had work to do, and his work needed a clear mind.

Breathing slow, breathing deep, he laid his gloved hands on the patio doors. And pushed that clear mind inside the house.

He had that talent, and always had.

His mother had tried to pray it out of him; his father had tried to logic it out of him.

They failed.

One day, one day down the road, he'd pay them back, pay them back for not giving him a big-ass house like this to grow up in, a pool to splash in.

He'd pay them back for cooking burgers on a crap charcoal grill instead of steaks on a big, shiny one.

But until that day, it was more than enough to live free, to use that talent to take from the rich and give to himself.

No dog in the house. Not now, but there'd been one. And kids, one, maybe two, but not now.

The only people inside now slept, as he predicted, upstairs.

And yet, he felt something like breath on the back of his neck, like someone watching, watching so close they were all but inside him.

A line of sweat dribbled down his temple at the thought, forced him to look behind.

Fuck that, he thought.

He'd seen no signs warning of a security system, and saw no signs of one.

He'd worked with his tightfisted old man one summer, installing security systems in big MFMs like this one, so he knew what to look for.

What to do if he found something.

But the only thing on the wide glass doors was a lock.

Rather than pick it—his skills were top-notch there—he got the glass cutter out of his backpack.

It didn't take long to slip his hand carefully through the circle he'd made and twist open the lock.

Once inside, he looked around at the big kitchen, the giant wall TV, the wide, L-shaped sofa they called a sectional.

He could see straight into the living room, the fireplace, another couch, chairs. Tables, lamps. Everything polished and pretty.

He should've lived in a house like this. These people weren't any better than he was. They just got lucky, and liked to shove that in his face.

In his heart he wanted to smash it all, but he had to keep that mind clear.

There was the mudroom—as if this type ever had mud on their shoes—with a door that would lead into the garage.

And a home office—like they actually worked for a living.

A whole wall of pictures. Look at them, smiling for the camera! Frolicking at the beach or . . .

He stopped at the photo of the girl. The girl who looked a lot like the rich bitch, except . . .

Something in the eyes, something that made his breath go shallow, clouded into his mind. Like she looked straight at him.

Into him.

Made his blood run cold; walked icy fingers up his spine.

His hands balled into fists, and for a moment he lost his sense of the house, of the people sleeping upstairs.

He had to relax his hands, wipe the sweat coating his palms on his jeans.

He had to relax his mind to see.

"Too bad you're not here. Too goddamn bad," he muttered. "I'd take care of you, too."

He imagined she had a trust fund, her and the boy—probably *baby brother*. Oh, he'd have taken care of them good, but they were probably at some rich-kid camp.

For another moment he lost track, just staring at that picture, into those blue eyes. They made his hands tremble, made him want to smash his fist into the face, close those blue eyes.

He had to turn his back on it, get his breath back, clear his mind.

Work to do, he reminded himself, scales to balance.

Drawing the pistol, he started up the stairs.

The roll of thunder didn't wake her, nor did the muffled pop of the gun firing. Trapped in the dream, Thea screamed and screamed. But like the rest, the scream stayed inside her head. She screamed, sobbed, helplessly watching until she finally ripped herself free.

In a flash of lightning, she sat shaking in bed, unable to draw enough breath to cry out. Forgetting she was nearly a teenager, she clawed her way out of bed. Her legs simply folded, so she dropped to the floor, dizzy, her stomach churning.

So cold her teeth began to chatter, she pushed herself up.

The floor seemed to tilt and rock like the deck of a boat caught in the storm that still raged outside.

She had to brace a hand on the wall as she walked to her grandmother's room.

She wanted Grammie's arms around her, Grammie's hand stroking her hair, Grammie's voice telling her it had been just a bad dream.

But when she reached the doorway of the bedroom, she saw Lucy sitting on the side of her bed. She heard her crying. She saw her shaking.

"Grammie. Grammie."

For the rest of her life, she'd remember that moment, the exact instant their eyes met. Eyes of the same color and shape, eyes drenched with tears and shock and grief.

And the spark that flashed between them, so sharp, so bright, like the lightning.

And the instant that followed that spark, when she knew her parents were dead.

She spilled to the floor like water from a cup.

Then Lucy's arms were around her. Lucy's hand stroked her hair.

But she didn't say the words because they would have been a lie.

"I saw—I saw—"

"Oh, God, Thea." Lucy rocked her, rocked them both on the floor in the doorway. "Darling, my baby."

She could hear Lucy's breath hitching in and out, feel the wild gallop of her heart.

"I have to call the sheriff. You hold on to me now. You hold on tight. He'll call the police up in Virginia so they can . . . they can check."

"You saw it, too. You saw it, too. But—"

"Let me call now. Hold on to me."

"I feel sick."

"I know, I know."

Because Thea's head lolled, and the floor rocked, Lucy half carried her to the bed.

"Try to breathe slow. If you have to get sick, don't you worry about it. Hold on to me, that's my girl, breathe slow. The dizzy'll pass."

When they got to the bed, Lucy wrapped a throw around her. "Put your head between your knees, breathe slow. It'll pass."

She did what Lucy said while the room spun. And she heard her pick up the phone on the night table.

Her grandmother's voice sounded strange, like she spoke inside a big, empty room where everything sounded hollow and echoed.

"Tate, it's Lucy Lannigan. I need you to do me a favor."

Thea let the words wash over her while, just as Lucy told her it would, the dizzy started to pass.

The cold went with it, flooded away in a blast of heat that slicked every inch of her skin.

"Here, darling, you lie down. I'm going to make you some tea."

"Don't leave me alone. Please, don't leave me alone."

"The tea's going to help. You trust me on that, Thea. Do you want to come down with me? Are you able?"

Nodding, she leaned against Lucy. "I won't be sick."

"Let's not wake Rem, all right?" Lucy put an arm around her, and the arm still shook. "Here's the steps. We'll go slow."

"I'm not dizzy now. I won't be sick." Outside her, everything felt hot. Inside, everything went numb. "I saw. I saw, and you saw, too. It wasn't a bad dream."

"I pray it was. You're going to sit at the table, and I'll make the tea. We haven't talked about what we have inside us, you and me, darling. Your mama—"

"She doesn't like it."

"It worries her, that's all. It worries her. Sit down now. Sheriff Mc-Kinnon, he's going to call the police up there, and they'll go check. And—and won't we feel foolish when they call and say everything's just fine?"

"Grammie—"

"Sometimes, lots of times, darling, what we've got inside shows what hasn't happened yet."

"But it's not that." Tears streamed again so she had to choke the words out through them. "They're gone, Grammie. I can feel it. So can you."

Her hair loose and wild around her shoulders, her face pale with shock, Lucy crossed her hands over her mouth as if to hold back a scream. "I didn't see clear."

"I did. I was there. I was there with them. I could see, and I could hear, and I could smell and feel. I was screaming, but they didn't hear me. I think, maybe, he did."

Suddenly exhausted, Thea laid her head on the table. "He killed them, and I was there."

"We're going to pray it was something yet to come, and by seeing, we changed it. We stopped it. That's all we can do now."

They could pray now, Thea thought, and they could pray forever. But it wouldn't change it. Through the numbness, she felt her grandmother's grief—a wild, terrified thing—and said nothing.

Lucy pulled out every ounce of strength and measured the hawthorn tea. She had to think of the child now, tend to the child now, and think of nothing else.

This child, she told herself, the child at the table swamped in shock and grief, and not the baby she'd carried inside her, given birth to. Not the child she'd loved with every beat of her heart, not the good, good man that child had grown up to marry, one she'd loved just as if she'd carried him inside her.

This child needed her to be strong, so strong she'd be.

This child she should've talked to about the gift long before this. To help prepare her, because she'd known, she'd seen that gift shining so bright, so strong.

Can't change what's already slipped away behind you, Lucy reminded herself. Right now, this child needed her strength to help her cope with that they both knew.

Her own grief had to wait.

She set the teacups on the table, stroked a hand over Thea's hair. "Drink a little, honeypot. I promise it helps."

"I can't feel anything inside me. It's like everything inside me went away."

"It's a way we protect ourselves." But it would come back, Lucy thought, it would all come screaming back. "So drink a little now, and I need you to listen to me. All right?"

Thea lifted her head, picked up the tea. She nodded.

"There are going to be questions about why I asked for the police. Thea, I need to hope it's your mama who calls and asks those questions. I need that hope."

Thea sipped some of the tea, nodded again.

"But whoever asks them, you best leave it to me to answer."

"Why?"

"Some people, they get greedy when they know you've got a gift, and they sure can hound you. Others, they don't believe in it, and they can say hard things."

"I know that already."

Lucy sighed, and the sound was pure regret. "I haven't done right by you on this, darling. I'm sorry for it."

"Mom worried. It scared her."

"That's right."

A little color had seeped back into those soft, young cheeks, Lucy thought. Not a lot, but a little at least. But the eyes didn't look so young now, and the emptiness in them told Lucy that numbness still held.

"What do we do, Grammie?"

"I—"

The knock on the front door had Lucy's heart folding in on itself, like paper balled in a fist. She could try to smooth it out again, and would have to, for this child, for the one sleeping upstairs.

But it would never be the same.

She started to tell Thea to go back upstairs and wait, but knew the wrongness of it. So she rose, reached for Thea's hand.

"Hold on to me."

They left the tea on the table and, hands linked, walked together to the door.

Chapter Four

Though the hard edge of the storm had softened, the wind still whipped through the trees and sent them swaying. The rain, thin now, left the air drenched and hazed. Thunder over the hills dropped to an irritable mutter.

Tate McKinnon, a solidly built man, his dark skin barely lined though he'd moved into his fifties, stood on the front porch in his uniform. His eyes, a deep brown, held sorrow.

He'd brought a young female deputy with him, also in uniform. Though she'd known Tate most of her life, and he was the next thing to family, Lucy understood he'd brought a woman because he felt she might need one.

Everything changed in that moment, before a word was spoken. She'd known, just as Thea had said, but that sharp and painful change waited for this moment.

There would always be a before, and there would come an after. And this moment forever separated them.

"Tate," she said as Thea's hand tightened in hers. "And it's, ah, Deputy Driscoll, isn't it? I know your mama."

"Yes, ma'am."

"Lucy."

Lips pressed together, Lucy nodded at Tate. "Y'all come in. We should sit down."

Tate shifted his gaze from Lucy to Thea, then back to Lucy again.

She just nodded again. "We should all sit down." When they stepped inside, she closed the door behind them. Steeled herself. "In the front room."

She led the way, then sat on the couch, wrapped her arm around Thea.

Tate took a chair, then the deputy—Alice, Lucy remembered. Alice, named for her grandmother.

Lucy held Thea close as she looked into Tate's eyes. She didn't need the words to know, but he had to say them.

"I'm sorry, Lucy." His voice was a rumble, like the thunder over the hills. "I'm so sorry to tell you Cora and John are dead."

"He killed them." Thea burst out with it even though Lucy gave her a warning squeeze.

"Who?" Alice demanded, and ignored the cool look Tate sent her.

"I don't know. I don't know who, but he cut a hole in the back door, the sliders, and reached in and unlocked it. He hated the house and he wanted the house. He hated them and he wanted them dead."

"How do you know that?"

"Deputy." The warning in Tate's voice carried enough weight to silence her.

"Lucy, the Fredericksburg police are investigating, and they'll want to talk to you, probably the kids, too. I know this is as hard a time as hard times get, but maybe you could answer some questions for me now. It might be easier to talk to me to start with."

"All right. All right, Tate."

"I want to ask you if Cora or John said anything about being worried, about any threats."

"No, they didn't, and we just talked to them last night. I just had this feeling tonight about them, so I—"

"They didn't know him," Thea interrupted. "He didn't know them, but he hated them anyway."

"Thea . . ." Lucy trailed off, and feeling the trembling under her arm, her poor little girl, she made herself accept the after.

Not just her after, she thought. But Thea's after.

"You go ahead, darling. You go ahead and tell what you saw and what you know."

"He was so mad, Grammie, at them. Even though he didn't know them. He hated they had a fancy, big-ass house. That's what he thought in his head . . . and the watch, Mom's watch Dad gave her for their anniversary. She only wore it for special. I don't know how he knew about it, exactly, but—"

She broke off, cuddled closer to Lucy. "I didn't really see until he was cutting the hole in the door, the one that goes out of the kitchen to the patio, the pool. He was mad about the pool, too, and the—and the grill."

"How do you know that?" Alice asked, and this time, Tate let it go.

"Because I saw it, and I felt it." Hot tears spilled down her cheeks to be wiped away with an angry fist. "I dreamed it, and I was there. Right behind him, and he didn't like that. Breathing down his neck—he could feel . . . He didn't see me like I did him, but he felt something."

"Let her be now, Deputy." Tate looked at Thea with kind eyes. "You go ahead, Thea. You tell us what you can."

"He got madder as he walked through the house. It all made him mad, should've been his. Like these people worked for a fucking living."

She paused, flushed a little. "I'm sorry, but he thought that."

"That's all right, darling." Lucy kissed the top of her head. "You don't worry about that."

"He walked down toward the stairs, then he saw the pictures on the wall. Dad calls it the family gallery, and they made him mad. But then he saw my picture. He didn't like it, didn't like feeling like I could look right at him. Like he knew I could see him. Like he felt me."

"Did he, Thea?"

"I don't know, Grammie. I swear I don't know for sure. But . . . it scared him, and I know he wanted to hurt me. He wished I was there, so he could. He had a gun. He walked up the stairs, and got madder and . . . happier? Mad and happy, going up the stairs with the gun.

"They were sleeping."

She saw it now as clearly as she had in the dream, and told it the same way.

He walked into the room where they slept, in the cool of the air-conditioning. Her father lay on his back, her mother on her side facing him. Pillows stacked on the floor. Her mom liked lots of pretty pillows on the bed when it was made up in the morning.

He picked one up, and she could feel him smiling as he put the pillow over her father's face and shot through it.

Because her breath caught, Lucy held her tighter.

"I screamed and screamed, but no one could hear me."

"If you saw all this—"

"Alice, hush," Tate ordered. "You go on when you're ready, honey."

She breathed in, breathed out, and went on. Seeing it again as she spoke.

The gun made a kind of ugly pop. Feathers flew out, and her father jerked, like he had a bad dream. Then went very still.

Her mother stirred, started to reach out, but he came around the bed, fast, very fast, and put the gun under her chin.

Scream, bitch, and I'll shoot you in the face just like I did him. Where's the fancy-ass watch? Where's the safe? What's the combination?

She started to scream Dad's name, and the man hit her in the face with the gun. She cried for Dad, tried to reach him, and the man hit her again.

Tell me and I won't hurt you again.

But that was a lie.

She heard her mother's voice in her head, so clear. She heard the fear, the shock, the grief.

It's on the dresser, over there on the dresser. Oh God, John. John.

She reached for Dad's hand, and squeezed it, hard, hard.

The safe's in the closet over there. The combination's nine-two-nine-four. That's the day they met, September second, nineteen ninety-four. *Take whatever you want.*

He said: *Gonna.*

And slapped a pillow over her face and shot her, just like Dad.

Now, Thea leaned her head against Lucy's body.

"I was screaming, but it didn't come out of my head. He went to the closet, and he took out the money, and he thought: Five grand, not bad. And he took Dad's good watch, and the pink diamond studs he gave Mom when I was born, because I was a girl, and the blue diamond ones for Rem, because he was a boy. And the diamond hoop earrings he gave her one Christmas, and the gold bracelet she bought herself one day."

When she paused, pressed her face against Lucy's arm, Tate spoke gently.

"Did you see his face, honey? Can you say what he looked like?"

"I was behind him, always behind him, and it was like, almost like I was looking with his eyes for some of it. He took the money from her purse, and from Dad's wallet, and the keys from Dad's dresser. Then he went to Mom's dresser for the watch. He felt good when he picked it up. Happy. He smiled when he looked up, into the mirror.

"I saw his face then, and something in him knew it, and he was mad and scared. He turned around fast, and his heart beat really fast, too. I could still see him. I could see him, then he ran. He ran and left them there, in the bed, with the pillows over their faces."

Though tears had coursed down her face throughout her retelling, now Thea clung to Lucy and sobbed.

"I've got you, darling. I've got you. Deputy . . . Alice," Lucy corrected. "Would you go into the kitchen and get my granddaughter a glass of water please?"

"Of course."

Lucy recognized the look on her face, in her eyes before Alice left the room. That look of suspicion and fear and the need not to believe.

"I'm so sorry, Thea," Tate said. "I'm so very sorry."

"I couldn't stop him."

"That's going to be our job now. If you can tell me what he looks like, that'll help us do our job. If you're willing, I'm going to send for a police artist, and we'll see if we can get a sort of picture of him."

Alice came back with the water, and for all her suspicions and fear, spoke kindly.

"Don't drink too fast, okay? You take your time. Take little sips."

"Thank you." Thea knuckled a tear away before she drank. Then rested her head on Lucy's shoulder.

"He was older than me, but not very old. Like twenty? Or not even. He had blondish hair, messy, straggly messy, I guess. He had blue eyes, but not dark, not even like medium. Really light blue, like washed-out?"

"All right." Tate nodded at her. "Was he a white boy then, Thea?"

"Yes, sir. Pale white, like he doesn't get in the sun much. Not very tall.

I don't know how to say. Taller than me, but not as tall as Grammie, and . . . his nose was skinny. Long and skinny. When he smiled, I saw his two front teeth were crooked. Like they crossed over each other some, and his lip poked out a little bit."

She tapped her top lip. Then rubbed the same hand at her temple, squeezed her eyes shut as if in pain.

"He thought . . . he thought how he was going to the beach. He thought how he'd scored big, and had a fancy new ride to drive down to Myrtle Beach."

"Lucy, it would help if we knew the makes and models of the cars Cora and John drove."

"BMWs. Cora's is a sedan, dark blue, and she's only had it about a year now. John's is an SUV, and it's about three years old, I think. About that. I don't know the license plates."

"That's all right."

When he signaled Alice, she rose, started to take her phone out of her pocket.

"We don't get very good cell service here. You can use the phone in the kitchen."

"Yes, ma'am."

"Now, Thea, is there anything else you remember or can tell me? You never saw this man before this?"

"No, sir. But . . . His hands. They were even whiter than the rest of him. He was wearing those gloves the doctors wear, and when he came in, he left a bag and a backpack on the kitchen floor. He put the thing he used to cut the glass back in the backpack before he started upstairs.

"It was the watch that started it. I don't know why or how exactly, but it was the watch."

"That's all right. Lucy, can you . . . corroborate any of this?"

"I didn't see nearly as clear, Tate, and I never saw his face. But I saw what he did to John and Cora. I saw the gun in his hand—with those white gloves. It was a nine-millimeter."

He rose when Alice came back.

"Is there anything we can do for you, Lucy? Do you want me to call your boys?"

"No, they need to hear it from me. See they find him, Tate. See they find who took my children."

"Anything and everything we can do, we'll do. You think of anything, you need anything, you call. No, we'll show ourselves out."

When they walked out, the rain had stopped.

"They'd already put out an APB on the SUV," Alice told Tate. "The BMW registered to John Fox wasn't at the house. How the hell did that girl know all that?"

"You weren't born here, Alice, but you've lived here long enough to have heard about Lucy Lannigan."

"Some, and I don't believe in that stuff."

"Up to you." He got behind the wheel. "But she was in this house, her and that little girl, when this happened. We already knew they were murdered in their bed, pillows over their faces, single gunshot to the face. The son of a bitch."

He slammed a fist on the steering wheel. "She said he took her father's keys, and it's the SUV, John Fox's, they're looking for. Goddamn it."

"I feel sick for that little girl, losing her parents this way. But listening to her telling it the way she did, it gave me the creeps."

He shot her one look, cool and mild, as he drove. "You'd best get over that. This isn't our investigation, but those are our people. If you're going to work our part of it with me, you'd best get over that right quick."

Inside the house, Lucy held Thea. "I can give you something to help you sleep awhile."

"I don't want to sleep."

"How about you come up with me, lie down in my bed? Darling, I've got to call your uncles." Her voice shook a little on the words. "That's something I have to do."

"Can I stay in your bed tonight?"

"Of course you can. Come on now."

"We have to tell Rem."

"Let's wait till morning. That can wait till morning. He's going to need your help, Thea. So am I. We're all going to need each other. We all have to help each other."

"They never hurt anybody, Grammie." Eyes swollen from weeping lifted to Lucy's. "They never even spanked me or Rem. Even when I guess we deserved it."

"I know, I know. Sometimes there's no understanding. Sometimes something's so cruel it seems impossible. Lie down, honeypot, maybe close your eyes. You don't have to sleep. Just rest."

"I want them. I want Mom and Dad."

"Oh, so do I."

She sat, stroking Thea's hair. "Find a memory of them, a happy memory. Go into that for a while and rest."

She sat and stroked. Then she stretched the phone's cord as far away from the bed as she could to call her sons.

While she told them, while they wept and she wept, she watched her granddaughter finally drift to sleep, drift into a dream, a soft one.

"I only need a minute, darling." She murmured it as she brushed a kiss over Thea's cheek. "I'll only be a minute."

In her bare feet, she ran down the steps, then out the front door she left open behind her. The wet grass soaked the hem of her sleeping pants as she ran across the road, into the trees.

Where she screamed and screamed and screamed until the mountains shuddered with her grief.

Lucy didn't expect to sleep, so took the single hour of oblivion with gratitude. She'd need strength to get through the day, and that hour helped.

She rose in the predawn light, even more grateful Thea slept and Rem slept on. The thought of Rem and what she'd have to tell him brought tears rushing into her throat.

She swallowed them back as she dressed. Her animals needed tending. And when they woke, so would the children.

After yanking her hair back in a tail, she wrote Thea a note.

I'm just outside, darling, doing the chores.

On her way down, she peeked into Rem's room. He slept flat on his stomach, arms and legs spread out like a starfish. Cocoa yawned, stretched, then padded out to join Duck and Goose.

Tails wagged.

Just a boy, she thought, barely ten. A boy who still smelled of forests and all the wild, wonderful things in it.

She left him sleeping.

She'd let the dogs out. She'd make coffee—she needed it—then see to her animals.

In the kitchen, she turned on the light, started the coffee just like any ordinary day. Just as she would if Cora and John were still on this earth with her.

Fighting more tears, she walked to the screen door to let the dogs out, to just breathe in the morning mountain air.

The sun, she knew, would be peeking over the eastern hills, but in this western view the light held back in a quiet, pearly gray.

In that pearly gray she caught movement by the barn. A movement that walked on two legs. Her first thought was the shotgun locked in the closet in the mudroom. She could have it out and loaded in one quick minute.

She had children to protect.

Then she recognized that gangly silhouette, and stepped out on the porch.

"Will McKinnon."

"Yes, ma'am, Miss Lucy. Didn't mean to give you a start."

At seventeen, Will didn't have his father's solid build. A walking beanpole with a head full of twists, he carried a lidded pail of milk.

"I milked Aster. I'll take her on out to the pasture there. And I'll see to Molly and your ladies."

He didn't have his father's build, but he had Tate's eyes. Wide and deep and now filled with sympathy.

"Oh, Miss Lucy, I'm so sorry." He stopped at the porch. "I'm so sorry about what happened. I'm going to take care of things out here. I don't want you worrying about it."

She managed a slippery grip on composure as the gray faded toward light with the rising sun.

"Did your daddy send you?"

"No, ma'am. But he said it was fine if I came by and just took care of things for you. I didn't want to wake you so I didn't knock."

Lucy stepped down to where he stood and took the milk pail, set it on the porch. Then she wrapped her arms around him.

After a brief hesitation, he wrapped his around her.

"I'm just so awful sorry. I'll take care of the milking and such for you, Miss Lucy. You shouldn't ought to worry about it today."

"Thank you, Will. You've made this hard day just a little easier for me."

"I can do it as long as you need, and anything else needs doing. You just have to tell me."

"This morning's enough for now. It's helped me when I needed help the most. I'll take care of the milk." Stepping back, she patted his cheek. "I can make you a hot breakfast. I've already got coffee on."

"No, 'um, don't you worry about that either. I know you've got your grandkids. I'm just going to leave Molly's milk and the eggs on the porch here."

"You have a kind heart, Will. It's going to take you to some good places." She went onto the porch, picked up the milk pail. "You brought a little light into my dark today."

She went back in, then stopped short when she saw Thea and her sleep-starved eyes standing by the kitchen table.

"Who was that?"

Lucy set the pail on the counter. "That was Will, Sheriff McKinnon's boy. He's taking care of the chores for us this morning."

"Did you ask him to?"

"I didn't have to. He's a good young man, a kind one. He sees to things here when I come up . . ."

"When you come for Christmas," Thea finished. "But you won't come for Christmas anymore."

"Thea—"

"When I woke up, for a few seconds I didn't remember. I didn't remember what happened. I didn't remember about Mom and Dad. Then I did. You weren't there, and for a few seconds I was scared you were gone, too."

"Oh, darling. I'm so sorry."

"No, Grammie. You left a note right there on the pillow, so I wasn't scared very long."

To keep her hands busy, to will them not to tremble, Lucy started filtering the milk.

"I won't leave you or Rem alone, and that's a promise. Sit down, honeypot. I'll make breakfast in a minute."

"I'm not hungry, Grammie."

"I know, neither am I. But we're going to have to eat a little anyway. We need to eat and sleep so we can get through this."

"I dreamed a memory, like you said. I dreamed the day we got here, and eating fried chicken and buttermilk biscuits. The dogs were wagging, and everybody was talking and laughing. We were all happy."

"That's a good one." Lucy thought about screaming out her grief again, but she couldn't.

She had children to protect.

"You can pick a good one anytime you need."

She put the jug of fresh milk in the milk cooler before reaching for a mug for coffee.

"Can I have coffee, too?"

Lucy looked back into those sleep-starved, grieving eyes. "How about I make you a mug of what my mama always called coffee milk?"

"Okay."

Thea said nothing as Lucy fixed up a mug—a lot of milk and sugar with enough coffee to flavor it. She just sat, watching Lucy's every move. Under the table, her hands twisted together.

Instead of starting breakfast, Lucy sat at the table, took her first sip of morning coffee.

Thea tasted hers. "It's good."

"And I'm probably starting you on a lifetime addiction. Thea, I see worry on you. Tell me what worries you."

Thea took another sip, then a long breath. "I—I need to know—"

They both heard Rem bounding down the stairs like a pack of wild dogs.

Lucy closed her eyes. She would crush his childhood, break his young, happy heart. She had no choice.

He came rushing in, all grins and energy. As if some of that energy came from an electric socket, his hair stuck out in all directions.

"There's somebody outside and he's feeding the ladies. I saw out the window. Did you hire somebody, Grammie?"

"No. That's Will, and he's doing me a favor."

"I can help him, then we can all have buckwheat pancakes, 'cause I'm starving."

"Will's going to take care of it this morning. I need you to sit down here with us."

He looked from face to face, and what he saw had the grin falling away from his. "What's wrong? Did I do something wrong? I didn't do anything wrong."

"No, sweet potato, you didn't do anything wrong. Sit down here with us." When he did, she took his hands in hers. "I have to tell you something, and it's very hard."

"Are you sick or something? You look sick."

"I'm not sick, not the way you mean." And now, she thought, just like for her, for Thea, there would always be a before and after. "My darling, your mama and daddy, they got hurt."

"They got in an accident? Are they okay? They're okay, right?"

His eyes begged her to say yes, yes, of course. And Lucy couldn't find the words.

"It wasn't an accident. It's best saying it fast, Grammie. Somebody broke into the house and killed them. He killed them."

"Don't you say that." The pleading went straight to fury as he tried to yank his hands free. "That's mean. That's a lie. You—you're a lying bitch!"

Thea didn't flinch, just kept her eyes on his face.

"It's not a lie," Lucy said, as gently as she could. "I hate telling you it's truth. Thea's hurting. I'm hurting, and I'm sorry that hurt's in you now."

"It's not true!" He wailed it as tears popped out of his eyes. "They're coming to take us home in a week. And later we're all going to the beach."

Saying nothing, Lucy got up. She lifted him out of the chair, and though he struggled at first, she sat with him in her lap. Rocked him as she had as a baby.

"It's not true, Grammie."

When he began to sob, Thea got up. She wrapped her arms around both of them and let her own tears come.

"I'm going to call them. I'm going to call them on the phone."

"They're not there, darling. They're gone."

"How do you know for sure? Did you call? Did you call them?"

"I saw it. I saw him." Thea swiped away tears with the back of her arm. "I saw it all."

"You're not supposed to do that!" Outraged and desperate, Rem shoved at her. "Mom doesn't like it."

"I didn't want to. I couldn't help it."

"That doesn't make it true."

"Rem. Rem." Lucy shifted, took his face firmly in her hands. His angry, tear-streaked, terrified face. "I saw, too. We called the police, and what we saw is true. I'd give my life, I swear to you, if it wasn't."

"But why! They didn't hurt anybody."

"He hated them." Thea sat again, gripped her hands tight together. "He didn't know them, but he hated them anyway. He wanted Mom's anniversary watch and money and her earrings, and Dad's car. He just wanted things, but more than the things, he wanted to hurt them. Just because they had them."

"Did the police find him and put him in jail?"

"Sheriff McKinnon will tell us as soon as they do."

Now, through the tears, he stared at his sister. "Are they going to? Are they?"

"I don't—"

"Don't say you don't know!" His fury slapped at her like angry hands. "If you can see stuff like a freak, why can't you see that?"

As Thea laid her head on the table, weeping again, Lucy looked into her grandson's eyes. She said nothing but his name.

"I'm sorry." He slid off Lucy's lap. "I'm sorry, I'm sorry. I didn't mean it." With more tears, he sat on the floor and hugged Thea's legs. "I didn't mean it. I swear. I'm sorry. I'm sorry."

When Thea got down on the floor with him, when they held each other, cried on each other's shoulders, Lucy got up. She fetched the milk and eggs Will, in his kindness, had left on the back porch.

He'd fed the dogs, too, given them fresh water, she noted. Bless him.

She let her grandchildren give each other comfort in shared grief, and she dealt with the milk, the eggs.

When she sat again, they came to her.

She held them both, kissed them both.

"Y'all sit down now. I'm going to make us some scrambled eggs on toast. That'll go down easiest, I think."

"I'm not hungry, Grammie."

"I know." She kissed Rem again. "But we need to eat a little."

"Grammie, I need to know— We need to know," Thea corrected. "What's going to happen? What happens now?"

"Yes, you do. I'm going to make us some breakfast, and we'll talk about that."

Chapter Five

Thea ate what she could. Food didn't stem the grief, but the soft scrambled eggs on a slice of sourdough toast helped lessen some of her fears.

Part of her thought it seemed wrong and selfish to even think about herself, but the other part knew she'd carry the fear and worry until she knew.

And Rem was two years younger, so she had to look out for him, too.

And Grammie—Grammie looked so tired, so sad. *We all have to help each other*, Thea remembered.

"All right." Lucy reached out on both sides, to pat their hands. "I appreciate you ate a little. I know you have questions, so maybe you can try to eat a little more while I try to answer them. You want to know what happens now, and I can answer some of it."

"Will they make us go back?" It blurted out, that fear. "And get fostered, even separated because—"

"Right off, no. No to all of that, so put that worry aside. Not long after you were born, Thea, your parents had wills drawn up. Because they had you. And they asked me then, and every time they've updated that will since, if I'd take care of you, and Rem, too. If anything happened to them, if you could live with me. So that's what happens if you both want it to."

"We can live here, with you?"

Lucy nodded at Rem. "I'm your grammie, and I'll be your legal guardian, and you can live right here, live with me as long as you want."

Thea's shoulders shuddered as she looked down at her plate.

"Nobody's going to take you away, my darlings. Nobody's going to separate you. I promise you that, as solemn a promise as I've ever made."

"I thought maybe we'd have to go with Dad's parents, because they're rich. They don't even like us, so maybe they'd make us go to foster."

"You're mine. You'll stay mine. Put that worry aside."

"Cocoa, too?"

"Yes, Rem, Cocoa, too. Let me ask you, do you want to go back to Virginia, get your things? And anything else that you want to have here with you?"

"I don't ever want to go back there." Thea lifted her head again, eyes fierce as she snapped out the words. "I don't ever want to go in the house again. He killed them there."

"Then you don't have to. Your uncles will go, and they'll get all your things. They'll get anything else you want. It's yours now. Your mama and daddy looked out for you, always. The house, all of it, it's yours, in a trust."

"Can I have Dad's drawing board?"

Everything in Lucy softened when she looked at Rem. "Of course you can. I think that would please him, very much. You take all the time you need, the both of you, to think about what you might want."

"The house, it'll just sit there empty?"

"It could, Thea, if that's what you want. We could put everything in storage and rent it, if you want that. We could sell it, if you want that."

"I don't ever want to go back. Do you?"

Rem shook his head.

"We want to sell it."

"All right. You take a few days to think about that, then we'll talk to the lawyers about it."

"Can they come here, too? Mom and Dad." As he asked, tears swirled into Rem's eyes. Then in Thea's as she reached out, gripped his hand. "If we're not going back, can they come here? They shouldn't . . ."

"They shouldn't be buried in Virginia." Still gripping his hand, Thea finished for Rem. "They should be here, with all of us."

Lucy pressed her fingers to her mouth, just nodded until she could speak again. "I think that's what they'd want, too. I'll see to it. I'm going to ask both of you not to worry. Or if worry comes, to tell me so we can fix it. We have to help each other now, do our best for each other."

Rem poked at his eggs. "I'm sorry I called you the *b* word and a freak. I'll never ever do it again."

"That's a fine apology, Rem, and a good promise to try to keep. Y'all are going to get mad at each other here and there, now and then. Brothers and sisters do. And that's all right because under it, you're always going to love each other."

She took a long breath before poking at her own eggs. "I need to call your daddy's mother, to express my condolences. I have to ask you both to speak with your other grandparents, to be kind."

"She doesn't love us, or Mom." Thea spoke flatly. No rancor, no heat, just fact.

"Now, Thea—"

"She doesn't. I'd've felt it, the way I feel you love Dad, and always did. And us, and Mom."

"People feel love in different ways, but she's still his mother. We'll give her and her husband that respect."

"She won't respect you."

The words, and the cool, flat tone, were so adult, Lucy's brows lifted. She did her best to answer in kind.

"Well, if she doesn't, that's on her, isn't it? Somebody else does wrong doesn't mean we do."

When the phone rang, she rose to answer.

"Tate, have they . . ." She looked back at the children. "All right, yes. She's right here, let me ask her. Thea, honey, they've sent down a police artist from Virginia, and Sheriff McKinnon wants to bring the artist here to talk to you. Is that all right with you?"

"Okay. I can try."

"That's fine, Tate." She listened awhile, rubbing her free hand on her other arm. "That's good to know. Yes. Tate, I'm so grateful to Will. I know, I do, he is all of that. If I do, I will. We'll see you soon."

She hung up. "Y'all go up and get dressed."

"Will you stay with me when they come?"

"Yes, I will."

"What was good to know? We need to know, too."

"The police found the car he drove before, in a driveway on the street behind the house. He'd stolen that one, too."

"Did he kill somebody else?"

"Yes, he did, Rem. I'm afraid he did."

"I can see him, Grammie. I can tell the police artist what he looks like."

"I believe you can and you will, Thea. Go on up now and get dressed."

Thea put on jeans because shorts seemed wrong, then braided her hair because it seemed tidier. She didn't want the police artist to treat her like a child, or a freak.

To keep busy, she made her bed, then her grandmother's, since she'd slept in both.

As she finished, Rem came to hover in the doorway.

"You have to tell me what happened. What you saw."

"Not now, Rem. I will," she said before he could argue. "I swear." To seal it, she swiped her finger over her heart. "But I can't say it all again right now. I don't want to be all shaky when I talk to the artist."

"But you will." His eyes, so like their father's, arrowed into her. "You promised, crossed your heart."

"I double promise." She swiped her heart again. "Maybe we'll take a walk later and I'll tell you, so Grammie doesn't have to hear it all again."

"We need to shake on it."

That actually made her roll her eyes, but she shook. Then heard the knock. "Oh God, that's them now."

"Don't be scared. I'll stay with you, too."

She wasn't scared, but didn't say so. She was nervous she'd get something wrong, something important, and he'd get away. So she couldn't get anything wrong. She wouldn't.

The sheriff stood with a woman, and she hadn't expected a woman.

Her mom would've given her a look about that.

The artist was a woman, barely as tall as Thea, with straight dark hair that came to her chin and dark eyes.

"Thea, Rem," Lucy began, "this is Detective Wu."

"You can call me Mai." She held out a slender, delicate hand. "I'm sorry to meet you this way. I'm very sorry for your loss."

"I can see him."

"I understand."

Not only a woman she hadn't expected, but none of the judgment she'd prepared for.

"I thought you could work in the kitchen." Lucy laid a hand on Thea's shoulder. "There's a good table there."

"Wherever Thea's most comfortable."

"The kitchen's good."

"Just back here. Can I get you coffee, tea?"

"Just water for me, if you don't mind. This is perfect." Mai set a case on the table. "I've never been to this part of the country before. It's beautiful."

She sat, somehow managed to pet all three dogs at once.

"Rem, let the dogs out."

"Oh, not on my account. They're so sweet. Do you want them outside, Thea?"

"No, they're okay."

"I know this is hard." Mai opened the case, took out a sketchbook, some pencils, erasers. "I want you to try to relax. Just sit and breathe. Do I hear chickens? Don't the dogs bother them?"

"They guard them from foxes and hawks, even bears."

"Sweet, smart, and brave. When you're ready, Thea, why don't you tell me the first thing about his face you think of?"

"His eyes."

"What about them?"

"They're so pale. Pale, pale blue, but there's so much dark behind them."

"What about their shape?" Idly, or so it seemed, Mai drew different shapes on the page.

Thea pointed to one. "But a little wider? This way wider," she added and held up her thumb and forefinger to indicate top to bottom.

Mai drew another shape, got a nod. She turned a page, sketched the eyes. "What comes to your mind next?"

"Can I close my eyes? I think I can see him better if I close my eyes."

"Of course."

With her eyes closed, Thea brought the face into her head.

"His two front teeth overlap some." She tapped her own. "So his top lip pokes out a little."

Keeping her eyes closed, with Duck lying under the table with his head on her foot, she went detail by detail.

She heard the summer breeze stirring, the chickens humming, birds calling. But she kept the face right there, right there, behind her closed eyes.

"Could you take a look, Thea? See if this is close?"

When she opened her eyes, her breath caught. "It is, yes, it really is, but . . . His face is thinner, and his chin is a little more pointed."

"All right, I'll fix that. Thea, look at me. Relax again, relax your shoulders, breathe. You're doing an amazing job. You're really helping me do mine."

"I—I can't draw faces very well."

"Good thing I can. Is this better?"

"His eyebrows are straighter. I forgot to say that before."

"More like this?"

She nodded, eyes wide, breath short. "It's him. It's him. I swear."

Lucy laid her hands on Thea's shoulders, rubbed. "Take those breaths again. He can't hurt you."

"But he wants to. He has my picture, too. He's looked at it a lot. He's sleeping." She reached back to grip Lucy's hand. "He drove a long way, but he got too tired to go all the way to the beach. Didn't want to get pulled over, better to stop at some crap motel."

"Can you see him now?" Mai asked her.

"Not really, not exactly, but he's sleeping. It's dark in the room. He closed the cheap-ass curtains with the dumbass flowers on them. Room around the back, around the back because it's quieter and he wants to sleep. Accident on 95 held him up some, but still nearly made it to . . . to Fayetteville. Can't check into the house at the beach until after three anyway. Get some sleep, then a couple more hours on the road, and he'll be there."

She breathed out. "He's sleeping now," she said again.

"Lucy, you got a scanner on your computer?" Tate asked.

"I've never used it."

"Mind if I do?" He took the sketch Mai gave him, then followed Lucy out of the room.

"Sweet, smart, and brave," Mai said. "That's you, too, Thea."

She didn't feel sweet, smart, and brave, but tired and sad and confused. When Mai left and before their grandmother came back, Rem leaned toward her.

"Can we go for a walk now?"

She wanted to snap at him to leave her alone, just leave her alone because her head hurt. But he looked at her with eyes so like their dad's, and so full of need.

"Okay, I guess."

They went out the back with the dogs happy to tag along. Because she wanted to get through it and out again, Thea started right away.

"He cut a hole in the patio sliders."

As she got through it, Rem cried again, but the tears came hot out of angry eyes.

"When they catch him, maybe they'll kill him." Rem knuckled the tears away. "He's a—a motherfucker."

Too tired for shock that Rem not only knew the word but said it right out loud, she just looked at him. "Better not let Grammie hear you say that word. That's the massive bad word. Or words."

She wasn't sure which.

"I bet she thinks the same, and you do, too." Balling his fists, he shouted at the sky. "Motherfucker, motherfucker, motherfucker!"

Now shock got through, shock that a laugh tried to bubble up in her throat. "Shut up." She gave him an elbow jab. "You're going to get us in trouble."

The angry red faded from his cheeks. "I don't care. It made me feel better."

"I guess it made me feel better, too. I'm tired, Rem. I don't want to talk anymore right now."

"What do you want to do?"

"I don't know. I just don't know."

She sat on the ground beside the chicken coop, drew up her knees, lowered her head to them.

After a moment, Rem sat next to her, then draped an arm around her shoulders.

From inside the screen door, Lucy watched them. She didn't need the sight to know Thea had told Rem what she'd seen. And since there wasn't a thing wrong with her ears, she'd heard Rem's rage, and the pain inside it.

Now look at him, she thought, doing what he could to comfort his sister.

They'd get through it, somehow the three of them would get through.

She glanced at the clock. Barely eleven? How could the day drag so when it had so much in it?

Barely eight out in California. She supposed it best to wait until noon to call out there—so nine in California.

She called the number Tate gave her for the medical examiner to find out when she could have her daughter and son-in-law sent home to her. Then worked down the terrible list of arrangements, buying gravesites, setting a date for the funeral, and all the rest.

She'd left it to her sons to tell the rest of the family, and called Waylon to tell him what she'd arranged.

When the children came back in, she opened her arms to take them both in.

"I'm about to call your grandparents in San Diego."

Thea just burrowed in. "I'm so tired, Grammie. I don't want to talk to them. Please, can I just lie down on the couch?"

"I don't want to talk to them either."

"All right." Enough, she thought. They've both had enough. "I'll tell them you're both sleeping. Go lie down, and Rem, you go sit quiet awhile, close your eyes so you don't make me a liar."

Lucy braced herself, stared at the phone for a full minute before she made herself pick it up. She dialed the number, then sat at the kitchen table.

"Fox residence."

"Yes, hello. I'd like to speak with Mrs. Fox."

"Neither Mr. nor Mrs. Fox are accepting calls this morning. If you'd like to leave your name and number, they'll return your call when it's convenient."

"This is Lucy Lannigan. I'm Cora's mother. I want them to know the children, Thea and Rem, are with me, and to extend my sympathies for our mutual loss."

"One moment, please."

They had holding music, like their home was a business. She found that a wonder as she rubbed at her temple and the nagging headache.

"This is Christine Fox."

The voice brought the image of the woman. Tall, stately, and as cold as a January storm.

"I'll speak to Althea and Remington."

"They're sleeping. If I could have them call you a little later."

"Sleeping? Isn't it past noon where you are?"

"They've had a very difficult morning. We all have. I can't begin to tell you how dear John was to me. Christine, we've lost our children, and I can't—"

"Why are Althea and Remington with you in—it's Kentucky, isn't it?"

"Yes, and they were here on their summer visit. I can only thank God they weren't in the house when—"

"We'll arrange for them to be flown out to San Diego, along with their father's remains. I'm sure you understand," Christine continued in a voice clipped and final. "The memorial service will be very private."

Not one word, not one of sympathy. Not one thought of Cora.

Well then, Lucy thought, you're about to get back some of your own.

"You're not going to do any of those things."

"I beg your pardon?"

"You can beg for it, but you won't get it. You won't separate John and Cora in death any more than you could in life. They loved each other and their children enough to make me their legal guardian. The children stay with me, and because the children want it, John and Cora will be buried here, together."

Silence held, and Lucy used it to stop herself from raging out as Rem had by the chicken coop.

"You expect to raise Althea and Remington alone, on some backwater, hillbilly farm?"

"I do, and I will. That's what John and Cora wanted. It's what the children want."

"I won't allow it, and have no doubt the courts will agree with me. We can provide them with an excellent education in a respected boarding school while you'll toss them into some ramshackle public schoolhouse. We'll see they're raised properly."

"What color are Rem's eyes? What's Thea do every night before going to sleep?"

"That's irrelevant."

"It's as relevant as it gets." She'd pushed up to pace without being aware of it. "You want to put these kids through a custody battle after their parents were murdered in their own bed? You want to go against their dead parents' wishes so you can put them in some damn boarding school?

"You want to fight me on this? Bless your heart, you bring it on, because for them, I'll fight dirty. I'll start by calling the papers and the TV stations out there in California, and telling them how the people who live so high and mighty sent their granddaughter twelve dollars for her birthday while they bought a horse for one of their other grandchildren."

"It's none of your business what we—"

"Bullshit it's not my business. It's my only business now. I'll make sure everyone knows how you planned to separate your dead son from my dead daughter. How you're planning to put their orphaned children in boarding schools."

"Our reputation—"

"Will be shit before I'm done. I swear on my life, you'll end up covered in the shit I'll shovel over your precious reputation. You, who've never once tucked them into bed, or rocked them, made a meal for them, loved them, listened to them. You treated my daughter, their mother, your son's wife of thirteen years, like she was nothing. And it's God's truth you didn't treat your own son much better."

"How dare you?"

With her mouth twisted into a sneer, Lucy laughed.

"Oh, you have no idea what I'll dare. I'm an Appalachian woman, born and bred. You try to take these children, children you don't know or love or give two damns about? I'll ruin you, I promise you. Why, when I'm done airing your dirty laundry, you'll be giving parties nobody comes to. Next gala you go to? People'll be whispering about you behind their hands."

"We'll see about that."

"Drag these children into this, and you'll see enough to make your eyes burn. John understood you better than I realized. And that's why he made the guardianship ironclad, why he named you and your husband, his siblings in his will, and I will quote:

"'Under no circumstances are those named below to serve as legal guardians of the minor children, as they are not fit to care for the minor children.' Get your high-class lawyers, you go ahead, because I think that'll hold up in court and embarrass the living hell out of you."

"If you dare to take this to the media, I'll sue you for libel."

"I'd love it. I swear to God, I'd love you to try just that."

Her heart pounded, but with fury, not fear.

"You'd have to prove I was lying, wouldn't you? Since I'm not, you go ahead. I've got John's own words on a legal document. I've got these kids, who only have to tell the truth to show what kind of people you are. I've got the fact that not once, not once since Thea was born, have you gotten your fat ass out to visit. Twelve years, and you couldn't be bothered. And add a couple more with you treating my daughter, the woman John loved and married and had babies with, like dirt."

Riding on rage, she flipped through her tattered phone book. "I've got John and Cora's lawyer's name and number right here. Why don't you call, and he'll tell you how far you'll get with this? And while you're doing that, I'll just look up the top paper, TV, and radio stations in San Diego and cut your precious reputation to ribbons."

"You want them so much, keep them. And know they'll get nothing more from us."

"Oh, I think Thea'll be just fine without thirteen more dollars her next birthday."

When Christine hung up, Lucy snarled at the phone. "You snake-eyed, blackhearted hell bitch."

When she turned to put the phone down, Thea and Rem slid into the kitchen.

"Oh, sweet Jesus! You're supposed to be resting."

"You were sort of yelling." Rem's wide eyes fixed on her face.

"I didn't mean to." With a vicious headshake, Lucy hissed out her breath. "No, I damn well did."

"You were really mad. I didn't know you could get so really mad."

"Well, I can. When it's called for." She shook a finger at Rem. "So remember that, and don't make me so really mad."

"I kinda liked it. You looked like a superhero."

Thea reached down, took Rem's hand. "Can they take us away?"

"No, my darlings, they can't and they won't. That's a promise I can make and know I can keep. I talked to the lawyer in Virginia while you were outside. You're mine. We're each other's. And that's how it's going to be."

"Are you going to call the papers?"

"I won't need to now." Crossing over, she stroked Thea's hair, then ruffled Rem's.

"'Cause you scared her."

"That's right, Rem. I scared the crap right out of her."

When he giggled, the weight on her heart lightened.

"You said she had a fat ass."

"I did, and I don't know if she does or doesn't, but it's what came to me at the time. I said cruel things, and lord help me, I'm not even a little bit sorry for it."

"Grammie?" Thea's hand tightened on Rem's. "Do we still have to call her and talk to her?"

"No. There'll be times I have to make you do what you don't much want to, but that's not gonna be one of them."

"We love you, Grammie."

"Oh, Rem, I couldn't love you more if you were covered in chocolate."

She held them both in the kitchen where she'd once been a young wife, a young mother, a young widow.

Now, not so young, she'd need to be mother, father, and grammie to two precious children.

"How about the two of you go out and pick some green tomatoes, and I'll make some batter? We'll fry them up. And after, if you've thought of things, we'll start making that list of what you want."

"Dad's drawing board."

"Top of the list."

"When they get them back, can I have the earrings Dad gave Mom when I was born? I got my ears pierced last year, and I could wear them for special."

"Those are good wants."

"You can have the ones he gave for me, Grammie. I'm not getting holes punched in my ears."

"I'd be proud to wear them, for special. Go on, get us a couple good tomatoes."

On the way out, Thea paused at the door. "They didn't really want us."

"No, baby, they didn't. But I do."

Lucy got out the cornmeal, her container of saved bacon grease. Then just took a moment before getting the rest.

The burning mad had cooled to a steady calm.

They'd get through, she thought. Through today and tomorrow and all that came after.

Chapter Six

Ray slept until nearly two in the afternoon. And why not, the way he figured it. He hadn't checked in until around four in the freaking morning, so he'd paid for the crap room.

He had that nice new ride, plenty of cash. He'd take a hot shower to get himself going. Then he'd hit a Mickey D's for a Big Mac, some fries, a jumbo Coke.

He only had a couple more hours on the road, and that would hold him.

But he lay a few minutes more.

He didn't like he'd dreamed somebody watched him sleep. Gave him the fucking creeps, and the creeps pissed him off.

He rolled over to pick up the picture he'd taken from the MFM in Virginia, the one of the girl.

"Don't know why I took this, and that's another pisser. Except you piss me off, little blue-eyed bitch. Too bad you weren't there when I took care of Mommy and Daddy. Maybe I'll see if I can hunt you up one of these days and take care of you."

He smashed the glass against the bedside table. Shattering it made him feel better. Feel good.

Then he picked up the watch that had started it all. Turning it over again, he read the engraving.

"'For All Time.' Well, your time ran out, asshole."

His now, until he sold it. Then the money would be his. And that's how it was done.

If he worked at it, and held it, he could see it in its fancy box, watch her hands opening it. Even hear her gasp, her voice, though that sounded like she spoke in a tunnel under a river.

Oh my God, John! It's beautiful. Are you crazy?

We made our first decade, the man said. *This is for that, and all the ones to come. Read the back.*

Now her voice sounded all teary, amusing him.

Oh, John. Now you're making me cry. I love you, too. For all time.

The pushing to see brought on a headache, right behind his eyes. Not a bad one, but enough to have him dropping the watch onto the bed and getting up to dig out the bottle of Advil he kept handy for just this reason.

He flopped back on the mattress to give the tablets a few minutes to start working. Blanked his mind, closed his eyes.

He drifted off for another twenty minutes.

Shouldn't've pushed it, he admitted. He still had to get where he wanted to go, and stop somewhere to load some food into the place.

But the twenty minutes out took care of the headache.

He yawned, stretched, idly scratched his balls, and headed to the shower.

Cheap-ass soap for a cheap-ass motel, but the water ran hot.

He'd pick up some good soap when he got supplies for his vacation. Some fancy-man soap.

And he'd find someone over twenty-one he could bribe to buy him a case of beer. He pictured himself sitting on the deck of the house he'd found and booked online. Drinking a beer, soaking up some sun, watching people.

He wouldn't kill anybody then and there—he wasn't an idiot—but he could watch, push a little, and take his pick.

Get the license plate number and state off the car in their driveway, the make, the model. Or if they left it unlocked, just get an address off the registration.

He knew from experience people got careless on vacations, and an unlocked car wasn't hard to find.

But he'd take a couple days, oh yeah, to sit out, drink some beer, and relax. Too much pushing brought on those headaches, and sometimes a nosebleed or a dribble of blood from his ear.

So he needed some downtime. Goddamn, he'd worked for it!

He rubbed the cheap soap on his balls, considered taking a few more minutes to jerk off. But that could wait for the beach, too.

The soap spurted out of his hand when he heard something crash.

Before he could think what to do next, the shower curtain skidded back, and he had a gun in his face.

"Hey, Ray, you're under arrest."

"What the hell is this!"

"It's the police, Ray, and let me repeat and expand. You're under arrest for Murder One, two counts. Then there's related charges like nighttime breaking and entering, burglary, grand theft auto. You're going to want to step out of the tub, really carefully."

"Lawyer."

"Oh yeah, you can have one, but I'm going to read you your rights anyway."

"Got the watch here on the bed," someone called out from the bedroom. "The kid's picture. Key to the BMW and all the rest."

"Gotcha, Ray. Out of the tub. Somebody hand him a towel so I don't have to look at his junk when I Mirandize him."

Lucy found Tate and Alice on her front porch again. When she saw them, she pressed a hand to her mouth.

"They got him. We wanted to tell you in person." Because she trembled, he took Lucy's arm. "Why don't you sit out here on the porch, and I'll tell you."

"Yes. Yes. I've got fresh lemonade."

"Don't you trouble."

"We'll get it." Thea spoke from behind her, where both kids stood at the base of the stairs.

They could move quiet as ghosts, Lucy thought, when they wanted.

"We'll get it," Thea repeated, "if you don't tell what happened until we bring it out."

Lucy nodded. "You have a right to hear it, too. We'll wait for you."

She sat in one of the chairs she used when the mood struck so she drank her morning coffee and watched the sunrise.

The dogs came around to wag and sniff.

"Tate, could you carry that chair over to this side? That'll make three, but there's more around the kitchen table."

"I can stand, ma'am," Alice told her.

Rem carried the pitcher out, his tongue caught between his teeth as he concentrated on not spilling any. Thea came behind him with ice-filled glasses on a tray.

"I can pour it, Grammie."

"All right. Rem, come sit here with me. Me and this big chair could use some company."

The ice crackled as Thea poured. She had always liked the sound it made, and today, she considered that sound a kind of celebration. Not really a happy one, but a kind of one.

She passed the glasses out. "Deputy, you can sit here."

"No, honey, you sit there. I'm fine."

When she had, Tate began, and some of it she could see before he said it. But she only listened.

"He checked into a motel off 95, the other side of Fayetteville, like you said, Thea. About four in the morning. Looks like he slept late today. The police were already checking motels along the route. After what you told me, they started working that area hard."

"They believed me."

"I did. And they had the sketch, showed it around. Turns out the night man worked a double, so that was some luck, seeing as he recognized the face, when he'd checked him in. Even without the luck, they'd've found your daddy's car. Parked around the back, and right in front of the room he took."

Room 205, Thea thought. She could see it now.

"They busted in and found him naked as a jaybird in the shower. And they found the things you said he took from your house. They found the gun."

"Did they kill him?" Rem asked.

"No. Remember, he was naked, unarmed, but they arrested him on the spot, and he's on his way back to Fredericksburg. They got him cold, you understand that. He's going to get a lawyer, and he's entitled to one, but they got him cold. He'll be going to prison for the rest of his life."

"I know how you feel right now," Alice said to Rem. "But he's only eighteen years old. The longer he lives in prison, the more he pays. Me, I'm hoping he lives a long life."

"What's it like in prison?"

"I've never been on the wrong side of it, but you're locked up, and you eat when they tell you to eat, what they tell you to eat. You wear what they tell you to wear, and every day that's the same. You've got a toilet in your cell, and you have to do your business with no privacy."

"Eew."

"Right? You can't go out of the cell whenever you want, or outside whenever you want. When they let you outside, it's walled in, with guards and with barbed wire on top of the wall."

"That's right, and there are people like him in there with him. People who like to hurt," Tate continued. "People who've killed. It's a dangerous place."

"Are you sure he'll have to stay there all his life?"

Tate shifted to Thea.

"Honey, they've got the glass cutter he used, a box of white medical gloves, they've got the car, and all the rest. They've got the gun he used. They'll find out where he got that gun. And they've got the other car, parked on the other street, and that they've already tied to two more murders in Maryland."

"He killed somebody for the car."

"Yes, he did, so they'll charge him there, too. He won't get out of prison. He's going to die in there, and like Alice here, I hope that's a long way away.

"Now, the detective who had this case up in Fredericksburg is still going to want to talk to you."

"Will these children have to go into court, Tate?"

"I can't say for absolute yet, but they got him cold, Lucy, and I don't see a reason for that. My sense is he'll try for a deal."

"What does that mean?"

Tate shifted back to Thea.

"Virginia has the death penalty for first-degree murder, and he has two counts there, and we've got a pile of evidence. I think he'll say guilty if it saves his life. He'll trade execution for two life sentences without the possibility of parole."

"Even murderers cling to their own life," Alice added.

"Do you have any other questions?"

"Does he go to prison for the people in Maryland, too?"

"I expect that's going to add more years on, as he still had some of the things he took from them. I think we can count on more years there. Anything else?"

"Not right now, Sheriff." Thea looked at Rem, who shook his head. "Thank you for believing me and helping them catch him."

"You caught him, Thea. The police did their job, and they did it well. But it's you who caught him. You remember that."

Tate set down his glass, rose. "We're going to get on. If you need anything from me, you just call."

"We're grateful to both of you. And the police artist." Lucy got to her feet. "I hope you'll let her know we're grateful."

"I'll do that. Lucy, Leeanne sends her love and sympathy to all y'all. If you need any help with anything, you call her. Will's set to come around in the morning, and for as long as you want."

"I could use one more day, then I think we'll need to get back to routine. But he only gives me one more day if he comes in for breakfast after."

"I'll let him know."

When they'd driven off, Lucy poured more lemonade. "Can you tell me how you feel?"

"It feels good they caught him, and he'll go to prison forever. But . . ." Rem trailed off.

"It doesn't bring your mama and daddy back to us."

"We're never going to see them again."

"That's not altogether true. We'll all have them in here." She laid a hand on her heart. "And in here." Against her temple. "We'll see them in our hearts and minds, and all the memories."

"We can't ever make new ones."

"No, Thea, we can't, which makes the ones we have more precious. I have one of when your mama brought your daddy here to meet me and her brothers. On spring break it was, and John brought me flowers, so I knew right off he was a smart young man. Tulips yellow and bright as sunshine. We were standing right here on this porch when he gave them to me.

"Do you want to know what he said, first thing?" When they both nodded, she smiled. "He said not 'Pleased to meet you,' like you might expect. He said how Cora looked just like me, and she was the most beautiful woman in the world."

She sipped her lemonade. "Your mama wasn't the only one who fell for John Fox on the spot."

On a sigh, she rose. "Let's go feed our animals, then we'll cook up some dinner and feed ourselves. By tomorrow, people'll bring food."

"Why?" Rem asked.

"Because that's what neighbors do when you've lost someone."

Leeanne McKinnon, along with Abby from Appalachian Crafts, arrived together the next day before noon. They brought a chicken and rice casserole and blueberry cornbread cobbler.

They wouldn't stay more than a minute, but both hugged Lucy hard.

"If you need anything, a trip to the market, laundry done, a shoulder to lean on."

"I can call on you." Lucy hugged Leeanne again. "I've always been able to call on you. Both of you." And hugged Abby.

Leeanne, tall and thin like Will, looked at the children. "My number's in your grammie's book, so you use it if you need to. The three of us all went to school together, and we've been friends all these years. Old friends? That's next thing to kin, so y'all call if we can help with anything."

Her eyes, more golden than brown like Will's, went shiny with tears. And Thea saw the two women clutch hands as they walked to the car.

"You went to school together?"

"That we did, honeypot."

"But . . ." Thea trailed off.

"But what?"

"Well, Will's only seventeen."

"Leeanne and Tate got started on family a little later than I did. Will's got two older brothers, and they've got a girl younger than Will, about your age. She was what we call a happy surprise."

"Didn't she know she was having a baby? Because, you know." Rem held out his hands. "You get really big in the belly."

"Of course she knew, but she and Tate didn't expect to be expecting again. Then they had Madrigal. She's a caution, that girl. Maybe later this summer, Miss Leeanne can bring her over so you can meet her."

"How old were you when you had Mom?"

"Sixteen." Lucy laughed when Thea's mouth dropped open. "Zachariah and me? We just couldn't wait to get started. And we were lucky. We never stopped loving each other as some do when they can't wait."

More came, just as Lucy had predicted. They brought casseroles and pies and summer salads. They brought comfort.

A man with bright red hair and a red beard brought three fish in a big bucket of ice.

Rem made excited noises when Lucy got out her fish fillet knife and scaler. "You're going to cut them up!"

"Watch and learn. We got us some nice largemouth bass. First I have to scale them. And these scales fly all over, so we're doing it outside. Then I'm going to fillet them."

"What's that mean?"

"Watch and learn."

"Gross!" And Rem looked delighted, eyes huge, while Lucy scaled the fish.

Thea watched so she could learn, but it didn't feel really delightful.

When Lucy cut off the head and tail, Rem all but went into spasms. "Can I do one? Can I?"

"This knife's as sharp as they come, so we're going to be careful." She held the knife with him. Then looked at Thea.

"No, let Rem do the last one, too."

Lucy guided him through the next steps, so they had a pile of fish guts, a pile of bones, and chunks of fish meat.

"Now we're going to soak these pieces in salt water for about half an hour."

"Why?"

"To draw out all the blood."

"Yuck, yuck, yuck. Fish blood." Rem practically sang it.

"And we clean up our table and tools while it's soaking."

She turned to Thea, smiled. "Lots of people don't want to know where their food comes from. And that's just fine. But around here, it's all part of the cycle."

She liked the last parts of the cycle better. Helping make the coating, watching it fry up.

They had it with hush puppies and chowchow and some of the rice and broccoli casserole a neighbor brought them.

She couldn't write in her journal, and couldn't stop the tears when Lucy came to tuck her in.

Without a word, Lucy sat down and gathered her in.

"We did regular stuff all day, just normal. And sometimes I didn't think about them. We sat outside and ate cobbler, and heard a coyote up in the hills. When Rem tried to sound like one, I laughed. It's like I didn't care."

"No, darling, no, no, my precious girl. Living is what we have to do, and what they'd want. Because they loved us, they'd want us to live."

She eased Thea back, patted away the tears. "Grieving takes its own ways, its own time. Whenever you need to cry, you cry. But you have to laugh, too. You have to eat and sleep and wash your face, brush your hair, and all that regular stuff."

"I don't want them to think we don't care."

"They never would. Here, let's lie down awhile."

Lucy lay down with her and stroked her hair in that way that always made Thea feel warm inside.

"They made you and Rem out of love. You honor that love, you honor those who made you, by living a good, strong life. A happy one as much as you can. And when you find love, you hold on to it the way they did."

"I don't want to find it when I'm sixteen."

When Lucy laughed, the warmth spread, and Thea smiled.

"I'd as soon you didn't either. But I'll remind you of this when you're sixteen and think you're in love."

"How do you know the difference?"

"It's hard to tell at that age, so like I said, your granddaddy and me, we got lucky because it was true and real and deep, that love."

"You still love him."

"I do, and always will. When it's the kind of love that holds through the years, the troubles, and the joys? It's more than the heat and flutters inside you. I'd say it's like something roots in you, roots deep. It grows, and it blooms. It can't bloom without those roots."

"I want him to be handsome."

"Of course you do."

"And kind, like Dad." Thea's eyes started to droop.

"Kind beats even handsome. What else?"

"I hope he's smart." Those heavy eyes closed. "Likes books and music and animals. And he has to live here because I don't want to move away."

As she drifted into sleep, Lucy stayed awhile longer, stroking Thea's hair.

I want all that for you, too, she thought. In its time, I want all that and more for you.

Love hadn't taken root in her yet, but her grandmother's words had. She could cry when she needed to, and she would. But she would do what Lucy said, and live a good life to honor those who made her.

To start that good life, she got up even before her grandmother. She dressed and, with the dogs on her heels, went downstairs, let them out.

She'd watched her grandmother make coffee often enough she knew how it worked, so she made coffee. It would be ready for her grammie when she came down.

It was more dark than light when she went down, but she could see well enough to lead Aster into the barn. She scooped out grain, added the hay, then got down to the process of milking.

It felt good, she thought. Good to just get up and do it.

She thought how her mom had known how to milk a cow, but didn't really like to. How her father had learned how, and did.

As she walked back with the pail just as the sun lifted over the eastern hills, Lucy stepped out on the back porch.

"Girl, you got an early start."

"I wanted to."

"You made the coffee."

"I think I did it right. Can I have some coffee milk?"

"You surely can. Let me take that pail, and we'll go have our coffee."

"I'm going to feed the chickens first, and get the eggs. Rem really likes milking Molly, so he can do that. I want to live a good life, Grammie, and honor them. I'm trying to start today."

"Oh, my sweet child." Lucy pressed the back of her hand to her lips. "You're going to make me cry now. Pride tears. I'll take the pail. You go feed the ladies, and we'll have coffee when you're done."

When she was done, they sat with their coffee at the kitchen table.

"Waylon and Caleb are going to start driving down with the things you and Rem wanted. They'll be here tonight if they can, or tomorrow. The lawyer— Do you want to hear about all that?"

"Yeah."

"You're old enough to get up on your own to make my coffee and tend the animals, you're old enough to know what's going on around you. The lawyer said it was fine to take what they're bringing. It's going to take longer to settle everything. The estate it's called, and your mom and dad named me the executor of their estate. That means I work with the lawyers to get it all settled up."

"Get what settled? We can stay here. You said—"

"That's a different thing, and already settled. Thea." Lucy waited a beat. "That part's never going to change. I wouldn't lie to you about something so important."

"I know. I just . . . I get scared."

"Don't be scared about that. I just had to sign some papers. He emailed them, and I signed and did that scanner business. This is about the rest. The house, what's in it, their cars, and the bank accounts and all that."

"Okay."

"It can take a year or two to get it all settled."

"Why?"

"God knows, darling. It's lawyers, and making sure everything's done right and proper. I'm telling you so you know you and Rem have time to be sure what you want to do about all that. When you're ready to go to college, you'll have the means. They made sure of that. Beyond that, beyond the house, there's a considerable amount of money that'll come to you and Rem one day. I'm going to do my best to school you both on how to handle that."

Blowing out some air, Lucy sat back. "Your grandpa was a good provider. A hardworking man. And I didn't sit on my hands. My business does just fine. But I'm going to tell you the pure truth. All this is more money than I've known in my lifetime. We're all of us going to respect that."

"Are we rich?"

Lucy took another sip of coffee. From where she sat, Thea could see her trying to work out what she wanted to say and how to say it.

Then she said, "Hell with it. You're sitting here drinking coffee with me, so I'm going to give you more pure truth. I try not to speak ill of people, and that ill can come back on you threefold. But it needs saying. Marshall and Christine Fox—'cause never again will I call them your grandparents—are the kind of rich people call wealthy. And they're poorer in who they are than anyone living up in those hills struggling to keep a roof over their heads or fuel in the fire.

"Do you understand what I mean?"

Thea realized Lucy still held a lot of anger in that direction. And it made her feel warm and safe.

"I understand."

"You're going to be rich in who you are, you and Rem. I think you already are. Unless you're plumb stupid, which you aren't, you'll never have to struggle for the roof or the fuel."

She sighed again. "I'll be working with the lawyer and the financial adviser your parents had looking after all that, and an accountant, and Jesus only knows."

Thea saw the tears swim into Lucy's eyes, and the struggle to hold them back.

"You said to cry when you need to."

"I did. I did say that." So let the tears come. "It's my baby I'll bury in a few more days, and the man I loved like my own child. I have to do right by their babies. I'm going to make mistakes, because people always do, and I'm no better than the next. But I have to do right by you and Rem. And here I am, loading you down with all this when you'll bury your mama and daddy in those few days."

"No, Grammie, I want to know. It helps to know. I— Grammie, I can see your hurt, all dark red, like bleeding inside. And when I see it, it helps to know. Like needing to do the regular stuff. Like that."

Lucy reached across the table for her hand, and for the second time, Thea felt a flash, a spark. "I need to teach you, do right by you there, too. I promise, I will."

They both looked over as Rem clambered in with his eyes glazed with sleep and tears. "I dreamed they were back, then I woke up."

"Oh hell." Lucy reached out for him with one arm, and for Thea with the other. "Let's all have us a good cry, share these tears. Then Rem'll go milk Molly and Thea and I can make breakfast."

Later, when they went out the front to weed and water, they found a mason jar filled with wildflowers and a round of bread wrapped in a cloth.

"This is kindness," Lucy said. "This is richness."

"Do you know who left them, Grammie?"

"I do, Rem. Remember the lady we visited, and her little girl had ringworm? The bread's for what I brought her, and the flowers are for your parents. This here's stottie cake—it's bread but some call it cake. You take it back in the kitchen, and we'll make some sandwiches with it for lunch with that sun tea we've got going."

"Cake sandwiches!" He grabbed it up, ran inside.

"At this rate we won't have to cook for a week."

"Can we make candles later?" Regular stuff, Thea thought.

"That's a fine idea. We'll do just that."

Chapter Seven

Because Detective Phil Musk won the toss on the rental car at the airport in Kentucky, Detective Chuck Howard suffered through his partner's driving.

Worse, the airport sat a full hour from Redbud Hollow, and Musk never drove one damn mile an hour over the posted limit.

He liked Musk, trusted him without a ghost of a doubt, even admired his dog-with-a-bone stubbornness, attention to detail, and suspicious mind.

But he drove like an old woman.

"At this rate, we may get there by nightfall."

"Enjoy the scenery, Chuck. It's pretty country."

"We're not here for the scenery. We don't need to be down here in Nowhere Kentucky anyway. For Christ's sake, we got our guy, Phil. He knows it, his lawyer knows it, or they wouldn't have taken the deal."

"Life times two's still better than the needle or the chair."

"So he'll live and die inside. Now we're down here going to interview the grieving mother and a twelve-year-old? He confessed, right down the line. We had evidence to stick right up his ass."

"And why'd we have that evidence, why'd we find him so fucking easy? The kid dreamed it? Bullshit, Chuck."

Musk took his eyes off the road long enough to give his partner the hard eye.

"That grieving mother's got guardianship of the kids, and the kids are going to roll in the dough. Dreamed it all? Give me a fucking break.

Riggs did the murders, and yeah, we got him. But the rest?" Eyes trained on the road, Musk shook his head. "It doesn't smell right. None of it."

"If this Lucinda Lannigan—who doesn't have a mark on her record—set this all up, convinced the kid to say what she did, why didn't Riggs roll on her?"

"Don't know, and maybe it wasn't Lannigan, maybe it was the kid."

"Christ."

Because he'd given it considerable thought, Musk bore down into it.

"Kids that age can be devious, can be murderous. You know that as well as I do. The kid's down here with grandma and baby brother, and Riggs picks that time to murder the parents?"

"He'll be charged in Maryland, too, to ice the cake," Howard reminded him. "The Mercedes, the jewelry, the MO. Two more murders."

"Harder to tie him to those. Claims he bought the gun off the street in Baltimore, says he found the Mercedes, keys in it, out of gas when he tried hitching on some back road in rural Maryland."

Deliberately, Howard sniffed the air. "Now I smell bullshit."

"Yeah, and they'll wrap him. But they can't wrap him on those like we did on this one. We talk to the kid, the grandmother, and we get the truth. Local sheriff, he's too close to it, and when's the last time he's investigated a double murder? That would be never," Musk said helpfully.

Howard searched for patience. "It's a stretch, Phil, and you know how much of a stretch."

"Dreaming it all's a bigger stretch. It's a Mister Fantastic stretch. We've got to wrap this up, Chuck. We don't want that little bastard coming back later, crying he was framed by a twelve-year-old kid."

Howard hissed out a breath because there, he couldn't argue.

"I'm driving back when we're done with this."

In the kitchen, Thea and Rem helped work on a batch of candles. Lucy called the finished product Just Peachy for its scent and color. First they set the containers up, some travel tins that came with lids, some squat mason jars, and two bigger glass jars that had swirls of pink and orange. The bigger would get three wicks—Lucy said they gave a nice fragrance throw—and were Thea's favorite.

They'd set the wicks, and had the top of them secured to little sticks that lay over the rim of the jars and tins. Because they had to sit and cool and harden for a whole day, they sat on a sheet of brown paper on the counter in the workroom part of the kitchen.

If they had time, they'd do another batch of lavender.

They melted soy wax in the big double boiler. When Lucy made candles with beeswax, she let them stand on their own for their natural color and scent.

Thea added the scented oil, and Rem the coloring.

It all smelled good enough to eat.

As they poured the last of the tins, the dogs scrambled up to bark, and someone knocked on the front door.

"I'll get it, Grammie!"

Rem rushed to the front door with the dogs. Like the back door and the one off the side, only the screen door was closed, so he could look right through. He saw two men outside, in suits. Both had brown hair, but one was taller, and the taller one had some gray stuff in his hair.

"Everybody, stop! Sit!"

All three dogs sat, and though Duck made noises in his throat, all stopped barking.

Rem said, "Hello."

"Hi there." The taller one smiled at him. "I'm Detective Howard, and this is Detective Musk."

Obviously fascinated, Rem pushed open the door to study the badges. Then he looked up. "Are you the police who caught the"—he looked behind him, gauging the hearing distance to his grandmother—"the bastard who killed my mom and dad?"

"We were part of that, yeah. We're really sorry about your mom and dad. Is your grandmother home?"

"Sure. I don't get to stay by myself even though I'm ten. We're making candles."

"Can we come in and talk to her, to you and your sister?"

"Okay. At first I wanted you to kill him when you caught him, but then Deputy Driscoll said what prison was like, and how he'd be there forever. So that's even worse. I guess. Is it?"

Musk looked down. "If he lives to be a hundred and fifty, he'll still be in prison. I have to figure that's worse. Those are nice dogs."

"This one's Cocoa, she came with me and Thea. That's Duck and that's Goose. They won't bite you, since I told them to sit."

But when he opened the screen door again, they tore out like the house was on fire.

"They need to run around awhile."

He led them back as Lucy stepped into the main kitchen with Thea. "Now, that's a job well done. We can—"

She broke off when she saw two strange men with Rem.

Automatically, she nudged Thea behind her, reached for Rem's hand.

"Can I help you with something?"

Protective, Howard thought. Guard the kids first.

"We're the police, Ms. Lannigan. Detectives Howard and Musk, out of Fredericksburg."

He noted she relaxed, visibly, even as one arm went around each child.

"Oh. We weren't expecting . . . We're some of a mess. We were candle-making."

"Smells real good in here." Musk put on his easy smile. "Like . . . peaches?"

"Yes, that's exactly right. Ah, we've got some iced sun tea, or I can make you coffee."

"It's a rare day I turn down coffee, but it's a hot one. That tea sounds good, if it's no trouble."

"No trouble. Rem, why don't you take the detectives to the front room while we get the tea."

"Here's just fine." Howard gestured to the kitchen table. "We just have some follow-up questions, but first I want to tell all of you we're sorry for your loss."

"We appreciate that. Rem, you can take a counter stool, all right?"

"The youngest always gets the shaft."

Howard couldn't help but grin at him. "Tell me." He poked a thumb at his chest. "Youngest of three."

Lucy took her best glasses from the cupboard. "Sheriff McKinnon came to tell us when you caught him. Can you tell us if there's going to be a trial?"

"He confessed to everything," Howard told her. "For a full confession, we took the death penalty off the table. He'll serve two consecutive life sentences. No chance of parole."

Lucy pressed a hand to her throat, nodded while the girl stuck by her like a shadow. She took the big glass jug from the refrigerator, poured the tea over the ice in the glasses.

Crackle.

"It's a relief to hear that. I'm—we're obliged you've come all this way to tell us. Did you drive from Virginia?"

"No, ma'am." Musk took the glass she offered. "We flew down to the regional airport."

"A good hour's drive from there, isn't it? We've got some . . ." She paused, breathed out. "Some chocolate pecan pie a neighbor brought by."

"We're fine," Howard assured her. "We'll try not to take much of your time. We understand you're the children's legal guardian."

"That's right."

"And the executor of their estate."

"Yes."

"Would you mind telling us when that was decided?"

"Oh, well, Cora and John had wills made right after Thea came along, and asked me if I'd agree to it."

"You're a widow, Ms. Lannigan."

"Yes, I lost my husband eighteen years ago come November eighteenth."

"Your son-in-law has parents."

Musk let that statement lay. Before Lucy responded, Rem did. "They don't like us."

"Rem—"

"Well, Grammie, you say tell the truth even when it hurts, and they don't like us."

He hooked his sneakers around the stool, shrugged.

"They never came to see us, and they didn't send me anything for my birthday, and the last time we went out there—I didn't tell anybody—but I heard them say Thea was going to turn out just like her mother, how she'd never be a lady, and I'd just be a ruffian.

"I had to look that up, and that's a lie! And when Grammie called her to talk about what happened, she said she was going to take Dad, just Dad, out there to bury, away from Mom, and how she was going to put us in boarding school. Grammie got mad, madder than I've seen her *ever*, and said she wouldn't do any of that, and if they tried, she'd cover their reputations with poop. But she didn't say 'poop.'"

"Rem! That's enough." But the light in Lucy's eyes spoke of humor and admiration. "The detectives didn't come all this way to hear that."

"Actually," Howard said, "it answers the question."

"First Grammie said we had to talk to her, and him, too, because they lost their son, and they're our grandparents. But after that, she said we didn't have to. We didn't want to anyway, did we, Thea?"

Thea just shook her head, kept her head down.

"The relationship between your son-in-law, daughter, and his parents was adversarial?"

With weary in her eyes, Lucy looked at Musk. "I wouldn't say adversarial. There wasn't anything there. Cora and John loved each other, deeply. They loved their children, and they built a fine life together. That didn't matter to John's parents. He chose something and someone they didn't want, and that mattered more."

"As I understand it, Thea, you and your brother come to stay here for a couple weeks every summer?"

"Yes, sir." She didn't look at Musk.

"That's something you want to do?"

"Yes, sir."

"Even though you've got a swimming pool and friends back home? Video games, and a big-screen TV? What do you like doing here for two weeks?"

When Thea looked up, her eyes were deep and blue, and met Musk's dead on. "We milk Molly and Aster, and feed the ladies. We go for walks in the hills, and make soaps and candles, and homemade ice cream. We sit out and look at the stars. I'm going to learn how to make an apple stack cake. Grammie always made one for my dad because it was his favorite. Grammie plays music, and she's teaching Rem how to play the banjo because he wants to."

"Sounds like a lot of fun," Howard commented.

"It's our favorite two weeks of the year," Rem put in. "Well, maybe next to Christmas, but Grammie comes for Christmas."

Musk went back to Thea. "Was there any trouble at home before you left to come down?"

"No."

"You described Ray Riggs in detail to the police artist." Musk added the easy smile. "It really helped us find him. Where had you seen him before?"

"When he cut the hole in the sliders and came into the house."

"But you were here when that happened, weren't you?"

"Yes. I was dreaming. I didn't see his face when he cut the hole. I saw it after he shot them, I saw it in the mirror when he picked up Mom's anniversary watch. When he looked in it," she continued, her gaze steady on Musk's. "When he got scared because he felt somebody was looking at him. Before he went down and took my picture off the wall because a part of him knew it was me, and he wanted to hurt me like he did Mom and Dad."

"Now, that doesn't make much sense, does it?"

Still easy, still smiling.

"How you saw him in the mirror when you weren't there. How you knew just what he took from the scene, how you knew just what he did."

Lucy put a hand on Thea's shoulder. "Are you calling this child a liar?"

"Ms. Lannigan, there's no doubt Ray Riggs murdered John and Cora Fox. We want to make sure he pays for that. We want to make sure he spends the rest of his life in prison."

"And you've said he would," Lucy countered.

"We know he murdered your daughter and son-in-law. It's important we have all the facts, to be certain he acted alone."

Alarm leeched color from Lucy's face. "You think he might've had an accomplice?"

"I'm wondering if Thea might have seen Riggs before, may have spoken with him. If that's not the case, well, I have to consider the fact you're now the legal guardian of two minors with substantial trusts.

Executor of a substantial estate who has considerable influence over those children.

"I have to wonder if you met with Ray Riggs, made an arrangement. You told Thea what to say, and she's saying it."

Alarm flipped to rage.

"You would sit here, in my kitchen, in front of these children, and accuse me of conspiring to have my own child murdered in her bed? Have John murdered? Use this girl that way?"

"Facts, Ms. Lannigan."

In his line of work, Musk knew temper often served as a trip wire. So he pushed.

"If you didn't have part in it, this girl—and twelve can be an age where a girl resents her parents—gave details she could only know if she was there. She wasn't there, so the next logical conclusion is she took out that resentment using Riggs."

Lucy got slowly to her feet. "How dare you? How dare you speak to and about this beautiful, grieving child this way? Sit here, smiling at her when you have that blackness in your mind and heart?"

"I'm doing my job, and my job is to get full justice for John and Cora Fox."

"They have to go, Grammie." With his hands fisted at his sides, Rem jumped off the stool. "They have to get the hell out of here right now!"

"Yes, they do. Get out of my house, and don't you ever come around these children again. Don't you talk about justice when you've sliced a knife in these children's hearts."

"We can go, but if you're sticking with dreams, we'll come back, and we'll talk to Riggs again, get the truth out of him. We'll come back with Child Services."

"You got divorced last year, and you're still sad about it." Her eyes trained on Musk, Thea spoke quietly. "Mostly because you don't get to see the twins—Rogan and Logan, they're eight—as much as before. People call you Phil, or Musk, but when your mom was mad, she called you Philip Henry Musk. You broke your arm when you were eleven. You were riding your bike too fast and hit a root coming through the sidewalk, and flew right off and broke your arm. This one."

She rubbed a hand on her left arm, then looked at Howard.

"You're Chuck and your wife is Lissa. Kevin's six and Cody's three—you have their pictures in your wallet, and you're starting to think you and Lissa should have one more, try for a girl. You're mad at him right now, at Detective Musk. You didn't want to come down here. You didn't like the way he let his stubbornness and his anger push him to handle it this way. Riggs'll rot in prison. You can't explain what I told the sheriff, but everything else told you there's nothing here to . . . to tie us to it."

She looked back at Musk. "I'm not mad at you for it. Grammie, Rem, don't be so mad. He saw them after, in bed. They were holding hands." Her voice trembled now, tears swirled with it. "He saw how they were holding hands with bloody pillows over their faces, and that went in him, it went deep. And you said to Detective Howard . . ."

She closed her wet eyes, and let it come. "'We're going to find the fucker who did this, Chuck. If it takes the rest of our lives, we're going to find this fucker and take him down.'"

"Jesus Christ."

"Shut up, Phil. I mean it, shut up." Howard leaned toward Thea. "Thea, I'm going to apologize to you, to your grandmother, to your brother as sincerely as I know how. I'm sorry for what you had to see that night. I'm sorry for what and who you lost. I'm sorry we put you through this."

"He really does want justice for them, so I'm not mad. But . . ."

She turned to Musk again, who sat, his face pale and stunned. "My grandmother loved our parents as much as we did. She was a mother to my dad when his never was. She's changing her life to keep us because they asked her to, because she loves us.

"Don't you ever, ever say bad things about my grandmother again."

Musk started to speak, then held up a hand to stop his partner from cutting him off. "Give me a break, Chuck. I'm sorry. I've never had an experience of anything like this. I don't believe—didn't believe . . . I'm sorry."

"Thea's accepted your apologies, so we will, too. Now I'd like you to show yourselves out."

When they rose to leave, Thea took another breath. "Detective Howard? Be careful on the blue stairs. I don't know what it means, but be careful on the blue stairs."

A little chilled, he nodded.

Outside, Musk rubbed his hands over his face. "I need a drink. A serious drink."

"We'll get one at the airport."

At the car, Musk looked over the hood at his partner. "Something about them holding hands like that got to me, Chuck. I couldn't let it go."

"Let it go now, Phil. Case closed."

In the kitchen, Lucy pressed a kiss to the top of Thea's head. "I'm so proud of you, Thea, and you, Rem, of the way you stood up."

"They scared me, I think. And I didn't want them to be here. I didn't want to talk to them, to talk about it all again. So I tried not to think, and I could see . . . just knew things about them. Because the more they talked, the more I got upset and tried not to think."

She closed her eyes. "I've got a headache, Grammie."

"I know. I'm going to give you something to help with that. Do you want to lie down awhile?"

"Can I just go outside and sit on the porch?"

"I'll go with you, Thea. I'll be quiet, promise." Tears, from anger and grief, still stood in Rem's eyes. "I'll go with you."

"I had to say those things I knew about them so they knew we weren't lying. But when I started to know some, I couldn't stop. Even when it started to hurt, I couldn't stop."

"I'll help you with that, too. I think you're beyond my gifts, darling, but I can help you. You go sit awhile, and, Rem, until Thea wants to talk, you keep that promise."

"I will."

The cool basil tea helped the headache. When Rem said he could feed the animals all by himself, Thea sat with Lucy.

"You have a strong gift, darling."

"Why does it have to hurt?"

"There's always a price, I guess, but there are ways to lower that price. Like there are ways not to see or know until you need to or want to. Today, you needed to, so it came over you, and you weren't ready for the strength of it."

"Did Mom have it?"

"I think she did, but she gave it back. She pushed it out, and she had a right to."

"I don't want to give it back."

"Neither did I. But I stopped using all of it to keep the peace."

"For Mom."

Lucy smiled a little as she nodded. "She was my baby girl, my firstborn."

"She didn't want to be different. Not that way."

"I think that's true. And it scared her to think she might know things she didn't want to know. Or I might."

"It doesn't scare me like that, Grammie."

"That's good. It's something you respect, even though some people will steer clear of you for it, or say hard things. Something you don't ever use to play tricks or hurt somebody."

"I wanted the detective to stop saying those things, thinking those things."

"I got too mad," Lucy admitted. "I wanted them out and gone, so I didn't do what I should've to show them what was what."

She rubbed Thea's shoulder. "But you did. You were clearing your mind, working not to think about what they talked about, wanted us to talk about. A clear mind can help it come right through. Getting upset, scared, that's another way. But the best, the clearest, the one that hurts less? Is just opening up to it. Like, all right then, come on in!"

"Like just opening a door—sort of?"

"That's just it. When we sleep, we're open, so the dreams come. If you don't want them to come, you can close them out. Most of the time."

"How?"

"It sounds silly, but certain herbs under the pillow, or a charm bag over the bed. A phrase you say three times running, certain scents you breathe in before sleep. Your gift doesn't want to hurt you, Thea. It's part of you. So you work with that part of you."

She lifted Thea's hand, kissed it. "We'll practice. Now look at that boy, doing the chores so we can sit here like ladies of luxury. Ruffian? My great-aunt Maggie's ass."

When Thea giggled, Lucy laughed with her. "She's got a big one. There's the phone." Lucy held up a finger, closed her eyes. "It's Waylon." Then winked at Thea.

"I've still got it."

Even with the packing up into the U-Haul truck, the traveling, Thea's uncles arrived before noon the next day.

Seeing them brought Thea twin pangs. Happiness in seeing them, sorrow in the why of it.

Waylon lifted her right up, held her tight. He had some scruff on his face and smelled a little of the cigarettes he was always trying to quit.

He looked really tired, and so did Caleb when he held her face in his hands and kissed her.

They hugged Rem, too, and both of them held on to Grammie even longer. Thea saw Waylon's shoulders shake when he pressed his face down to his mother's shoulder.

And how her grandmother stroked his hair, scruffy like his face, the way she did Thea's when she needed comfort.

"You boys come inside now, sit down awhile. You've had a long few days. We made some lemonade, and we've got plenty to eat."

"We've been sitting, Mama." Since the dogs whined for it, Caleb gave all three a quick rub. "How about we save the lemonade and food till we unload the truck?"

"Did you get my dad's drawing board?"

"We sure did." Waylon shoved sunglasses on wet eyes before he ruffled Rem's hair.

"Can I have that in my room, Grammie?"

"That's just fine."

Thea didn't know how she felt, not exactly, about carrying boxes of her clothes and things inside. She wanted her things, but it made it all real again.

She'd never go back to the house in Virginia.

"We don't have to put everything away just right now. Y'all can put the computer stuff in the sewing room. I've got it cleared out."

"That's your room, Grammie."

"I don't do the kind of sewing I once did." Lucy patted a hand on Thea's shoulder. "So set everything in there for the time being. I'm thinking I'll see about having the attic fixed up enough so we can put all that up there, like a game room. But let's just get it all there for right now."

In her room, looking at the boxes of clothes, of things, Thea didn't know where to start.

"This one's got your name on it, too. I'm going to give those boys credit for packing up right." Lucy came in, set the box down. "I know this room's smaller than what you're used to, but—"

"No, Grammie, it's not that. You don't have to change things for me, for Rem. Like your sewing room and the attic."

"I'm not changing them just for you and Rem. I'm changing some things for us. For the three of us. For Waylon and Caleb when they come to visit. For the families I hope they make one day."

She sat on the bed, patted the space beside her. "I've been living here alone for a time now, so I didn't need much to change. Things are different now, and it's time for some changes. I'm telling you, Thea, it helps my heart to make them. It helps my heart because I know in it, your mama and daddy would be pleased with those changes.

"Rem's in there working with Caleb to set up that PlayStation. You could do it quicker."

"Maybe." Then Thea lifted her shoulders. "Yeah, I could."

"But the doing it's helping both of them."

"Because we have to live."

"That's right."

Time, Thea thought, to ask what was most on her mind.

"When are they sending Mom and Dad?"

"Why don't we go on down, put some food together? We can all talk about it after some lunch. We'll talk about all of it together."

Chapter Eight

They ate and talked about Caleb moving to New York, drank lemonade and talked about Waylon's latest travels.

When they'd cleared the table, Lucy told her sons they'd more than earned a beer.

"We need to talk about the arrangements I've made." With everyone around the table again, Lucy began. "I can change things, if anyone wants something else or different. I want to make sure I've made the right choices. First, Cora and John are coming home here tomorrow."

"Can we see them?"

Lucy shook her head at Rem. "No, darling. I'm sorry."

"Because of the way he killed them."

Waylon's face went to stone, but his eyes flooded with rage. Beside him, Caleb laid a hand on his arm.

"That's right. We're going to have pictures of them. Your uncles brought their pictures, and you can both have as many as you want. We'll pick ones we want to put out for the funeral."

"Can we do a gallery wall here, Grammie? Not just with their pictures. I mean with everybody's?"

"Rem, that's such a good idea." Lucy beamed at him. "We'll go through my picture albums sometime soon and start on that.

"The funeral home, they're going to pick up"—she hesitated, then went on—"the caskets from the airport. Cora had white and pink hydrangeas in her bridal bouquet because she favored them, so we're having those at the service, and at the gravesite. I thought we'd have just one stone because they're together and always will be."

She cleared her throat. "In my first anger and grief, I thought about having it say something like *taken from us through cruelty*, but that's not how we should remember them. So I thought, something that honors them. I thought what John put on Cora's anniversary watch. *For All Time*."

"That's perfect, Mama," Caleb told her.

"None of us are big churchgoers so I thought having the service right in the funeral home's the best. Caleb, Waylon, I'm going to ask you both for something hard. Caleb, I'm asking you to do their eulogy, to get up there and speak for all of us, if you think you can."

He didn't speak, just nodded.

"Waylon, the hard I'm asking you? That song, 'Endless Love,' they had at their wedding for their first dance. I'm asking you to sing that for them, and for us, just like you did for the wedding."

"Mama." He closed his eyes, then, like his brother, nodded. "Of course I will."

"Is all of that all right with you, Thea, and you, Rem?"

"Can one of the pictures be their wedding picture, the one on the gallery wall in Virginia?" Thea asked. "If we're having the flowers and the song . . ."

"That's just perfect."

"Can Cocoa come? They loved Cocoa."

"Well, I'll find out about that, Rem. If she can't come in the funeral home, she can sure come to the gravesite. We'll have the funeral day after tomorrow, and after, people will come back here. The eating places in town are sending food. They won't take money for it. But I'm going to make a ham and an apple stack cake. Cora favored my ham, and John surely loved my apple stack cake. I've got a list of what I need at the market, if one of you boys would drive in and get that for us."

"I'll take care of that, Mama," Waylon told her.

"I appreciate that. I'll give you a check you can fill out when—"

"No, you won't. Don't say that to me, Mama. Don't. Cora was my sister, John was a brother to me."

When his eyes went teary, Lucy rose and went to him. "You're right."

From behind his chair, she hugged him, kissed his shaggy hair. "We all have to say goodbye in the best way we can. If I've left something out, or you want something else, just say."

"Will a lot of people come?"

"I expect they will, Rem. And your granny's coming up tomorrow with Stretch, and my brother, my sisters, your cousins. Your mama and daddy had friends in Virginia, and some of them are coming, too."

"A lot of people," Caleb confirmed. "When they're all in here, if y'all just need to get away from them for a little bit of a while, just want the quiet? Then you go on up to your room and take that quiet. If you need something else, you just find me or Waylon."

"Give me your list, Mama, and I'll do your fetching. How about taking a ride with me in Grammie's truck, Rem? You, too, Thea, if you want."

"That's okay. I want to put my things away. And I want to help make the apple stack cake. I want to learn how. I'm going up now, Grammie, to put my things away."

And to think a little, she added to herself. To think about how many people would come to the house. She needed her grandmother to teach her how to hold back all that grief and mad. She felt so much from her uncles. As calm as Caleb made himself look and sound, she'd felt as much grief and mad from him as Waylon showed on his face.

All from them, from her grandmother, from Rem, inside herself got so heavy.

It hadn't been like this before, not before that night. She needed to know how to hold some of it back because it almost felt like it could crush her.

She needed to learn.

She waited to ask until Lucy came to tuck her in that night.

"You said there'd be a lot of people."

"Yes."

"You said the gift doesn't want to hurt me, and I should open myself to it. But when we were all talking after lunch, and a couple of other times today, it—it did hurt, Grammy. Uncle Caleb feels the way Uncle Waylon does, even though he doesn't show it as much. And with lots more people—"

"I understand. Sometimes you have to close a window."

She nodded to the open one letting in the night air.

"If you closed that window, you'd still see outside, see the rain if it's raining, or the sun or the wind in the trees. But you wouldn't feel it nearly as much as you would if that window stayed open. This is the kind of time where you need to close that window."

"How?"

"You've done it plenty already. Maybe not as thoughtfully or deliberately. Accepting what you have doesn't mean you have to use it every day. If you need more than a window, imagine a door, close it up, turn the lock. It's yours, Thea. Maybe you decide, all right, I can open the window a little bit, or leave the door ajar. Or you don't because you need that quiet Uncle Caleb talked about."

"Do you leave it open or closed?"

"Oh, I guess mostly a little open. Sometimes all the way open or all the way closed."

"If I can, I want to keep it closed when we have the funeral."

"Then that's what you do. And if you need help, you come to me. All right now?"

When Thea nodded, Lucy leaned down to kiss her. "Dream something happy now, or something full of adventure. Don't carry weight into sleep."

Thea closed her eyes, imagined a window. It stormed outside. The rain, the tears. The wind, the grief. The thunder, the mad.

And imagined herself closing the window.

On the day of the funeral, Thea put on the black dress she and her mother had picked out for the spring chorus concert at school. She'd felt so grown-up wearing it, and the shoes with the short, stacked heels.

She knew she'd never wear either again.

She braided her hair, and put on the earrings the police had given back to her uncles.

Granny had come with her well-to-do second husband everybody called Stretch. She'd heard her grandmother, and her mother, too, call Carrie Lynn O'Malley Riley Brown a force of nature.

Standing a full six feet tall with a long spill of bright red hair and sharp green eyes, she looked like one.

She'd cried, and when Thea let the window open a crack, she saw a heart that carried deep scars.

The aunts and uncles and cousins brought more tears with them.

Because Waylon and Caleb had driven down in the U-Haul and they only had her grandmother's truck, Stretch rented cars for driving down to the funeral home, to the graves, and back home again.

She sat in the back of one beside her grandmother, Rem on the other side in his best and only suit.

Waylon drove, with Caleb in the seat beside him and Cocoa between.

The funeral home sat on the far end of town, a big redbrick building with white trim and windows that shined in the sun. It stood on a slope of a manicured lawn, and to Thea's eye, did look like a house.

A man with gray hair opened the door to them. He wore a black suit and shiny black shoes, and spoke in the quiet voice you're supposed to use in church.

Thea decided not to listen, because her heart started to beat so fast.

Everything smelled like flowers; everything felt too hot.

She wanted to run back outside and keep running, but gripped her grandmother's hand, as Rem did on the other side. With Cocoa on the leash, they all followed the man into a big room where the sun beamed through the windows, and folding chairs sat in line after line after line.

A table held the pictures they'd picked out and more flowers. Two big white vases held the pink and white hydrangeas beside an easel with the picture Stretch had enlarged.

Her mother in her wedding dress, and her dad in his wedding suit. She knew it was from their first dance because it had hung on the gallery wall.

They looked at each other. She'd heard her grandmother once say you could see the stars in their eyes.

She made herself look at the caskets as they walked toward them down the aisle between the lines of chairs.

Boxes, polished up, more hydrangeas flowing over them.

With her parents inside.

She remembered how they'd looked the day they'd left for home.

It seemed like a minute ago. It seemed like a year ago.

Even with the window closed as tight as she could, she knew Rem started to cry. She knew tears ran down her grandmother's face. Her uncles' grief layered over her own.

Lucy looked at her, pressed her lips to Thea's cheek, and some of the terrible weight lifted.

They let the rest of the family come in next. Though Rem went with Caleb, Lucy kept Thea's hand firm in her own.

Even when they sat in the front row of all those chairs, Lucy held Thea's hand.

More and more people came. Even when all the chairs filled, others stood in the back. The man in the black suit walked to the front. He spoke about knowing Cora since she'd been a little girl, about meeting John. How everyone here felt their loss, the tragic loss to their families, to their young children, to the community.

Waylon got up, strapped on his guitar. He'd shaved his face smooth, tamed his hair.

"This is Cora and John's song, the one they danced to first as husband and wife."

He played it slow, and when he sang the lyrics, Lucy's hand trembled in Thea's.

This time Thea gripped tighter.

Waylon didn't cry until he sat back down again.

Then Caleb went up. He was very pale, and somehow more handsome with it.

"There are people in the world who make it better just by being in it. People who bring joy, bring love, simply because they have joy and love in them.

"Cora and John made the world better. They brought joy and they brought love. They were taken from the world, from their children, from all of us by a senseless and brutal act.

"And still, they bring joy, they bring love. Through our grief we feel that joy, that love because they send it to us. To all of us, friends, neighbors from near and far. They send it to our family.

"To you, Mama, to you, Waylon, and especially to you, Thea and Rem. Their loss cuts so deep, it's hard to get through and believe that.

But we do, and we will. The light they brought into the world, it's never going out. It shines on in their children."

When Caleb sat again, the man in the black suit invited anyone who wanted to say a few words to come up.

Plenty did, to say kind things or tell a funny or sweet story.

But as Thea sat, her heart stopped pounding. Waylon's song, Caleb's words seemed to flow right into her. And somehow they dulled the sharp, cutting edge of pain she'd fought against since she put on the black dress.

The cemetery lay outside the town proper, with its stones and monuments on rolling hills.

The man in the black suit spoke again, then both Caleb and Waylon got up.

"What are they going to do, Grammie?"

"I don't know, Rem."

They stood together on the sun-washed hill with the flower-draped coffins behind them.

"We're here to say goodbye to Cora and John. Mama and Daddy raised us with music, so Caleb and I, we decided we'd sing them off. Not with a sad song, but a song about life, and the love in it."

They sang, a cappella, "In My Life."

At the first line, Lucy choked back a sob. She swallowed the tears, let out a long, long sigh.

She kissed Rem's hand, then Thea's. The three of them sat, joined, while her sons' voices carried over the rolling hills.

After, people came up to offer condolences, embraces, but eventually they stood alone together, brothers, mother, children.

"I want to say how proud I am of you, my boys. For the song in the service, Waylon, for your words, Caleb. How they're going to stay with me for the rest of my days. And for what you did here. None of that was easy for you to do, but you did it for them, and for me, and these children.

"Let's go on home now. People will already be there, and we're grateful to the friends who stayed back from the gravesite to greet them. Let's go on home, and we'll come back when the stone's set. We'll bring flowers."

*   *   *

People filled the house, spilled onto the porches, wandered on the grass, front and back. They ate ham, collard greens, cornbread, casseroles, and cake. They drank sweet tea and lemonade and beer and wine.

Younger kids ran around outside with the dogs. With Lucy's permission, Rem changed out of his suit, but Thea kept her dress on. Since it would be the last time she wore it, she decided she'd keep it on until people left.

But she did take some of the quiet time in her room. Better for it, she came down. Even with the window opened only a crack, she could tell the grief didn't weigh as heavy. People wanted to tell stories about her mom and dad, especially her mom, that made that weight a little lighter.

She met a man who'd gone to college with her parents, who'd been best man at their wedding.

"You won't remember me," he said. "I haven't seen you since you were about five or six, not in person. I moved to Chicago, so I didn't get to see your mom and dad much after that. This is my wife, Melissa."

"They went to your wedding. We were here with Grammie, so they went to your wedding in Chicago. Not last summer, but maybe the one before that."

"That's exactly right. He was my best man, like I was his."

"You came all the way from Chicago?"

"I loved him," he said simply. "Your mom, too."

She'd thought it would hurt, all the people, all the feelings, but it helped, at least a little.

Somebody convinced Waylon to get his guitar, and somebody else got another, and somebody else a banjo. So music started on the front porch while little kids and dogs raced around back.

And that helped somehow, too.

She walked outside to sit on the back porch swing. Not really quiet time with the kids shouting, the music playing, all the voices carrying out the windows.

But enough just to sit in the air.

A girl came out. She had a head full of braids with white beads on the ends. She wore a black skirt that brushed her knees and a white top with flowers on the collar.

Carrying a big red plastic cup, she sat right down beside Thea.

"I'm Maddy," she announced. "It's really Madrigal, but that's a whole mouthful. My mama's a friend of your grammie's, and my daddy's the sheriff."

"Oh. I'm Thea."

"I know. I'm real sorry about what happened to your mama and your daddy. I hope the man who killed them gets warts and boils on his pecker."

The laugh just burst out of Thea, and Maddy smiled.

"Well, I do. My mama always says how you shouldn't wish bad on others, but I bet she wouldn't mind if he got those boils and warts. You want some of my lemonade?"

At Thea's hesitation, Maddy smiled again. "It's okay. I got rid of all my cooties. We're the same age, so we're going to be going to school together. Might as well be friends."

Thea took the cup, sipped. Cold, tart, and just right.

Just like that, on the day she buried her parents, she met a lifelong friend.

From the kitchen window, Lucy watched them. Then reached back for her lifelong friend. "Look out here, Leeanne, look at our girls. Thea's smiling again, and meaning it."

"Maddy'll shake the sads out of anyone. She just won't quit. If she's decided to be Thea's friend, Thea doesn't have a chance."

"She needs friends. So will Rem. Good Christ, Leeanne, don't let me be too old to do all this right by those children."

"I'll remind you, Lucinda Lannigan, I've got a twelve-year-old, too."

On a light laugh, Lucy sliced more ham. It helped to keep her hands busy.

"I've been at it a lot longer."

"That's experience, not age. You raised a fine daughter and two fine sons. And when Zachariah left us, you did it on your own. I don't know anyone in this world, Lucy, who'll do all of this more right by them than you."

"Thea needs a friend who'll hold her up like you do me."

"Trust me." Leeanne peeked out the window again, watched Maddy and Thea on the porch swing. "She's got one."

It took a long time for the house to empty out but for family, and longer yet before it came down to only Waylon and Caleb.

Lucy's friends had tucked away all the food left and cleaned the kitchen to a shine.

"Waylon, do your old mama a favor and get her a glass of that wine."

"I don't have an old mama, but I'll get my beautiful mama some wine. Which? I think Stretch bought out a wine store in Atlanta."

"If Stretch bought it, it's bound to be good. You pick." She let out a groan as she toed off her shoes. "I don't know the last time I had dress-up shoes on for so long. Thanks," she added as Waylon set a glass of wine in front of her.

She took a sip, glanced around. "They didn't leave a thing for me to do. And didn't Will see that the animals were tended. I'm not sure I know what to do when nothing needs doing."

"You sit and drink that wine," Caleb told her.

"Then I will."

"Can I have some?"

Rem's question got a resounding no from every adult in the room.

"How come? Kids in France drink wine."

"You find your way to France, sweet potato, you can have some."

"I think maybe I will. They eat snails, too. I'd try a snail." He gave Thea a superior look. "Bet you wouldn't."

"You make gagging noises if you've got spinach on your plate. You're not eating any snails."

"I would in France. French snails are different or people wouldn't eat them over there."

"Then you've got to wear a beret," Caleb told him.

"What's that?"

"It's a hat. You wear it cocked." He demonstrated with his hands.

"Probably an ascot. That's a fancy tie," Waylon explained. "Like a scarf."

"Ties suck, but I'd wear the hat thing and the ascot. I'd eat snails and drink wine, and say merci beaucoup because that's French for thanks."

"What if you don't like the snails?"

Rem frowned at Waylon a moment. "I'd spit them out and say whatever's yuck in French. How do you say yuck in French?"

"*Merde*'s close enough."

Now Waylon frowned at Caleb. "How the hell do you know that?"

"The theater, brother. You learn all kinds of things in the theater."

Under the table while the other three talked, Thea took her grand-mother's hand. And smiled.

This, she realized, was what needing to live meant.

That night, after Grammie tucked her in, she lay trying to dream herself to sleep. But then she sat up, turned on her light. For the first time since her parents' death, she picked up her journal.

She wrote out everything she could remember, even about that night. She wrote about Ray Riggs, about the deputy, the detectives. She wrote about Will, about making candles. She wrote about opening or closing the window, about the funeral. About Maddy and her uncles.

About words spoken, songs sung.

She wrote it out of herself, into the journal, until she had hardly any pages left.

She'd ask her grandmother if she could get another journal.

After she finally set it aside, turned off the light, she slept.

And slept quiet and calm and easy while everyone in the house slept around her.

Waylon and Caleb stayed three more days. They ran errands, helped with the animals, and both did their best to work with Lucy on the paperwork and decisions involving the estate.

"Cora and John did well for themselves, but holy hell, Mama, I didn't know John brought that kind of money with him."

"He never flaunted it," she said to Waylon as the three of them sat in her little office. "They couldn't take the money away from him, but they sure withheld everything else. Not one of them came to his funeral. Their son, their brother. Not a one of them has called or written those children to offer comfort."

"There's a simple solution." Caleb shrugged. "They don't exist, not in our world. They just don't exist. John was ours, your son, our brother, and he always will be."

"That's a damn good solution." Lucy rubbed tired eyes, pushed at the hair she hadn't taken time to braid. "I'm using it. You boys have been such a help to me with this. I figured myself a pretty sharp business-woman, but I'm getting an education on accounting and lawyering and big-wheel finances here."

"We can stay a few more days, Mama."

"Waylon, you and Caleb have lives to get back to. I really want you back here for Christmas this year, as it'll be a hard one, and those kids need family around. But now, you've got lives to get back to. I've got those accountants and lawyers and big-wheel financial advisers to pull me through this."

"You call if you need to bitch some about all that."

On a laugh, she patted Caleb's hand. "You might regret that offer, 'cause I'm taking it. And I'm taking the advice both of you gave me. Those children are never going to want to live in the house where their parents were killed. I'm foolish for hesitating about selling it for them."

"Doesn't make it any easier to sell off what Cora and John worked to build."

"No, Waylon, it doesn't."

Such a lovely house, she thought. One they'd filled with light and love.

Knowing what needed doing didn't make it easier. But it made it right.

"This is what they'd want. It's what both of you think, and it's what Thea and Rem told me they wanted. I do worry some about all their things."

"Mama." Caleb waited until she looked at him. "The kids said what they wanted, and you told us what you knew both Cora and John set store by. Things you passed down to them, things they gave each other that held real meaning to them. The rest? Just things, Mama."

"You're right, and I know it. So I'll do what the lawyer said we could. Hiring on that company he recommended that goes in and appraises all that. They'll handle an estate sale, and that'll be that. That's what's best."

"They asked you to take this on because they knew you could, and you would. But what Caleb said before goes for me, too. You need to bitch some, you call."

"All right then." She closed the last file folder. "I know it's late, but how about we sit out on the porch awhile, have a little sipping whiskey?"

In the morning, after chores, after breakfast, the brothers tossed their bags in the U-Haul.

"I want calls when you both land in your spots, you hear?" She hugged them both. "Oh, I miss you both already."

"Home for Christmas, Mama." Waylon scooped Thea off her feet. "You take care of your grammie for me."

"I will."

"And you?" Rem got a bear hug. "You're the man of the house."

"And they outnumber you, so stand strong, my brother." Caleb kissed both of Rem's cheeks, then Thea's.

They stood, as they had at another goodbye, as the truck drove away.

"It's all right to say it, Grammie," Thea told her. "It's the three of us now."

"It's the three of us. Well, I need to make the liquid soap people are so fond of. Since making it right from start to finish takes a couple days, I'm gonna use some child labor."

"Days! Don't you just melt it?"

"No, Rem, you don't. But I'm going to show you how. The way I figure it, you're employees of Mountain Magic now. We gotta talk salary."

"Oh, Grammie," Thea began, but Rem waved his arms in the air.

"We get paid?"

"A body needs some spending money. We'll negotiate."

"I'm older. I should get more."

"No way! I'm the man of the house, and men get more than girls."

"Just listen to y'all." Lucy shook her head as they walked back to the house. "I'll tell you right off, I don't run my business with any bias against age or sex. I pay you both just the exact same. I'm thinking, oh, ten cents an hour."

"Ten cents!"

"That's what they call my floor, Rem." She pushed open the screen door. All three dogs rushed in before they did. "Now, start negotiating."

Chapter Nine

Ray Riggs hated prison. Some of that hate rooted itself in a deep, dark fear. Fear of never getting out.

Due to the double murder, and charges pending on more, he'd earned a no-detour trip to Virginia's supermax.

During transport, he'd caught a whiff of one of the guard's thoughts about him, how he was a punk-ass no-account who'd deserved the needle.

His aborted attempt to attack the guard earned him some bruises.

Bruises were nothing, nothing compared to the spit-drying fear of seeing segregation.

Not cells with bars, but doors, blue doors with a single skinny window. Behind those doors, inmates shouted, banged, some cackled. And the noise boomed and echoed as they shuffled him along in his cuffs and leg shackles.

He couldn't be here, couldn't stay here. They couldn't keep him here.

He fought, couldn't stop himself, but they made him kneel down just inside one of those doors.

He saw the horrible room with its bunk, its toilet, its high little window of frosted glass.

No, he couldn't stay in here.

His lawyer fucked him over, that's what happened. He'd get out, kill the bastard.

He didn't hear what the guards told him as they unlocked his shackles. He didn't care.

He wouldn't stay in here.

When they locked him in, he pounded on the door, screaming, adding to those echoes until he couldn't scream anymore.

Later, food came through a slot in the door, but he didn't eat it.

He'd heard about hunger strikes. He'd go on a hunger strike, and get the TV people and all those bleeding-heart assholes on his side.

That night he heard voices in his head, taunting him.

And by morning, he was too hungry not to eat what came through the slot.

Later, they made him kneel again, shackled him again. They took him down to a big mesh cage, like he was an animal.

"You get an hour to exercise," the guard told him.

"Fuck you. I want to make a phone call." He'd call that asshole lawyer and let him know what was coming.

"You don't have phone privileges. One hour, Ray." The cage door closed behind them.

He didn't exercise. He sat instead on the bench bolted to the floor. In the cage beside his, some Black guy wearing a yellow ski cap over dreads did push-ups.

He looked strong. Ray figured he needed somebody strong on his side. He'd start with this guy, put a gang together. They'd overpower the guards and escape.

"Hey." Ray hissed the word out. "I'm working on a way out of here. Could use some help."

The other inmate never paused, didn't even glance in Ray's direction. "Fuck off."

"I'm getting the hell out of here!" Screaming it, he threw himself at the mesh.

"Hey, man." The Black guy continued with his push-ups. "This crazy mofo's interfering with my endorphins."

"Settle down, Ray."

But he wouldn't, he couldn't, and ended up back behind the door with the voices screaming in his head.

That night, he wept himself to sleep, where dreams chased him like hounds.

When he woke, shaking, the silence bit more viciously than the hounds.

He took his mind on a journey where he sat with a cold beer on the terrace of a fancy-ass house and looked out at the water. When it calmed him, finally calmed him, he reminded himself he could go wherever he wanted in his head.

He just had to find a way to use that to get the rest of him out.

He'd been born with a calculating and knowing mind, a special talent. It was time he started using it.

He let his mind wander, from cell to cell, from inmate to inmate. Some of what he picked up had his whole body shaking, and the scope of the push had blood dribbling from his nose, his ear.

He kept at it. The headache nearly made him scream, but he didn't quit.

Ray Riggs was no quitter.

He shouldn't even be here. They should never have caught him. Someone had to pay for that, and someone would. But first he had to survive.

So he ate what came through the slot. He didn't fight when they came to the door, but shuffled down for his hour a day in the mesh cage and sat, brooding, thinking.

He read the guards, looking for openings, any opening, but found none. Just scattered thoughts about the next smoke break or money worries, or wives and women.

He read other inmates but found no hope of help from any. Just roiling rage, hopeless resignation, regrets, resentments.

And many he feared too much to read.

He sweated through the nights, so many voices, and sometimes dreamed of the face of the kid, the girl, the picture on the wall he'd taken.

She'd done this to him. He'd caught something about her, about her pointing the finger, from the detectives when they'd dragged him out of the motel.

But he'd been too shocked, too scared to catch more than a whiff.

Now he had time, nothing but time, to think back on it. To think of that smirking little girl.

She hadn't been there—he *knew* that—so what the fuck.

But that picture on the wall. Hadn't she looked right at him?

And for just a second, in the mirror when he had that goddamn watch in his hands . . .

Riggs shot up. He'd seen her. He'd seen that little bitch. In his head. Behind him in the mirror.

Both.

She *had* been there, just like he could go where he wanted in his head.

She was like him, that had to be it. She was like him. She'd seen his face, she'd watched what he'd done. And she'd used that to put him in this cell.

Oh, he'd dream of her, all right. He'd dream of that little bitch. And he'd find a way to make her pay.

He closed his eyes, brought the picture into his head, and for the first time, slept almost peacefully.

But instead of in a picture, she slept in a bed with white sheets. He thought he heard rain, just a distant rainfall, thought he saw curtains stirring at an open window.

When he shifted on his cot, wanting more because the breeze felt cool and sweet, she shifted in the bed.

While he dreamed of her, she dreamed of him.

And she looked down on him, the man who'd killed her parents. He slept with one arm dangling off the side of the cot. Sweat stuck some of his shaggy hair to his cheek. She could smell the hair, the sweat. She could hear him breathing.

She could breathe, but her parents couldn't.

And still, and still, what the deputy said about prison rang true. It was like a cage, the little window, the hard, bare floor, the hard, bare walls. He couldn't close a door when he used the toilet or walk outside to listen to the night sounds if he couldn't sleep. Or turn on a light and read a book.

She could hear men snoring, all in their cots, in their cells. Trapped like Riggs was inside four hard walls.

She walked to the door, put her hands on it. Looked out as she imagined he would look out, at more and more cage doors, for all of his life.

He could breathe, she thought again. He could sneeze and snore and sweat. But he couldn't really live.

Her parents danced together, held hands when they died together.

Riggs would never have anyone to love him, to hold hands with him or make babies with him, no one to walk in the woods with him or kiss him good night.

Maybe that was worse than death.

She was glad she'd seen and felt and heard where he'd spend his life that wasn't a real life at all.

When she turned back, his eyes were open and on her.

Her breath caught; her stomach trembled. But she made herself stare right at him.

She'd be grown-up. She'd be . . . dignified.

"I see you. Little bitch, I see you."

"I just wanted a look at your new home. It really suits you."

"I'll find you, and when I do, you'll wish you'd been home in bed when I did your parents. You'd have died quick, and now you won't."

His hate poured off him, and covered her like a blanket made of tiny needles.

"I can leave, you can't. You don't scare me."

As she pushed herself awake, she heard him say, "I will."

Hugging her elbows tight, she sat in the dark. He wouldn't make her turn the light on like a baby. Dark or not, she sat in bed in Grammie's house—no, *her* house, too, now. She sat in her own house while the soft rain brought a soft breeze through the window.

And he, miles and miles away, slept—somehow she knew he still slept—sweating on a cot in a cell.

In the morning she'd put on whatever clothes she wanted and walk outside. She'd do cartwheels on the grass still wet from the rain, play with dogs, feed chickens.

He'd never do those things.

So she wouldn't be afraid.

Because the dream had dried out her throat, she got up, ran the water cold in the bathroom, scooped some into her hand, into her mouth.

Part of her wanted to go into her grandmother's room, climb into her bed. But she wouldn't.

Straightening, she studied herself in the mirror.

"Don't make it a lie. You said he didn't scare you. Don't make it a lie."

She walked back to her room, slipped into bed.

She listened to the soothing sound of the rain, and carried it with her into sleep.

In the morning, she did those cartwheels just because. And she waited until breakfast before she told the story. She'd decided Rem, even though he was younger, had a right to hear it, too.

"You were there?" Eyes wide, Rem stared at her. "In jail?"

"It's prison." She'd looked up the difference. "And it's not the same as I'm sitting here. It's like a dream, but not exactly that either."

"Her mind went there. Her gift took her there."

"How come I don't get a gift like that?" Sulking, Rem pushed at his eggs. "I want one."

"Well, sweet potato, it seems this gift runs through the women in the family, and you're the man of the house. Now let your sister tell us the rest."

Before she did, Thea pulled out something their father used to say to Rem when he complained girls got all the breaks. "You can pee outside, standing up."

And that cracked a smile.

"It's not like with bars, like the movies. There's a door and a window in it, only a few inches wide."

She continued, finished, then hunched her shoulders. "I said I wasn't scared, but I was. At first."

"I'd've been scared, too," Rem told her. "I might've peed standing up, in my pants."

"He saw you, spoke to you, heard you when you talked back?"

"He did, Grammie. Then I made myself wake up."

"It's best if you don't go back there, have this happen again. So we'll work on that today. But here's something to remember, Thea. You were in charge, start to finish. I'm thinking he's scared of you."

Maybe, Thea thought, but she wanted to work on never, ever going back.

Unless she chose to go back.

Lucy showed her how to make a little bag out of two pieces of cloth, needle and thread.

"While you make the pouch, think pretty thoughts, happy ones."

Since she'd never sewed before, Thea found the process very cool, so happy thoughts came easy. One minute you had nothing, the next you had a little bag. And after weaving the bigger needle with a skinny cord, you had a way to tie it up.

Then Lucy put cloves and cardamon and salt in a little wooden bowl, and lit a white candle.

"This is a mortar, and this is a pestle. Use the pestle to grind that up into a powder. And pretty thoughts."

More cool as she heard the pods and tiny balls crunch under the pestle.

"That's good! You've got a fine hand at it. What we do now is add some rosemary and some peppermint from the garden, and this dried lemon peel."

"It smells nice." Rem took several sniffs. "Can I make one, too?"

"Sure you can. Thea's going to finish this up, then you can make one for yourself."

"You make one for you, Grammie. Then we all have one."

"You know what, Rem. I believe I will. Fill the bag, Thea, and put your intent and your faith with it. They count just as much as the rest. That's good, that's fine. Now, when you hang it by your bed tonight, you'll say this, three times:

"Sleep, peaceful sleep, be with me tonight, and stay with me till the morning light."

Thea repeated it, nodded. "How do you know how to do all this, Grammie?"

"My mama taught me, like her mama taught her and on back a long, long ways. Kitchen magic. It's part of these hills. It's part of who we are."

She helped Rem make his, then made her own.

"Tonight, at tuck-in time, we'll hang them and say the words. But now, I think the three of us and the three dogs should take a walk. Summer doesn't last forever."

The days passed, as days will, and every night Thea said the words three times. Her sleep stayed peaceful.

They went to the town park to watch fireworks on the Fourth, and Thea got to hang out with Maddy, and some other girls. Rem found some boys his own age, and ignored her. And that was fine with Thea.

On the last days of summer, Maddy came to visit, or she went to Maddy's house. Rem's new friends Dwayne and Billy Joe did the same.

They took walks and paid calls. They made peach ice cream and gathered black walnuts.

Lucy hired a man she called Knobby, who had more hair on his face than on his head, to fix up the attic.

"It doesn't have to be fancy, Knobby. I want the kids to have this space. You're gonna need to pull electric up here, and the internet business so they can do the game console."

He scratched his impressive brown beard. "Gotta insulate, Miss Lucy, or those kids'll fry in the summer, shiver all winter."

"You do that. But I want the beams showing. Got character that way. Floors are fine, and solid with it. I'm getting one of those TVs that go up on the wall, so I'm going to want you to hang that when I do."

With a grin, he shot a finger at her. "Sounding fancy now." And she laughed.

"Just fancy enough. I'll have the kids pick out the paint color once you start on the Sheetrock. There'll likely be some lively debate on that."

"Lucy, Modeen and I, we think about you. You know how fond we were of Cora, and of John when he came along."

"I know you were. I feel those thoughts, Knobby, and they comfort me."

"How're those children doing?"

"They're getting through, Knobby. They've made some friends, and I'm so thankful for it. Don't get much quiet around here now, but I don't mind that a bit. They're good as gold. I'm biased on that, and it's not like I don't have moments when I think: How can they argue about anything under the sun? They're good as gold."

"And how're you doing, Lucy?"

"Getting through, Knobby. We're all getting through. Now, how much do you think this'll set me back?"

He scratched his beard. And they began negotiations.

July blurred right into August, and Knobby and his helper got things going. Lucy drove the kids clear into Pikeville for back-to-school shopping.

She'd had both of them put on long pants and jeans from their dressers and closets. It didn't take long to see every pair hit high-water. And Rem's feet, when she checked, were squeezed into his shoes.

They spent an afternoon putting donation boxes together. And a good portion of the next in Pikeville at the mall.

They loaded up on school supplies.

Thea loved new school supplies, with everything fresh and clean and neat. Rem didn't care about them, and cared even less about new clothes.

But he did like the new sneakers.

"You need to get him two pair, Grammie. He'll get one pair all wet or full of mud, so he needs another while the first get dry or cleaned up and dry."

"How'd I forget that?" Smiling, Lucy tossed back hair she'd left loose today, and the white streak shimmered like a wave in a black sea.

"Your uncle Waylon was just the same. Caleb, he could play just as hard, and his shoes would look fresh from the box. Pick another pair, Rem, then this old grammie needs some lunch and sit-down time."

As they drove home, Thea thought about starting school. She'd made a couple friends—Maddy for sure—but she'd still be the new girl.

She'd never been the new girl in school before. And Redbud Hollow had a small school. Everyone knew each other already.

She didn't think she was shy, but she didn't want to wear the wrong thing, or do her hair the wrong way. She just wanted to fit in, and she was already taller than most of the boys her age.

So she stuck out.

And she barely had breasts. They'd come out a little, but not like Maddy's.

"What's on that mind of yours, darling?"

"Oh, I'm just thinking about starting school. I don't know how any of it works here, or if I'll fit in."

"My girl fits in anywhere she wants to. And she happens to be friends with Madrigal McKinnon. You trust me, Maddy'll breeze you right through the first awkward day."

"Are you sure?"

"You know how I say your granny's a force of nature? Maddy's pint-sized, but the same."

"I'm a force of nature."

Lucy flicked a glance in the rearview. "Oh, you are that, Rem. You are all of that."

At home, Lucy helped Rem put his new things away because he didn't care where anything went. Thea cared, so it made her feel better about school starting to put everything in its place. She hung tops and shirts the way her mother had liked to: by color. Then pants that weren't jeans. She'd have hung her jeans, too, because she liked to, but she didn't have room for those and for skirts and dresses.

In Virginia her closet had been a walk-in with an organizing system. When she thought of it, grief for her parents rose up sharp and quick.

She sat on the floor of the skinny closet and cried until the worst of it dulled.

As it lessened, she stood on a hard floor with terrible sounds echoing.

Some men walked around her, men in uniforms, but didn't see her. She saw big cages. A man in prison blues paced in one, muttering to himself.

And his thoughts, thoughts that pelted her like little rocks, were dark and bitter.

Riggs, small, skinny, so white he looked like a ghost of a man, sat in another big cage on a bench.

Riggs didn't see her, he didn't feel her, not while he pushed his mind toward the other man, toward those guards.

He zeroed in on a guard named Douberman, so she piggybacked on what he read.

His wife's knocked up with their third kid, and he heads over to West Virginia every other Tuesday on his day off. He's got a regular whore over there he hires to meet up with him in a motel. He gets off on the dominatrix thing.

Maybe, maybe find a way to use that, shake him down.

Bored, Riggs glanced toward the other inmate. Crazy bastard. Pacing, screaming the other twenty-three hours a fucking day. Always getting his meds adjusted.

Maybe I can get him to kill himself. Maybe I'll just take a mind walk tonight and get him to strangle himself with his sheets.

That'd be fun.

Then, to boost his mood, to revisit that indescribable rush of power, he thought about the people he'd killed.

She came back to her room, a little shaky, a little breathless.

Others? There were others, like her mom and dad? Curling up, she hugged herself, struggling to stop the shakes, the rise of panic.

She was in her own room, sitting in the closet of her own room. She could see the sunlight on the floor and hear Rem laugh across the hall.

Riggs couldn't touch her. He sat in a cage, and he couldn't see the sunlight.

He'd killed more people, and he'd thought of each one like, like trophies in a case.

Did the police know?

He wanted to do it again, kill again. For the fun of it, she realized.

Could he do that? Could he somehow push someone to suicide?

Could she stop him?

While her grandmother worked with Rem, Thea went downstairs to the kitchen phone and looked up Detective Howard's number in her grandmother's book.

"Detective Howard."

"Um, Detective Howard, this is Thea Fox."

"Hey there, Thea. How are you?"

"I'm . . . okay. I . . . Detective Howard, there were others."

"Others?"

"More people, like my parents. Riggs killed more people before.

Before. And there's another inmate at the prison, Jerome Foster, and Riggs wants to kill him, and—"

"Thea. I need you to slow down. Take a breath. Slow down."

"I'm—I'm going to get some water."

She poured some out of the tap, chugged it down. Then nearly sicked it back up again.

"Okay," she managed. "Okay."

"Have you been in contact with Riggs, Thea?"

"Not exactly. I just know. And he knows about a guard who's cheating on his wife and wants to try to use that for something. Um. Douberman. I just know. He knows things, too. He has what I do."

"You're saying Riggs is psychic?"

"It's why he took my picture. He knew there was something. He knows I helped put him in prison. He killed other people before my parents."

"We linked him to a double murder in Maryland."

"Before that, before. Three—three—three—"

She squeezed her eyes shut, bore down. "Three times before."

"Three other murders?"

"Five people. Two like my parents, and one a girl. He was thinking about them. He was in a big cage, and he was thinking about them. One was . . . something, some place like Brinmaw, and she—the woman, the wife—was thinking about the alarm code. He got into the big house because she had to think about it, so he knew the code. He used a knife, he killed them with a knife. Oh God, oh God, so much blood.

"I can't breathe."

"Thea, I want you to sit down. Sit down and put your head between your knees."

"Okay." It felt like trying to breathe through a collapsed straw. But the weird gray at the edges of her vision faded.

"Where's your grandmother?"

She sucked in the next breath, and felt some of the weight lift from her chest. "Upstairs. He got the gun there, at the Brinmaw place, the one he used to kill the people in Maryland, then my parents. But before, I think before . . . Albany."

"New York?"

"Yes—no. New Albany. He was older, the man. Terrance. No, no, a terrace. Summer, night air. I don't know. I can't think right now. My head hurts."

"All right, Thea. This is enough. I want you to sit until you feel steady, then go get your grandmother."

"He wants to try to kill this other prisoner this way because . . . he's bored. I didn't know what else to do."

"Okay, Thea. We're going to look into this, all of it."

"You will?"

"Yes, and I want you to do me a favor. I want you to stay as far away from Riggs, in every way, as you can."

"I'm trying." A tear spilled out. "I didn't mean to go there. I saw the big mesh cages. And all the blue doors, but I didn't mean to."

This time, she thought. The first time, she had. At least a little.

"It's all right. You leave this to me now. I want you to tell your grandmother what happened."

"I will. Thank you."

After hanging up, she straightened, and saw Lucy.

"I'm sorry. I didn't mean to—"

"Shh." Lucy hugged her in, hugged her tight. "It's all right."

"I was upset, thinking about Mom and Dad. And it just happened. Grammie, there were more people. He killed more people, and I saw . . . He has the gift, too. He used it, he used it to kill people. He's still using his gift to try to."

"And he'll pay a price for it. Did he see you?"

"No. He was too busy looking for people to hurt, and thinking about the ones he had."

"And you did what you could to try to help." Brushing Thea's hair back, she waited until Thea's eyes met hers. "Because that's what the gift is meant for. Helping. So you put this away now, darling."

"Grammie. I could see how awful it is, how awful he feels. I was glad to see it."

"Do you think I'd blame you for it?" Lucy eased back, brushed tears off Thea's cheeks. "Blame you for it when I'm glad to know it? Why didn't you come get me?"

"I was going to tell you after, but I . . . I wanted to do this part myself."

"Growing up on me already?" Lucy pressed a kiss to Thea's forehead. "Try not to do it too fast. I'm proud of you. This took courage, and it shows what you're made of. It honors what you've been given."

"I don't want to go back there. I'll try not to."

"Good, and I'll try to help you. But if you do, Thea, remember you're in control. You're free. He's not, and never will be again. You're stronger, and you always will be."

A few days later, on a hazy Saturday afternoon, the detectives knocked at the door. When Lucy saw them, her heart sank. She had to remind herself Thea's courage had opened this door, and she had no right to close it.

"Ms. Lannigan," Musk began. "We'd like to speak with you and Thea. A follow-up on information she provided."

"Yes." Lucy opened the screen door. "She's twelve. She's only twelve."

"Ma'am."

Howard put a hand on his partner's arm to stop him.

"Phil and I drove down on our own time. We took personal time for this, Ms. Lannigan, because it is personal. And part of why we're here is to thank her for contacting me."

"It's Lucy," she said, and sighed. "Come on back. She's out on the porch working on her drawing. Rem's over at a friend's, and that's probably for the best. I've got fresh lemonade."

"That'd be welcome."

When the back screen opened, Thea studied the sketch on her pad. "I think this one's better." Then looked up. Stood up.

"You came. Did he kill that man?"

"Jerome Foster's on suicide watch," Howard told her. "It's the best we can do there, right now. Thea, I want to thank you for calling me. You didn't have to take that on."

"Yes, I did." She looked over as Lucy came out with a tray. "Grammie."

"Let me take that for you." Musk took the tray with the pitcher of lemonade and glasses, the plate of shortbread cookies.

"You did what was right, Thea. The detectives drove all this way on their own time to thank you for it."

"And because we think you deserve to know what we know because of it, and what's being done. Okay if we sit?" Howard asked her.

"Yeah. Yes. It was Bryn Mawr. I looked it up."

"That's right. Bryn Mawr, Pennsylvania. James and Deborah Cohen. About a year ago. It's still an open case. That means—"

"You didn't know who did it," Thea finished. "He did it. Ray Riggs."

"That's right. We couldn't trace the gun he used to kill your parents because it wasn't registered. With the information you gave us, we could do a little digging, and we've confirmed Deborah Cohen had a weapon of that make and model, unregistered. Her brother got it for her at a gun sale. It was never recovered, and initially not reported as missing."

Musk cleared his throat, accepted the glass Lucy offered.

"New Albany, Ohio," Musk said. "Stuart and Marsha Wheeling, another open case. The, ah, investigators concluded the killer climbed a trellis onto a second-story balcony and entered the unlocked doors to the main bedroom. Eighteen months ago."

"He killed the woman first because the man was old. He used a hammer on her. He meant to just knock her out, but he hit her too hard and couldn't stop."

Saying nothing, Lucy sat next to Thea on the swing, took her hand.

"Because he used different methods, different methods of entry, he took time to do considerable property damage in the Cohen home, the cases weren't linked."

Musk looked at his partner, who nodded.

"Now, due to a high-confidence tip from an anonymous source, those cases are getting a closer look with Riggs as the prime suspect. I want you to know we'll never use your name as that source."

Relief, the flood of it, had Lucy closing her eyes.

"He knows. Riggs knows I saw, with my parents. He knows I told you everything."

"You said he has what you have."

"He uses it to kill people because he likes it. He's always liked to kill things, even when he was a kid."

"Yeah, we have witness statements from his childhood behavior. It's one of the reasons he is where he is. Thea, you said you saw where he is. You saw the prison. It's not a place, even with this thing he has, he'll ever walk out of."

"He was going to try to bribe that guard."

"It would take a lot more than that, but that's been handled, too. This prison is a supermax, set up for the worst of the worst, but anytime you're worried, or get scared, or just need to talk about it, you can call me."

Howard took out a card. "My personal number's on there, too. Twenty-four/seven, Thea. You call." He set the card on the tray. "Now I'm going to ask you one more hard thing. You said there was a girl."

"I don't know her name. I don't think he remembers it or maybe he didn't know it. I know she was the first he killed. He'd hurt other people, like this kid, a gay kid, but he didn't beat him up so bad because he was gay, or not really. It was because he was smaller and weaker, and he could. But the girl . . ."

Thea drank some lemonade, settled herself. "She was on the street. Young, like him."

Musk started to speak, but Lucy shook her head.

"It was cold, and rainy, too," Thea continued. "He had a room because he'd stolen money, from his parents, his grandparents, even the kid he beat up before he left home. He always meant to go back, hurt his parents. He hated them. They never did anything terrible to him, but he hated them. And the girl, she'd run away like him, and he said she could stay in his room for the night if she . . . You know, um, had sex with him."

"Okay."

"But he couldn't make it work, and he heard her thinking how he couldn't, and how he was a loser or something. He hit her. He hit her really hard in the face. Then he grabbed the lamp, the lamp with the green metal base beside the bed, and he hit her with that.

"Grammie."

"I'm right here."

"She couldn't fight back then, and the blood was on her face from where the lamp cut her. He strangled her when she couldn't fight back. And he liked watching her eyes when she died. He liked it more than killing cats or dogs or birds. He put her in the closet, and wiped down the room. He took the sheets in case of DNA. He packed his things, and he took them and the sheets, and he left her there."

"Do you know where this happened?"

"I think maybe Toledo, or he was going there after. I'm not sure. It all came so fast, and it scared me, and—"

"That's fine, that's good. That's so helpful."

"I don't think he remembers her name, so I can't know it, but I saw her face because he did. I tried to draw it. I'm not really good with faces."

She went to the last pages of her sketch pad, and offered it to Howard.

"I'm going to disagree with you there. This is good."

Artistic pride snuck through the distress. "You think?"

"I do."

"She had blond hair with dark roots—I tried to show that, and the streaks? She had blue streaks. Her eyes were brown."

"Can we take this page?"

"Sure. It was a motel, I think, and the door was brown, like fake wood. The number on it was 137."

Carefully, Howard tore out the page. "I don't suppose you're interested in becoming a cop."

"No, sir," Thea said definitely. "No."

"I'm going to say this with admiration, Thea. That's too damn bad. I hope you can put this away now, and leave it to us. Thanks for your help, and for your time. We'll get out of your way, but I'm grabbing one of these cookies."

"You said you drove down from Fredericksburg?"

"Yes, ma'am. Lucy," Howard corrected.

"Surely you're not driving all the way back tonight."

"No, we're staying the night at the . . ." He glanced at his partner.

"Welcome Inn," Musk provided.

"The innkeeper's my third cousin. She serves a fine breakfast."

"We'll take advantage of that before we head home in the morning."

"Well, tonight, you're staying for supper."

"We don't want to put you out."

"You came all this way, on your own time. You're staying for supper.

Now, since you're off duty, can I get you a beer, or can I offer you some Kentucky lemonade?"

"Isn't that what we're drinking?"

Lucy shook her head at Musk. "It ain't Kentucky lemonade till you add the bourbon."

Howard looked at Thea before he answered, and when she smiled, let out a long sigh. "Lucy, I could sure use a glass of that."

Chapter Ten

Lucy kept the kids out of the attic during the finish work of what she thought of as the Foxes' Den. Because it drove Rem crazy, Thea decided to embrace the restriction.

It made her feel superior and more adult.

Over the last few days of it, Rem asked a million questions.

"Just say what color they're painting the walls. Is it my interesting orange, or Thea's stupid blue?"

"Maybe, since the two of you squabbled so much over those paint samples, I told them to paint it an ugly old brown. Now, if you can't pick tomatoes and talk at the same time, stick with the picking."

"But when are they going to be finished? It's taking forever."

"That'd be up to Knobby. You want it fast, or you want it good?"

"Why can't it be fast and good?"

Straightening, Lucy stretched her back, adjusted her wide-brimmed hat.

"The same reason these tomatoes didn't grow and ripen fast so we could pick them and can them for good soups and stews we'll eat over the fall and winter."

"What's the reason?"

"Because it's the way of things."

He did an eye roll as he picked another tomato. "Why do you say 'can them' when you're going to put them in glass jars?"

"I guess that's just the way of things, too."

But now, damn it, she wondered the same herself.

Breathing in the scents of late summer harvest, she looked around the garden.

"We'll take those leather breeches in tonight—and I expect they're called that, Mister Question, because when the snap beans dry out right like that, they sort of look like leather breeches."

"Did you plant all this yourself, Grammie?"

Lucy glanced at Thea. "I get a pair of willing hands and a strong back to help me in the spring. Now I've got two more. You'll get a taste of it when we plant our winter crop, but next spring, you'll see how it all starts."

Taking a short break, Lucy lifted her face to the sun.

"There's satisfaction in that, and more when you do the harvesting. More still when you reach for a jar of something on a cold night that you grew and put by with your own hands."

They hadn't grown vegetables in Virginia, Thea thought, and twisted a tomato from the vine the way her grandmother taught her. But she'd helped plant flowers every spring. And she'd liked watching them grow.

She wondered if whoever bought the house would plant flowers.

She hoped they would.

And she hoped the police and the courts all made Riggs pay for those other people he'd killed. She knew the name of the girl now, because Detective Howard had called to tell her.

She'd been Jessica Lynn Vernon, and she'd been fifteen.

She'd never plant flowers or pick tomatoes or reach for a jar of what she'd put by on a cold winter night.

I did the best I could for her, Thea thought. She trusted the detectives to do the best they could.

Now, once again, she put it aside, or tried. As she held the tomato up to her nose, drawing in its scent, she scanned the green of the hills.

She'd see it all change in the fall, through the winter, and into spring. She'd watch the redbuds bloom next year. She could miss her parents—she'd always miss them—and be grateful for the smell of a fresh-picked tomato, for the deep, dreamy summer green of the hills, and the hazy mountains beyond.

* * *

The last week before school, Thea hardly thought of anything else. The thought of being singled out, not accepted or fitting in filled her with such anxiety she wondered if she could talk her grandmother into homeschooling her.

When the idea took root, she crafted her argument and launched it early one morning before Rem got up.

Lucy came down to find Thea had made the coffee.

"One of your early bird days?"

"I could get up early every day and make the coffee, then bring Aster in for milking. I could do a lot more to help if you homeschooled me. Lots of kids get homeschooled."

"Hmm. I see I'm going to need this coffee straight off."

"I'll get it for you. I can make breakfast, too. I don't mind at all. We can make a schedule for lessons, and assignments. They have programs online and everything."

"You've given this considerable thought."

"I'm a good student. I got mostly As. And if I'm homeschooled, I could learn more about farming and making the soap and everything for your business."

With the ease of experience, Lucy twisted her hair up, secured it with the band she took off her wrist.

"That's true. You could do all that. And while you were doing all that, you'd miss out on being around young people your own age, learning different things from different teachers, going to school activities, learning about the different ways other young people think and live and act."

"I don't care about any of that."

Because nobody would talk to her anyway! And they'd all look at her funny because she didn't have any Kentucky in her voice, and she'd picked out the wrong shoes, and wore her hair wrong.

"I just want to stay here. I'll study, and I'll work and learn and help, and—"

"Slow down, darling. You're nervous about starting something new, and that's a natural thing. You're worried somebody'll make fun of you or be mean to you. It's a fact that sort of thing can happen anytime or anywhere in this life. But I'm going to tell you something."

Thea's eyes stung with tears when Lucy cupped her face.

"I'm going to tell you, not because I'm your grammie, but because I know who you are. You're going to be just fine. More than fine."

"But what if I'm not? What if nobody likes me because I'm not from here, and I don't sound like they do when I talk? Or I don't dress right?"

"Your blood kin's from here as far back as anybody's. But that's not the point, darling. We'll make a deal, all right? You give it two weeks. You go to school, and be who you are. If after those two weeks you feel the same, I'll look into it, and we'll talk about it. Promise me those two weeks, and I'll promise you that."

Thea's belly hitched, and her breath with it. "I don't want them to stare at me and say that's the girl whose mom and dad got murdered."

Lucy pulled her in. "Some of them may. And some of those who do will reach out to you because they have good hearts. You reach back if they do."

"What if—"

"What if a giraffe had a short neck and a zebra had spots?"

Thea could only sigh. "Just two weeks?"

"Just two weeks."

"Don't tell Rem about it."

"It stays between us."

Satisfied, and absolutely certain in two weeks' time she'd stay right there on the little farm, homeschooled, Thea got through the day without a worry.

And the very next day, after the chores, Lucy made an announcement.

"Today's the day," she said, "of the Big Reveal."

"Right now!" Rem leaped from the table.

"After you finish your breakfast."

"I'm all done!"

Lucy just pointed to his plate.

"You didn't tell us it was finished."

"I had a little fussing to do up there," she told Thea. "Just a bit of fussing after y'all went to bed."

"Did you hook up the PlayStation?"

"You don't have much longer to wait to find out, unless you keep ignoring those eggs and breakfast potatoes on your plate."

Rem shoved more in his mouth. "We can go up there anytime we want and play games?"

"You can go up there when you've done chores, when you're not in school, when it's before your bedtime, and you don't give me grief. You can play games on that thing after you do schoolwork. And I expect you won't hole up there for hours at a time and leave your poor grammie alone."

"You can play, too!"

"We'll see about that."

"I really am done, Grammie."

"Close enough. Hold on! Don't you go racing out of here, Rem. You take care of your plate like always. Then I'm leading the way. It's my Big Reveal."

When she did, Rem nearly stepped on her heels.

"It took forever! I don't see why it took so long."

"You're supposed to say thank you," Thea reminded him.

"I haven't seen it yet."

"Thank you can wait till you do."

Lucy paused at the top of the attic stairs. "Revealing the Foxes' Den." And pushed open the door.

Thea rolled her eyes when Rem raced right in. But she wasn't far behind.

And whatever she'd expected, it hadn't been this.

Half of the big attic was everything bright and new, with the sloping wall on one side painted her blue, the wall on the other Rem's orange. Each side had a desk built right into it, with shelves on either end.

The floor, all polished up, held a big hooked rug that married those same colors. A couch sat on it with a chair on either side, facing a wall that hadn't been there before. A blue slipcover for the couch, orange for the chairs. A stack of floor pillows rested in the corner.

Lucy flipped a switch and the ceiling lights sprang on.

The new wall held a flat-screen that faced the couch. Under the screen, the unit Knobby had built held the game console.

Instead of racing forward, Rem turned, threw his arms around Lucy. "Thank you, Grammie. Thank you so much! This is the best ever."

"Worth the wait?"

"It's beautiful," Thea murmured. "It's so nice. It's all so nice. You didn't say about the wall. Where are all your things, Grammie? The things you save up here?"

"Behind that wall, and there's plenty of room for them. If I want to put something in, take something out, I just open that pocket door Knobby put in. Thea, you can bring up your laptop for the desk if you want. Y'all can do schoolwork up here, if you want. That's up to you.

"Now, I'm telling you, if you bring food and drink up here, as I expect you will, you'd best bring the dishes down again. That's a hard and fast rule of the Foxes' Den. And keeping it clean's on both of you."

"Can we try out a game now? You can play, too, Grammie."

"I appreciate that, Rem, but I have one more surprise before we try this place out. Maddy and Billy Joe are coming over this afternoon. They'll be staying for supper, and for a sleepover."

"Dibs on the Foxes' Den! We're not sleeping over up here with girls."

"We're not sleeping over here with boys. We'll sleep in a bed while you're on the couch or the floor. Thanks, Grammie. I really love it. I really do."

"First chance you get, you thank Knobby. He put a lot of work and time and thought into making this special for you."

"Because good takes time," Rem said.

"A fine lesson learned. Now get that PlayStation going, and show me how it's done."

They had Grammie's pizza and homemade peach ice cream. They held a tournament, and to Rem's shock and mortification, the girls edged out the boys.

It griped him, and always would, that when it came to Mario Kart, and pretty much every video game, Thea ruled.

"Rematch," he demanded.

"Maybe tomorrow, and you'll still lose."

"Let's go down to your room, Thea. It's called retiring from the field as winners." Maddy did a shoulder bump. "We're number one."

"Cowards!"

"Losers." And with that, Maddy hooked arms with Thea and retired from the field. "Girl," she added as they walked down, "you're a genuine joystick wizard." She waited until they'd reached Thea's room and closed the door. "Do you use any of that extra special of yours for the game?"

"No." At least she didn't think so. "I just like playing. It's like a story, and you're the hero."

"'Cause you're a joystick wizard." Maddy, her hair in one big poof of a tail today, flopped on the bed. "We really have to go back to school in just two more days."

Thea flopped with her. "If I don't like it after two weeks, Grammie's going to homeschool me."

"What'd you want to do that for? You miss out on everything." Rolling onto her stomach, Maddy looked down at Thea's face. "You still gotta do the schoolwork, take tests, and write those essays. I hate writing essays. But you don't get to hang out with your friends and see what's going on."

"I don't have any friends except you."

"I'm enough for anybody, but Sheryl Anne likes you, and Ruby does."

"Everybody already knows everybody. I don't."

"How're you gonna know everybody if you don't go to school with the rest of us?" She gave Thea a poke. "You're just a little scared, that's all."

"I'm the girl whose parents got murdered."

The poke turned into a stroke.

"Nobody's going to make fun of you about that. And if anybody does?" Maddy's eyes fired. "I'll punch them right in the face. Swear to God, I will. What you got is some basic social anxiety."

"Seriously?" Thea's eyes rolled as she shook her head. "Where do you get that stuff?"

"My cousin Jasper has it. I heard my mama say, and then I heard Daddy say: *How come they had to use fancy words for being shy?* You're just feeling shy is all."

"I never used to be shy."

"Good, so you'll likely get over it. How're you going to get a boyfriend if you don't go to school with boys?"

"I'm not really thinking about boyfriends right now. I don't know any boys except Rem's friends."

"They're too young for a boyfriend. You don't want to be a cradle robber."

"Oh, Maddy! As if."

"Plus, they're goofy."

"Yeah, they are."

"Who wants a goofy boyfriend? You'll meet more boys in school, and I'll steer you clear of ones not worth your time. Me, I'm going to have lots and lots of boyfriends right up till I decide to get married."

Maddy flopped over again.

"And I'm not getting married until I find one that's handsome. If he's not real handsome, he has to be hot, and if he's not real hot, he at least has to be cute. So I'm having lots of boyfriends so I can weed through them till I find one I decide's worth marrying."

"That's going to take a while."

"Oh, at least till I'm thirty, I figure. Maybe thirty-five." Maddy shot a finger at the ceiling. "A woman's got a life to live."

"Grammie had my mom when she was sixteen."

Maddy shifted her dark eyes to Thea. "I love Miss Lucy like crazy, but that's wacky. You think they maybe had to get married and all that?"

Though the bedroom door was closed, Thea glanced that way. "I wondered, so I looked up when she and my grandfather got married, and my mom was born almost a year later. Like ten and a half months, so I guess they didn't have to. Grammie said they just loved each other so much they couldn't wait."

"I can wait," Maddy said definitely, "before I settle for one man. Wouldn't mind if he was rich, and he can't be stupid or mean or I kick him right to the curb. Handsome doesn't make up for stupid or mean."

Pushing up, Maddy sat cross-legged. "Anyway, plenty of boyfriends, and I want to have sex with at least three before I pick. You gotta be compatible in the sex stuff or you end up divorced or cheating."

"Maddy!" Shocked, thrilled, Thea shoved up to mirror her friend's pose. "You'll be a slut!"

"No such thing! A boy goes around having some sex, they say how he's sowing his wild oats. Well, girls got oats, too. I'll sow mine when I want to. But not till I've dated—just dated—at least half a dozen.

"Now school."

Maddy flipped subjects so quick, Thea's head spun.

"We're going to eat lunch together every day. Plus, we're going to have some classes together. And you're going to know everybody by the first week. You're going to make friends, but you'd better not make a best best friend. Because that's already me."

Thea knew lunch period equaled the Great Humiliation Zone without friends.

"You'll eat lunch with me every day?"

"Promise. Now kick that homeschooling idea in the ass, and let's pick out what you're wearing the first day."

Since Thea couldn't stop time, the first day came. With her stomach churning, she dressed as Maddy decreed. Denim skirt, white tee, her pink Converse sneakers. She wore her mother's pink studs, and did her hair—Maddy approved—in a side braid that fell over her left shoulder.

Rem tossed on shorts, a tee, tied his new shoelaces, and considered it done.

"Look at the pair of you! You're going to indulge your grammie and let me take pictures. I want to memorialize your first day. I swear I don't know what I'm going to do with all the quiet around here until you get home."

When the school bus rolled up, Lucy kissed them both. "You have a good first day, and I want to hear all about it."

Thea clung a little; she couldn't help it. Lucy murmured in her ear.

"If you're worried about taking the bus, I can drive you in."

Thea understood the meaning of *gauntlet* now. Maddy lived in town, and didn't ride the bus. Rem already ran toward it, thrilled to embrace the experience.

She couldn't let her little brother be braver than she was.

"No, Grammie, it's fine."

She walked the gauntlet as the bus driver waved and called out to Lucy. To the bus, onto the bus, down the aisle between mostly empty seats. They rode the winding road, climbing up, heading down, making more stops. Kids piled on; the noise level rose.

Two girls sat behind her and giggled together.

They'd nearly reached town before someone sat beside her. The girl said, "Hey," then immediately shifted to talk to other kids.

Thea suffered the thirty-five-minute bus ride without speaking a word.

When they reached the school, she filed off. Rem deserted her for a group of boys. She started the second gauntlet while around her kids greeted each other, laughing, talking, mock groaning about school.

Maddy came up behind her, hooked an arm around Thea's waist.

"God, it was awful! Nobody talked to me the whole way."

"Did you talk to anybody?"

"No, but—"

"Social anxiety," Maddy said wisely. "We don't have homeroom together because of the alphabet, but I asked Mama to check, and we have first and third and sixth period together. Hey, Julianne!" she called out as she steered Thea through the heavy front door. "Like the new do! This is my friend Thea."

She called out to others as they walked, and explained the layout to Thea as they went.

The offices, the doors to the gym, the auditorium where they had assemblies and the concerts.

Compared to her school in Virginia everything here was smaller, older. At least she'd never get lost.

"Okay, this is your homeroom. Mine's right across there. So after the bell rings to go to the first class, we'll meet right out here. Now go on in there and talk to somebody."

Without a choice, Thea went in and started to head straight to the back where she'd have a better chance of invisibility.

But she stopped herself when she got to the middle and slid into a desk.

Her ears rang; her heart thumped. So she gripped her hands in her lap under the desk and tried desperately to look normal.

Eventually someone dropped into the desk beside her. The girl with short red hair wore snug, cropped jeans and a bright green shirt. Her nails matched the shirt.

She propped her chin on her fist and appeared bored to the bone.

But she looked everywhere, including at Thea. She gave Thea a long once-over that made Thea want to sink into the earth and pull it over her head.

"I like your shoes."

The shock of the words nearly left Thea speechless.

"Thanks."

"My grandmother says redheads can't wear pink, but hell with that. I like pink. You're new, right?"

"Yes."

"You'll get used to it. We've got Mrs. Haverson for homeroom. She teaches history and makes it boring. I'm Gracie."

"Thea. I'm Thea."

"Well, Thea, welcome to the last year, thank you, Jesus, of middle school hell."

By the time Thea got back on the bus to ride home, she'd kicked the idea of homeschool in the ass.

She survived that last year of middle school hell with a circle of friends. She turned thirteen—at last. She had her first boyfriend, her first breakup. Her vow to never love another didn't last through Christmas of her freshman year in high school.

In her other world, as she sometimes thought of the world of Riggs, prison, detectives, the police traced Riggs from his home outside of Bowling Green to Toledo, to the motel and the room where he killed Jessica Lynn Vernon.

"Once we tied him to it," Howard told her on the phone, "he laid it all out. Where he'd picked her up, how he'd taken a bus to Akron after."

"He was proud of it. It gave him a way to relive it again, to feel it all again."

"I think you're right."

She knew she was right.

"Charging him with another murder, that gives him a . . ."

"A shine," Howard finished.

"A shine. Yeah."

"Are you doing okay, Thea?"

"I'm doing fine, thanks. He pushes at me sometimes, especially when he's bored." She didn't add Riggs was bored a lot. "But I don't let him in."

"Good. Don't. You've still got my number. Use it anytime."

"Thank you. Um . . . congratulations on the baby. Fiona's a pretty name. You're thinking about her really hard," Thea explained.

"And you get that through the phone?"

"Really hard. It just sort of came through. And the blue stairs. Just be careful on the blue stairs."

"All right, Thea. Give my best to your grandmother. And call anytime."

Knowing she'd done her best for Jessica Lynn Vernon, Thea did what she could to close the door on that other world.

At fourteen she cut her hair to chin length, an impulse she regretted for months after. She won an award in math, an accomplishment that both thrilled and embarrassed her.

When she was fifteen, they lost Aster and grieved. The best of best friends, Maddy brought them flowers.

They called the new cow Betty Lou.

Waylon married a rawboned blonde named Kyra Lightfoot who had a wonderful wild laugh and played the fiddle.

She developed an obsession with a rock band—four young guys who called themselves Code Red. And most particularly the lead singer, songwriter, and all-around hottie (according to Maddy) Tyler Brennan.

He starred in dozens of her dreams and cast every boy she knew in his shadow.

So for her sixteenth birthday, Lucy took her, Maddy, and Gracie to their concert in Louisville.

And there he was onstage, tall and lean in ripped jeans and a black tee, his wild mop of hair the color of the sipping whiskey her grandmother sometimes poured.

The music, his music, simply filled her. She considered her heart lost to him forever.

In her journal, she wrote that no matter how long she lived, she'd never have a better birthday.

As her senior year approached, she knew what she wanted to do with her life. College loomed, and she focused on computer science at the University of Kentucky. With a double major in art.

She'd add an online course in computer game design.

Because that was the dream. She'd design, maybe even develop video games.

Another dream included somehow meeting Tyler Brennan, having him fall in love with her. They'd marry and have three children and live on a small farm near her grandmother.

He'd write and play his music; she'd design games.

And they'd live happily ever after.

Waylon and Kyra gave Lucy another granddaughter and had a second baby coming. Caleb landed a co-starring role as a charming yet dedicated police detective in a TV series called *Case Files* filmed in New York.

On the fifth anniversary of her parents' death, she stood, as always, with Lucy and Rem at their graves. As always, they laid hydrangeas against the stone.

Rem stood two inches taller than Thea's five-nine, and didn't appear to have finished growing as she had. He had their father's eyes, but the rest of him looked like Caleb.

Thea knew the girls swooned over him.

At the end of the summer, she'd leave them both when she went to college. She'd leave Maddy, too, who would head to Duke to begin her journey toward becoming a doctor.

Gracie had her waitress job and a boyfriend she'd moved in with. So she'd stay right in Redbud Hollow, at least for now.

Most of her friends would scatter, she knew. Some already had.

But she'd come back. She'd always come back to the hills and the forests, to the farm, to her parents' grave.

"They'd be so proud of you." Lucy gripped Thea's hand, and Rem's. "So proud of both of you."

"I can't even picture the house in Fredericksburg anymore."

Thea glanced at Rem, and thought: I can.

She went back sometimes, in dreams, to see them as they'd been. Just as she went back to the prison to look at the half life Riggs led.

"I can't really remember it."

"You remember them," Lucy told him. "That's what matters. And look at you, baseball star already *and* making the honor roll every semester in your sophomore year. And you, going off to college to study what I couldn't understand if I lived to be a thousand. I swear I don't know how I'm going to run the online part of the business you talked me into starting without you right here."

"I've got you covered, Grammie."

"You'd better, Rem."

"You're more computer literate than you'll admit," Thea told her. "And you can call or text or FaceTime me if you need help. I'll be home for Thanksgiving and Christmas and . . ."

Thea pressed a hand to her belly.

"Don't you start getting nervous. You're going to shine. Both of you, the two Waylon and Kyra've given me. And if Caleb ever decides to give me more, they'll shine, too."

Thea dreamed of the house in Virginia that night. And though the house stood empty, she heard her mother's voice, her father's laugh. Distant, distant as if smothered by the shadows.

Then it flooded back, all flooded back as she stood outside the house, not empty, no, not empty, behind Riggs.

She could walk in behind him, see it all again. Hear it, feel it.

Instead, she turned away, let herself drift, let her mind travel. Let her gift take her to his cell.

He slept, but fitful, jerking on his cot, muttering in his sleep.

He wore his hair short now, and his face was as pale as the moon. Still thin, she noted, but getting some flab around the middle. Soft in the middle, she thought, but hard in the face. He looked older than his twenty-three years.

He has a toothache, she realized, but he's afraid to say, afraid of the dentist. He scored some pills—opioids—but they've worn off, and that tooth's throbbing.

"Wake up, Ray."

His eyes flashed open on a moan. Then their eyes met.

"Remember me?"

"Little bitch." On a wince, he pressed a hand to his right jaw. "Get the fuck out of here. I'll kill you."

"Yeah, you remember me. They're going to yank that tooth. It's going to hurt like a bitch until they do. And it'll hurt like a bitch for days after."

He rolled to sitting. "Fuck you. Get out of my head."

"You don't look so good. Don't smell so good either. I can smell that tooth rotting in your head. Anyway, I'm just checking in to say good-bye. I won't be back. I've got a life to live."

"I'm gonna kill you slow." Still cradling his jaw, he pushed at her, pushed what he wanted to do against her mind.

She didn't flinch.

"Keep dreaming, Ray. Oh, your nose is bleeding."

She willed herself awake to stare up at the ceiling of her bedroom. Her heart didn't pound; her head didn't ache.

Rising, she rehung the charm bag she'd taken down before she'd gone to bed. She'd wanted this one last time.

She said the words, repeated them three times, then got back into bed.

Time to let it go, she thought. Time to look forward instead of back.

Thea closed her eyes and slipped into sleep, dreaming the dreams she built herself.

PART II
Living

Live all you can; it's a mistake not to.
—HENRY JAMES

Deep into that darkness peering, long I stood there,
wondering, fearing,
Doubting, dreaming dreams no mortal ever dared to dream before.
—EDGAR ALLAN POE

Chapter Eleven

At the end of her junior year, Thea assessed her college life.

In her freshman year, she'd survived frequent bouts of homesickness as well as Mandy, the Roommate from Hell.

Mandy, who liked to have phone sex—loud phone sex—with her boyfriend at two in the morning. Mandy, who spent most Sunday mornings puking up her Saturday night partying. Mandy, who appeared to have a religious objection to clothes hangers and wastebaskets.

Thea'd had sex for the first time, and had nearly decided it wasn't as advertised. The second time changed her mind. The boy, or maybe just the sex, made her feel things she'd never felt before. Had her seeing stars and hearing bells ring.

But she'd made the mistake of convincing herself she loved the boy—Asher Billings, another computer nerd.

In the heat of sex and love, she'd told him about her gift.

His initial laugh hadn't hurt, or not much. But what followed had cut though the core of her.

Freak, *weird-ass loony*, and worse. Worse yet, he'd dumped her and told others. Between the scorn and the stares, she'd nearly run home.

Home was safe. Home where people accepted who she was.

"Don't you *think* about letting that jerk chase you off!"

Maddy FaceTimed two minutes after Thea's misery midnight text.

"I'm over him, okay? I'm over him, but he's got people talking about me, and this girl I don't even *know* came up to me today in the coffee shop and said I was the devil's spawn, and—"

"Are you?"

"Of course not, but—"

"Then fuck her, fuck all like her. You know who you are, Thea Fox, so fuck them. You stick, you hear? You stick and show them what you're made of."

"I shouldn't have told him. I thought if we were going to be together, really together, he should know, well, what I'm made of."

"He showed you what he's made of. Pig shit's what he's made of, and you won't step in it again. You get your guts up, Thea, and don't let his kind take away what you love."

"I wish you were here."

"I sort of am. Now, what're you gonna do?"

"I'm going to get up in the morning and go to class. I need what I'm learning here to have what I want. So fuck all of them."

She'd told herself she'd learned a hard lesson, and one she'd never, ever repeat.

She wouldn't step in pig shit again.

Love didn't always mean trust or acceptance or understanding. And what she had was hers, and no one else's business.

But that was then, and she'd gotten through it.

She'd made a small circle of companions—not quite friends—which made her sophomore year a much different and happier experience.

She'd learned, and learned a lot—improving her art skills, her coding skills, her writing skills.

And not once had she gone back to that prison cell, not once had she gone into the mind of the man who'd killed her parents.

She'd felt him try to slip into hers, and the cold chills or flashes of heat those attempts brought with them.

She'd kept the window closed, and a charm bag over her bed.

And she'd learned home was Redbud Hollow.

Now, with her last final of her junior year behind her, and her bags already packed, she wanted nothing more than being there. Being home.

One stop left to make, she thought, and tried to tamp down the worry that her Game Design professor had texted he wanted to meet.

If she'd screwed up her final, she had to hope he'd give her a chance to fix it. She'd worked so damn hard, bringing that long-ago dream of adventure and magic into a complete story with solid graphics, testing the coding, the levels and play countless times.

If she'd tanked it, she'd fix it.

She had another day to move out of the dorm, and she'd have it to herself. She'd fix whatever she'd screwed up.

Even if she blew the final—ill-conceived idea, poorly executed—she wouldn't fail the class. Her grades throughout the semester would pull her through.

The building, nearly empty, as most students had headed out and summer classes had yet to begin, echoed in her head.

Anxiety, she admitted. She couldn't push it back.

Professor Cheng's office door stood open. He sat behind his workstation, frowning at one of his three monitors.

When she knocked on the doorjamb, he looked up. His eyes behind his square-lens glasses showed nothing but annoyance.

As her stomach sank, he held up a finger for her to wait.

He swiped something on the touch screen, then sat back.

"Come in, Ms. Fox. Shut the door."

He never called a student by their first name, but the directive to close the door had her stomach sinking even deeper.

"You wanted to see me, Professor?"

"I wouldn't have texted you otherwise, would I? Sit. We need to discuss your final project."

"Yes, sir. Professor Cheng, I believe my work in your class has shown I put in the effort. Up until the final, I've carried a ninety-six percent average. I hope you'll give me the chance to correct whatever errors I made in the final project, whether in the engineering or in the concept, design, and development."

She cleared her nervous throat. "I took your class this term to help refine my skills. I hope—I think—I hope to find a career in game design and development."

He sat in silence, then lifted an eyebrow. "Are you finished?"

"I— Yes, sir."

"Good. Normally I might ask a student who turned in a project such as yours if they employed outside help. But you're correct, your work this term has been excellent. You can expect, when the grade for your final is added, that average to rise to a ninety-eight.

"I assume you can do the math."

"Oh." The air went out of her lungs, then filled them again. "Oh."

"Succinct. It's a rare thing for me to grade a final at a hundred. I questioned doing so here, debating with myself on doing so because I enjoyed playing the game."

His chair creaked as he sat back, tapped his fingers together.

"But then, that would be one of the points of a game. Enjoyment. The graphics are clean, crisp, and creative. The narrative flows, the dialogue is clever and suited to the characters. You developed the characters well."

"Thank you."

"Your coding is solid, not a single glitch. You're careful and you're thorough."

"When I started here, I thought I'd aim for a job in IT."

"No doubt you'd find one. But now you hope, think, hope to make a career in game design and development."

"I know it's a competitive industry, one that demands—"

He held up a finger again to stop her.

"Are you afraid of competition or hard work, long hours, Ms. Fox?"

"No."

"Then I might be able to help you. I have a connection at Milken. I assume you're familiar?"

"Sure. Yes. They're one of the top video game companies, globally."

"I'd like to send my connection, who happens to be my cousin, your game."

Her mind went completely blank. "I'm sorry?"

"Why?"

"I . . . You want to send *Endon* to Milken?"

"With your permission. And this is a first. I have provided students who earned them with references and recommendations. I would certainly do so for you. But this is the first time in my ten years at the university I will have offered to send a student's project to my cousin. I would never do so unless I believed in that project. My cousin is fully aware I would never take advantage of our family relationship, so he will give the game his personal attention, and give it his honest and professional review."

"I—"

"There's no crying in my office, Ms. Fox."

So she squeezed her eyes tight on the tears, nodded, kept nodding until she managed to control them. "Yes, thank you. You have my permission."

"Good. I'll send him your contact information. I imagine it will take time before someone lets you know, one way or the other. That's all, Ms. Fox."

Though her knees wobbled, she rose.

"I can't thank you enough, Professor Cheng. I—"

"There's no guarantee."

"No, but it's an opportunity. I'm very grateful."

She walked out on a cloud of shock, joy, and disbelief. Because her eyes teared up again, she pulled out her sunglasses.

She started to take out her phone. She had to tell her grandmother, Rem, Maddy. Everybody!

But no, no. She shoved the phone away again. She had to tell them in person. She'd be home in a few hours. So would Rem, fresh off his first year at Columbia, and Maddy from Durham, where she'd wrapped up her premed requirement in three years.

Overachiever.

Then Maddy would head to New York and Columbia Medical School.

Life was so different now. Everything changing. Rem, the business major; Maddy, the doctor-in-training. And Thea might just have a career doing something she loved.

God, she couldn't wait to get home.

She quickened her steps to a jog. She'd go up, grab the last of her things, shove them in the car with the rest, and be on her way.

She pulled up short, then simply froze when she saw the two men standing outside her building. Detective Howard had more gray sprinkled through his hair now, and Musk had touches of it at his temples.

But they looked the same, really much the same as they had eight years before when they'd first come to the farm.

Fear, bright and hot, washed through the ice, and she ran.

"He got out. He got out."

"No. No." Howard took her arm. "He's exactly where he belongs. We're not here about Riggs, about anything to do with your family. I'm sorry we scared you."

Obviously uncomfortable, Musk shifted. "We're here to ask you for a favor. Could we go in for a few minutes?"

"I'm going home. I just need to get the last of my things and turn in my keys."

"We'll try not to take too long. Thea." Howard waited until she looked back at him. "We wouldn't have come if it wasn't important."

Saying nothing, she led them inside.

Nearly empty, she thought as she took the stairs. Everyone going home for the summer. All she wanted was to go home for the summer. See her people, see the mountains.

"My dorm mates have already left. Everything's packed up. I don't have anything to offer you."

She unlocked the door to the communal living area of the quad.

"It's a nice space." Howard tried a smile. "You wouldn't believe the dump heap dorm I lived in back in my day. Can we sit down?"

"All right." She took a chair so they had the couch.

Everything personal already packed, she thought. Nothing of her remained. No photos, no flowers, no dishes, none of the art she and her art major dorm mate had hung on the walls.

Better that way. Nothing personal, and whatever the detectives brought, she wouldn't allow it to become personal.

Howard, especially Detective Howard, had been kind to her over the years, she reminded herself. The least she could do was listen.

"Before we talk to you about why we came, I want to thank you for saving my life." Howard leaned forward. "I never told you. I guess I didn't want to pile on, but I think this is a good time.

"Nearly three years after we first met, Detective Musk and I were pursuing a suspect. He was armed, had already proven to be dangerous. I was in the lead, Phil at my six—behind me," he qualified. "We were heading down a flight of stairs. Painted blue. I heard your voice in my head telling me to be careful about blue stairs. It pulled me up short. Just for a second. Just a second. The bullet missed me by inches. It wouldn't have if I hadn't pulled up. I wouldn't have pulled up unless you'd warned me."

"I'm glad you're all right."

"So am I. And we were able to stop him. I've thought about that moment a lot over the years. Thought about you, Thea, and your family. You helped put Riggs away. You helped us get justice for his other victims.

"You saved my life."

"You helped me."

"And you helped us. Now we're here to ask for your help again."

"I had a lot of doubts about coming here, coming to you," Musk began. "I pushed you pretty damn hard after your parents died, and you just a kid. You've got plenty of reasons to resent that. I hope you can put it aside. There's a fifteen-year-old girl whose life might depend on it."

"I know why you pushed, so I can't resent it. But I don't understand. What girl?"

"Her name's Shiloh Durning. She was abducted two days ago on her way home from school. She's on the track team, and she stayed after school to run. Somewhere between the school and home—less than a mile away—someone took her."

"She's the fourth girl taken this way over the last sixteen months," Howard continued. "All between fifteen and sixteen, all blondes with slim builds. He keeps them for four days, and he hurts them, Thea. On the fourth day, he kills them and dumps their bodies."

"We have a task force working it," Musk told her, "and we've got the FBI involved. We know he must know the area, that he must have a place private enough to keep them. We believe he's a white male between twenty-five and thirty-five, meticulous, organized, who lives alone."

"Our profile gives us a picture of him, but not a physical one. Shiloh's time's running out, Thea."

"I still don't understand what you want from me."

Howard took a small evidence bag from his pocket. "These are her lucky earrings. Little lightning bolts? She only wears them when she's in a race. Maybe you'll get something from them."

Instinctively, Thea crossed her arms, hugged her elbows. "I don't do that here. Nobody here knows about what I have."

Nobody who counts, she corrected.

"And I don't know if I can . . . see that way."

"If you could just try," Musk began, but Howard put a hand on his arm.

"It's fucking unfair, I know it. Coming here like this, asking you. But that's what we're doing. Three girls are dead because we can't find him. We don't want Shiloh to be the fourth. She's fifteen. You'd have gone to the same high school if your life hadn't changed. She has a younger brother, like you. She has parents who love her, like yours loved you."

She kept the window closed here, she thought. Closed and locked. She'd made that deal with herself after Asher had crushed her.

She'd kept the deal for three years.

Just another college student, going to class, sweating over assignments, going to parties, flirting with boys.

But that lock had already slipped, she realized, because she could feel the frustration, the desperation, the cold anger from the two men who sat across from her.

"Do you have a picture of her?"

Musk pulled out his phone, brought one up to show her.

"She's a pretty girl. So were the others. Chrissy Bates, fifteen; Harley Adamson, sixteen; Michaela Lowe, two days shy of sixteen."

"I don't know if I can do this. I don't know if I can help."

But she held her hand out for the earrings.

"No, let me take them out. I'll take them out. Keep the picture on the phone. And be quiet. Just be quiet."

Before she opened the bag, she thought of her grandmother, who'd taught her how to open, how to close. How to look, how not to.

She took the earrings out, held them in her palm. Looking at the photo, she stroked her fingers over the little gold lightning bolts.

And threw open the window.

Oh, so much blew in.

Her dorm mates, their voices, their feelings, their hopes, their fears.

Not now, not now. Not your minds, not your fears.

Hers.

Shiloh.

"She wants to improve her time on the 1600 meter. She has the endurance, the strategy, just wants to cut a little off her time. She got nipped in the last race by less than two seconds. Need to cut three off. Wants the track record, wants it bad. Three seconds will do it.

"She feels so strong when she runs! So strong, so free, so full. She wishes Jack would ask her out. She flirts with him, trying not to be too obvious. He flirts back, but when is he going to ask her out?

"God, if she flunked that Spanish test, her parents will kill her. But Jesus please us, it's not like she didn't study her brains out!

"She wants to . . . Oh, oh!"

When she went pale as glass, Howard leaned toward her. "Thea."

"Be quiet! She's so afraid, and cold. It's so cold. It's hard to breathe with the tape over her mouth. It hurts, everything hurts. The zip ties hurt her wrists, her ankles. She wants her mom. She wants her mom. She's naked, and she's cold. He'll rape her again when he comes back. He'll come down the stairs. He'll hold the knife to her throat, let it cut just a little.

"'Make a peep, girlie, and I'll slice straight through.'

"He makes her drink something, fake chocolate?"

Because she could taste it, Thea rubbed her hand at her throat. "For nutrition. Then he puts the tape on again, and he rapes her."

As Thea's eyes filled, she hugged herself, rocked.

"He takes her to the shower, nasty, it has mold.

"It smells bad. She smells bad. He runs the water cold, and she cries. He hits her when she cries, but he likes it. He likes when she cries, she can tell. He has brown eyes and brown hair. She studies him when she can make herself. If she gets away, she can tell what he looks like.

"She's afraid she won't get away.

"He makes her use the toilet while he stands and watches. Then he ties her back on the bed. In a basement, with pipes on the ceiling and one of those windows that's just aboveground. It's filthy, inside and out. She can't see anything, and no one would see her even if they looked. Wooden steps go up.

"Wait."

Thea shifted, did what she could to dull the girl's fear that lived in her now, too.

"He showed her a badge, right outside the school. But she knows now he's not the police. There was never a missing little boy, never a picture he wanted to show her. At the car, he hit her, hit her hard, but she saw the car. Green, four-door. Not new. She doesn't know cars, neither do I, but dark green, four doors.

"Wait," Thea said again, and pulled the girl back.

"His mother's house. He tells her something . . . dead mother, likes her better that way. He grew up in that house. She got it in the divorce. Let me see," she murmured, "let me see.

"A garage. Attached garage. That's how he takes them in so the neighbors don't see. He keeps the lawn mowed, keeps to himself. Two-story, brick, old. Inside, it's falling apart, but he keeps the outside looking good. The house is like him. There's a red maple in the front yard, and pink azaleas for foundation plants.

"The house number is 1331. It's not far from the school. She's in the basement."

Thea pushed the earrings at Howard. "Please, take them. I can't do any more."

"Let me get you some water."

"I left a Coke in the refrigerator, for the drive home."

As he got up, Musk moved away, talked low into his phone. She heard him describe the house, the car, then snap at someone to find both.

"Here you go." Howard handed her the Coke, the bottle blissfully cold when she rubbed it over her forehead. "I don't want to leave until you feel steadier."

"I'll be fine. I'm going home."

"How about you drink that first, then Phil and I will carry the rest of your things down for you."

"She doesn't know what time it is. She's not sure what day it is."

"We're going to find her. Thanks to you, we're going to get her back to her family. We're going to get him, and he won't hurt another girl."

"She could've been me if things had been different, if there'd never been a Riggs. You knew that. You used that."

"I did."

She opened her purse, took out a pad and a pencil. "I'm not as good as the police artist," she said as she began to sketch. "Brown hair, short, neat, stylish, I guess, on the conservative side. Brown eyes, wide set.

He's good-looking, like the house on the outside. A nice smile. Ears close to the head. Some stubble—stylish again."

She handed the pad to Howard.

"This is good. It's damn good." He took a picture of it with his phone. "Can I have it?"

"I don't want it. I'd really like to get on the road."

"We'll take your things down. Musk."

Still holding the phone, Musk turned. "Lawrence James Heberman, 1331 Laurel Lane. He owns a 2010 green four-door Chevy. And he fits the profile like a fucking glove, Chuck."

He walked to Thea. "I've got a little girl. She's five."

"Yes, you remarried, had a daughter. Congratulations."

"Howard has a daughter, too. They'll both be fifteen one day. If you ever need anything. Hell, you want somebody to pick up your dry cleaning, paint your house, mow your lawn, you just call. I swear to God, I'll be there.

"We need to get to the airport. Your friend the fed's getting us on a plane."

"Let's get Thea's things in her car, get her headed home."

She stopped halfway there to buy something for the headache that wouldn't quite fade, and a ginger ale to try to stem the queasiness.

And saw the text on her phone from Howard.

Shiloh's safe, and her family's with her. Heberman's in custody. I wanted you to know you saved another life. I sincerely wish you everything good in yours.

Thea sat in the car a moment, read the text again.

And realized the headache had faded after all.

However three years of college had changed her life, the farm remained constant. Small changes here with a fresh coat of paint, her grandmother's new truck in the driveway.

And, to her surprise, two floppy-eared puppies who raced around the house well ahead of the slower-moving Goose and Cocoa.

"Oh my God!" The little girl popped right out of her as she pushed out of the car and crouched down for puppy greetings, then the enthusiastic welcome by the older dogs.

All but buried in dogs, she looked over as Lucy came out of the house. And to her eye, no one had ever looked more wonderful.

Tall and slim in jeans and a red shirt rolled to the elbow, with her hair bundled up, she seemed simply ageless, as constant as the farm.

"There's that girl!"

As Lucy came down from the porch, Thea detached herself from the dogs to hurry toward her. "Grammie."

The first embrace wrapped her in strong arms, in the scent of rosemary and fresh bread. In scents of home.

"I missed you. It's so good to be home."

"Let me get a look at you." Lucy drew her back. "You just get prettier every day."

"Because I look like you."

"Well, I can't deny it." Laughing, Lucy hugged her again. "You've had a long drive. Let's get you inside and settled."

"You've got two puppies."

"They came as a set, brother and sister." As the puppies scrabbled at her legs, Lucy shook her head. "I had a weak moment, but the fact is since we lost Duck last winter, and Goose and Cocoa are getting on, we needed a little lively. I've got a soft spot for coonhounds."

"They're adorable."

"That's Tweedle, and his sister Dee, though I wonder if I should've gone with Dum instead. But I'm hoping she finds her good sense before long. Now, let's get your bags inside. I know how you run. You'll want to unpack."

"I'm not all the way home till I do. And I want to be all the way home."

"We'll get that done, then sit ourselves down with a glass of wine—even though you're not quite legal—and you can tell me everything about everything. You can finish up the telling over chicken and slicks."

"That sounds so good. I've missed your cooking, too."

"Rem'll be here before supper tomorrow, so there'll be more cooking. He favors my pork chops."

"Who wouldn't?"

The house smelled of the slowly simmering chicken and aromatics, of the orange oil on freshly polished wood.

And her room carried the scent of lilacs from the flowers in the blue mason jar on the dresser.

Even the breeze through the window whispered welcome.

"Maddy should be back the day after tomorrow," Thea said as she hung up and tucked away clothes.

"Her family's about bursting with pride. Top five percent of her class, and getting it done in three years. It'll be nice for her and Rem to be close by each other next year. And, hell, I'm about bursting, so I'm going to tell you before we sit down. Caleb and Selma are finally getting married."

"That's big news! When?"

"They're going to do it quick and quiet in New York in a week or so, then take themselves off for a honeymoon. Then they're coming here so we can have a party. A double party. I'm getting another grandbaby before Christmas."

"Oh! Not big news. Huge! I've only met her a couple times, but I record their show every week. They look so good together. I know Rem likes her a lot."

"Caleb loves her, and she loves him back. I could tell it the first time I saw them together. They've taken their sweet time about it, but they're on their time, not mine."

"The charming police detective and the no-nonsense prosecutor. Their fans will go wild."

"Which is why they're doing it quick and quiet."

Hands on hips, Lucy looked around. "Seems you're all the way home. Let's go down and you can start on the everything."

"Not a lot of everything before today. Etta broke up with Adam again, Lily got her internship, Chelsea's going to Italy with her family."

"I want to hear about your friends, too, but start with you. I've got store-bought as well as my apple wine."

"I'll go with Grammie's. That chicken already smells good."

"I'd just pulled the breasts out so they wouldn't toughen when you drove up. We've got another forty minutes or so for the rest to simmer."

Lucy poured the wine, gave the pot a stir. Cookies came out of the jar and onto a plate.

Thea knew the house rules. First day home, she sat while her grandmother fussed.

"Now. What's this about today?"

"Two things. I guess I'll take them in order of appearance. Professor Cheng—he's Game Design—texted he wanted me to come to his office. Naturally, I worked myself up into a state, I guess that's how I'm built, about tanking my finals project."

"I don't believe that for a minute. You worked so hard on it, and Rem said it rocked hard—that's a quote."

"Rem's my brother, and Professor Cheng's a hard-ass. I learned a lot from him, maybe because he's a hard-ass."

"What did he have to say?"

Thea lifted her glass in toast. "A hundred percent. Believe me, he doesn't toss those around like Mardi Gras beads."

On a hoot, Lucy clapped her hands together. "Oh, Thea, I'm so proud!"

"There's more. His cousin works for Milken."

"The games people?"

"Yeah, and he's going to send my game to his cousin. He said he's never done that before."

Lucy sat back. "You mean to say they might make your game?"

"I don't know about that, but if I get any kind of feedback from them, it's gold, Grammie. And maybe a connection when I get my degree."

"I should've gotten champagne."

"We won't jinx it. It's an opportunity, and inside I'm dancing. But we won't jinx it."

"I'll be lighting a candle and sending out light with intent that my girl gets what she's earned and deserves. No jinx there."

"I'll take it. Then there was something else. When I floated back to the dorm to get my things, Detectives Howard and Musk were waiting for me."

Lucy's hand shot out to grip hers. "Riggs. But . . . no, not Riggs."

"No, nothing about him. They told me that right away because I thought the same. It was about a girl who'd been abducted."

She told it all, beginning to end.

When she finished, Lucy rose to pour them each a second glass. "That girl's safe because you followed your heart and your conscience."

"I didn't want to, Grammie. I really wanted them to go away, leave me alone. But . . ."

"You followed your heart and your conscience," Lucy repeated. "You helped when help was needed."

"And you helped me open to seeing that way, by touching or holding. It hurt, Grammie. I mean I could feel her pain, her terror. Removed from it, but still feeling her, knowing it."

Lucy nodded. "It's part of the price."

"But once I started, I couldn't stop, whatever the price. The things he'd done to her? We know there's cruelty in the world, we've lived through it. But, Grammie, the things he'd done to her, what he would do to her."

Pausing, she breathed out, drank some wine. "I understand how I could see his car, because she did. And the basement, because she did. And him, because she did. But she didn't see the house from the outside. She didn't see the inside except for the basement. But I did.

"I didn't see through him, not like Riggs. It wasn't like that."

"You stepped back, so you could see. You put yourself there, with her, then stepped back to see more."

"I don't know how."

"Honeypot, you do, or you couldn't and wouldn't have done it. I don't have a gift that shines that bright, but you do. How did it make you feel?"

"Sick, shaky, my head ached."

"That's physical. How did it make you feel?"

"Worried, scared. Scared for her. What if I was wrong? What if they didn't find her in time? I wanted to be here, to be home and not be worried and scared for a girl I'd never met, but I knew. I knew her now. I had to stop on the way here to get something for my head. But before I got out, I got the text that she was safe. And my headache went away. Just like that."

"You connected to her, shared her fear and pain. The gift carries weight, you knew that, but you lifted it up. When you knew she was safe, you could let it go."

"What about . . . when I don't want to lift it up?"

"You follow your heart and your conscience. It's a choice, Thea. It's always going to be your choice, just like it's your gift."

"I really needed to talk to you. I really needed to come home."

Chapter Twelve

Rem's homecoming, delayed for a day, as Caleb had his quick and quiet wedding with him as best man, brought Rem's usual chaos and joy.

He didn't unpack, a process Thea knew would take him the better part of a week.

He stood at six-three, and looked so much like Caleb, it dazzled. But he had their father's eyes.

He surrounded himself with the dogs, roughhousing like a twelve-year-old. He lifted his grandmother up and swung her in circles, and nearly cracked Thea's ribs with his hug.

"Can I have a beer, Grammie? You probably suspect I've had one or two in my checkered past."

"I've had that suspicion, so I laid some in. Go on and get one. Then I want to hear about the wedding."

"Nothing to it." He popped the top on a beer. "They decided, *Hey, let's just do it now,* and it took like five minutes. But I've got pictures."

He took out his phone, hit the app, handed it over.

"Oh, look, Thea! Don't they look happy? And my boy so handsome in his suit, and his bride just a vision in her pretty dress. Oh, and this one here, see the way they look at each other. That says everything you need to hear. I need you to print this one out for me, Rem, so I can frame it."

"No problem. Man, it's really seriously good to be home. I like New York. I like it a lot, but there really is no fricking place like home."

"Since you mention it, I've got something to talk to the two of you about. Let's sit out on the porch."

When they did, the dogs rushed them. After the chaos Rem joined in, Lucy gave the word.

"Y'all sit! Sit and settle."

The puppies sat, for about two minutes, then raced off to wrestle in the yard. Cocoa lay across Rem's feet, and Goose snored under Lucy's chair.

"I'm going to say first, I'm as happy as those lunatic puppies to have both of you home. I'm proud as I can be with how you're making your way, but that doesn't mean I don't miss you when you're gone."

Content, she looked out over the gardens, the fields. "This place has been my home most of my life, and it's always going to be yours. Now, I wondered if y'all might want to make your homes elsewhere. New York, like Caleb, Atlanta, like my mama, traveling around, like Waylon did before the children came. Not that he and Kyra and the family don't still get out and about, but they've made their home. Somehow I've come to think, and you tell me if I'm wrong, that's not what you're after."

"This is where I want to be, Grammie," Thea told her. "Like Rem, I like New York whenever we've visited Caleb, and I like other places I've been. But I'm happiest here."

"It's home." Rem nodded. "I want to see other places, sure, but this is where I want to come back to."

"If that's the case, I want to say you can live here as long as you want. Hell, if you start your own family, we'll just build the house bigger. We got room for that. But I'm thinking down the road and how you might, and most likely will, want places of your own. It happens circumstances gave me an idea on that."

"I hope that's a long road. I'm not even legal to drink this beer in a bar yet."

"Time moves fast, darling. A minute ago you were sitting out here wanting to be an astronaut. Y'all remember Miss Leona from down the road a little ways?"

"The little yellow house. She likes your oatmeal soap. Rem mowed her yard in the summer all through high school."

"She always had cookies and sweet tea for me. Is she okay?"

"She is. Getting up there, though, and a widow these last eight years. Used to plant a big garden, and raise some beef cattle, keep chickens. Nowadays, she plants small, has some help with that. She sold off the cattle. Too much for a woman alone nearing eighty. I suspect some past that, as she won't say."

"If you want us to give her a hand this summer," Rem began, and Lucy patted his hand.

"I expect she'd be grateful. She asked me to come see her, talk some business, so I did. She's got fifteen good acres where the house sits, the old barn and such, the fields, and some wooded land where the stream goes through. She wants to sell off all but five, hoping to keep that in the family when she passes, and wondered if I'd have an interest in those ten acres."

"What would you do with ten acres?" Thea wondered. "Nearly a mile away?"

"About three-quarters of a mile, and I'm not thinking of it for me." Lucy smiled out at her land. "No, this is enough for me. Five acres for each of you, though, that's interesting to me. You'd have a place to plant a home, build a house that suits you, if you're still of a mind to. Sell it, if you change your mind. Either way, a good investment, I think. It's good land, and I'm selfish enough to like it's close."

"Buy five acres," Rem murmured.

"The business major's mind's working. There'd be legal what all. Survey, right-of-way, as you'd need to put a road back to your properties. She'd toss that right-of-way in. I'm going to say it's hurting her heart to see the land go wasted. You'd need wells and septic and getting the electric back there. It'll take time, but if you have an interest, you have that time, and you have the money to make what you want of it."

"What do you think, Thea?"

She looked at her brother. "I'm trying to think about something I never thought about."

"Thinking's what you should do. Why don't the two of you take a walk on down there, have a look, have that thinking and talking-about-it time. And, Thea, you have other things to tell Rem."

"What?"

"Not yet. I'm thinking." Thea got to her feet. "Let's take that walk."

Lucy whistled for the pups. "I'll take them inside so they don't trail you."

They hadn't reached the road before Rem spoke. "I want to buy it."

"Rem, we haven't thought about it for five minutes. You've got three more years of college."

"It's a good investment, and one we can see and feel. One we can use. And you've only got one more year. Making the deal, getting a lane put in and the rest, getting a house designed and built? That'll take longer.

"You're not going anywhere, Thea. I know you."

She looked out toward the hills, the woods that climbed them.

"No, I'm not going anywhere. I guess part of me didn't want to look past living at Grammie's little farm."

"Well, look now."

When she did, she could imagine herself, maybe a pretty cottage, gardens, and the quiet of it. She could keep chickens, maybe a goat or a milk cow.

"Why do you want it?" she countered. "And don't say just for the investment."

"Because this is home. I wouldn't build on it, at least not for a long while. Grammie can use my help, with the little farm, with managing her business, and with the rest. I'm nowhere near ready for a house, but you are."

"Maybe."

"What are you supposed to tell me?"

"After we look at the property."

And it was so damn pretty, she thought when they stood on the road that looked over it.

The yellow house stood well back from that road, and its porch sagged more than a little in the middle. Thea could see where the roof had been patched.

"The house needs some work," Rem observed. "I'll see if I can get Billy Joe to give me a hand, see if we can fix it up some for her."

He put an arm around Thea's shoulder. "Miss Leona always has cookies and sweet tea."

"The barn needs some help, too, and that shed's not going to stand through the next good storm until it's shored up."

"We'll see what we can do. But look at the land, Thea."

"I'm looking," she murmured. The way it climbed and rolled, the summer green of it.

And already knew her answer.

"We'd have to decide my five acres and yours."

"I knew it! You get dibs on this one because it'll matter more to you. And I've got years to decide how to use mine. We're going to be land-owners. Ain't that a kick in the ass?"

It was, and brought it back to her how much things could change, and just how fast.

"Let's go tell her."

"Now?"

"Now's good." Before she could object, Rem started back toward the house with its sagging porch. She hurried to catch up as he knocked.

The woman who answered gave them one long look out of faded green eyes. Then smiled. "Goodness, girl, aren't you the image of your granny! I knew her since she was barely higher than my knee. And look how tall you got, boy. You come by to cut my grass?"

"I can sure do that for you, Miss Leona."

"It could use it, and you always did a fine job. Come in, come in. Just brush that cat out of the way and sit in the parlor here. I've got short-bread cookies and sweet tea."

"I'll help you with that, Miss Leona."

"No, no." She waved Thea into a parlor with an aged brick fireplace, a sofa covered with white daisies and red poppies. Next to one of the two wingback chairs sat a knitting basket.

"You sit now. I'm pleased to have some company."

So they sat, and eventually ate shortbread cookies and did the ex-pected visiting chat.

Rem launched the ball.

"Miss Leona, Grammie told us you're thinking about selling off some land."

"Made up my mind to. I can't keep it up, and hate seeing it fallow.

My grandson says I should sell the lot, move into a retirement place up north in Philadelphia where he is. That ain't never happening."

She waved a gnarled finger, then sipped at her tea with a hand with the slightest tremor.

Eighty-six now, Thea thought. Not nearing her eighties, but more than halfway through them.

"I came to this house as a bride, gave birth to my children here, raised them up. Me and George, we worked this land together, lived our lives here. I intend to end mine here when the good Lord calls me home."

"We'd like to buy the land you want to sell, Thea and I."

"Is that a fact?" Smiling again, and that smile reached right into those faded eyes, she set her glass on a needlepoint coaster. "That's welcome news. I'd sure welcome having some young neighbors. It's the land," she said, "not the money. Though I expect a fair deal for it. My son sends me a check monthly. And more, my great-grandson, why, he's taken over all my bills."

Sipping tea, she shook her head over it.

"Won't hear any guff about it from me. He's a good boy. He visits when he can, and doesn't he fly me all the way up there every Christmas so's I stay in his big, pretty house, where he treats me like a queen? It's not the money, but I've got my mind set that land won't keep sitting there pining."

"If it's all right with you, I can put a contract together. You can have your lawyer look it over."

Miss Leona fluffed at her white ball of hair. "What'd I want a lawyer for? You figure I think Lucinda Lannigan's grandchildren would try pulling one on me? Why, she'd skin your hides for it, then tan 'em into leather for a new coat."

She named a price, nodded. "That's what I want for it. You can put that in the contract, that's fine. But if that's what you'll pay, we'll shake on it here and now."

Rem held out a hand, and shook hers gently.

"You, too, girl. Men don't run every blessed thing."

Thea held out a hand. "Thank you, Miss Leona, for trusting us with your land. I promise we'll take good care of it."

"You're Lucinda's blood, all right. I trust you will, and I'll hold you to it."

Back on the road, Rem wrapped an arm around Thea's shoulders again. "We just bought ten acres."

"And I feel right about it. I wasn't sure I would, but it feels absolutely right. Do you know how all of this works?"

"I'll find out. That's what I do. Now, for Christ's sake, tell me what you're supposed to tell me."

When she told him about the game, he stopped. And did a wild dance in the middle of the road.

"Holy shit, holy shit, holy hot shit. I told you it rocked. I knew this would happen."

"That makes one of us."

"Because you wouldn't look. Your business," he added. "Man, if I had what you have, I'd've looked. Anyway, I don't need the sight to know they're going to want to buy it, but you're not going to sell it."

"First, don't jinx it! And why the hell wouldn't I sell it?"

"Because that's just a lump of money and no control. What you're going to do is lease it to them. Give them the rights for— I need to find out how long it should be, and how much you get on each sale or download."

"But—"

He waved her off like a fly.

"You'll let me negotiate this. You're the talent, but I'm the business. And if they want more of your talent, they're going to have to hire you."

He nodded to himself as they walked. "I can work this. I can make this work."

Since she didn't believe any of it would happen—just some feedback and the connection—she let him talk his talk until he wound down.

"There's something else."

His absolute delight drained away as she told him about the detectives, the young girl.

"Are you okay?"

"Yes, she's safe."

"Yeah, and I'm really glad she is. But are *you* okay? She's safe because they came to you, safe because you put yourself out there to help her. It couldn't've been easy to do what you did. It has to cost you."

On a sigh, she hooked her arm around his waist, leaned her head to his shoulder. "How am I supposed to pretend my brother's a jerk when you say that? When you understand that? But I am okay. Whatever it cost in the moment, that's outweighed knowing I could do something."

"I know I joke about getting ripped off in the psychic department, but I don't know how I'd handle what you and Grammie have."

"It wasn't always a joke."

"True." It made him smile to remember. "Really pissed me off when I was a kid. Plus, you wouldn't do me any little favors."

"Right, like looking to see what the questions were going to be on your science test."

"Just so I could target my study area."

"Cheating."

"Is it, though? And later, I just wanted you to see if Nadine Peterson had a thing for me before I asked her to homecoming."

"Intrusive."

"Maybe, a little. But no guy likes getting rejected."

"Rejection builds character."

"Bullshit." Laughing, he rubbed his knuckles over the top of her head. "I'd probably have gone wild with it. Can I get that girl I'm hot for naked? Swami says: *Yes.*"

"Swami?"

"I'd absolutely call myself Swami. Can I get a little look-see at the final for my Probability and Statistics class, which I deeply regret taking? Swami says: *Bet your ass.*"

"You wouldn't, though. You wouldn't because you like a challenge."

"Probability and Statistics about busted my brain. The professor hasn't posted the grade for the final yet, or the semester average." He gave his sister a winning smile. "Maybe you could just take a quick look?"

"No."

"So strict. Anyway, I'm going to text another prof—Business Law. See if he can give me some advice on drawing up the contract of sale and all that."

"We've got lawyers, Rem."

"Yeah, but I want to see if I can do it."

"I know we need one, the contract, but I liked the handshake on it."

"Me, too." Taking her hand, he swung it as they walked. "And that's one of the reasons we both want to be here. Let's go tell Grammie we're going to be neighbors forever."

"And you'll mooch dinner off her forever."

"You forgot breakfast."

As they turned toward the farm, the puppies came running.

"No, wait, give me eight or ten years, I'll build my house and mooch breakfast off you."

He got right down to wrestle with the dogs, and grinned up at her. "But I'll babysit your three kids. It's three I remember, once you marry Tyler Brennan."

"You read my journal!" She gave him a kick in the ass.

"First, ow." He rubbed two dog bellies at once. "Second, no. Not that I didn't think about it, but I calculated the twin wraths of you and Grammie as not worth it. But I knew how to eavesdrop. You told Maddy all about it."

"See, you are a jerk. And I was fifteen."

"Or sixteen, maybe. If I remember right, Maddy was all into Jaden Smith."

"You were hot for Buffy. Watched that in syndication and mooned over Buffy Summers."

"What do you mean *was* hot for? Sexiest vampire slayer ever. I still catch a rerun now and then."

Rising, he grabbed Thea's hand with one damp from puppy licks.

"You know Buffy isn't real."

"In my heart she is. I'm starving. I heard pork chops for supper."

She fell back into routine, and loved it. Mornings seeing the sunrise, tending the animals, walks in the hills, gardening. Finally spending time with Maddy again.

One rainy afternoon they sprawled in the Foxes' Den as they had since childhood. Maddy had cut off her braids and wore her hair in a glorious 'fro. On the last day of premed, she'd added a tattoo of an abacus to her left biceps.

Otherwise, Thea thought, she was the same.

"I can't count the number of times you trounced me, and everybody else, at every video game known to man. And look now, you're going to be making the games."

"I hope."

"You'll do it, Joystick Wizard."

"Nobody from Milken's contacted me."

"Hasn't been a week."

"A week today. Not that I'm counting. And you, Dr. McKinnon."

"Not yet, but I will be. There's a rumor going around town about some doctor, maybe out of Hazard, maybe opening a clinic in Redbud Hollow."

"Really?"

"A lot of maybes. Like maybe he's going to buy the old Darson place and make it into one. I'd be glad if it's so, and a little pissed off because I wanted to open one. If I could swing it once I finish medical school."

"You're going to stay then." Joy popped like champagne. "You said you were thinking about trying for a hospital in Louisville."

Maddy shrugged. "I got over that. My family's here, and look at my brother, Deputy Will. You're here. My best best friend for all time. I'm going to be ready to come home when I've got my degree. Now it looks like I may have to try for a job in somebody else's clinic, or give private practice a try."

"Either way, I'm your first patient."

"And you're for sure staying, seeing as you bought five acres."

"Working on it. Rem's handling all that—he wants to, and I don't. The surveyor's already been there. We had to figure out where I want my five, and Rem his."

"I want to see! Let's walk down there now."

"It's raining."

"Some wet won't hurt us. I want to see where my Maddy's-staying-over room's going to be." Rising, Maddy reached down and hauled Thea to her feet. "And I definitely have to approve the plans for your house. I don't want you thinking too small."

"I don't need a big house."

"You need a good-sized kitchen, seeing as you like to cook, and an office, and a game room. A game room studio. You need those for your work. A main suite," she continued as she led Thea downstairs, "because you'd be a fool not to have one. At least two more bedrooms, another full bath and a half one, too.

"You're still doing yoga, right?"

"Yeah."

"A place for that. And you ought to do one of those wraparound porches."

"I . . ." Thea imagined that, and the views all around. "I ought to.

"Let me tell Grammie we're going out, in the rain, to tromp around five acres."

She caught the scent before she walked in the kitchen, and found Lucy and Rem about to pour out a batch of soap.

"You should've told me you were working. I'd have helped."

"I enlisted this one, and nearly done now. You girls hungry?"

"I could be," Maddy said. "But first Thea's going to show me her five acres. It's one of my favorite things, Miss Lucy, the way your house always smells of something good. My soap and candles were the envy of my dorm."

"That's good to hear. If y'all wait till we're finished, we'll go along. I've got some balm for Miss Leona's arthritis I can take her."

"When I'm a doctor in town, you're going be my main competition."

The phone in Thea's pocket signaled. After taking it out, she stared at the readout.

"Oh God, it's Milken."

"Jumping Jesus, Thea!" Maddy punched Thea's shoulder. "Answer it."

"I will. I am. Ah, hello?"

"Thea Fox?"

"Yes, this is Thea."

"This is Bradley Case. I'm general manager of development at Milken. Is this a good time for you?"

"Yes. Thank you for calling."

"Mr. Cheng passed *Endon* on to me. Your professor sent it to him—with your permission?"

"Yes." Because everyone stood staring at her, she turned away. "I appreciate you taking the time to review the game."

"You designed and developed *Endon* yourself?"

"Yes."

"For a college project?"

"Yes."

Maddy hissed, "Say something besides yes!"

"Can I call you Thea?"

She started to say yes, switched it up. "Of course."

"It's impressive, Thea. The game play, the graphics, the narrative. I've had a team play it at its varying levels, and shared their conclusions and mine with Ms. Kendall, CEO. We're interested in buying your game."

"You're . . ." She spoke each word slowly. "You're interested in buying my game?"

Immediately, Rem surged forward, shook his head, his finger at her.

"Yes, we are. We'd like to set up a meeting with you to discuss it. I realize you don't have an agent or representative, so—"

"Actually, I have . . . He's right here."

She shoved the phone at Rem. *Name*, Rem mouthed, and pointed at the phone.

"Bradley Case."

"Mr. Case, this is Remington Fox, Thea's business manager. I'm also her brother," he said cheerfully, and wandered away as he spoke. "Yes, that's right. It does."

"Oh my God, what have I done? I just handed my eighteen-year-old brother the phone. The most important call of my life, and I hand him the phone."

"Almost nineteen, and his business smarts are a lot older than eighteen." Lucy rubbed a hand on Thea's shoulder. "Listening to him's brought me almost more business from online than I can handle. I'm thinking about hiring on a crafter."

"Let him go for it, Thea." Maddy gave her a hip bump. "Worst thing is they hear him out and tell him no. That won't stop you from selling the game to them if you want."

Thea paced. "It won't. It absolutely won't. I can call him back, tell him my brother's crazy, and I'd be thrilled to have Milken produce my game."

Rem wandered back, offered her the phone.

"Mr. Case— He's gone."

"Yeah, we concluded our preliminary discussion. We've got a video call meeting day after tomorrow, ten o'clock. He needs to take my counter-offer up the chain—though he's pretty far up, so not much chain over his head."

"Your counteroffer?"

"Yeah. I told you you're not selling, you're leasing the rights to them for ten years—with an option to renew. We'll negotiate your advance, and your percentage of the sales. Since you have a sequel planned— You do, right?"

"Just in my head." And at the moment, that head felt numb.

"Good enough. Since, if they want any future *Endon* games, or any other games designed by Thea Fox, they should hire her at a salary commensurate with her talent, creativity, and skills."

"Listen to my boy." Laughing, Lucy gave him a smacking kiss on the cheek. "'Commensurate.'"

"What did he say?"

"That he'd take it up the chain. He also told me they'd already decided to recruit you. Now I say we hold off till tomorrow and the sun for going to see the land, and instead we sit down here and work out what you want, and what you should get.

"I've done some research on it."

Thea dropped down at the kitchen table and pulled out one of her brother's favorite exclamations.

"Holy hot shit."

Chapter Thirteen

She wrote it all in her journal, then read what she'd written just so she could feel the thrill again.

She'd sold—no, leased—her first game. And she'd be paid for it. She had to sign the contract, but she'd be paid for what had once been only a dream.

More, so much more than the money, she had the vindication that her work had value. Milken Entertainment considered her work, her game, her dream worthy.

They wanted some tweaks—improving the music, the sound effects. They had a whole department for that. They'd hire experienced voice actors for the dialogue, which made sense, and could only enhance the gaming experience.

They'd have first refusal on any spin-offs or sequels, while hiring her as a paid intern for her final year in college.

When she graduated, if her work continued to meet their standards, they'd offer her a position as a game designer.

She could have a career, an actual career, doing something she loved.

It seemed impossible, so she read her own words one more time.

Maybe it was being home, maybe it was the thrill and the nerves winding through it, the vision of a future that held so much of what she wanted, but she forgot to hang the pouch and say the words.

She turned off her light, closed her eyes, and began to build her dream.

Part Two of the world of *Endon*, with Zed and Twink and Gwen, the fearless farm girl Mila, the resurrection of the evil Mog.

She wondered if she could find someone to teach her how to use a sword, to execute the moves, to actually feel what her characters felt. Wouldn't knowing add more realism and thrill to her battle scenes?

Maybe take a mixed martial arts class, too. The more she knew, the more her characters would resonate.

She saw another character—a young man, young warrior, half human, half elf. Not of one world or the other, he sought to defend both. With no ingrained tribal allegiance, no place he felt fully at home, he wandered those worlds, a sword at his side, a quiver on his back.

Ty, she thought.

No, Tye, and, amused at herself, began to draw him in her head to resemble her childhood crush.

She drifted into the magic forest, and dreamed.

Riggs found her there as she stood in dappled sunlight, among the wildflowers that reached for it, the colorful fruit that dripped like jewels from branches, among the moss that coated the trees and rocks in the shadows.

"There you are. You've been hiding from me. What the fuck is this place?"

"You're not welcome here."

"I'm here, aren't I?" In his prison blues with his hair straggling nearly to his shoulders again, standing in the dappled sunlight, ghost pale, he smiled and showed those overlapping front teeth.

"You've grown up some since the last time. Still no tits or ass to speak of."

She heard the stream she'd dreamed burble behind her, and the breeze whispering through the trees. A bird, as blue as a sapphire, winged by with a trill of a song.

This was her world. He couldn't hurt her here, she reminded herself. And he couldn't make her afraid again.

Her world, she thought again. And she controlled it.

Someone had used their fists on his face recently, she noted. He had a black eye and raw red and purple bruising on his jaw.

"Looks like someone gave you a pounding, Ray."

"Shut the fuck up. I handle myself."

"Not from the look of your face at this moment. Oh, you got out of seg for a while, got some yard time. And picked the wrong guy to take on. So you're back in segregation."

Steady—maybe her heart beat too fast, but she remained steady—she took a step toward him.

"Push into my head, Ray, I push into yours. You're not real popular in Red Onion. Even murderers and rapists don't like you very much. They don't like the way you look at them, the way you know things."

"They'll get theirs. Payback's coming. Coming for you, too. You thought you could hide from me, but you can't. I found you. I'll keep finding you. And one day I'll get my hands on you. Your face won't look pretty after I'm done."

"Sure, Ray. Now if you don't mind, this is my place."

She opened as wide as she could to what she had, fisted her hands.

"Get out!"

She woke, not with fear but satisfaction. The vague headache would pass, and the results were more than worth the price.

He'd pushed into her mind, into her dream, but she'd pushed him out again. It cost her, but she'd done it.

And she'd seen him, bruised and battered. Seen enough to know he continued to pay for all the lives he'd taken.

She found satisfaction there, too.

With her equipment set up in the Foxes' Den, Thea sat down to work on the new game already formed in her mind. She hoped to have at least a start on the GDD—the game design document—before the meeting. But before she began to lay out the details of the game design, she wanted to create her new character.

Not muscular like Zed, but tall, wiry. His build, his elf blood would make him agile and quick. He'd wear his hair, the color of good Kentucky bourbon, about chin length and shaggy.

Narrow face, sharp cheekbones, she thought as she sketched. Long-lidded eyes, as green as the forest shadows. Tip them up a little at the outside corners, she decided. Another nod to the elf inside him.

She sketched the face straight on, in profile, drew the back of his head, and decided to layer on a braid over the shaggy, down the center.

As she finished a sketch, she pinned it to the board beside her desk, studied, went back to drawing.

Full-length, and she dressed him in mud-brown breeches, darker brown boots that folded over at the top just below mid-shin. The shirt—not quite a tunic—fell at his hips. She belted it, added a sword. After some debate she decided to color it green, like his eyes, like the forest shadows he could slip through all but unseen.

Sitting back, she stretched her cramping fingers and studied the dozen sketches on her board.

Maybe a tattoo. Biceps, shoulder blade, back of the hand? Not sure, she admitted. Should she add a thick leather bracelet, given to him by his elfin mother, as his human father forged his sword?

She didn't only need his physical appearance, but his background, lineage, history, power points, and weaknesses to create a full character and detail it in the GDD.

Tye, son of Gregor the smith and Lia the elf. A warrior born, a wanderer looking for a battle, a cause, his place.

"Maybe, maybe, maybe. But I know one thing. You're in love with Mila, the farm girl. Is that a problem for you? I think it is, at first. Should be fun for me."

Time to start with the basics, she thought, and swiveled back to her computer to start the document.

As she worked in the blissful quiet, she heard someone coming up the stairs. Not Grammie—too heavy in the feet.

"Working, Rem," she said without turning around.

"Yeah, and you've hogged the Den for about four hours."

Hands in his pockets, he wandered over to her board. "Hey, who's this? New guy? You know, he looks sort of familiar."

She'd just keep the prototype to herself. It was a little embarrassing.

"Half human, half elf. Nomadic warrior and defender of Endon. Badass, romantic interest for Mila."

"That's cool. Look, we have to outline our strategy for the meeting tomorrow."

"We need a strategy?"

"The fact you have to ask proves you need me." He dropped onto the couch. "Take a break. First thing, tell me what you want, exactly what you want, so we can work toward getting it."

"I'm already getting more than I expected."

Legs stretched out, Rem crossed them at the ankles of his battered high-top Chucks.

"More proof you need me."

When she gave up, saved her work, then swiveled around, he shot a finger at her. "What do you want, Thea? A job at Milken, sure, but what do you want to do?"

"I want to design games, like I'm trying to do now. And I want to develop them."

"What's the difference?"

She sent him the pitying look only one sibling could give another. "The fact that you ask proves you don't know enough about the industry."

"So educate me. Give me a thumbnail."

"Fine. The designer, that's . . . like an architect. They draw the blueprint. The idea, the concept comes there, the creative process of designing every element of the game. The developer's like the contractor, see? They build it from the blueprint—the game design document."

"Got it. You want to do both parts?"

"Developing's more than one part, really. It's usually teams and departments."

"You didn't have a team for *Endon*."

"No, but I'd been working on it—off and on—for three years. And I had the concept, the basic storyline, for years more. It's like Milken's going to bring in their music department, and voices. I'm fine with that. I'm actually thrilled with that. But I don't want to just design, then turn it over, get called in when there's a hitch or glitch."

What did she want? To be good at what she did, and get even better. And to imagine people in a space like this, like the Foxes' Den, enjoying what she created.

"I want . . . basically what I'm getting with *Endon*. I design and develop a game, they take it, improve it—adjust or change anything that needs it. Package it, promote it. I don't know if that's realistic, but—"

"We'll find out. What else?"

"I need to work here. That's the only deal-breaker for me. I'm not moving to New York or Seattle."

"Are you willing to travel to New York or Seattle, if and when a face-to-face is needed?"

"Sure. Most of what I do I can do right here, but I can travel when and if. I just won't move away for a job. Not for any job, Rem, even this one. And this one is . . ." She closed her eyes. "Oh boy, this one."

Then she looked at her brother again. "But I need this place, this place where I first dreamed about *Endon*, where I feel rooted. I need Grammie. She always helps anchor me."

"Then we'll get you those things."

She started to laugh, then didn't because she actually believed he would. "What do you want, Rem?"

"I'm doing what I want, and I'm going to get better at it."

The fact that he nearly echoed her thoughts struck her deep.

At the core, she realized, they were so much the same.

"After I do," he continued, "after college, I want to take three or four weeks and travel all over Europe."

"And eat snails in France?"

"Bet your ass—but I'm skipping the beret and ascot. Probably," he qualified.

"Either way, we need a picture."

"I'll make sure it's family gallery worthy. Then I want to come back home, maybe get my MBA, full-time business manager, part-time farmhand."

He shot her his grin. "Tailor-made for me. Build that house one of these days, and find the lucky girl I want to share it with me."

Thea grinned back. "What does she look like?"

"To be determined, but must love dogs."

"A given. Speaking of dogs, I've ignored them, and Grammie, longer than I meant to. I'll get back to this tonight."

When she had the quiet again.

* * *

And when she had the quiet again, she held on to it until nearly two in the morning. She spent a chunk of that time with her software and sketches, translating her image of Tye Smith, wanderer and warrior, from paper to screen.

Of course, he needed a horse, but not just any horse. A warhorse. Dilis. Dilis the loyal and true.

By the time she'd determined the size, shape, color, personality of the horse, her mind blurred enough for her to admit she needed to stop.

More, she knew, would come to her in dreams.

She dressed carefully for the meeting, a collared white shirt, her hair back in what she thought equaled a professional and non-distracting tail. Her mother's pink diamond studs for luck.

After some debate, they settled on holding their part at the kitchen table. It said, Thea thought, who she was, and the powers that be might as well know that from the start.

"I'll stay out of the way."

"Oh, don't leave, Grammie. You're moral support."

"I'll stay, honeypot, but out of the way. And the dogs stay outside so they don't fuss around."

"Ready?" Rem asked her.

"I actually am."

"Then let's log in."

She got her first look—except from online photos—at Bradley Case. He had a flop of brown hair, Buddy Holly glasses, and a tiny silver hoop in his right ear.

"Good to see you, Thea, and you, Rem. Let me introduce you around."

As he put names and positions to the other three people on-screen, Thea scribbled those names and positions on a pad to the side of her laptop.

They talked about the game—and there she felt confident.

She could answer questions about characters, world rules, obstacles, power points, choices, coding, game play without missing a beat.

She listened to suggestions for changes or improvements, made more notes.

"Actually, I'm bringing Mog back in the next game." She said it absently as she scribbled notes.

"You have plans for the next?" Bradley asked her.

"Oh, sorry, yes. I started the GDD yesterday, and have the first layer. Also another main character I'm bringing in. I can bring those up if you want, but it's only a start, and maybe a little rough."

"Bring them up. Give us the pitch."

The pitch, she thought, and her belly clutched. She did better writing it out than talking it out. But she had to learn.

"Endon's been at peace for nearly a year," she began, "when the seers prophesy a new threat, and an old one. And a stranger comes to the forest."

She ran it through as best she could, tried to keep it brief.

"I don't have the narrative locked down. I work better when I let it flow. But the character of Tye Smith will be key, as well as the new big bad, Barstav the Giant, conjured by Mog."

"Before we go on," Rem interrupted, "Thea intends to design and develop this game as she did the first. Then submit it for your review and consideration. And, of course, will be open to any changes you feel necessary."

Bradley just lifted an eyebrow under his flop of hair. "We'll keep that in mind."

She let Rem take over, talk terms, compensation, percentages, salary, bonuses. Her eyes widened when he brought up merchandizing, but she let it roll.

An hour later, she closed her laptop.

"Did I really just sell—I mean lease—my first game to Milken Entertainment?"

"Yeah, congrats." He offered her a fist to bump. "Some nitty-gritty to work out, and you'll want a lawyer to look over the contract when it's finalized."

Frowning, he drummed his fingers on the table. "If I knew more, we could probably have done better there. But I think it's fair. You're just getting started."

"I'm in awe. In serious awe of both of you." Lucy got up from her counter stool to hug them. "You were each speaking a different language. I didn't understand the half of it."

"I got an internship."

"Salary's kinda crap."

She punched Rem and laughed. "The salary's the least of it. I'll work on other games—entry-level work, but work. Get experience. And I can keep working on my own."

"They were interested," Rem said. "I watched them, and they liked the new idea."

"It's a good concept, and I can make it work. I know what I'm doing there. Like I know how to milk a cow. But . . . Oh my God! They're going to produce my game. My game! People will play my game."

"I don't care what the time of day is, I'm opening that champagne I bought."

"You got champagne?"

"I did." Lucy nodded at Rem, then at Thea. "Tucked it into the fridge in the craft kitchen so as not to jinx all this. I'm going to drink champagne and toast my brilliant grandchildren. Then I'm calling your uncles and everybody else I know and bragging on you."

Touched, Thea put a hand on her heart. "Oh, Grammie."

"Try to stop me."

"I sure won't. And since I'm man of the house," Rem reminded them, "I'll open the champagne."

The summer moved fast. Celebrations for Thea, then another celebration when the rest of the family arrived, for Caleb, his bride, and the baby on the way.

More remote meetings made Thea realize that the life her grandmother had told her to live had entered a new phase. She continued work on the new game, now titled *Endon: Mog's Revenge*, did her part around the little farm, and made her first completely solo apple stack cake.

She added wings to the warhorse because when they unfurled for her, she knew Dilis had been meant to have them.

She lined up her courses, found a beginner's class off campus for swordplay, and one on campus for mixed martial arts.

And signed up for both. She'd make time, and believed her work would be better if she experienced some of the moves and actions she programmed for her characters.

Just before she left for college, she turned in her GDD for review. And crossed her fingers.

If the summer had flown by, her last year of college blurred. She learned, from her professors, from her internship, took plenty of knocks in mixed martial arts, and bought her first sword.

She spent spring break in New York, meeting supervisors, department heads, colleagues. It gave her a few days with Caleb and Selma, and snuggle time with her infant nephew.

She watched the city, and found, as she always did on her visits here, the excitement, the color and movement appealing.

One day, she thought, she'd set a game in a great city like this.

But New York was Caleb's place, she thought, not hers.

She heard the baby cry, and slipped out of her room to walk to the nursery.

"Is it time for your midnight snack, handsome? I think it's Daddy's turn, so let's give him a minute. Your mama pumped some fresh a few hours ago. Oh, I'll miss this," she said as she picked him up to gather him close and walk.

"Tell me I will." Caleb yawned in the doorway.

She turned to smile at him with his tousled head of hair, sleep-deprived eyes.

"Bet you will. If you get the bottle, I'll do the rest. It's my last night, so I'd really like to."

"Twist my arm."

He brought the bottle, and when the baby greedily found the nipple, sighed. "Just look at him. Who knew you could love anybody this much? Especially when they don't do much more than eat, poop, cry, sleep."

He kissed the baby's cheek, then Thea's.

"We're going to miss you, and not just for the help. So far all the talk about baby nurses, au pairs, nannies stays just that. Talk."

"You're not ready."

"Not yet. He's so . . . new. But since the show's been picked up for another season—"

"Of course it has."

"We'll have to do more than talk. He sure takes to you. Too bad you're not in the au pair market."

"They'd like me to come back for a few days before they launch the game this summer. So if I've got a room, you've got a babysitter."

"You've got a room regardless, but we'll take the babysitting."

Caleb skimmed a hand over her hair, then gave it a tug. "No chance you'll move here?"

"About as much as there is of you moving back to the Hollow. You love to be there, enjoy it while you are, but."

"But," he agreed.

"You've got me now, so go on back and get some sleep."

"If he doesn't settle back down—"

"Oh, he'll settle. I've got the touch."

When she graduated, they all came. She hadn't expected it. Waylon and Kyra with their three, Caleb and Selma and the chubby-cheeked Dylan. Her grandmother shedding tears as Rem handed her tissues.

On that long last drive away from campus, Lucy went with her.

"It's a whole new world for you now, darling."

"Most of me's ready for it. I need to go to headquarters in a couple of weeks. Three, maybe four days. But I'm so ready to just be home."

"I'm hoping you'll take on a passenger north."

"Really?" The idea had her bouncing in her seat.

"Rem said he'd take care of things at home, and I know he can and will. I'd so like see this headquarters of yours for myself. And have a few more days with my youngest grandbaby."

"I'd love it! I can't wait to show you around Milken. It's such a cool place. The tech's just crazy, and the people are so smart, so creative."

"Just like my oldest granddaughter."

"I'm getting there. I've got a favor to ask you, Grammie."

"Today when I'm bursting with pride's a good time to ask for a favor."

"I'd like a few months, maybe a year or so before I really start planning the house. It's such a big step, and I want to do it right. I've got so much going on, I'm afraid I won't do it right. I'll be working full-time now, and want to give it my best. With the launch, then working on the new game and whatever projects they might give me. I'm going to upgrade all my equipment, and—"

"You don't worry about any of that. You'll stay until you're ready for your own."

She stayed, a few months, then a year. And nearly two more while she settled on a design for the house, then through the building of it.

Twice during those years, Howard and Musk traveled down, on their own time, to ask for her help. And she gave it. If Riggs pushed at her, she pushed back.

She never went back to the prison. Her life now looked forward, and she told herself Riggs lived in the past, locked in it.

Then it stood, her two-story cottage of mountain green with a blue front door, with its wraparound porch, tucked back in the rolling hills. She'd added the small deck Maddy insisted on just outside the French doors of her main bedroom.

And already imagined herself sitting out there on quiet nights, on quiet mornings.

She considered her gaming studio a source of pride, and had arranged it so its windows faced the hills—and the chicken coop Knobby built her.

She'd get a half dozen hens, but leave the milk cow and goat to her grandmother.

And one of these days, a dog. Settle first, she thought, standing, looking, the keys warm in her hand.

Settle through this fall and its riot of color, and through the winter when the wind blew cold and fires simmered in the hearths.

She'd put wind chimes and witch bottles all around, add some fairy lights to the trio of young redbuds in her front yard.

And plant a garden, her own garden, next spring.

She'd fill her home with flowers, candles, and pretty things. She'd tend the land around it.

She'd worked for this, yes. But she wouldn't have it without what her parents had given her, what her grandmother had given her.

This home was hers, she thought, but never hers alone.

She'd do good work in it, she promised herself, and make good food so she deserved the kitchen she'd designed over countless dreamy days and nights. Cook meals for her family, and be a good neighbor to Miss Leona.

She had work she loved, and she was good at her work. Maybe it still surprised her she and Milken had built a franchise with the *Endon* series of games, but even the surprise of it satisfied.

She thought of that day in her grandmother's kitchen, and Rem talking about merchandizing.

Well, she thought now, he'd been damn smart to lock that in.

She worked hard—that seemed to be a Fox/Lannigan/Riley trait. She'd decided the luck of enjoying the work came from the same sources.

Now another phase of her life stretched behind her, she realized. And another beckoned, just ahead.

In the kicky October breeze, she stood on land that belonged to her, then slowly walked to the house she'd built in her dreams.

Unlocking the door she didn't intend to lock again, she went in to light the fires and the candles.

Chapter Fourteen

Until the day she died, three years after Thea moved into the house, Leona lived a good, strong life.

Around ten on that windy February night, Thea felt her go, just slip away from one world and into the next.

She left Thea a pretty teapot decorated with dragonflies Thea knew Leona had prized.

Thea missed her, missed seeing smoke curl from the chimney, a light in the window.

Bunk, Thea's Bernese mountain dog, missed her, too, and the biscuit she'd always have for him when he paid her a call.

That spring, when Thea planted her garden, she wondered how long the house would stay empty. Leona left it, and all in it, to her great-grandson. He hadn't come to the funeral—something about his little boy being sick—but she wondered why he had yet to make the trip down. Either to take over his inheritance or make arrangements to sell.

She did her work, tended her garden and her chickens, walked down with Bunk to Lucy's often.

Every year on the anniversary of her parents' death, she stood with Lucy and Rem and put hydrangeas on their grave.

And every night on that day, the lock on her window slipped. Ray Riggs came calling.

She'd blocked him out countless times over the years, but on that night he always slipped through. She understood he knew her weaknesses, read hers as she read his. Whatever strange twist of fate had bound them together refused to break.

"Maybe, darling, you don't really want it to."

In the craft kitchen, she helped Lucy with a new batch of soap.

"Why wouldn't I?"

"It's a kind of reassurance, isn't it, that he's still paying? He's still locked away."

"They'd tell me if he wasn't. But . . . I don't know, maybe you're right. I start thinking about him when we get into June like this. Maybe it's me giving him the opening and not just him taking it."

"You said it didn't scare you. He doesn't scare you."

"No, he doesn't. It disturbs me. But when I see him, when he's inside my head that way and I see him, hear him? I guess it's better to deal with the truth. It gives me a kind of satisfaction, and a kind of comfort. A dark one I'm not proud of."

"Why shouldn't it?"

"Fifteen years this month, Grammie. There's no price he can pay that makes up for what he did, but fifteen years? I can't seem to move on."

"That's nonsense."

Lucy finished the pouring, stepped back. She brushed back her hair. She still favored the one thick braid, and the dramatic white streak had been joined by threads of white through that raven black.

"You've built a life, honeypot, and a good one. You've used your gift well, sparingly and well. If you use it for this, when thoughts of your parents come so close? Why shouldn't you?"

As Lucy spoke, they began the cleanup together.

"He's an evil man, Thea, with the gift inside him twisted into something dark. That I believe with all my heart. So you let him in that one night, and doing that assures you he's where he belongs.

"If I could do the same, I would."

"Really?" She'd never imagined her grandmother wanting, or needing, that kind of payment.

"He took my children from me. Fifteen minutes or fifteen years, that doesn't change. I don't know if I could've forgiven him if he'd asked for forgiveness, if he'd truly atoned. But he hasn't, so I don't forgive."

"No, he hasn't. He's not capable of atonement." She took a long, easy breath. "The past is his world because he has no real present, no future. And in the past, he had power.

"It helps, Grammie, to know you feel the way I do."

"Maybe this time of year especially. It hits this time of year. But." Turning, she gripped Thea's hands. "While we can't lock the past away, not when it holds the ones we love, we have a real present, and a future. And that's where we look.

"Now, let's have some lemonade on the porch. We earned it. I swear, Rem's business management works me off my feet."

Thea laughed, and felt her mood lighten. "You wouldn't have it any other way."

"I can't deny it. Here I am with employees."

"Who you could let take over the work. You never will."

They took their glasses out to sit where Thea had sat so many summer nights studying the stars, listening to the hills whisper.

Now her dog, the mountain of him, wrestled with Tweedle and Dee. The chickens hummed, and old Betty Lou, too old to produce milk, cropped at the grass in the field.

Young Rosie, her replacement, dozed on her feet in the sun.

"I wonder if Rem's ever going to build a house."

"He's making some noises about it," Lucy told her. "More serious type of noises. He's just twenty-five."

"I was a year younger when I moved into mine."

"Different for you, darling. He wanted that travel, and he got it."

"And actually ate those snails."

"More a matter of pride, you ask me, than enjoyment. Now, I'm not saying he hasn't gotten some spoiled having good meals regular, but he's a big help to me. He more than earns his pancakes. And he's a sociable sort. You need your quiet and your space. He'll build when it's time for it."

"I miss having Miss Leona down the lane. Miss just knowing she was there, puttering around her house, sitting in her chair with her knitting.

"You haven't heard anything about what's happening with her house?"

"Not a thing, not yet. But I think it takes time, all the lawyer business takes time. All I heard is the great-grandson's got a little boy, maybe four? Four or five, and no wife to help share that with."

"She never talked about family much. The great-grandson more, but still . . . Except how he made sure she came for Christmas, and he came to visit when he could, called her every week, and saw she didn't do without anything."

"If he ever comes around, I hope he appreciates how good you were to her."

"We were neighbors."

"I know you did her marketing this last year, and saw she had company when she wanted it. Rem, too, seeing her lawn got mowed, doing repairs for her."

"He did it for the cookies. I miss her cookies. She never failed to have them ready."

"She's with George now. He came to see her often in her last months. She told me," Lucy added when Thea looked at her. "But she didn't have to. I could feel him around her during that time. She was ready to go, to let go and move on. Having George close made it easy for her."

"Do you ever feel Mom?"

"Oh, darling, all the time. My sweet little girl, my beautiful young woman. Your daddy, too, as he was mine. And it comforts me."

"I never went back to the house in Virginia. I knew what happened that night would block out everything else we had there. But when I see them or feel them, it's always here, on the little farm. And they're always together. That comforts me.

"Now I've got to get on."

"Rem'll be home for supper. You could stay."

"Not today. I gave myself the morning, but I've got work, and I know you do. I have to run into town tomorrow, so if you need anything, let me know."

She rose. "Come on, Bunk, time to go." Leaning down, she hugged Lucy hard. "You and Rem come down Saturday, if he doesn't have a date, and have supper at my place. It happens I have my grammie's secret fried chicken recipe, and I'm in the mood."

"We'll be there. I'll bring dessert."

Thea started down the road, the dog beside her. At nearly two, Bunk (short for Rambunctious) stood over two feet tall, weighed in at close to a hundred twenty pounds. A strong tricolored mountain with a joyful disposition.

He trotted along beside her, waving his bushy, white-tipped tail.

While training him had been a challenge, he was, to Thea's mind, as perfect a companion as she could wish for.

When she stroked a hand over his head, he looked up at her with big brown eyes full of love. As if he considered her the perfect companion in turn.

"It's a pretty afternoon, right? But I've got to spend some of it in the studio."

She felt clearer, as she always did after a visit to her grandmother. And the walk, to and from, never failed to energize her.

A summer afternoon, everything blue and green. The hills rising, wildflowers blooming. Clothes at her grandmother's nearest neighbors' hanging on the line.

If she didn't have work, she'd sit out on her own porch and just enjoy the day with her dog. Later, she promised herself, in the evening. Porch sitting with a glass of wine, watching her garden grow.

As she walked, she pulled the tie she'd used during the soap-making out of her hair. As the hair fell around her shoulders, she laughed as Bunk began to sniff the air.

"What you got? A fox, a rabbit? No chasing the wildlife unless they're after the chickens or the garden. We've talked about that."

His tail switched as she rounded the corner. She spotted the big SUV in front of Miss Leona's, and the man, the little boy. The boy let out a squeal, started running just as Bunk let out a delighted woof and did the same.

She heard the man call out: "Braydon, stop!" but it didn't do him much good. He charged after the boy, had him scooped up by the time she'd snapped at Bunk to *stop* and *sit*—and succeeded.

"Daddy, doggie! Daddy, doggie!"

"He's harmless." But Thea got a grip on Bunk's collar as he trembled with joy because she felt the fear pumping off the man for the boy. "He loves kids."

"For breakfast?"

She started to laugh, then when the boy tried to dive free of his father's arms, she got her first real look at Miss Leona's great-grandson.

The sixteen-year-old girl inside her would have let out a squeal to rival the little boy's if she hadn't managed to hold it in.

Code Red might have disbanded nearly five years before, but she knew Tyler Brennan's face.

And here he stood, a little boy in his arms, on the side of the road, about a quarter mile from her house. Hair she'd always thought of as top-shelf bourbon fell in disordered waves. His face, chiseled, just gorgeous, wore a two- or three-day stubble. At the moment those long green eyes aimed straight at Bunk with deep suspicion.

Thea did her best to quell the teenager bouncing and babbling inside her.

"Bunk's as gentle as he is big." It helped her behave herself to focus on the boy, a miniature version of his father. "Maybe you'd like to say, 'Hi, Bunk,' and wave."

"Hi, Bunk!" The little boy waved enthusiastically. "Hi, Bunk. Want to play, Daddy!"

"Say hi, Bunk."

At Thea's words, the dog lifted his right paw, waved it in the air. His eyes shined with love under the rust-colored markings, and if a dog could grin, Bunk grinned.

"I know his size is intimidating," Thea began.

"You think?"

"His heart's just as big. I'm Thea Fox. I live back up the lane a bit. Bunk loved visiting Miss Leona."

Ty's attention shifted from the dog to the woman. "You're Thea. Granny talked about you and your family. I appreciate, a lot, everything you did for her."

"We loved her," Thea said simply. "She didn't talk a lot about her family, but I know how much it meant to her you called every week, and arranged for her to spend Christmas with the rest of you up north."

"I couldn't make it to the funeral. Bray was sick, and couldn't travel. Then . . ." He looked back at the house, trailed off. "Anyway. I'm Tyler Brennan, her great-grandson."

"I know. I might as well say it. I'm a big fan of Code Red. My grandmother took me and two good friends to your concert in Louisville for my sixteenth birthday."

"I thought you looked familiar." He smiled, and the tiny dimple at the right corner of his mouth came out with it.

The teenage girl inside all but fainted.

"Well, when y'all did 'Ever Yours,' I knew you sang it to me. Bunk," she said quietly when he edged closer.

"Doggie. Daddy, *please*!"

"Me first. You ride."

Braydon agilely climbed around to ride his father's back. "I really need this hand," he said, but held it out for Bunk to sniff.

Skipping the sniff part of the introduction, Bunk angled so Ty's hand lay on top of his head, then pressed against it until that hand rubbed.

"Okay, pal, you be gentle."

Bray slid down Ty's back, pushed through his legs. And all but fell on Bunk. "*Love* doggie!"

"I'd say that's mutual. He really does love kids." She could see boxes in the big car. "You drove down from Philadelphia?"

"Yeah. Tell me why I thought that was a good idea with a four-year-old."

"Well, you'll want your car here, so there's that. Still, a long trip. I'm sure you're tired, so I won't keep you. If there's anything I can do while you're here, I'm about a quarter mile back, right off this lane."

"Appreciate it. Say bye, Bray."

"Wanna go with Bunk."

"Bunk has to take his nap." Thea caught Ty's look of gratitude for the easy out. "But he'll come back and visit another time. Say bye, Bunk."

The dog sat, waved his paw.

"We're just up the lane," she reminded Ty. "Welcome to Redbud Hollow."

She had to force herself not to look back. All these years, she thought, Miss Leona had never said anything about Tyler Brennan, rock star, songwriter, Grammy winner, being her great-grandson.

Of course, she couldn't recall gushing over him and his music to Miss Leona.

But still!

Now her teenage crush would stay—a few days, a couple weeks?—almost within shouting distance. With his little boy. She hadn't known he had a little boy. Of course, she hadn't kept up with Tyler Brennan's life and times.

Very much.

She thought of the work she had to do, and she'd do it. But that didn't mean she couldn't throw some dinner together. After all, the man had come all the way from Philadelphia, with a preschooler in tow.

The least she could do as a neighbor was save him from making a meal.

He didn't know if the giant dog napped, but by the time Ty had made up a bed, Bray conked.

He said a quiet hallelujah.

While his son slept, he unpacked the essentials. Stored away the food basics he'd stopped for in what turned out to be a pristine refrigerator, pristine cupboards.

He'd expected to have to deal with some of the cleaning himself, and wondered if he owed the long-legged Thea and her family yet another thanks.

The estate lawyer had dealt with all Leona's files and paperwork. His granny had been meticulous there. And her instructions upon her death clearly spelled out.

She'd wanted him to have this house, this land. He wondered: If she'd died before Braydon came into his life, would he have sold it? Kept it for a kind of vacation hideaway?

He honestly didn't know.

But Braydon had come into his life, and a woman he'd loved had wanted this for him.

So they'd see.

They had the summer ahead of them to see how they'd fit.

His parents thought he'd lost his mind. But then again, they'd thought the same thing when he'd wanted to make music his life's work.

His grandmother had stepped far away from Redbud Hollow, and had no emotional attachment here. While fond of her mother, Willa Rowe Brennan hadn't felt a strong connection to her roots.

And since he'd been born and raised in Philadelphia, Ty's father had felt no connection at all.

Obligation, yes. William Tyler Brennan had done what he considered his duty to his grandmother in Kentucky.

For whatever reason, Ty always had felt the connection. To the woman, certainly. And to the place? He wasn't sure except he'd enjoyed his brief visits.

Not even brief ones in the last few years, he admitted, and felt that pang of regret. But Braydon, and complications, and life.

Remembering those visits, he walked through the house. Less than half—considerably less than half—the size of his place in Philadelphia, but he could fix that if he and Bray decided to stay.

Some rearranging needed, especially when his piano arrived. Cheaper and more efficient to buy one locally, but he was attached to his own. Oddly enough, he'd written "Ever Yours," the song Thea had mentioned, on that piano, and it had been Code Red's first major hit.

So much room, he thought, for Bray to run. And yeah, maybe nearly time to get the puppy his boy yearned for.

A reasonably sized puppy that would grow into a reasonably sized dog. And not an enormous, white-chested black mountain.

He went upstairs again, looked in on Bray. Out like a light, and no surprise there. In the bedroom he'd chosen, he made up the bed. Thought about taking a shower, but made the mistake of stretching out first. Just for a minute.

Just for a minute lasted an hour until Bray bounced on him.

"Time to wake up!"

"What? Why?"

Wrapping his arms around Bray, he shifted, snuggled him in, made Bray giggle.

After the expected wrestling and rib-tickling, Ty hauled him up.

"I'm hungry!"

"Yeah, me, too." And he didn't have it in him to drive into town, find dinner as he'd half planned.

But he had peanut butter, jelly, bread, some lunch meat, milk, frozen pizza, and cans of SpaghettiOs, ravioli.

They'd absolutely not starve.

"Let's go down and figure it out."

Bray, all energy, bounced in his father's arms. "Can we go see Bunk?"

"Let's give that a day or two, pal. We've got to get organized."

"I'm organized."

"Yeah, well, I'm not. We're going to take it easy tonight, but tomorrow we're men at work."

Had to make room for the piano—first priority. Figure out where to put what. He knew his granny had kept a garden, but he didn't see himself planting anything. If they stayed, maybe. But there was a lawn to mow, and general yard work.

The third bedroom didn't rank above a good-sized closet. The size and the proximity to Bray's bedroom made it a bad choice for a studio.

Since he couldn't see them using the dining room for dining, that seemed the logical choice.

He'd figure it out.

Right now, he wanted a beer. It might not be the best accompaniment for SpaghettiOs, but he wanted a damn beer.

He'd just opened the fridge when someone knocked on the front door.

"I get! I get!"

"Braydon, what's the rule?"

Bray blew out a small wind of air. "Don't open the door without Daddy."

"Right." Ty closed the fridge, took Bray's hand to walk to the door.

The long-legged dark-haired beauty and her enormous dog stood on the porch.

Bray immediately fell on the dog's neck again.

"I just wanted to drop something off. Traveling in, unpacking, I thought you might not have the time or energy to make dinner."

She offered him a wicker basket that smelled like heaven.

"What is that smell? It's amazing."

"Oh, it's just some skillet pork chops and potatoes."

"Pork chops? You made us pork chops? Seriously? Sorry, come in."

"No, no, thanks. I just wanted to drop it off. And there's some eggs for tomorrow, in case you don't have any. I have chickens."

"You have chickens." She looked like a blue-eyed country goddess, he thought, and she had chickens.

"Chickens poop eggs," Bray said.

"They sort of do. But these are nice and clean. I hope y'all enjoy. You can drop the basket and dish back anytime. Just leave them on the porch if I'm not home. Come on, Bunk."

For a minute, as she walked back to a spiffy red convertible, his addled brain couldn't come up with her name. Then it did.

"Thea. Thank you. You saved two starving men from a sad dinner of canned pasta."

She smiled as the dog leaped into the back seat. "Glad I could come to the rescue."

After she drove back up the gravel lane, Ty closed the door.

"My man? We're about to eat like kings."

He took the basket into the kitchen, opened it.

Besides the amazing scent of a hot meal, she'd tucked in a candle that smelled like vanilla beans, and a little clutch of flowers in a tiny bottle.

"Like kings," he said again.

Thea couldn't help herself. The one person on the planet who'd understand her current state of disbelief wrapped in euphoria had been her best friend for fifteen years.

She texted Maddy.

What are you doing?

The response took just under a minute, but in Thea's current state felt like an hour.

Giving thanks my shift at the clinic's now over, and trying to decide whether to make myself a peanut butter and banana sandwich or open a can of ravioli.

Forget those slightly disgusting food choices and come here. I made pork chops. AND!!! I have big news.

What news?

Big must tell you in person news. Come over. I also have wine.

I'm in for the chops and the wine. Give me a hint on the news.

Nope. You get nothing until you get here.

I'd say that's mean except I'm getting food and drink. Omw.

Considering Maddy had an apartment in town, Thea judged she had more than enough time to set the table, put on music—obviously Code Red—feed Bunk and the chickens.

She'd just poured the wine when Maddy came in the front door.

"There's a car at Miss Leona's. The great-grandson? That's the big news?"

"Part of it." Thea handed over a glass of wine.

Maddy wore her hair in locs these days. She'd changed out of her doctor-at-work clothes into calf-length sweatpants and a short-sleeved hoodie, both in bright, bold pink.

She had half a dozen studs running along both earlobes.

"I'm sitting. On my feet since eight this morning. Sitting out on your porch so I can enjoy my wine and you spill the news I don't have to be psychic to see you can barely hold in."

She ran a hand over Bunk as she strolled out. Then let out a huge sigh as she sat in one of Thea's summer-sky-blue porch chairs.

"I'm guessing you met him, so what's he like? Got a kid, right? How long are they staying? Putting the house up for sale? I'd buy it myself so we could Mr. Rogers it. Won't you be my neighbor? But you're just too far out from the clinic."

"And Doctor Dreamboat. When are you going to give Arlo a break and marry him?"

Maddy smiled her smug smile. "I'm closing in on living together.

Maybe, say, this fall. We'll give that a year once I do, and see how it goes." She slid a look toward Thea. "Or you could just tell me."

"I'm not Madame Carlotta with her crystal ball. And I'm not looking into your future if I could. But"—Thea toasted with her wine, then drank—"I know a close-to-perfect match when I see one."

"Why only 'close to'?"

"I'm not sure there are many absolutely perfect ones."

Her parents, she thought, but they'd been robbed of all the decades they might have had together.

"Okay, I've stalled you long enough. What's with the next gen down the lane? Tall, dark, and handsome?"

"Tall, handsome, and the little boy's not only a mirror image, but adorable. They drove down from Philadelphia with a lot of boxes in the car, so I think they're planning on staying awhile."

She sipped wine again. "I didn't look, at least not deliberately, but I could feel how much he loves his son. Bunk scared him—not the boy but the dad."

"Sweetest dog ever." Maddy made kissy noises that had Bunk's tail swishing. "But he's big as a house, so I see that as first reaction."

"He loved Miss Leona, too, the great-grandson. Just a lot of emotion I didn't manage to block out. Love, guilt, regret."

Eyes narrowed, Maddy pointed. "You, Thea Fox, are smitten! You who never get smitten got smitten in five minutes."

"Oh, it's been a lot longer than five minutes. He's been in my life and heart for years."

"I know everyone who's been in your life and heart, and none of them are Miss Leona's great-grandson."

"Well, you missed one." Tilting her head, Thea listened to the music rocking through the windows. "One look," she sang, "one word, one touch, and lightning strikes."

"Save the concert. Who the hell is he?"

Thea laughed. "You must be tired not to catch on. Miss Leona's great-grandson is . . . drumroll. Tyler Brennan. Code Red, Maddy. My teenage crush Tyler Brennan."

"Get *out*!" Reaching over, Maddy gave Thea's arm a slap. "No possible way."

"I couldn't believe it myself, but there he was. God, *God*! He's so good-looking even all rumpled from traveling. I almost squealed. Inside I did, many times, but I managed to maintain. Then there was a giggle, right in here." She tapped her fingers at the base of her throat. "I held it back. Barely. I might've drooled," she considered. "I really hope not, but I might've."

"Holy hot shit. Miss Leona had a rock star in the family and never said?"

"I don't think she thought of him that way. Plus, she didn't talk much about her family. Little things, like going up for Christmas, or how he called her every week. But she didn't share a lot in that area."

Thea lifted her shoulders, let them fall. "I took them down half the skillet pork chops and potatoes and leather breeches."

"Come on. Are you serious?"

"I'd have done that even if he hadn't been Ty Brennan. He'd driven down here with a little boy, looked so tired, had all that unloading to do. But I'm not ashamed to admit I kept thinking how I was making dinner for Ty Brennan when I made dinner for Ty Brennan, and Braydon. His son's Braydon."

"It's going to take me awhile to wrap my head around this. Are you going to make a move on him?"

"Oh, stop." Laughing, Thea shook back her hair. "We're neighbors, and that's thrill enough, even though that's probably temporary. And the really adorable little boy must have a mother somewhere."

"My knowledge of him and the band isn't as extensive as yours, but I know he kept his personal life private—must've gotten that from Miss Leona. And since the band broke up, I haven't heard much about it."

"He's been mostly songwriting the last few years. But that's all I know. I've been a little too busy for celebrity crushes."

"We could find out. No, not that way," she said at Thea's look. "Google knows all, tells all. Or close enough."

"I'm not going to google him. That's just rude."

"I have no problem being rude."

Maddy pulled out her phone, and googled.

"Not a whole lot after the basic history, where he grew up, forming the band, hitting it big at nineteen. I'm not seeing any mention of the kid here, so that's keeping the door locked. But, Jesus, Thea, I didn't know he'd written all these. Hasn't recorded or performed in the last couple, three years, but he's written some hits. Like 'Crazytown.' I love that song. Oh, and 'No Regrets.'"

"Put that away. Let's go eat."

"Since I'm starving, I'll dig more later. This was definitely big, in-person news. One more thing," Maddy said as she rose. "If you don't put some moves on him, you're going to regret it forever."

"He's a single father—most likely—trying to settle his great-grandmother's affairs, and obviously a very private person."

"So what? If he blocks the move, you accept. But if he doesn't?" Maddy added a shoulder wiggle. "Teenage dream fulfilled."

"Shut up and come eat your pork chops."

Chapter Fifteen

She dreamed of him that night, dreamed of Ty sitting on her porch playing his guitar while the sunset turned the western sky into a palette of pinks and golds.

The summer breeze wafted the scents of lavender, rosemary, heliotrope. It set the witch bottles on their branches ringing, and the wind chimes sent out a quiet bong.

Of course he sang "Ever Yours," the song that had always made her heart sigh, and when he sang, he smiled at her. Only her, those green eyes full of warmth.

A harmless dream, so she burrowed into it, feeling light, happy, maybe just a little foolish.

In the way of her dreams, she saw him so clearly. The way his hair fell, always carelessly sexy. The line of his jaw, the long fingers moving over frets and strings.

The shape of his mouth, then the feel of it when he leaned over to touch it lightly to hers.

Just a dream, and harmless, even though that light kiss stirred inside her so in sleep, she sighed.

The shadows in the woods lengthened as the sun dipped lower and lower behind the mountains.

And in those woods, something cried out as the predator took the prey.

The pink and gold of the sky turned to a bruised gray as storm clouds rolled in.

Ray Riggs stepped out of the woods.

He wore his prison blues, and though his face remained thin, it held a doughiness. Deep lines scored the sides of his mouth, fanned out from those pale blue eyes.

Still those eyes smiled, smiled with nothing to do with humor.

"Got yourself some guitar-playing pansy? Waiting for moonlight so he can fuck you? Want your romance before you roll over for him?"

"We have to go inside. Ty, we have to go inside and lock the doors."

But Ty kept playing his guitar.

"He don't see me, you stupid bitch. I'm in your head, just like always. Watch this."

He had a gun in his hand. The gun, the same gun he'd used to murder her parents. She leaped up, screaming even as he fired.

But he didn't fire at her. The guitar fell as blood bloomed on Ty's shirt. He looked at her, no warmth left in those green eyes.

"It's your fault," he said. "You let him in. This is your fault."

She dropped to her knees beside him as he died, as his blood ran warm on her hands.

"I'll find a way." Riggs cackled out a laugh as he faded back into the trees. "Won't be long now. I'll find you, and I'll find a way."

Sobbing, shaking, she shot up in bed. Moonlight streamed through the windows as she stared at her hands.

No blood. No blood, but God, she could feel it on her skin, could almost smell it.

Bunk stood with his front paws on her bed, whining.

"A dream, just a dream. It's okay." She wrapped her arms around him as much to comfort herself as him.

Because it had felt like more than a dream. And it wasn't okay.

Before the moonlight faded into the first pale light of dawn, she'd finished two loads of laundry and scrubbed her kitchen from top to bottom. She needed movement and purpose more than sleep.

A batch of cornbread muffins added a good, homey aroma.

As the light strengthened, she fed her chickens.

"Good morning, ladies."

They clucked and swarmed around her as much for the attention as the feed to come. She stroked soft brown feathers, calling each by name, then left them pecking at their feed as she hunted up the morning's supply of eggs in the nesting boxes.

"Good job!"

With five eggs in her basket, she looked up at the sky—a bowl of blue softened by a complement of white clouds.

"Gorgeous morning," she told her hens. "But I think we'll have a quick, wicked storm this afternoon. Y'all take shelter now."

She left the coop, headed back to the house. Bunk stuck close to her side, as if he knew she wasn't as settled as she wanted to be.

When she reached the back porch, the dream flooded back into her mind. The music, the moonlight, that sense of quiet happiness. Until Riggs walked out of the woods.

Bringing blood and grief.

"He found a way in, Bunk. He found a way in, and found a way to scare me, to hurt me. But I'm not helpless, and I won't be. Just need to remind myself I'm not and won't be."

Maybe her first instinct was to go to her grandmother for hugs and reassurance. But she wasn't a child any longer either.

She'd become a successful, professional woman, she thought as she cleaned, dried, stored her eggs. She'd used her gift four times to save a life since Detectives Howard and Musk had come to her at college.

She'd made a difference to others, and she could handle herself. Physically, mentally, emotionally.

Work could wait a little longer, she decided. Better to clear her mind of those lingering images before she focused it on fleshing out the new concept for a game.

She went upstairs and changed into a sports bra, workout capris, then layered a simple white tank over it.

In her bare feet, she went into her studio and studied the swords displayed on her wall rack. After a brief internal debate, she chose a katana.

Though she had a large mirror on the wall she used for working out movements in a battle—armed or unarmed—she wanted more room. And she wanted the sun and air, the feel of the grass under her feet.

Bunk followed her back out, but because she'd belted on the sword, he sat on the porch.

She faced the woods, let herself imagine Riggs stepping out because it set her mood.

No sobbing, no shaking, but action. Defense.

"Come on then," she murmured.

Closing her hand over the long grip, she drew the curved sword and began.

In the past three years and counting, Ty had grown accustomed to early mornings. His kid, he'd learned, didn't believe in sleeping in.

Bray served as his often too-reliable alarm clock, with a happy bounce on his dad's sleeping body and a happily insistent: *Time to wake up!*

He had managed, through trial and error, to convince Bray that the numbers on the clock had to start with a six or seven before the bounce and announcement.

Occasionally, if Ty stirred awake enough to open his eyes prior to that six o'clock mark, he'd find Bray sitting on the bed beside him, waiting.

The fact that touched his heart made it clear to him that where Braydon Seth Brennan was concerned, he was a goner.

On the first morning in Kentucky, Bray woke him at six-sixteen.

Groggy, half wishing for the familiarity of his bedroom up north, Ty tried to cuddle the kid in.

"How about ten more minutes?"

"Six—one—six, Daddy! We're hungry!"

The "we" included Woof, the purple stuffed dog Bray had been clutching when Ty learned he had an eighteen-month-old son.

If Bray wanted breakfast, so did Woof.

"Okay, okay, I'm up."

He rolled out of bed in his boxers. At home, he'd have left it at that for the breakfast cycle, but who the hell knew who might knock on the damn door around here at any time of the day or night?

And Christ, he needed coffee.

206 | NORA ROBERTS

After Ty dragged on jeans, Bray hopped right on his back for the ride downstairs.

"Gotta put gas in the engine first."

Ty gave thanks he'd packed up his beloved coffee machine, and that his boy accepted coffee came first.

"Fill it up!" Bray wiggled down to the floor.

"Gonna."

As the coffee worked its hot, strong, black magic, Ty started to reach for a box of cereal. Then remembered the eggs his blue-eyed neighbor had provided, along with an amazing dinner, the flowers and candle on the little kitchen island.

He peeled a banana for Bray and Woof as a stopgap.

He could scramble eggs.

He supposed it was her love of baking that had convinced his granny to update her kitchen. Probably about a decade before, he calculated as he located a pan, but it had everything, including that little island where he knew she'd happily rolled out cookie dough.

Maybe it didn't approach his big, shiny kitchen in Philadelphia, but no question its smaller size and scope better suited his just-on-the-high-side-of-mediocre cooking skills. Nearly all of those acquired A.B.

After Braydon.

He made toast, cutting Bray's piece into triangles as preferred, added the eggs and a juice box.

By seven, Bray sat on the floor playing with his trucks, and Ty drank his second, more clarifying cup of coffee.

He started a list he titled:

WTF Needs Doing

Top of it, find a local pediatrician for Bray. Even if they only stayed through the summer, he needed a good doctor in case.

He'd need to at least research the local school in case they stayed longer.

A trip into town to buy fresh produce and all that—which meant a separate list.

He sure as hell needed to boost up the Wi-Fi and replace his granny's ancient TV. The cell service worked fine, a happy surprise.

He needed to organize the house the way he and Bray needed it.

Music studio. Playroom.

While Bray played, he got up to wander the main floor again.

He could put the piano in the front room, but the dining room gave him more privacy. Next to the kid playing trucks on the kitchen floor, privacy equaled top priority.

He studied his granny's overly formal dining room table, chairs, a kind of buffet, the half a million knickknacks on every surface.

He knew that set brought her a lot of pride, but he needed the space. Even if he could've snapped his fingers and added a studio to the house, he'd never find use in his lifestyle for the furniture, gone black over time and countless coats of shellac.

He'd donate it, he decided. She'd like that. She'd like knowing someone else used it, found pride in it.

Bray's hand tugged on his.

"Go see doggie. Please!"

"I've got a lot to do around here today, pal."

"Please!"

Bray wrapped his arms around Ty's legs and shot up a look that could've melted the iceberg that took down the *Titanic.*

He had to take the basket back anyway. And maybe she knew something about where he could donate stuff, about a doctor, and half the things he didn't know.

He might as well take advantage of a friendly neighbor.

"We've got to brush our teeth, get dressed."

"Okay! Come on, come on. This way!"

Though he stalled the process as much as possible, they started walking up the gravel lane by eight. Walking, Ty calculated, would stretch out the time a bit more, plus give Bray a chance to run, explore, work off some energy.

If the neighbor with the legs wasn't up and around, he could just leave the basket on the porch, as suggested.

"Should've written a note in case, damn it."

"Damn it!"

"Those are daddy words, remember?"

Bray shot him the most cheerful of looks. "I like daddy words."

Then halfway up the steep lane, he lifted his arms. Ty crouched for the piggyback.

After the turn, he saw the house. Pretty as a picture with its background of rising hills, of thick trees. Bigger than he'd assumed, since he knew from his granny that Thea lived alone.

She definitely liked color, he noted. And flowers.

A good-sized fairy-tale cottage, he decided, with a witchy sort of garden in front, weeping trees, a generous front porch with a swing and some tables and chairs.

More flowers in pots.

As they got closer, the big dog bounded around from the back.

Ty braced, as the dog looked fully capable of bowling him over, and Bray already wiggled to get down.

"Sit!" He put as much command in the single word as he could muster.

While the dog didn't stop until he'd reached them, he sat and looked up with love shining.

"Down, Daddy! Down, down, down!"

"Just wait."

Once again, Ty held out a hand. Bunk nuzzled it, tail thumping.

"Okay. Let's take it easy. Say hello first, Bray."

"Hello, Doggie."

"Bunk."

"Hello, Bunk!"

Bunk waved in return.

"Gentle, Bray."

When Bray's feet hit the ground, he body-wrapped the dog.

"Let's go knock so we can give the lady back her basket. And thank her for dinner."

He started to reach for Bray's hand, but the dog ran at the house, around it. And Bray shot off like a rocket after.

"Wait!"

Ty scooped Bray up on the run. The dog paused, looked back, wagged. Then kept going at a slower pace.

"Bunk!" Bray insisted.

"Yeah, okay."

Since the dog kept slowing, looking back, Ty figured following made sense.

He saw another garden—vegetable—a birdbath formed out of a three-headed dragon, more flowers, colorful bottles hanging from trees, then . . .

She had snug pants on those long legs, and her hair in a braid. On the grass in her bare feet, she did a kind of fluid dance.

With a sword.

With a two-handed grip, she sliced it through the air, pivoted, stabbed, spun, and swung it over her head, brought it down.

When the sun hit the blade, it gleamed.

Sweat dampened her white shirt between the shoulder blades as the muscles in her arms flexed. His neighbor, he noted, was ripped.

However much effort it took to dance with the sword, her face showed none.

She looked, Ty thought, oddly peaceful.

Well behind her, chickens pecked away in the yard of what looked like a chicken mansion.

She spun again, and saw them.

And said, "Oh!"

"You have a sword."

"Yes, I do." She sheathed it. "I was just practicing."

"With a sword."

"Yes." Using the thick band on her wrist, she dabbed at the sweat on her forehead. Smiling, she walked toward them. "Good morning. How was your first night?"

"We slept like rocks, probably because we ate like kings first. Thank you."

"You're welcome." She took the basket.

She's holding a wicker basket, Ty thought, and has a sword on her hip.

Who is this woman?

"I could use some lemonade. How about I get us all some lemonade?"

"Chickens!" Bray tried to wiggle down.

"You can go see them. They're very friendly."

"Like the dog?" Ty asked.

"And a lot smaller. I'll be right back."

What the hell, Ty thought, and set Bray down. His son ran off toward the chickens with the dog beside him as if they'd been friends since birth.

As he looked around, he thought she'd made a little paradise out of her land. No, more a sanctuary.

He appreciated a good sanctuary.

Colorful bottles and wind chimes hung from tree branches. What he recognized as a hummingbird feeder hooked to another, and already had some jewel-toned takers.

Stepping stones made wandering paths to a stone bench here, an iron one there.

She came back out with a tray holding a pitcher, glasses.

And without the sword.

Since Bray giggled at the chickens with one arm slung over the dog's neck, Ty stepped onto the porch.

"If we could just go back a minute? You practice with a sword?"

"I do sometimes. For my work."

"As a ninja assassin?"

She tipped her head side to side as she poured the lemonade over ice. "Well, actually . . ." She offered him a glass. "Occasionally. Sort of. I'm a game designer. Video games, and you will have battles, assassins, sword fights—at least in a lot of mine."

"Really?" He didn't have much time for gaming beyond what worked with Bray, but there'd been a time. "Like what?"

"The *Endon* series, *Dragon's Fire* series—"

"Get out! Seriously? You worked on those?"

"I did, do. You know them?"

"Well, yeah. Bray's just getting into the kids' *Endon* game. He's even got some of the little figures. He's mostly into trucks and cars right now, but he takes Baby Twink and Baby Tye for rides, and the Magic Forest play set's a hit with him."

"That's nice to hear. Would you like to sit?"

"I don't want to take up your time."

"I could use a break."

"For a second." When he sat, he saw her hesitate, nearly got up again. Then she sat.

"We really appreciate the dinner, and the eggs, and all of it." He glanced over at Bray. "I hope to hell this doesn't mean I have to get chickens now."

"He can come visit my ladies anytime. They really do like company."

"Looks like it. I have to hit the market for some supplies. Where would I do that?"

"Kushner's in Redbud Hollow, straight through to the end of town. There's a bigger supermarket, but that's a good twenty miles out. You should see if Kushner's suits you first."

"Great. Got it. You wouldn't happen to know if there's a good pediatrician in the area. He had his checkup a couple months ago, but I'd feel better if I had one on tap."

"The clinic in town. They added a pediatrician about a year ago. My friend's a doctor there, and speaks highly of him. Dr. Franklin. Another friend takes her kids there now, and I know she's happy with him."

"Dr. Franklin. Okay. One more thing, if you don't mind."

"Of course I don't."

"Some of my granny's things. I just can't use them. Some of the things I need are on their way down, and I need to make room."

"You want to have a yard sale?"

"No." He kept one eye on Bray, who now sat in front of the chicken mansion with the dog. "No, I wouldn't feel right selling her things. I'm hoping to donate them. Somehow."

"Ah." Sipping her lemonade, Thea nodded. "Miss Leona would like that. Let me talk to Maddy, my friend the doctor. The clinic does house calls, and she'd probably know who could use what you want to donate. And would accept the donation."

"I really appreciate the help. I'll let you get to work, and start on my own." He set down his empty glass. "Damn good lemonade. What brand? I'll look for it."

She just beamed at him. "I guess it's Lucy's brand. My grandmother. It's her recipe."

"Lemonade from lemons. That's a concept. Hey, Bray, we gotta go."

"Bunk wants to come, too!"

"Bunk has to do his chores," Thea said easily. "Here, have some lemonade and wait just a minute." She gestured Ty toward the door. "I can let Bunk come down to see him this afternoon if you like."

"Bray would sure like."

"Okay, hold on." She went inside and came back with two dog biscuits. "Why don't you give him this one now, Bray. And put the other in your pocket. When he comes to see you, you can give him the other."

An eye on the biscuits, Bunk sat.

Ty started breathing again when the dog took it politely out of the child's hand.

"He'll come back when I whistle," Thea said.

"When you whistle."

"He'll hear me. If it's time for him to go before then, just tell him to go home. Just *Go home*, and he will."

After the child version of a bear hug for the dog, Bray climbed up to ride Ty's back.

"Did you forget something, Bray?"

"Nuh-uh."

"About dinner last night, and what to say to Ms. Fox."

"Okay! Thank you. We ate and ate."

"You're welcome. You come back and see the chickens whenever your daddy says you can."

"I like the chickens. Can I have chickens, Daddy?"

"And here we go." But he shot Thea a smile before carting the boy off.

When they'd left, Thea sat where she was, one hand on Bunk's head. "Nice to have neighbors again, isn't it? Close enough to be friendly, distant enough to keep the quiet."

But staring off into the wood, she thought about Riggs—nothing friendly there, and the distance could evaporate without warning.

She'd had that moment, that moment of breathlessness when Ty had sat on her back porch chair—the same chair in her dream. Riggs's doing, she reminded herself. Twisting a silly little fantasy into a bloody nightmare.

"It doesn't matter. He doesn't matter. Or doesn't," she corrected, "unless I let him."

Fifteen years, she thought, and he stayed locked in a cell while she sat with her dog on her back porch.

That was reality.

"Time for work."

After carrying the tray inside, dealing with the glasses, she went up to shower off the sword session. She dressed for her day in ancient jeans, a red T-shirt for color energy.

Oh, the joys of working at home!

Still barefoot, she walked into her studio, where Bunk did his circle three times before sprawling on his studio bed for his morning nap.

She'd spent months working with a team on *Aftermath*, a multi-layered, postapocalyptic game with live actors. That had necessitated multiple trips to New York, deep, often freewheeling collaboration, and long hours.

It hadn't been her concept, nor had she been involved on the ground floor. Bradley had pulled her in to help smooth out the narrative, punch up the dialogue and world-building.

Set to launch in September, *Aftermath* would offer gamers twenty to thirty hours of gameplay in a dark, desolate, often brutal world where the human race fought, struggled, and connived for survival.

She'd enjoyed it, and she'd learned a great deal. But she found herself more than ready to dive into something a little lighter, and where she held the wheel from the start.

Before she sat, she stood studying her board, the sketches. Potential characters, landscapes, buildings she envisioned for her parallel worlds.

One ruled by dark forces, the other by light. But of course, shadows loomed in both.

Then, through the actions of one—on either side—the portal between opened, the worlds collided, and the battle began.

She'd seen it all clearly, the young thief Cairn, light and dark, stealing the glowing green stone from its high, secret perch in the Tower of the Ancients, the flash and clash of lightning and howling wind as he raced away with that dangerous prize in his bag.

And the portal, deep in the High Forest, locked centuries before by the Council of Sorcery, releasing a long-held breath as it opened again, seeping light into the dark, dark into the light.

She sat, booted up her main computer at the sturdy desk with its long L she'd had Knobby make for this exact space, this exact purpose.

Using *The Portal* as her working title for the project, she started the first file with the concept.

She worked well into the afternoon, pausing to let Bunk out, to eat a carton of yogurt as she paced and considered details.

She worked in the quiet, switched to the laptop on the L of the desk for art, back to the desktop for mapping and level planning.

Choose your side, she thought. The lightness of Lewin, the darkness of Niwel.

Fun, she thought, rolling the stiffness out of her shoulders. Play solo or multiplayer, play competitively.

Leaning back, she closed her eyes.

Snag energy sources, healing herbs, power bonuses, weapons, or stumble into a bog, fall into a trap, lose your supplies or perhaps your life in the Lake of Dread.

She drifted a moment, tired in mind and body from the work and the interrupted sleep.

And he pushed at her, slyly, like cold, pinching fingers along her skin.

She heard Riggs laugh even as her eyes snapped open. Her stomach quaked as she shoved to her feet. She pushed back, as hard as she could, hard enough to have pain stabbing through her left temple.

She knew fear, had to accept it, had to accept he'd somehow gotten stronger. He'd pried through her blocks twice now in less than a day.

And what she'd felt from him was a kind of glee that he could.

He'd found a way, she admitted. Now, so would she.

Chapter Sixteen

After some internal debate, Thea decided she'd wait until Saturday to tell her family about Riggs. The three of them could talk about it, talk it out, over dinner. Until then, she'd keep to herself, and she'd keep working on her physical and mental strength.

She shelved her new game concept for later, and pulled out another she'd filed at concept stage. Now, with Riggs in mind, she began to flesh it out.

She'd felt him. She'd heard his fingers scratching at her locked window, but held him back. He hadn't walked into her dreams again.

She sent Bunk down to visit Bray in the afternoons, then whistled him home again. And now and again she heard a drift of music or the boy's laughter as it floated up to her on the air. Though she hadn't seen Ty or his son since they'd returned her dish and basket, those sounds of life, easy and ordinary, brought her contentment.

Still, since Riggs's recent torments coincided with their arrival in Redbud Hollow, she kept her distance. Kept to her routine. Kept to the quiet.

On Saturday, she dipped chicken pieces in an egg-milk mixture, then shook piece by piece in the flour and herbs in a paper bag. Just like her grandmother taught her.

While the chicken browned and sizzled in hot oil, she started on the biscuit dough. The potato salad she'd made earlier blended its flavors in the refrigerator. She'd fry up some okra and serve her family a fine early summer meal.

With enough left over, she calculated, Rem could take some home for a midnight snack.

While she had the chicken keeping warm on a platter, the biscuits ready for the oven, she whisked up gravy in the skillet. They'd eat outside, she decided, as the day just called for it. She'd whistle Bunk home when she took out the plates to set the picnic table.

Even as she thought it, Bunk came charging in the front door.

A second later, Bray charged after him, with Ty scrambling behind.

"Sorry. I'm sorry." He stopped short. "They got away from me."

"That's just fine. Did y'all have fun?"

"We played fetch. Daddy's arm fell off. I drew this. For you."

As Bray thrust a picture at her, Thea turned down the heat in the skillet and took it.

She decided he'd used every crayon in the pack to scribble circles and jagged lines and loops.

"For me? It's just beautiful." She couldn't help but read him. He was so full of life, and pure cheerful energy. "And it's Bunk!"

As Ty just blinked at her, she crouched. "And here you are, and your daddy. Is he tossing a red ball?"

"We got it from the store, for Bunk."

"I know he appreciates it. I need to put this picture right up on my refrigerator. It's the best art gallery going."

"Daddy does, too. Can I see the chickens?"

"Bray, Ms. Fox is busy."

"Not very busy." Straightening up, Thea used refrigerator magnets to display the drawing. "Unless you're in a hurry, I'm about finished up here."

"Please!" The leg hug, the look. "See the chickens, please, Daddy."

"For a minute."

As Bray ran off, Bunk with him, Ty heard his mother's voice.

You spoil him, Tyler.

Yeah, well, so what?

"I'm sorry," he said again. "Barging in this way. I hate when people barge in."

"I think Bunk did the barging, and the door was open." He looked so frazzled, she had to smile. "Can I get you something? I've got wine, beer, sweet tea."

"No, really. We'll only stay a minute." He walked over to look out the open back doors, keeping an eye on Bray.

And looked a little disheveled with the frazzled, Thea thought. Like a man whose arm had fallen off playing fetch with a boy and a dog.

He'd bought a ball for her dog.

"I'm just going to finish up this gravy. Are you settling in?"

"It's been . . . a lot. I was able to donate Granny's dining room furniture—that was big, and thanks for the help there. A few other things, still have some to go. A bunch to go, in reality, but I'm avoiding too much reality."

"I often find that helpful myself."

He glanced back at her. "Having the dog come down for a couple hours in the afternoon's been a godsend. He really is a damn good dog, and he's a hell of a babysitter. Plus, Bray's laid off his pleas for a puppy. That gives me some breathing room in that area."

He wandered a little. "You've got a nice house, outside and in. It looks like you. And I don't know exactly what that means, but it does."

"Since I spent a long time planning it, I'd say it's a compliment."

Bunk let out a series of joyful barks. When Ty looked out, he saw the big dog running toward the front of the house. And Bray racing after.

He shot out the door after them. Once again, Thea lowered the heat, then hurried out.

"It's going to be my family," she began, and when she caught up, Lucy already had the boy on her hip.

"Look what I found." She sent Ty a reassuring smile. "I don't suppose you'll let me keep him." Still holding the boy. "You're Leona's great-grandson. I'm Lucy, Thea's grandmother, and this is Rem, her brother. It's nice to meet you."

"You, too. I'll take him. Bray, you're not supposed to run toward the road."

"I stop. Don't go in the road. I stop."

"He did," Rem confirmed, and offered his hand. "Tyler freaking Brennan. I heard a rumor. Now I'm waiting for Buffy Summers to move to the Hollow and make all my dreams come true. Teenage crush," Rem told him with a grin. "The Slayer ruined me for anyone else. You were Thea's."

"Thank you, Rem, for bringing humiliation to the table."

"Hey, what are brothers for? And you two staying for dinner means I'm not outnumbered for a change."

"Oh, we were just heading back."

"Do you like fried chicken?" Thea asked Ty. "Potato salad, buttermilk biscuits, fried okra?"

"I . . . I don't think I've ever had fried okra."

"You've got Appalachian blood in your veins, and never had fried okra?" Shaking her head, Lucy hooked her arm in his free one. "You're in for a treat. My granddaughter's a very fine cook, seeing as she learned from me."

"I really don't want to . . . Did you say 'granddaughter'?"

Lucy batted her eyes. "And he's a charmer. Let's you and me have a glass of wine."

As charmers went, Ty figured Lucy Lannigan hit top of the list. After the initial cold sweat jolt of seeing his son in a stranger's arms, he relaxed so when they sat on the porch and she just plucked Bray onto her knee he didn't worry.

"Got doggie," Bray told her. "Got chickens."

"Yes, she does. Now, you have your daddy walk you down the road a bit to my house. I've got chickens, too, and two doggies, two cows, and a goat."

"Cows go moo."

"That's exactly right. I hope you will," Lucy said to Ty as Bray scrambled down to play with Bunk. "I do enjoy having little ones around. My younger grandchildren come around when they can, but it's not nearly often enough to suit me."

Rem brought out wine. "Thea says ten minutes, and it's nice enough to eat outside. I'm drafted to set the table."

"You sit." Lucy patted Ty's arm as he started to get up. "Keep me company. That boy's a fountain of energy, isn't he? And looks just like his daddy."

"I could say the same about you and your granddaughter. Rem, too. He reminds me of someone though. Can't quite . . . well, hell."

When it struck him, Ty looked over at Rem, then back at Lucy. "Caleb Lannigan."

"My younger son. Do you know him?"

"Only his work. I binged two episodes of *Off Time* last night after Bray crashed. Is Waylon Lannigan related?"

"My older son."

"That's a kick in the head. I know his work, too. Session musician out of Nashville. And his wife did the violin work on 'Busting Out.' That's one of mine."

Lucy sipped her wine. "It's a small world or a big one. It all depends on where you're sitting."

In about ten minutes, he was sitting at a bright red picnic table with a spread that put his plans to make sloppy joes and tater tots to shame.

And he watched in amazement as Bray, who he rarely persuaded to eat anything beyond peas and carrots in the vegetable family, consumed fried okra like gummy bears.

"I like biscuits."

"Would you like another?" Thea asked the boy.

"Okay."

"How about we split one? Half for you," Ty said, "and half for me."

"Put lotsa butter. It's yum."

"It really is. What kind is it? We'll switch."

"Lannigan-Fox brand. I milked the cow," Lucy explained. "Thea made the butter."

Ty's eyebrows drew together. "With, like, a churn?"

Laughing, Thea made the churning motion. "Not the kind you mean. Same concept."

"When do you make time to design games?"

"Oh, it's all in a day's."

"Long days," Ty assumed. "You mowed Granny's lawn," he said to Rem.

"Sure. Still available if you need it."

"Thanks. I've got it. But it meant a lot to know there were people close by looking out for her."

"You looked out for her, too." Lucy patted his arm. "You made sure she didn't go without. Helped her be independent, and that meant the world to her. She lived a good long life because she could live it in her home, where her memories lived with her."

"I hated to see her place empty whenever I went by. How long are you planning to stay?"

Ty shifted back to Rem. "The summer, at least. I didn't know how Bray would do with the move, but so far . . ."

"Done!" Bray announced, and started to wiggle off the bench.

"Hold it, Flash. What do you say first?"

Bray lifted his shoulders to his ears.

"Thank you for dinner," Ty prompted.

"Thank you. I like butter."

"Next batch, I'll bring you some," Thea promised. "You know, it's about time to feed my chickens. Do you want to help?"

The boy's bottle-green eyes went wide. "Okay!"

"We'll clear this up, honeypot, and work up an appetite for the peach cobbler I brought along."

"If you're staying more than a couple months, or thinking about selling, the place could use a few things."

Ty nodded at Rem. "I've noticed."

"I was going to do a little painting for her this spring, just to help her out, but who you really want is Knobby."

"I want Knobby?"

"Yeah, contractor. Good solid work. Come on down to Grammie's sometime. I'll show you the Foxes' Den. Pretty sure that's where Thea really dug in the roots toward game design and development. She slayed all comers."

"Still does," Lucy reminded him.

"Yeah, well, she's a professional."

Ty helped clear the table, earning some Lucy points, as he seemed to know what he was about in that area.

"Chickens are funny. They got names," Bray added before he demolished a bowl of cobbler as if he hadn't eaten all day. A minute later, he was off and running.

"You sit with Ty, Grammie. Rem's on kitchen duty with me."

"My lot in life." But he followed Thea inside.

"If you don't mind me saying, you and your son have a lovely rhythm between you. It's not easy to raise a child on your own, but you're doing a fine job of it."

"Do you think?" A worry, a constant one, that he'd screw it all up dogged him.

"I know what I see, and I see a happy boy, a bright one, and a man who's learned how to grow those eyes in the back of his head."

"With Bray, I need them on the sides, too. He never stops."

Lucy laughed. "I know how that goes. That was Waylon. That boy never stayed planted. Now, I know I'm biased on it, but this is a good place to raise children. I raised three of my own here, and then the two in the house when they lost their parents."

"I didn't realize they'd lost their parents."

Watching the little boy play with the dog, Lucy sipped her tea.

"Thea twelve, Rem ten when it happened. Fifteen years ago next week. A blink of an eye, and forever."

"I'm sorry."

"Being together got us through. And they've built such good lives. They could've built those lives anywhere, but chose here. I'm grateful for that every day. You're the same. You can build a good life, and help your boy build his anywhere. If it's not here, you'll find your place."

She relaxed him, Ty thought, as if he'd known her for years.

"I guess that's why we're here, to see if this is our place. Pretty sure wherever it is, there'll have to be chickens and a dog."

Thea's laugh floated out the open doors, had him glancing back.

Lucy just sipped her tea. "It's good you're taking the summer to find out."

"That's the plan. So . . . Knobby? I'll add him to the list."

He waited until Thea came out again to rise.

"I've got to get Bray home. Thanks for letting us crash your family dinner."

"It's not crashing when you're invited. I'm glad you could stay."

"Your chicken beats the Colonel's all to hell. And I like the Colonel's. Great meeting you, Rem, and you, Lucy."

"You bring that boy down to see me."

"I will. Bray, time to go home."

"Nooooo, Daddy!"

"Pal of mine, you need a bath."

The whine changed to hope. "Bubbles and trucks?"

"And plenty of them."

"Three books?"

Ty held up two fingers, which Bray counted. "Aw."

"Lots of bubbles and trucks and two books." He hauled Bray up. "Let's ride."

When Bray climbed around to his back, Ty gave him a hitch to secure. "Thanks again. Bray?"

"Bye! Bye!" Then bounced and laughed when Bunk waved. "Bye, bye, bye!" He sang it out as Ty started home.

Rem had the good sense to wait until they were out of earshot.

"Okay, did you squeal like a little girl and bounce up and down when you met him?"

Thea afforded Rem a single, withering stare. "I certainly did not."

Inside, sure, but that didn't count. Nobody knew that but her.

Well, and Maddy.

"Didn't act like a rock star, did he? Or how you figure a rock star would act, I guess."

"He doesn't perform anymore, or hasn't since Code Red broke up."

Rem grinned at her. "You shed some tears over that."

"Maybe. I'm over it."

"He's a very solid young man," Lucy said. "And a good father. That boy's just brimming with light."

"Serious cute quotient," Rem agreed. "Wonder where the mother is."

"No, I didn't look and won't. Neither will Grammie, because she's too polite. If he wants to share that eventually, he will. And don't poke in your way either," Thea warned.

Obviously amused, Rem gestured with his beer. "What's my way?"

"So, Ty, what's the story with Braydon's mom?"

"Direct's best."

"Direct is often rude."

"Not when you're charming with it, the way I am."

At Thea's snort, Lucy shook her head. "Leave your sister be, and walk your grammie home. Thea, this was just what I needed tonight. Good food, good company, fresh air, and a little-boy bonus."

She kissed Thea's cheek, added a hug.

"It's what I needed, too. Even though it included you." She drilled a finger into Rem's stomach.

"Me, too. Even though with the extras, I only have one little wing and thigh to take home and mow down later. I'll get them on the way out."

Thea walked with them through the house to the front porch. And waved them down the lane.

She'd intended to talk to both of them over dinner about the dream, about Riggs, about all of it. When Ty joined them, she'd thought after dinner.

But then she hadn't wanted to spoil the mood. Theirs or her own.

It could wait, she told herself. And if he found a way in tonight, she'd just shove him back out the damn window again.

Ray Riggs popped one of his dwindling supply of oxy. Though he didn't know when he'd be able to score more, it felt like someone had clamped a vise on his head.

He could take it, he would take it, but not tonight. Tonight, he needed some nice, dark oblivion.

He could take it because when the pain flashed instead of crushed like tonight, he had more. Just more.

Fifteen years, he thought. The little cunt had had him caged for fifteen years.

And for what?

Taking out her parents, who'd have pushed and squeezed her into their mold? She was better off without them. He'd done her a fucking favor.

He had to pay her back for that, for fifteen long years. And he'd pay her back for taunting him the way she had. And worse, for ignoring him.

He wouldn't let her forget him, and since this new level of pain helped him remind her, he'd take the pain.

But not tonight.

Tonight he needed that sweet, sweet high.

He'd spent nearly six months—what did he have but time?—bullshitting his way out of seg a second time. Read the ones who think they have it over you, he figured, and you get it over them.

He'd needed some goddamn light, some goddamn air, so he'd taken the time, done the work.

He'd had that time in the yard, in the light, in the air, for nearly a month. Out of blues and into khakis, roaming the yard, plotting, planning.

He'd find a way out, and when he did, he'd find that bitch and make her pay.

He couldn't really remember what set him off. Some asshole saying something, thinking something. Oughta have more respect for a man who'd killed like he had, who done fifteen fucking years.

So he'd taught that bastard respect.

And the tearing in? It felt good, beating his fists against flesh and bone felt so damn good.

Until other fists beat against his.

A concussion, a couple busted ribs, a dislocated jaw? Bad, bad, but being back in seg was a hell of a lot worse.

Still, that beating had unlocked that pain, the pain that led to more.

He could do that more, and not just once a year now. Not just on the anniversary when she'd first pushed her way into his head.

He had taken it slow at first, barely peeking, glimpses, just glimpses of her. Mostly sleeping, but once when she'd stood at a big window looking out at a city at night.

Maybe New York, maybe Chicago. And another time when she'd milked a freaking cow.

Drifting into her mind was a kind of freedom. A freedom that burned like acid in his throat when he came back to himself, to his cage.

But that one night, the night he walked right in, when she'd seen him, felt him. Feared him. He'd run that show, you bet your ass. Made her see what he wanted her to see, made her see him kill some dipshit playing the guitar.

It had cost him, cost him in pain and the blood that slid out of his screaming ear.

Worth it, he thought now, smiling as he drifted. Worth every bit of it to hear her scream, to *feel* her fear fly out so it coated him like silk.

He just needed some time for the skull crushing to ease, and he'd do it again. Again and again, until he made it real.

He had to make a plan, a way to get not just his mind but his body out of the cage.

But getting out wasn't enough. Once he knew where to find her, once he found her, had her look right into his eyes as he killed her.

That would be enough.

Thea doubled down on her work. Once or twice she felt Riggs scratching at the window, but mentally yanked down a shade and blocked him out.

After some ten-hour days, a polished GDD, dozens of character sketches, she felt nearly ready to run it by her boss.

She already knew the game inside and out. She'd made sure of it.

But today wasn't for work. She never worked on this day in June. Today, she put on a simple summer dress and her mother's earrings. Outside, she cut a trio of hydrangeas, knowing her grandmother and brother would do the same.

"Stay, Bunk. You stay home now. Guard."

He whined a little, but flopped down on the front porch when she got into the car.

Not her indulgent convertible, not today. But the dignified sedan she thought of as mostly her winter car.

When she drove down the lane and passed Ty's house, she heard music. Something on the piano, something quick and edgy. She wished she could stop and just listen. Just let the day float by in music and sunlight.

She laid a hand over the pale pink flower heads on the seat beside her, and drove on.

Lucy and Rem didn't keep her waiting. Both came out of the house carrying sprays of hydrangeas. Rem got in the back, and Lucy held Thea's flowers and her own when she took the passenger seat.

"It's a pretty day to visit them."

"It is." Thea glanced in the rearview at her brother. He sat, silent, looking out the window.

Ten, she thought, so much younger and more tender than her twelve.

"Have you been all right?"

"I've been working, Grammie. I'm always all right when I'm working. But the other night . . ."

She braced herself, and told them.

"Goddamn it, Thea, why didn't you tell us?"

Because she knew her brother, she'd anticipated the explosion.

"I intended to when you came to dinner Saturday, but then Ty, Bray. It's not something I could bring up with them there. And after?"

She let out a breath. "After they left, I just didn't want to. Didn't want to talk about it, think about it. It was such a nice evening, I just didn't want to."

"If he could get into your dream, control it, he's stronger than he was."

"I know, Grammie. But that doesn't make him stronger than me. I've thought about it. I have a home, work, people. I have a life, and the freedom to live it. He doesn't have any of that. But he has time, nothing but time to sit and think and work on what he has, how to use it. So he's stronger than he was.

"He'll come tonight, like always, but I won't let him take control."

"I'll stay at your place tonight."

She shook her head at her brother. "I've got Bunk."

And I want you with Grammie, just in case, she thought.

Rem let out a sound of frustration. "What's Bunk going to do? Bite his dream ass?"

She flicked her gaze back to the mirror again.

"It's what I can do. It's what I'm going to do. I need to prove to him and to myself he can't scare me with his bullshit. It's bullshit, Rem, and I can't let him win. I can promise you I'm more than ready for him."

"You keep the charm bag over the bed, darling? And say the words?"

"I do, Grammie."

"Put up two more. Three's a strong number."

"Then I will. But not tonight. Let him come when he thinks I'm weak. He'll find out differently."

"I don't like it. I'm going to call Detective Howard."

"Rem—"

"He knows you, so he'll get it. Jesus, Thea, you've helped them plenty. Let them help you. It won't hurt to check with the warden."

"It's a good idea, and a good compromise. Let your brother look after you a little, Thea. I'll feel better for it, too."

"All right."

Riggs wouldn't hurt their family again, Thea vowed as she drove into the cemetery. He'd taken enough from them. He wouldn't get more.

When she parked, they got out of the car. They walked to the headstone together.

For All Time.

"Both Caleb and Waylon called this morning." Lucy laid her flowers on the grave. "They never forget. They're here with us now."

Rem laid his flowers. "Not once, not one time in fifteen years has Dad's family called or written. Not once."

"We're his family." Thea laid her flowers with Rem's, with Lucy's. Then took her grandmother's hand as Rem did on Lucy's other side.

"We're his family," she repeated. "With Caleb and Waylon and their families. We'll always be his family."

Chapter Seventeen

Ty dealt with family.

Dealing meant trying to keep Bray safe, happy, and, please God, occupied while he continued to sort through Leona's things. Sorting through so he could hopefully organize, make space, turn that space into a home.

Temporary or not, his boy deserved a home.

And with each day that passed, he started to think less about temporary.

The kid loved it there. He loved the yard, the squeaky floors in the house, the old barn Ty couldn't figure out what to do with.

He loved the porches, the trees, and the dog that came to play every afternoon.

Still, while the outside offered plenty of room to run, more than enough for the swing/slide/climb contraption Try was still researching, the house itself didn't.

If they stayed, it meant adding on, at some point.

They didn't need huge, but while the dining room could serve as a studio for now, he didn't want to work right off the kitchen for the long term.

For serious work, he needed a serious space.

And privileged or not, he'd really like having his own bathroom.

Those could wait until he reached a hundred percent on the Be Sure meter.

Plus, he'd probably have to learn to cook a little more than he had in his current repertoire, as delivery was off the table.

But his kid's happiness took the number one spot, and Jesus, his kid was happy.

After he'd spent most of another afternoon hauling and sorting, Ty looked around at piles of boxes. Some packed to go, some yet unpacked from the delivery van.

At that moment, it all seemed overwhelming.

Leona had loved her little things, and she'd had a long life to collect a lot of them. For the most part, he'd separated out what he felt mattered, had mattered to her. And hadn't she kept the birthday card he'd made for her when he'd been about eight. Out of purple construction paper, a weird and crooked yellow flower glued on the front. And his own sloppy print.

HAPPY BiRTHdAY!
TO ThE BEST GRANY.
LOVe TY

How could he toss that out? And where the hell should he keep it? Along with every card and letter and postcard he'd ever sent her?

For now he decided back in the faded fabric box where she'd kept them all.

He'd loved her, he'd really loved her, but until he'd come here, started going through her things, he hadn't realized how much she'd loved him.

And that was more overwhelming.

She'd left him everything she had because she knew he'd honor and respect it.

"I'm trying, Granny."

But right now, he needed a break not just from the work but the emotional toll of it.

When he looked outside and watched his little boy tossing the ball—decent arm for a four-year-old—for the big-ass dog, he knew how to take it.

He picked up the little pink vase he'd given Leona for Christmas when he'd been about ten. Taking it outside, he set it on the table on the back porch.

Bray charged at him—and so did the big-ass dog.

"Throw the ball, Daddy. Fetch with Bunk!"

So he spent the next twenty minutes throwing the ball, watching boy and dog give chase. And decided on the spot for the play set. He'd settle on one tonight, order it, and get that done.

"It's about time for Bunk to go home."

"No, Daddy!"

"How about we walk him back? You can pick some flowers for Thea on the way."

"What for?"

"Because it's nice, and I have this vase to put them in."

A sly smile followed. "Chickens?"

"We'll see. How about one of those flowers?"

Just clovers that had popped up since he'd last mowed the lawn, but it gave Bray a mission.

By the time they'd topped the rise, made the turn, the vase was stuffed with clover, little wild daisies, buttercups, and grass. And Bray rode his father's back.

He considered her wraparound porch as they walked, and wondered—if they stayed—if he should do something like it. Or just a bigger porch/ deck on the back for the grill he still had to buy.

He could grill reasonably well.

And made a mental note to order one along with that play set.

Lowering Bray, Ty handed him the vase. "Here you go. These are from you."

"I picked the flowers."

"That's right," Ty said, and knocked on the screen door.

Through the screen, he saw her coming, and felt the tug he imagined all men felt when a really pretty woman in a summer dress walked their way.

She'd scooped her hair back in a tail. She had a long neck to go with those long legs. Her smile said welcome, and he could admit that was something that got him every time.

"Look here, two handsome men at my door."

When she opened the screen, the dog bolted in, and Bray shoved the vase at her.

"You get this."

"I do? They're just beautiful."

"I picked the flowers."

"He goes for the weeds," Ty explained, and she smiled again.

"Weeds are just wildflowers in the wrong place. And these are in the exact right place. Come in. You had a long walk on a warm afternoon. I bet you're thirsty."

"I am!"

"I knew there was a reason I made lemonade, and sugar cookies."

"Cookies!"

All innocence, Thea looked at Ty. "Oops."

"It's fine."

"Y'all come on back."

A really nice house, Ty thought again as he scoped out the living room with its warm sand-colored walls, the dreamy landscapes, the fireplace framed in deep blue marble, its thick mantel. She'd flanked it with built-ins that offered open shelves and lower cabinets, all in natural wood.

Cozy, cushy, easy furniture.

He really had to think about replacing his Granny's old, half-sprung sofa.

Open space, plenty of light. A kind of sitting room/library on one side, and . . .

"Wow, this is where you work."

She'd given herself space—exactly what he wanted for himself, and what he'd given up in Philadelphia.

A good, solid workstation, one he assumed she needed for all the equipment. What he considered a thinking couch, and a wall of mirrors he couldn't explain.

A wall rack holding three—count them, three—swords.

"You have more swords."

"I do."

And nunchucks, he noted, some sort of bamboo stick, and an actual spear. All, fortunately, up out of reach of his son.

"Expecting a war?"

"I do design them."

"Yeah." He scanned the sketches on her board, others in frames. "I didn't realize you actually drew them. I figured you used the computer."

"I do both."

"It's Tye, Daddy! Twink, Gwen, Zed, and Mila. It's Mog. She's bad!"

"She's the worst," Thea agreed.

"I like Tye. He's brave and flies on a horse. But he's grown-up. He's little like me! Janey says he looks like me and everything."

"He plays the kids' version," Ty explained. "Janey is Scott's sister's daughter. She babysits some. He likes to be Tye in the game, and the play set."

"'Cause he looks like me, and he has a flying horse. Can I have the cookie?"

"You bet."

She led them back to the kitchen with its open plan expanding to a lounge, a dining room, its wide glass doors leading to the porch, the gardens, the yard.

After setting the little vase on the island, she poured lemonade, plated some golden cookies.

"I'm mentally stealing some of your house design if I do anything with mine."

"You're welcome to."

Bray downed his lemonade, then bit into a cookie. "This is yummy. Can I see the chickens?"

"I know they'd love to see you."

"Go ahead. Just a few minutes," Ty added as Bray and the rest of his cookie streaked out the door with Bunk beside him. "It looks like you were going out."

"No. Oh." She glanced down at her dress. "No, I had a family thing this morning, then had that urge to bake cookies. And now I feel a bigger urge to confess. There's a reason Scott's sister's daughter says Tye Smith looks like Bray. The child version."

Fascinated, Ty watched embarrassment flicker in her eyes.

"You see, when I had the idea to add his character to the second *Endon* game . . . It was right after my friend Maddy and I—the doctor?"

"Yeah, I've met her."

"Of course. Donations. She said."

More embarrassment, Ty noted.

"I don't remember how Code Red, and you, came up in that conversation with her. Exactly. But then I thought about the new character, and ended up basing him on you."

"Sorry, me?"

"What I mean is his physicality. His face, his, ah, frame, his build, his looks. So, his child version resembles Bray because, well, Bray looks like a child version of you."

"You based the character—the Wandering Warrior, right?—on me?"

"Yes, more or less. More than less. And it's getting hard to face moments of humiliation with you, so I'm getting it all out. I wanted handsome with a bit of an edge to it, but an edge that could turn on charm. I didn't want the big, beefy build like Zed, but a tall, lanky build, long fingers, that sort of top-shelf bourbon color hair, the green eyes. And that was you, so."

"Hold on a minute." He checked outside, saw boy, dog, chickens, and no threat. Then he turned around and walked back to her studio. Stood studying the drawing.

"My ears don't go like that." He gestured to add points to them.

"They would if your mother was an elf."

"Hmm."

"And you have long eyes."

"I have long eyes?"

"Yes." She sort of bit that out, amusing him. "I exaggerated them for character, for his elfin blood, added the braid down the back of his head, the tattoo, but otherwise . . ."

Ty moved a little closer to the drawing. "Well, son of a bitch. I never noticed it before. That's cool."

"It's cool?" She pressed her hands to her face, then ran them back over her hair. "I was afraid you'd think it was creepy. I was creepy."

"Try being in a rock band for about ten years, you'd know creepy. Having fans camp outside your house can start out cool until you can't go out without having them swarm. But that's not creepy so much as inconvenient. Having a teenage girl bribe a housekeeper for the key to your hotel room, then sneak in, strip naked, and get into bed with you?

"That's creepy."

"God, did that really happen?"

"Yeah. Having a video game character my kid likes based on me? That doesn't approach creepy and hits dead center of cool."

"Good. That's good."

He turned back to her. "Anything else I should know?"

"I can't think of anything at the moment."

"Well, if you do."

She still looked embarrassed, and he couldn't deny he got a kick out of it.

"Meanwhile, I didn't get a cookie yet."

She gestured toward the kitchen. "You'd do me a favor if you took some home. And some eggs, if you can use them. I'd take Miss Leona eggs. My ladies are reliable layers, so it's at least a couple dozen every week. Too many for me."

He tried a cookie. "We're definitely taking some of these home. Bray'll go for scrambled eggs a couple times a week."

"Great. I'll fix you up."

She still had Bray's drawing on her fridge, and that touched him. He'd lucked into a nice, quiet neighbor who didn't seem to mind a kid coming around now and then to laugh at her chickens.

When she started putting cookies in a container, he leaned on the island, took another. "The little vase was Granny's."

"Oh. I'll get it back to you."

"No, I'd like you to have it, if you'd want it. I'm still going through all her things, figuring out what matters, what doesn't. I gave her that for Christmas when I was a kid. I know how she felt about you, and think she'd like you to have it."

When she looked up at him, her eyes brimmed with tears.

"Shit, I didn't mean to—"

"No, no, it's the day." She swiped at tears that spilled. "I miss her. I really miss seeing her most days even just to wave if I was taking a walk. And seeing him out there?"

She gestured outside where Bray sat having what appeared to be a serious conversation with Bunk beside the chicken coop.

"It reminds me how much I loved doing just that starting about the same age when we—Rem and I—had our two-week summer visit with Grammie. How it was even better than Christmas, and counting the days until we'd drive down from Virginia. I loved my parents, but I couldn't wait till they drove off again, and it was just me and Rem and Grammie, the dogs, the chickens, the cow, the goat, the hills."

She let out a sigh. "It's the day," she repeated. "We lost my parents fifteen years ago today."

"God, Thea, I'm sorry. And I'm sorry we just dropped in this way."

"I hope you won't be, because it felt good to see you both at the door. You blew some of the clouds away. We go to lay flowers, the three of us, every morning on this day, then spend some time together.

"When I came home—I can never work on this day—I made cookies and lemonade to have something to do. After, I didn't know what the hell to do with myself. And there you were."

She used the heels of her hands now as the tears refused to stop. "And this morning, when I left to get Rem and Grammie, I heard you playing the piano, and it helped settle me. Hearing the music, knowing someone Miss Leona loved was inside her house, playing music."

Hesitating, Ty started to shove his hands in his pockets. Instead, he went with instinct and did what he'd do if Bray cried.

He went around the island, and held her.

"I'm sorry," she began.

"I hope you won't be." He echoed her words. "Seems like you need to get it out."

"I don't cry at their graves anymore. I know they're not there, and the stone, the flowers are for us. They're everywhere else, and that usually comforts me. But this day . . ."

"You were just a kid. That had to be brutal." He stroked a hand down her hair. "They had an accident?"

"No. No," she said again, and the tears drained out of her voice as she drew back. "They were murdered."

Shock flashed over his face, into his voice. "God, Thea."

"They were murdered in their bed while Rem and I were here with Grammie. He shot them for these earrings"—she closed a finger over her right earlobe—"and a watch and a few other things. He shot them because he could."

"Who?"

"His name is Ray Riggs, and he's in prison. He'll be in prison the rest of his life. And somehow, it's still not enough. At least not on this day."

"I'm sorry. Words don't cut it, but I'm sorry."

"I didn't expect to say all that, but I did. And you listened, and I feel steadier for it."

She picked up a cookie. "Thank you."

She still had tears on her lashes, Ty thought, when she smiled at him. They put a quick, hard dent in his heart.

"Sure. We should give you some space."

"Let me finish boxing up these cookies, and I'll get your eggs. I promise not to cry on your shoulder next time you come by. Of course, now you've fulfilled a sixteen-year-old's dream. Tyler Brennan put his arms around me."

He had to laugh. "You're a really interesting woman, Thea."

"Do you think so?" She got out a carton of eggs. "I so like being ordinary."

An odd goal, he thought. "I don't think you're ever going to hit that mark."

"I keep trying." She got out a cloth bag. "I'm going to give you some butter." She pulled a small lidded jar out of the fridge. "You can keep the jar, I have more. Or bring it back if you don't have use for it."

"If we bring it back, will more butter go into it?"

"That's very likely. You should take Bray down to Grammie. He'll like her dogs, and her ladies, and her cows and goat. I bet she'll teach him how to milk the goat."

"Excuse me?" He held up a finger. "She milks a goat?"

"It is a nanny. Grammie uses goat's milk for different things. And for her soap and candle-making, her lotions and such."

"She makes soap with goat's milk." He said it as if trying out words in a foreign language. "She milks a goat, and makes soap."

"Mountain Magic, that's her business. The candle I brought down's one of hers."

"It's great. She made it?"

"Mountain Magic," Thea said again. "I don't have any manly sort of soap on hand, but she'll give you some to try out. Be warned, it'll turn you into a customer."

"Seriously interesting women, both of you. And I get another care package. Listen, you've already fed us twice, now this. I can cook enough to keep Bray happy, but I don't think canned pasta and frozen peas compare. Do you like pizza?"

Her eyebrows lifted. "Am I alive and breathing?"

"Looks like. I need a few more days to get to the point where I'm not living in chaos. There's a pizza place in town—we've hit it a couple times. Next time we do, maybe you'd go with us."

"I'd love it." She handed him the bag. "I know about chaos. When you need to step out of it, take a walk down to Grammie's—that always clears mine. Or just a walk in the hills. And you're always welcome here."

"I appreciate it."

"I appreciate the shoulder to cry on when I didn't know I needed it."

When they stepped outside, Bray leaped up. "No, Daddy. Stay here."

"We need to head back, pal."

Thea produced a cookie Ty hadn't seen her pick up. "This one's for the walk home."

That cleared the sulk.

"Thank you. I'm gonna run! Bye, bye, bye!" And shot off.

"We're going to run," Ty said. He jogged after the boy, then half turned. "Oh, by the way, I've heard your whistle. Impressive."

Interesting woman, he thought again, and doing his best to keep the eggs from breaking, ran after his son.

On this night, she knew he'd come. Grateful for the interlude with man and boy, the moment of kindness and comfort offered, she found everything in her centered.

And focused.

Settled, she took a walk in the hills with Bunk. And planned.

And that night, she took her time preparing for bed, and the conflict to come.

Instead of hanging two more charm bags over her bed, she took the first down, set it aside.

Tonight wasn't for quiet sleep, but for action.

Her need for the quiet, for the ordinary kept her from taking action too often, and for too long. That changed tonight.

With Bunk already sprawled on his bed, Thea slipped into hers.

And did what she did best.

She built a dream.

The blue sea charged at the sugar-white sand. Palms waved their green fronds around the brown-haired rounds of coconuts. The stretch of beach rolled and rose up to thick jungle where birds of jewel colors winged and called. Vines tangled there, smothered in flowers of moon-glow white.

Tiny crabs, transparent as ghosts, scrabbled over the sand. Snakes, as bright as the birds, slithered silently among the vines.

Beasts with fangs and blade-sharp tusks roamed in its green shadows. Spiders, as fat as fists, weaved webs.

At the center of the island, the volcano rose, black as pitch against the blue of the sky. Clouds as thin as smoke ringed its peak.

It loomed silently now, its sides scored by rivers of lava that flowed when it chose to roar.

She stood on the beach in sturdy, knee-high boots over brown pants. She wore a many-pocketed vest over a long-sleeved shirt. Her belt carried a sleeve of water and sheaths for a jagged-edged knife, a short sword. Her hair hung in a single braid topped with a side-snap bush hat.

She scanned the water, pleased with the circling shark fins. Shells littered the verge of the beach like shards of colored glass.

Another island floated beyond that circle. Pristine, welcoming. Safe. There, salvation.

She waited until she felt Riggs scratching at the window. Then throwing it open, she pulled him in.

She'd outfitted him—fair was fair. His boots crunched over shells as he stumbled, disoriented, blinking against the strong sunlight.

"Hey there, Ray. Welcome to Perilous Island."

"What the fuck is this?"

"It must feel good to get out of that little room. Here you've got a pretty beach, a sea breeze, sunshine, no doors to lock you in. You're welcome."

Smiling she looked into those pale blue eyes. "Now let me explain the rules."

"Screw rules." When he rushed toward her, she only had to hold up a hand to lock his boots into the sand.

"That would be your first penalty, Ray. You have to wait for the go signal. But I'll let this one slide. Your goal is to reach that island."

"My goal is to beat you bloody. Then I'm going to choke the life out of you and watch you die."

"It's just those goals that got you here. But you'll have to catch me first. And survive. There's a boat on the leeward side, and you can use it to escape and reach Sanctuary Island. But the getting there? Well, Ray, they don't call it Perilous Island for nothing."

"This is bullshit."

"Is it? What it is, is a dangerous journey, so you'll want to stay alert. You're going to encounter predators, traps, challenges, obstacles. You'll also have the opportunity to locate weapons, power boosters, healing stones, a number of helpful tools."

He struggled to pull his feet free. "I said what the fuck is this!"

"My dream, my game, my rules. See Edina up there?" She gestured to the volcano. "She looks quiet now, but she's getting restless. If she blows before you reach the leeward side, well, Ray, your chances of getting out of this alive diminish, severely."

"I'm not playing some dumbass game."

"Then don't." Thea shrugged. "Either way, you'll feel the pain, the heat, the fear. You'll bleed and you'll break, Ray. Because as long as you're here, it's real."

"Bullshit."

"It won't take long for you to know it's real. There's the timer." Lifting a hand, she counted off: three, two, one. "And go. I'd wish you good luck, Ray, but that would be bullshit."

She raced into the jungle.

She'd played before. After all, she'd built the game. To offset her experience, she'd given her opponent unlimited lives. Not so much out of a sense of fair play, she admitted, but for her own satisfaction.

Drawing her sword, she hacked through a web, sent its deadly occupant flying. On a leap, she gripped a branch and swung over the hissing strike of a scarlet snake.

She heard Riggs thrashing behind her. And then his high-pitched scream.

He'd need those unlimited lives.

Jogging left, she snagged the first weapon, a bow and quiver of arrows.

At her best pace, at this low level of play—another sop to Riggs—it took three hours to reach the boat. Maybe a bit longer now, she calculated, since she had to pull him with her.

She could see him, stumbling along with the knife in his hand. Until a snake—sapphire this time—dropped out of a tree and sank fangs in his neck.

After she'd used the bow to take out a stalking tiger, its counterpart eviscerated Riggs.

His screams echoed as she grabbed a thick vine to swing over the snake pit. In practice, she'd lost a life falling into that pit more than once, so she tested her weight on the vine before taking the swing.

Fangs skidded along her boots, and those boots fought for purchase on the other side on slick grass.

Overcoming the obstacle gave her a power burst, and she used it to start the climb up the rocks near the Temple of Bones.

A risk, she knew, as skeletal hands would reach for her. But the quicksand usually proved riskier. Her hands ached, bled, nearly slipped. Bony fingers clamped over her wrist, nearly snapped it before she hacked those fingers into dust.

Her boots stamped on another hand as she inched her way up and up until, with sweat rolling down her face, she reached the top.

Scoring a health boost, she took the time to heal, and strategize.

Though her throat burned, she only sipped water. She could take the time to detour and refill, but Edina gave out her first rumble. While Ray thrashed in quicksand, she continued on.

Sweaty and breathless, she reached the rope bridge over the Rage. The river churned over jagged rocks, a fifty-foot drop that would cost her a life if she fell. But the fall, the swinging, unstable planks weren't the only perils.

She knew the perils of rushing from previous gameplay, so took careful steps. The attack of a bird of prey had her fighting for balance as she swung her sword. She decapitated the bird, but its razor-edge wing scored her shoulder.

The shock of pain dropped her to her knees, and she nearly spilled off the bridge. Flattening, gripping a broken plank, she used her last health boost.

She wouldn't make it across with her head swimming and her left arm nearly useless. And she'd lose Riggs. He'd pull out, pull away if she lost her focus.

By the time she reached the other side, took a stingy sip of water, she regretted not taking that detour to refill.

But Edina's rumble now shook the ground.

And Riggs, she noted, had just been gored by a wild boar.

His shrieks barely sounded human.

"You suck at this, Ray."

She had to make her descent—perilous, of course, but the beach and the boat waited below.

As she started down, Edina spewed fire. Thea clung to the rock wall, gripping until her fingers bled. She'd forgotten the climbing gloves in her vest again.

Rookie mistake.

But she made her way down, foothold by handhold, as flaming balls of rock flew out of the volcano, crashed into the jungle, onto the beach head, into the Rage.

She sprinted across the sand, untied the boat. Engaging the motor, she sped away and watched the island burn behind her. Waves of heat slapped the air. Panicked animals raced toward the sea, some burning as they ran.

Thea gave the sharks a wide berth, then pulled to shore on Sanctuary Island.

He'd never gotten out of the jungle.

"Stay out of my head, Ray. Stay clear of me or I'll bring you back to this. Or worse, I'll bring you back and keep you there.

"You can wake up now. Game over."

She rolled over in bed, checked the time.

Three hours and thirty-six minutes. And she felt every second of it. Her head ached, her muscles throbbed, her throat screamed with thirst.

But she'd made her point, to Riggs, to herself.

She could hurt him, and she would, without hesitation, without mercy.

Rising, she got a bottle of ibuprofen, took three, and downed two glasses of water. Though she didn't expect he'd try anything tonight, and hopefully never again, she hung her charm bag, and the two more she'd made.

She said the words.

Then slipped back into bed and into quiet dreams.

Chapter Eighteen

As June bumped into July, Ty decided to take that walk to the little farm down the road. It seemed much less stressful than facing the terrifying Ready to Assemble on the play set he'd bought Bray.

Hand him an instrument, he'd figure out how to play it. Hand him a hammer, and very bad things happened.

Given it was Saturday, he had to hope he wouldn't interrupt Lucy's work. Besides, she'd said to bring Bray, and seemed to mean it.

And his boy brimmed with excitement over the whole thing.

"Moo!" Bray strutted down the side of the road. "Pet the cow!"

There, Ty reserved judgment.

"Goat says naaaaa! Pet the goat."

"Maybe. Let's wait and see."

Did goats bite?

"Chickens go cluck, cluck. More chickens. Doggies, too, Daddy."

"So I hear."

Maybe, considering, the play set assembly would be less hazardous. But since he caught sight of the house, too late to turn back.

Nice place, he decided. It looked sturdy and homey and like it had been there forever.

Bray raised his arms. "Up!"

And ten paces later, wiggled. "Down!" As the dog mountain and two long-eared dogs ran around the house.

"Hold on a minute."

They stopped short of the road and wagged. Then, when Ty got close enough, sniffed at his shoes, his pants legs, and wagged some more.

"Okay, but we don't know if these two are used to kids, so let's be careful."

Bray's idea of careful was to try to grab all three dogs at once, laugh like a lunatic, and end up on the ground buried in dogs.

"Danger Guy. I'm raising Danger Guy."

"We run now!" And Bray took off so all three dogs ran after him.

When he squealed, Ty's heart stopped. Then went into overdrive as Bray shouted, "Cows," and, shifting directions, went into top speed.

"Braydon, stop! Now!"

The Serious Dad Voice did it, so Bray stopped seconds before the dogs bowled him over again.

"Cows, Daddy!"

"Yeah, I see them." He saw two cows, two really big cows. Two enormous cows behind a board fence that didn't look like it would hold them back if they wanted out.

Did two cows equal a stampede? He didn't want to find out.

"Look, this isn't our house. We have to talk to Miss Lucy first, okay?"

He heard the slap of a screen door, and looked over to see the lady herself on the back porch.

"Sorry," Ty began. "He took off before I could knock. He's got speed."

"So I see. Y'all finish that batch for me while I introduce this young man to Betty Lou and Rosie."

"You're working? I'm sorry again."

"No sorrys for giving me a break and having my grandchildren finish the work. How about we get some grain, Braydon, and you can give Betty Lou and Rosie a little snack?"

"Okay!"

"Now, unless you're interested in livestock, you hand over that boy and go on into the house. Get yourself a cold drink."

"I—"

Bray just reached out for her, made the decision. "Where's the goat?"

"Oh, we'll see Greta, too. I'm going to introduce you to all my girls."

"How come just girls?" Bray asked as Lucy carried him toward a barn.

"Boys don't give milk or lay eggs."

"Why?"

"Now, that's a good question for your daddy later on."

"Great. Yeah, that's great," Ty muttered, and walked to the house.

Clearly, Thea came by her love of gardening—or determination for it—naturally. Flowers and vegetables thrived here, too. And he spotted the goat watching him with its weird eyes from under a lean-to.

She had bottles hanging from branches, like Thea did, and bird feeders, a flower-shaped birdbath.

Another sanctuary.

Then the scent hit him. Another garden, he thought, coming from inside the house. Before he could knock, Rem called out.

"Come on in. We've got our hands full for another minute."

He stepped into the kitchen and saw a smaller kitchen off to the side. Thea, in shorts that set off her legs and a snug tank top that set off the rest of her, poured something bold red into glass jars.

Even wearing gloves that came to her elbows, and some sort of apron, she looked damn good.

Rem had his own set and poured something purple.

"Nearly done," Rem told him, blowing hair out of his eyes. "Got a hefty order in yesterday, so all hands on deck."

Ty stepped a little closer. "That's a lot of candles."

"Speaks to the success of Mountain Magic. Did soap first thing."

Ty saw filled molds on the opposite work counter. A soft pink, a pale purple, with flowers all over them. Or in them.

He slid his hands into his back pockets because he wanted to touch, and figured he shouldn't.

"Hot work."

"It's all that," Rem agreed. "That's the last of mine."

He carried the pot to the sink and started right in on cleaning it. "There's tea in the fridge. Maybe you could get some glasses, some ice and pour some out."

"Sure."

As he did, he heard Bray's voice, high, excited, asking a million questions.

Thea stepped out without the gloves and apron, a little dewy from the heat. And yeah, she looked damn good.

He handed her a glass.

"Thanks. Grammie's got two craftswomen working for her, but one's on vacation, and the other had a family thing this weekend. So."

"All hands on."

"That's right. The soap takes time to cure, so the order's going to almost wipe out her stock. Can't have that." She walked to the screen to look out. "Aren't they having the best time?"

"If your grandmother doesn't mind answering ten thousand questions."

"She always answered mine and Rem's, and never seemed to mind. How's the organizing coming?"

"Almost there. Now I've got a to-be-assembled play set for Bray sitting outside, intimidating me. I thought I might call on that contractor you told me about."

"Knobby?"

"I can do it." Wiping his hands on his jeans, Rem stepped in. "Not handy?"

"Not with tools. A screwdriver is about top of my skill set."

"I'm handy." And Rem rubbed those hands together. "Let me at it."

"Really? I don't want to—"

"He loves that sort of thing. I'm handy, too, if he needs an assistant."

"She is," Rem confirmed. Then grabbed a glass and downed it before going to the door. He shoved the screen open. "Hey, Grammie, Ty's got something needs put together at his place. Thea and I are going down to give him a hand with it. We're all done here."

"That's fine. You leave this boy with me. We haven't finished our visit. Have we, Bray?"

"Uh-uh. I stay with Grammie. Bye!"

"But—"

"You're doing her a favor." Rem slapped Ty on the shoulder. "Got tools? Besides a screwdriver?"

"Not to speak of."

"Mine are in my truck. We'll ride down in it."

* * *

They took over. And after a short period of bafflement, gratitude took over. They obviously knew what to do, how to do it, so delegated him as whatever came just below apprentice.

More, they clearly enjoyed the work, and beyond that, working with each other. As he carted precut lumber, tools, hardware, he tried to come up with a project he and his sister or his brother had done together.

And couldn't come up with one.

They got along fine, he reminded himself. But it seemed to him Thea and Rem shared a different kind of bond.

Not so surprising, really, he decided, considering how and when they'd lost their parents.

After a couple hours, Ty could see the bones of it, and concluded Bray would have started high school, possibly graduated, before he'd have finished it.

"I didn't realize it was so . . . much. He's just one kid."

"You're going to have more coming around once they see this. Got this little rock wall going, the swings and slide. Got your pretend grill down here—once we get to it. And that majorly cool upper deck clubhouse."

Grinning at it, Rem swiped sweat off his forehead with his forearm. "I'd've been all over this as a kid. Hell, I'm going to be all over it now."

"He's going to love it," Thea confirmed. "And it's good and sturdy. And here comes the lucky boy now, so you can get his opinion."

Bray's squeal said it all as he raced ahead of Lucy. "Wanna swing!"

"Not yet. It's not ready."

"Made progress." Lucy set a picnic basket on Miss Leona's old picnic table. "And isn't that going to be something? What a good daddy you've got. We figured it was time for the construction crew to take a lunch break, didn't we, Bray?"

"I had ham and biscuits and pie!"

"And we've got more."

"Perfect timing." So declaring, Rem set down his drill, winked at Bray. "If you talk Grammie into helping, we'll have you swinging by suppertime."

Somehow, they did.

With the three of them working, and his minimal help and steady supply of cold drinks, Bray had his debut swing by suppertime. He followed that up by clambering like a monkey up the little rock wall, hauling himself onto the upper deck and into the clubhouse, wheeing his way down the slide.

Almost as giddy as his son, Ty took pictures with his phone.

"One more favor? Could you all stand over there, in front of it? Crew shot."

After they posed for him, he tucked his phone away. "I'm never going to be able to thank you enough."

Thea glanced back to where Bray came down the slide again, laughing all the way.

"I think that does the job, right there."

"I'd offer to make dinner, but that feels more like punishment than reward. How about I take everybody out to dinner?"

"Oh, I appreciate that, Tyler." Behind Thea's back, Lucy took Rem's hand and squeezed. "But Rem and I, we've got a little business to work on over dinner tonight."

"Yeah, right. But I'm in for a serious rain check on that."

"Come on, drive your grammie home. We've got animals to feed. And you?" She crouched, crooked a finger at Bray. "You come see me again real soon."

"Bring my trucks."

Ty watched his son throw his arms around Lucy's neck.

She hugged him back, then rose to kiss Ty's cheek. "You've got a bright little jewel there, Tyler."

"I know. I— He's careful who he hugs like that."

She just smiled. "Grammies are easy to hug. Take me home, Rem."

When they walked around to Rem's truck, Ty turned to Thea. "Are you up for dinner?"

"I did hear something about pizza before." She nodded at Bray, currently heading up to slide yet again. "But you might have a hard time breaking him away from his new boy palace."

"Pizza would do it."

"Then give me about thirty minutes to feed Bunk and the chickens, clean up a bit. I'm in for pizza. Come on, Bunk."

The pizza bribe worked well enough, with the added incentive of a promised nighttime swing, for Ty to cart Bray into the shower with him for a quick cleanup.

When he drove up to Thea's, she came straight out. She'd changed into long pants and a shirt and looked as fresh as if she'd spent the whole day sitting in the shade reading a novel and sipping her amazing lemonade.

As she slid into the passenger seat, she filled the car with the scent of female. Subtle and intriguing.

And made him wonder when he'd last driven anywhere with a woman who wasn't related to him.

She shifted to look at Bray in his car seat.

"What kind of pizza do you like?"

"I like pizza."

"Me, too."

"I like pepperoni."

"Me, too! This bodes very well."

"Sometimes Daddy gets vegbles on it." He made an *ick* face.

"You know, Grammie does that sometimes, too. I just don't understand it. What's better than pepperoni pizza?"

"That's not helping."

She shrugged at Ty. "True facts matter. Did you have a good time at Grammie's?"

"I petted the cows and the goat. Doggies chased sticks. She had trucks! We played trucks."

"Rem's trucks. I see you have a truck with you."

"Monster truck."

In town, Ty parked, then dealt with extracting Bray from the car seat. Though traffic barely existed, he kept Bray on his hip while they crossed to the restaurant.

Inside, the siren's call of Italian cooking filled the air. And a summer Saturday night crowd filled plenty of tables and booths.

Since he knew the routine, Ty led the way to a four-top, grabbed a booster seat for Bray. Then, reading Thea's amusement, shrugged.

"We've been here a few times."

"I think they started up when I was about eight. I've been here more than a few. Hi, Pru."

"Hey there, Thea." The server with her bob of blond hair and pink nose stud put a coloring sheet and box of crayons in front of Bray. "We got your trucks tonight."

"I color trucks!"

"Bray?"

"Thank you," he remembered to say.

"You bet. Get y'all started with a drink?"

"Wine?" he asked Thea, and ordered two glasses of red at her nod and ice water for Bray. "Pepperoni pizza?"

"Braydon and I are soul mates there. You do as you will."

"Pepperoni pizza," Ty told Pru. "Large."

"I'll get that right in for you."

When Pru stepped back, she caught Thea's eye, pressed a hand on her heart, and rolled her own.

"How did a game designer learn how to use an electric drill like that?"

Thea shifted her attention back to him. "I could say life on the farm, which probably refined it. But my parents were handy. He was an architect and she an interior designer—well, exterior, too. They had a business together, and were hands-on. We were always around tools."

"I take it you weren't?"

"I don't think anyone in my family's ever held a drill. Doctors, lawyers, businesspeople, like that."

"But musical?"

"Not especially. Your basic piano lessons, and my sister played the viola for about five minutes. Thanks," he said when Pru brought the drinks.

"It's funny, isn't it? We're a musical family, and my uncle Waylon's made a career there. But otherwise, it's just a pastime for the rest of us. Caleb's pulled that out in a few roles, but he's never spotlighted it. And you, mostly nonmusical family? Apparently you hoarded all the talent."

"I made a blue truck."

Thea looked down at the drawing paper. "An excellent blue truck. Not all the artistic talent," she corrected.

"Thea!"

Maddy, hair a little wild, eyes very tired, arrowed from the door to the four-top. "Hey, Ty, hey, kiddo. Nice truck. Can I sit a second?"

She dropped into the chair next to Thea's. "And have a sip of this. It's been one."

She snagged Thea's wineglass, took one deep sip.

"Let me get you one," Ty said.

"Would you? Gratitude. Arlo's meeting me here. He's just finishing up. I escaped."

"Busy at the clinic today?" Thea asked.

"Get that right there." Maddy pointed to a spot between the curve of her neck and shoulder.

Shifting, Thea used her thumbs to go after the knot.

"Busy? No more than usual for a Saturday, until Alley Greer waddled in at about four, in labor, in the late stages thereof."

Maddy circled her head. "Thanks, that got it."

"Everyone okay?" Thea asked.

"Perfect baby girl, eight pounds, three ounces. But we had a scramble. She walked in after putting in a full day at the store, even though I told her it was time to take leave two weeks ago. But money's tight. Anyway, ready or not, that baby was coming.

"Thanks, Pru." Maddy lifted the glass Pru brought to Ty. "Thank you."

"I'd say you earned it."

"Boy, did I. We. Quirt—that's her man—he comes running in, as she called him when she was making her way down to us. He's panicked, and he hyperventilates five seconds after he rushes in and sees what's what. And keels over like a felled tree."

"Oh, Maddy." Thea laughed.

"Oh yeah. Now we've got Quirt out cold on the floor with a knot on his head the size of a golf ball, and Alley pushing the baby out, and crying 'cause she thinks he's dead—Quirt, that is. It's just me and Arlo at that time because everyone had gone home for the day."

She took another long drink. "So I stick with Alley, Arlo's dealing with Quirt and telling Alley how Quirt's just passed out is all. Then the baby comes, adds a nice set of lungs to the mix."

"How's Quirt?"

"Head like a rock, so he'll be fine. Arlo brought him around, got him up. Quint takes one look at the baby, bawls like one himself."

Maddy sighed as Thea felt most of the hard day slide off her friend's shoulders.

"A sweetness to that," she added. "But I boot him out before what happens after the baby comes happens so he doesn't pass out again."

"Babies poop in diapers," Bray informed them, and colored another truck.

"They do, all right. Good thing we had some on hand. After everything's said and done, we call Alley's mama. She's going to look after the three of them, so Arlo's driving them on home."

She drank again. "And how was your Saturday?"

"It feels somehow uneventful."

Smiling, Maddy settled back. "I'd like one of those sometime."

When the pizza arrived, Maddy started to slide out. "Let me get out of your way."

"Sit," Ty told her. "If delivering a baby doesn't earn pizza, nothing does."

Pleased, Thea closed her hand over Maddy's. "What did they name her?"

"Carleen Rose, after both their mamas. I don't want to horn in more than I have. Arlo's coming along in a few minutes."

"I'll get another chair."

When he got up to do just that, Maddy looked over at Thea. "I'm sorry. My mouth just ran."

"Don't be. This is nice. It's perfect." She took a slice off the serving pan, slid it onto a plate. "Here you go, Bray. The correct kind of pizza."

It turned into a little party when gangly, goateed Arlo arrived. More pizza, more wine, talk of new babies and play sets and monster trucks.

Ty relaxed into it. Small-town life, he supposed, had moments like this, if you decided to take them. He could give Bray this if they stayed. Good neighbors, a pizza place where a waitress knew a kid liked trucks, a visiting dog, a kind of honorary grandmother just down the road, a small school where an active, energetic boy would surely make friends.

A good place to raise kids, Lucy had said. It felt like it.

And, bonus, a quiet, private place to work.

The scale grew heavier on that side of things nearly every day.

Bray's eyes drooped by the time Ty strapped him back into his car seat. And still, he managed a slurry, "Nighttime swing."

"That's right, pal."

"He's already out," Thea murmured when Ty came around and got behind the wheel.

"Yeah, and he'll wake up about midnight, I figure, come in, and remind me I promised he could have a nighttime swing."

"And you'll take him out?"

"A promise is a promise."

She could imagine it, the father dragging himself out of bed to push his little boy on a swing under the stars.

"Grammie was right. He has a good daddy."

"He's everything."

"Exactly how it should be."

He glanced over. "I like your friends."

"Me, too. Do you miss yours? You were friends, not just bandmates."

"Still are friends—the best I've ever had. And yeah, sometimes, I miss just dropping down, having a beer, sharing a pizza. Everybody's busy, that's how it works. But we connect. We did a video call just yesterday. Mac's got his solo tour coming up, Scott's lady's expecting their second in January, and he's working on a book about Code Red—God help us all—and Blaze just signed to do a guest shot on a pilot. Some streaming show about werewolves."

"Well, I'll be all over that."

"You're a werewolf fan?"

"I wonder about anyone who isn't. Do you miss performing?"

"Now and again." His gaze flicked to the rearview mirror, and back to his son.

"If the breeze is right, I hear you playing. Faint, like dream music. And it's lovely. So that's almost a performance—for one."

"I'll take it. What I don't miss is touring. Mac thrived on it, so he's the first to go back into it. For me? It's nice knowing where you are when you wake up."

"Nice, I imagine, to walk into a pizza parlor and be able to eat like everyone else."

"You're not wrong. And it was nice to have you there. I'm getting a grill," he added as he turned into the lane and continued up. "Once I do, I want your family over. I can cook a steak on the grill. Steak, burgers, dogs. Haven't mastered chicken, but I will."

"My family's always ready for a summer barbecue. I really enjoyed this, all of it. Play set through pizza."

"So did I."

She opened her door, slipped out. "Good night, Ty."

"Good night."

He waited, heard the dog let out a woof as she walked to the door. Then she was inside.

He drove back down the lane, carried his sleeping boy into the house, and put him to bed.

Though the clock read closer to one, Bray remembered. As a promise mattered, Ty dragged himself up and gave his wide-awake son that nighttime swing.

Up on the rise, lights glimmered—those little lights she had on the trees on her front lawn, he thought, and a stronger one he thought must be from a window.

He wondered if Thea kept one on through the night, or if she worked late.

Either way, he liked seeing those lights shine from up the lane.

Chapter Nineteen

Through the long, bright days of July, Riggs stayed out of her head.

Thea decided if she could have dreamed a perfect summer, it would flow just like this one. Early mornings working in the gardens, then hours spent on a new project she believed in.

And now knew, from very personal experience, offered damn exciting gameplay.

Add flowers blooming in the sun, and soft rains slaking their thirst. They offered a bounty she could bring indoors and spread throughout her home.

And now and again, a wild and windy storm to blow in and leave the air sparkling clean.

She had her green hills with their mystical hint of blue rising, and wildflowers popping in sun spots on the floor of the woods.

Her quiet was disturbed in the best way with a boy's giddy laughter or music, sometimes both, carrying up to her on warm breezes.

With all that, she could mark July down as close to idyllic.

True to his word, Ty had her, Lucy, and Rem for steaks on the grill. Rem brought sweet corn fresh from the field, and Thea new potatoes from her garden roasted in homemade butter.

But Lucy's apple stack cake proved the biggest hit with the new neighbors.

"So yummy," Bray declared, and stuffed more in his mouth. "Grammie cake is yum."

"Grammie cake's freaking awesome."

Bray's eyes danced as he echoed his father. "Freaking awesome."

"Nobody makes an apple stack cake like Grammie," Rem agreed. "Thea comes close, but Grammie sets the bar."

"I've been making them, well, too many years to count. My mama taught me, then decided mine beat hers, so she said: *Lucy, you top your mama, so that's your doing now. I retire.* God knows she had enough to handle after my daddy passed—young, like my Zachariah. The mines took them both young. So I did most of the baking."

"You're better at it than Gran. And if you tell her I said that," Rem continued, "well, I'll run for the hills."

"Better run fast. She may not catch you, but if something comes to hand to throw, she'll knock you flat. Always had an arm on her, and deadly aim with it."

"Where is she now?" Ty asked.

"In Atlanta, living the high life with her second husband. Married, good lord, near to forty years now. A sweetheart of a man, and one with deep pockets who worships the ground she walks on."

"And you stayed."

"This is home for me. It never quite was for my mama after she lost Daddy. You'll meet them at Christmas. Everyone comes for Christmas."

"Santa comes here?"

"Why, of course he does, Bray. I can tell you he dotes on sugar cookies. And in that area, Thea's beat mine, so she'll give you some to set out for him this year."

"I'll do that," Thea agreed, "but it's best if you help me make them."

"I don't know how to."

"We're not big bakers."

Thea just smiled at Ty. "Then it's best you both help me. Santa knows when love and fun go into them. Rem and I baked them with my mom, and it was always fun."

"Where's your mom?" Bray asked her.

"She's in heaven."

"My mom went there, too. But I was a baby and don't 'member."

"She remembers you."

"Okay." Then he looked down at his plate. "Where'd my cake go?"

Laughing, Ty drilled a finger in his belly, then cut him another small slice.

"Are you going to play that banjo you brought along with you, Lucy?"

"I was hoping you'd ask. I'm betting you've got a guitar inside."

"I've got twelve. I can't seem to stop."

"Well, you go pick one. I say you and me sit on the porch and make some music while these two clear up the rest of the table."

While Bunk entertained Bray, Lucy took a chair on the porch, tuned up her banjo. Ty brought out a guitar.

"My goodness, that's a fine instrument."

"No matter how many I end up with, when I want acoustic, I reach for the Hummingbird." He fiddled with the tuning. "You start. I'll catch up."

"Since we're sitting where we're sitting, we'll play to that." Lucy sent him a wink and a smile. "Now, let's see what you've got, boy."

She hit the quick and fast notes of "Foggy Bottom Breakdown," and had Ty giving a low whistle.

"You don't fool around."

But he found the rhythm and the key, and went for it.

"Listen to that," Thea murmured. "Whoever thought Grammie'd sit on the porch of Miss Leona's place having a session with Tyler Brennan?"

"They sound damn good. That's the first I've heard about Bray's mother."

"I know. Is it harder to remember or not to?" Thea shook her head. "I wouldn't trade a single memory for anything, but he's such a happy kid."

"He's all that. So, now you know, field's clear."

"What field?"

"Don't be thick." Rem tapped his knuckles on her head.

"Don't be stupid," she shot back. "He's looking for a friend. Friends."

"I'm friends with women. Still want some touch."

Ignoring him, she wrapped the rest of the cake.

Lucy segued into "I'll Fly Away" as Thea stepped out. And added her voice.

"Somebody's got pipes," Ty commented.

With another wink, Lucy looked at Thea. "Take the harmony, darling."

"I'll fly away, oh Glory."

"More than one somebody." Then Ty shook his head as Rem stepped out, added his voice to the old mountain hymn.

"You're a hell of a trio."

"We've been at it since they were about your boy's age. Let's hear one of yours, Tyler. This time I'll catch up."

Thea recognized the song from the first bar.

"Just One."

"Just one breath," he sang in that easygoing tenor. "Just one look."

It didn't surprise her when her grandmother found notes to pluck to fill in. But it did when Lucy knew the words and sang with him.

"And I was lost, that's all it took."

And it took her back, Thea thought, and brought her here, to the moment all at the same time.

She watched something weave between the woman who'd given her home and the man who'd once filled a young girl's dreams. It was lovely to see that connection twine together.

"How about we switch?" He held the guitar out to Lucy.

"Oh my, I've never held an instrument so fine."

She passed him her banjo. "Do you know what to do with that one?"

"Oh, I know a few things." To make her laugh, he played the opening of "Dueling Banjos."

"I'm going to take that challenge."

They played, faster, faster, until even Bray stopped running to come closer and listen.

"Where'd you learn the banjo?"

Ty just shrugged. "Just sort of picked it up along the way."

"You picked it up mighty fine. My daddy taught me, and my uncle, that'd be Michael John Riley, could handle a guitar. Their sister, my aunt Mae, she burned up a fiddle, I swear. Plenty of nights we sat on the porch just like this and played half the night. A little sipping whiskey, or moonshine if Michael John brought a jug. Those were some days."

She sat back, sighed. "You've brought some good memories back, Ty, and given me some brand-new ones to hold. I'm taking them home with me."

"How about one more, just to cap it off. Your bluegrass again."

"All right. You may know this one from the movie, but it goes back a lot farther."

As before, Thea knew the song from the first guitar riff, and clapped her hands as Lucy belted out "I Am a Man of Constant Sorrow."

She gave Rem an elbow bump, and they joined for the response, in harmony, while Ty picked the banjo.

"Great song, great movie," Ty said at the end.

"And the right ending of a happy time." Lucy traded instruments again. "Thank you, gentlemen, for your hospitality." After passing Rem the banjo, she scooped Bray up for a hug, then wrapped her arms around Ty. "You're making a fine home here. A home's brighter, I think, when it's got plenty of books, plenty of music in it."

Then she cupped Ty's face in her hands. "Miss Leona was a smart woman. Rem, if you're staying, I can walk on home."

"I leave with the girl I came with." He closed her banjo in its case, lifted it. "Thanks, Ty. You've got some grill there. When I build my place, I'm getting one to match it. Need a lift, Thea?"

"Bunk and I are fine walking. I'll walk off that meal, and he'll walk off all the scraps people snuck him when they thought I wasn't looking. Night, Grammie."

She turned back to Ty. "And she's right, as always. This was a very happy time in the fine home you're making. Thanks for all of it."

Before she could call the dog, Ty sat again. "Know this one?"

At the opening chords, she laughed. "I know them all, from my stalker days."

"Sing it with me. From the morning light till the dark of night, it's always you."

"Always you, ever you. Through the rain, all through the pain, it's always you."

"Always you," Ty sang, watching her, "ever you. Key change, take the lead."

"When I can't see through the tears and I'm lost in all my fears, I turn to you. And you, you open your arms to me, you bring out the best in me."

"Always you, ever you."

He took the next verse, and they merged voices on the refrain.

When they sang the last note, he set the guitar aside.

"You never thought of doing something with that?" He tapped his throat.

"I just did."

"I mean professionally."

"No, that's not for me. I like singing on the porch, or in the parlor. I'm not shy really, but performing, seriously, that takes a different kind of skill and drive and need, I guess. I don't have it. I like the quiet."

"I hear that. Can I get you another glass of wine?"

"No, thanks. Plus, our kids are tired out."

He followed her direction, saw Bray curled up with the big dog on the deck of the porch. "He's like a light switch. On, then off."

They made a sweet picture, she thought, the boy and the dog. She'd take it with her.

"You need help getting him into bed?"

"No. It's routine." Bending, he picked up his boy, laid the limp weight of him over his shoulder.

"You're good at it." She leaned in to kiss Bray's head. Before she could back away, Ty took her arm. And took her mouth with his, lightly, very lightly. But he lingered while her heart did one long, slow roll inside her.

"I hope you don't mind."

"I don't." But, a little wobbly, she stepped back. "I don't mind. Come on, Bunk, time for home. Good night, Ty, and thanks for everything."

She laughed at herself as she nearly stumbled off the porch, then turned, walking backward with the laugh still in her eyes.

"Especially that last little thing."

She knew he watched her walk up the lane because she couldn't help herself and opened her mind to it. So she knew he watched her walking as dusk began to settle, and the last lights bled out of the sky.

He watched her as he stood on his back porch with a sleeping boy over his shoulder.

*   *   *

"What kind of a kiss?" Maddy demanded answers as she watched Thea try out different moves for a fight scene. "I mean, was it a good-night-neighbor sort of peck, or an mmm-mmm-baby kiss?"

"Between." Thea swung into a back kick. "Leaning toward good-night-neighbor." She fell back, blocked an imaginary blow, and tried a straight jab. "That's not working."

She paused, hands on hips of workout shorts, closed her eyes. "Roundhouse, better."

"Are you going to follow up?"

"With a jump kick, I think."

"The kiss, girl."

"He's got a kid to think of, Maddy, a boy who lost his mother. And I don't know if she and Ty were together when she died like that, or how long ago it happened. His life after Code Red's not just a closed book, it's padlocked."

"Not to you." Maddy waved a hand in the air. "I know, I know. Your willpower defeats me. Tell me this. Do you want to follow up?"

Giving up on the choreography, Thea sat on the porch steps with Maddy. "I'm saying this not as the teenager with a crush, but as me right now. Oh yeah, I do. I really like who he is. Kind, caring, funny, private. I like the way he puts Bray first, and not like it's duty. Because it's love. But."

Shaking her head, she laughed. "Singing with him like that. The saturated romance of that song, sunset, all of it. Well, she's still in there, that girl, and she was starstruck."

"What's wrong with that?"

"I don't know that there is anything wrong with it. It just is."

Reaching over, Maddy gave Thea's braid a tug. "Have you been sleeping okay?"

"Yes, don't worry about that, Dr. McKinnon. I'm pretty sure I scared the bastard off."

"Pretty brilliant, using a game. Mind game—get it?"

"Ha. It was a stupid risk, but I was so pissed. And it worked, so I'll say worth it. I've got to work out this fight. It's key."

"I'll let you get back to your brutality. I just came by because I'd dropped off Lucas and Rolan to play with Braydon."

"You what?"

"Will's boy Lucas is just five, Gracie's Rolan'll be five in a couple months. Bray needs some pals."

"You just dumped them down there?"

"What do you take me for?"

"Madrigal McKinnon, steamroller."

Lips pursed, Maddy nodded. "I'm not ashamed of that title. But I asked first."

Thea shoulder-bumped her. "And who says no to you?"

"Hardly anybody. And the hardly doesn't last long. Now we'll see how he handles three preschoolers for a couple hours. Marta's picking them up later. I can't believe she and Will are having another. Anyway, I took an hour off to perform my good deed, and I have to get back."

She rose, stretched. "And Sunday, just FYI, I'm moving in with Arlo."

"What?" Thea jumped up. "You didn't lead with that? You're really doing it. You said maybe in the fall."

"So I upped the schedule. I had to cave sometime. That man is quietly relentless."

"I call it patience."

"Po-tay-toe, po-tah-toe."

"I'm happy." She swung her arms around Maddy and squeezed. "This makes me happy. No! The word is *jubilant*. This makes me jubilant."

"I swore I wouldn't get married, if I did, until I was thirty-five."

Thea threw out her hands. "You're talking marriage now? I'm about to go from happy to jubilant to ecstatic!"

"No, well, he is." Maddy huffed out a breath. "And he'll win because I love the relentless son of a bitch."

"He's handsome," Thea pointed out. "Smart, kind, funny. And I believe you've indicated you're sexually compatible. Those were all on your list."

"Yeah, the man checks the boxes. I said I'd think about it after we lived together for a year, but I figure—and I know he figures because he knows me—I've got six months max before I cave on that."

"I think you completed your quota of many boyfriends along the way."

Maddy smiled a smug smile. "I did that."

"And you found your handsome, smart, kind, and all the rest, all rolled into Arlo Higgins."

"Not gonna lie. I did that, too. I've got to get back, even though I know I'll catch him gloating between appointments. And you? You should follow through. I've got next Wednesday off," she said as she walked away. "Let's do something."

"Shop for wedding dresses!" Thea called out.

Still walking, Maddy shot up her middle finger.

She didn't follow through. She knew how, of course, but felt any follow-through might be inappropriate at best, unwelcome at worst. And she had to consider the clash of her own feelings, those of the giddy teenage girl, and those of the cautious woman.

The girl? That was fantasy and easily dismissed. The woman? The here and now attraction was very real. And yet, he was a man building a new life in a new place with a child at the center.

And she was a woman with baggage, and secrets.

She heard his music almost daily, saw him now and again when she took a walk to clear her head. Her life stayed quiet and busy, as she liked it.

After two solid days of rain, the sort of days that urged her to burrow in and work as if the world didn't exist outside the game, she shut everything down.

"I see sunshine, Bunk. You go on out in it. I'm going to clean myself up." Swiveling in the chair to rub the dog, she caught sight of herself in the mirror.

"Well, God! I look like something the cat wouldn't bother to drag in."

She jogged upstairs to strip off the clothes she'd slept in. A long shower drained away the two days of rain, the work, the grab-and-go food she'd eaten at her workstation.

When she started to question the levels of play, she pushed it away. Let it sit, let it simmer, she told herself as she dressed. She'd take this glorious afternoon off, and run it all through again tomorrow.

Leaving her hair loose to dry in the sun, she started to put on boots for a hike in the hills. Then changed that to sneakers.

Since she hadn't seen a soul since she'd had lunch and gone shopping with Maddy—no wedding dresses—she knew she needed people again.

Outside, she rounded up Bunk. "Let's go see Grammie."

He knew the name, and ran in a happy circle before they started down the lane.

Halfway down, she spotted Ty on his back porch. He played a different guitar—a sleek black electric. Since she heard nothing, she assumed the sound ran through the headphones he wore.

Though Thea took her time, Bunk charged ahead. They'd hit about the usual time for his afternoon visit, one he'd missed on the rainy days. She'd planned to invite Bray to walk to Grammie's with her, but didn't see him.

And Ty, obviously deep in the music, didn't see Bunk's charge until the dog bounded onto the porch.

"Whoa. Hey, big guy."

"Sorry," Thea called out as Ty took off the headphones. "He's looking for his friend."

"Yeah, got that. He's crashed. Naps don't come around here often, but he's been up since . . . I don't want to think about it."

"We're just heading down to my grandmother's. The rain holed us up for a couple days."

"Tell me." His fingers worked on the silent strings as she walked closer. "We played *Adventures in Endor* five million times. I could hate you for that. But then I'd have to hate the Marvel Universe, Disney, *Sesame Street*, the makers of Candy Land, and a variety of cars, trucks, and construction vehicles.

"Too much energy."

"Rainy days and preschoolers."

"Make me want to beg my parents for forgiveness."

"You're working." She nodded toward a pile of sheet music with handwritten notes and lyrics. "We'll get out of your way."

"No—if you've got a minute. You're an actual adult human, and I started to wonder if I was the only one of those left on the planet."

"We've got a minute. Want to talk politics, world events, environmental issues?"

"Really don't. But I did want to . . . about the other night."

"It was great." She stepped onto the porch, took a seat.

Bunk deserted her to wander out to the play set and sniff for Bray.

"I wanted to say, with Bray, the move—it's looking like a serious move. I mean, I bought a new couch, and I'm looking into pre-K, so—"

"You have your hands full," she finished. And why, she thought, did she find him even more appealing for setting up boundaries?

"There's that. And . . . Bray mentioned his mother died. You've never asked about her. Any of you."

"It's for you to say or not. My family knows about loss, and how personal it is."

"Yeah, you would." Though his fingers stilled, he continued to hold the guitar. "She was a roadie on our last tour. Starla. She changed her name to that, legally. I don't know the name she was born with. She'd never say. Anyway, we were together for a while, toward the end of the tour, then back in Philadelphia. Nothing serious, just . . ."

"I'm an adult human," Thea reminded him. "I understand."

"We got along fine, until we didn't. She got really pissed when we decided to break up. Code Red, I mean. Or take a long break as we thought of it at first. We'd been at it, and hard, for almost ten years. Blaze was a mess—you'd have read about it—stoned more than half the time. Scott had a kid on the way, Mac wanted to try something on his own. I wanted to write and just be for a while. We didn't have a blowup like a lot of the press reported. We just needed a break, so we took it."

"It's a lot of pressure, the traveling, the performing. And so much of your life so public."

"Sounds whiny, but yeah. So rather than blow up, we talked it out, took the break. Blaze got into rehab, and I don't know if he would have otherwise. But Starla liked the rush, and wasn't going to give it up. She took off—no hearts broken."

"You didn't know," Thea realized. "You didn't know about Bray."

"She didn't either, not when she took off. That's what she told me when she came back, when Bray was eighteen months old. I believed her. When she found out she was pregnant, she'd been with a couple other guys, so wasn't sure who, you know? But she decided having a kid would be an adventure. She liked the rush," he murmured.

"He looks just like you."

"Yeah, there's that. She said he came out looking like me, so she put my name on the birth certificate. I'm grateful she did, even went to a lawyer, drew up papers, but that was later, after she found out she was terminal."

"I'm so sorry."

"Fuck cancer." He hissed out a breath. "She hadn't bothered with screenings, doctors, any of it, until it was too late. She said they'd given her six months, and she couldn't take care of Bray anymore, and she hands me this baby who looks back at me with my own eyes. She stayed a few days, then left a note, how Braydon was the one pure thing she'd done in her life."

"That had to be so hard for her."

"Yeah, she loved him. No question there." Absently, his fingers tapped the guitar strings as he spoke. "She didn't get the six. She had a hospice volunteer write me when she died, four months after she brought Bray to me."

"She knew you. She knew you'd look after him, love him, give him a home. She did what mothers do, the best she could for her child."

"I would've helped her. It still sits raw. She didn't have to die alone."

"She knew you," Thea repeated. "She knew that, and made a choice."

"We didn't love each other, not even close. But we made Bray."

"And there you were, all at once, with a toddler."

"Oh yeah." His fingers tapped the guitar strings again. "Those were some wild days. Wilder nights. I didn't know shit about taking care of a kid. The only thing I knew, absolutely, was I wouldn't expose him to the press, the bullshit stories they'd write about him. But changing diapers, figuring out how to get him to eat—and Jesus, cleaning him up after that? Why's he crying now, what's he trying to tell me, why won't he just go the fuck to sleep?"

She heard it in his voice, felt it from him. "You loved him, right from the start."

"I never knew you could love like that, like everything that ever mattered, ever would, was right there in this little human with a shitty diaper and mashed potatoes in his hair."

"How did your family react?"

"Shock, mixed with *this is what you get for living that life.*"

"You mean the life of a highly respected, award-winning, globally renowned musician?"

"Thanks for that, Code Red groupie."

"Just a minute." She shot a finger at him. "Code Red earned that respect, those awards and renown by working hard and creating damn good music, giving damn good performances. And since you've gone out on your own, the music you've written just glows, whether it rocks hard or flows into ballads. Don't diminish that, or my admiration of it."

He strummed a couple chords. "Well, that ego boost didn't hurt one bit. I don't mean to diminish my family either. They love Bray. Then again, bias aside, he's pretty hard not to love."

"I'd say impossible."

That earned a smile. "We're not like your family, just not woven together that tight. But they helped when I really needed it. They were right there for both of us. I was supposed to be a doctor or lawyer, or some kind of suit-and-tie guy, and I let them down there. That's the way it is," he said before Thea could object. "I ditch college for a guitar, take off to do exactly what I wanted. But they helped when I needed it.

"And here we are."

"Can I ask how they feel about where you are?"

"Ambivalent. My parents feel I'll get tired of living here just like— because they never understood what I did or what it took to do it—I got tired of recording, performing. Then I'll come back, put Bray in a good private school, get properly married, and get a respectable career started."

Her smile was both sympathetic and bolstering. "You're going to let them down again."

"Yeah, I am. Can I ask you how Lucy felt when you started game design?"

"When Milken leased the rights to *Endon*, she brought out the champagne she'd bought in hopes and we popped the cork."

"And there you go. Woven together tight. I want that with Bray."

"Oh, Tyler, you have that. You have that with Bray."

"You're good for me."

"Friends should be good for each other."

He looked over, met her gaze, held it until her stomach fluttered, wild butterflies, all the way up to her throat.

She saw the follow-through coming, leaned in to meet it.

The screen door slapped open. Rubbing sleep out of his eyes, hair everywhere, Bray said, "Daddy." Then his eyes popped wide, and he dropped the truck he held in one hand. "Bunk!"

They raced to each other as if war had separated them.

"Usurped by a giant dog."

"I'm going to add to that." Though her pulse still jumped, Thea pushed to her feet. "I'm going to steal your boy and take him and my giant dog to Grammie's."

"You don't have—"

"Try to stop me. You should go back to work."

"Why aren't you working?"

"Because I didn't spend the last two days playing video games, Candy Land and watching *Sesame Street*."

"And *Spider-Man* cartoons."

"Or that." Thea picked up the truck. "Give me a good reason besides *you don't have to*."

"I don't have one."

"All right then. Bray! Do you want to come with Bunk and me to see Grammie?"

"Okay! Bye, Daddy."

"Hey, hey, I get nothing?"

Grinning, Bray raced over, gave a hug, a smacking kiss. "Bye, Daddy."

Ty watched Bray take Thea's hand as they walked away, the giant dog beside him like a guard.

He felt a little pang, but it didn't last. Instead, he unplugged the headphones, turned his amp up a little.

As she walked, Thea heard him playing fast, tricky, unrestrained rock to the hills.

"Daddy plays guitar."

"He sure does." When Bray lifted his arms, she picked him up, set him on her hip for the walk. "He sure does."

Chapter Twenty

After Bray gobbled cookies and filled Lucy in on everything he'd done when it rained and rained, he ran—his usual speed—to see the animals.

Thea sat on the porch with her grandmother to help shell peas. She felt certain Ty knew she'd tell Lucy the story, and she did, quickly, quietly.

"That poor girl. So young. She did a brave and loving thing for her baby."

"I thought the same."

"I hope she can see what a fine job Ty's doing with that child. I thought a lot of Ty before you told me this. I think even more of him now."

As she shelled, she watched Bray talk to old Betty Lou.

"Another man might've said, *Oh no, no, I'm not taking this on, not changing my life, taking on a lifetime responsibility.* Or he might've cursed her, tossed her out. Maybe sent her off with a chunk of money. A lot of other ways it could've been.

"Makes me want to hug them both."

"His parents don't approve of him."

"Of that sweet little boy!"

"No, he said they love Bray. They don't really approve of Ty. Of what he's done with his life."

That didn't lessen Lucy's outrage. "Makes me think even more of him because I think less of who raised him up. That boy's got talent flowing over, and he put it to good use. He still is while raising a happy child all on his own."

"He shrugs it off, but it hurts him a little. I could feel that without trying. I don't know that it's like it was with Dad, but it made me think of how some just can't or won't love and accept who you are."

Amused, and more than a little in love, Lucy watched Bray race to talk to the chickens. "We're not kin, but we'll be family to them."

"He kissed me."

Lucy kept shelling peas. "I don't find that a surprise, honeypot. He looks at you with wondering in his eyes. Did you kiss him back?"

"It was . . . fleeting. I don't want to get mixed up, Grammie. I can remember how intense my feelings were for him when I was sixteen. But that was harmless, fantasy, innocent. Something else is stirring up now."

"Oh, darling, I was just about gone over Harrison Ford back in my day."

"Really?"

"And I still wouldn't turn him away from the door today—especially if he came calling wearing that Indiana Jones hat."

"Is that why you have the complete set of DVDs?"

Lucy sent her a sly, sidelong smile. "A woman's entitled to her fantasies. And a teenage girl, too. You didn't know him, not the man—well, hardly more than a boy himself back then. You knew his music, what they wrote about him, what he said in interviews and such, but that's an image. Now you know him."

"I'm starting to, so something else is stirring up. But I don't know how long Riggs will hold off pushing at me, or how to explain any of that. And I'd have to, wouldn't I? Wouldn't I have to if something comes of what's stirring up?"

"Would you want someone who didn't accept you for who you are?"

"No, but . . . I've been so careful. After I told Asher—"

"You didn't deserve what that boy said, what he did. And he sure as hell didn't deserve you."

"No, I didn't, and no, he didn't. But it left a mark."

Thea's hands worked on the shells as she thought it through. "I've told myself what happened with Asher was, in the long run, a good thing. It taught me to be more careful, and I have been. But I haven't been really serious about anyone since. I think this could be serious, for me."

"You'll do what you need when you need."

Over where Bray talked to the goat, Bunk let out a woof. His tail wagged with it, but he stayed beside the boy.

Lucy chin-pointed as she continued to shell.

"That's Nadine coming down from the hills, both kids in tow." She started to smile in welcome, then her face went to stone. "Goddamn it, she's sporting a black eye. Favoring her left hip."

"I see that."

Thea laid a hand on Lucy's, and together they saw more.

The angry man lashing out, the crying children, the woman weeping as she fell.

"Not for the first time." Lucy's voice rang cold. "And it won't be the last." Sighing, she set the peas aside and rose. "We'll do what we can for her."

She'd gone to school with Rem, Thea remembered. A year behind him, and now she had a little girl about Bray's age, a boy not quite two, and an aura of such resignation clouded over her it broke the heart.

Thea went in to get cookies for the children and sweet tea for their mother.

"Miss Lucy." Nadine shifted the thumb-sucking, towheaded baby on her hip. "I hope we're not disturbing you."

"No such thing. Why, Adalaide, that's the prettiest dress I ever saw."

"Mama made it."

"It's sure pretty. Let me see this little man. My, my, he's growing, isn't he? Curtis Lee, what's that thumb doing in your mouth?"

"I just can't get him to stop, Miss Lucy."

"Because it tastes so good. But look here, Thea's got something for you tastes even better. You sit down, Nadine, have some sweet tea."

"We shouldn't stay, Miss Lucy." Nadine tucked a stray wisp of strawberry blond hair behind her ear. "I was hoping I could get some of that balm you brought up last time, and some oatmeal soap. I got the money."

"You put your money away."

"We can't take the charity."

"Adalaide, this is Braydon. He lives just down the road, in what was Miss Leona's house. Bray, you take Adalaide over and tell her the names of all the chickens you can remember."

"Okay. Can I have a cookie, too?"

Thea handed him one.

"This is Bunk," he told the little girl. "He's the biggest dog in the world. We play fetch."

When the girl walked off with Bray, Lucy nodded. "You let those two children get acquainted, and that's payment. That boy's an honorary grandchild to me, and he needs playmates. Thea, take Curtis Lee. Nadine, you come inside. I'll make a cold poultice for that eye, and I want a look at your hip."

Tears rolled. "He didn't mean it, Miss Lucy. Jed didn't mean it. It's just he'd worked all day, and I hadn't finished the chores and the kids were acting up. I was feeling a little poorly and I didn't have supper ready either."

"And you think that's cause for your husband to use his fist on you?"

"He was sorry after. He didn't mean it."

Lucy handed the baby to Thea. "Come inside. You're carrying again, aren't you?"

"I don't know for sure. Maybe. Am I?"

Thea heard Lucy sigh again as she led Nadine into the kitchen.

Thea jiggled the baby, then carried him over to the coop with the other children to give Nadine and her grandmother privacy.

An hour later, Nadine walked toward home with a basket holding the balm, the soap, some fresh vegetables, some ginger tea for morning sickness, some biscuits and slices of roast chicken to feed her family supper.

"I had to take her money."

Thea rubbed Lucy's shoulder as Bray stood out in the yard waving and calling bye.

"You gave her more than she paid for, and let her keep her pride."

"She'll have another mouth to feed come spring."

"She won't leave him."

"She loves him. He never raises a hand to the children, she says, and I saw that for truth. What he needs is a good talking-to."

"Don't, Grammie."

"No, I know better. Only make it worse for her. I need some brightening. Braydon Brennan! Do you know where carrots come from?"

"Grocery store."

"Before they get there."

At his shrug, a mimic of his father's, she smiled. "Well, I'm going to show you."

Brightening happened when a little boy laughed so hard he fell on his ass in the garden when Lucy pulled up a carrot.

Thea took Bray home with another basket.

"Carrots grow in the ground. Tomatoes don't."

"That's exactly right."

"Peas come in a . . ."

"Shell."

"I like peas. I like carrots. Daddy gets them from the freezer and zaps them. I got so many friends. I got Lucas and Rolan and Adalaide. She's a girl."

"She is?"

"Uh-huh. I run now."

Since they'd reached the lane, Thea set him down, and shook out her arm. The kid had some weight to him.

"Daddy! I got carrots out of the ground!"

"What were they doing there?"

"I dunno, but I got them. And peas that come in a shell. I want peas and carrots for dinner."

"Sure." On the front porch, Ty scooped him up, kissed him.

"Adalaide has red hair, and she's a girl."

"Is she? Who's Adalaide?" he asked Thea.

"A girl about his age. She came down with her mother to get some balm and soap." She held out the basket. "From Grammie."

"Thanks. Ah." He looked inside. "We've got soap, too. And carrots, a couple tomatoes. I think maybe a turnip, an onion."

"I played farmer with Grammie."

"I see that."

"Peas, fresh shelled," Thea added. "In the container there."

"Wow."

"You don't know how to cook fresh peas and carrots."

"Not a clue."

He looked over at her, the tiny dimple coming out as he smiled. As they smiled, Thea corrected, boy and man, twin dimples.

"I was going to toss some burgers on the grill. If I toss one for you, you could demonstrate."

"I'll take a burger as payment, but you have to pay attention. It's not hard."

"So you say." He set Bray down. "Go on, get your trucks."

When the screen door slammed behind him, Ty took Thea's face in his hands. He held her gaze as he had before, then laid his mouth on hers.

No good-night-neighbor this time. Still light, light and slow and dreamily soft. Dreamily enough, Thea lifted her hands, curled them around his wrists as if to keep herself anchored.

"I wanted to finish that, from before. If I kissed you after dinner, you might think it was a thanks for making peas and carrots."

"A thanks for that would be nice, too."

"Come on in." He took her hand. "See my new couch."

After stepping in, she found herself seriously impressed.

He'd gone with a kind of wheat color on a low-slung couch that suited the size of the room, added two chairs in a subtle navy-and-wheat print. He'd arranged them with tables, lamps that said easy, cozy.

In the weeks while he'd put the house in order, he'd given the old wood floors a good lick of polish, spread a rug over it with deeper tones of that wheat, lighter of the blue.

A number of toy vehicles and figures were scattered over it.

"There was a terrible and tragic accident earlier."

"I see that, and I see this is a lot more than a new couch. I know you've been clearing and cleaning, but this is a transformation. And still you've kept some of Miss Leona's little treasures."

She saw the familiar on shelves, the mantel, the tables among framed photos, books, and mementos he must have brought with him.

"You did right by her. Right by Braydon, and made yourself a home. That's an accomplishment."

"It's a start. The walls need paint, and I should've dealt with that before the rest, but . . ."

"You're not ready to have a crew in here."

"Just not. And when I look at paint samples, my brain shuts down, so it'll wait. Meanwhile, Bray wants his room painted red. We're talking fire-engine red. So I'm holding off until I talk him out of it."

"I spent years planning my house, right down to dickering with myself over door hinges. Who notices door hinges? You've done a lot in a month's time. You need some pillows."

His hands slid into his pockets. "But do I really?"

"And a pretty throw for the couch. And right now, we need to peel these carrots."

She started back toward the kitchen, then stopped at what had been a little sitting room. At the moment it held a desk and chair, stacks of boxes.

"Home office-slash-library. Maybe. Not sure."

"A good spot for that."

She walked back to the kitchen, where Bunk sprawled on the floor and Bray used his long, wide back as a road for his truck.

She deemed the kitchen reasonably clean and moderately well organized. But the former dining room with its piano, guitar stands, guitar cases, control board, sound system, music cabinet, needed help.

"You need more space."

"Well, yeah. This works for now. If we hang around, I'll need to add on an actual studio. Maybe take that wall down. I don't know. Depends."

"I'd say it's easier to know and decide after you've lived in the space awhile."

"That's my thinking. Plus, procrastinating."

When he set the basket on the counter, she started unpacking it.

"You can set the oven on 425, and get that peeler."

"And by peeler, you mean?"

She looked over as he turned on the oven. "What you use to peel carrots, potatoes, and the like. I can use a paring knife, but I know Miss Leona had a peeler."

"A paring knife is . . . Okay, I'm messing with you." He opened a drawer, produced a potato peeler. "We also like carrots raw with dip, so peeler."

"All right, see if you can find another. Then all we need for these are butter, pepper, and thyme. The herb."

"I got butter. Not yours because we devoured that, but I've got butter and pepper. The only time I've got comes in minutes."

She shook her head. "Get some scissors and step outside with me a minute."

When he did, she pointed at what remained of Miss Leona's herb patch. "You got thyme right here. This patch needs weeding."

Frowning, Ty just stared at it. "You'd have to know what's a weed and what's a thing, then what the thing is."

"Yes, you would. We can have that lesson after dinner."

She snipped thyme.

As they went in, boy and dog ran out. "We run!"

"Stay where I can see you."

She walked Ty through the process, then slid the dish of carrots in the oven to roast in herbs and butter.

"Got potatoes?" she asked him.

"Sure." Opening a cupboard, he pulled out a box of instant mashed potatoes.

"Absolutely not. Ever. Put that away before I lose all respect for you."

"They're not that bad."

"Away. You're better off telling me you do wet work for the CIA than showing me dried-up boxed potato flakes."

"It was only one job—well, two, but they both had it coming. How about these?" After digging in the freezer, he held up bags. One of Tater Tots, one of frozen fries.

"Tyler, that just makes me sad. We'll go with the fries. I can doctor them up some. Put them back for now. The peas won't take long, but those carrots need a while. We can make the patties. Do you have an egg?"

"I've got a couple left. For what?"

"Since I'm here. We need a bowl for mixing the meat and egg, a little rosemary—you've got a nice little bush out there. Salt, pepper."

"I usually just sort of—" He lifted his hands, opened and closed those long fingers. "Smoosh."

"You can do that, or . . . Why don't you beat up an egg? I'll get the rosemary."

When she came back, she stripped the rosemary from the stem, chopped it fine. Standing hip-to-hip, she showed him how to mix it all in a bowl.

"You always smell so good."

"That's the rosemary."

"It doesn't hurt, but no, it's you. I've got a weakness for women who smell good."

She tipped her face up to his. "I'll have to thank Grammie's soaps and lotions for giving me that advantage."

As he lowered his head, Bray called out from outside the screen door.

"How come you kiss her? She got a hurt?"

"No. I'm kissing her because she's pretty, she smells good, and she's helping make dinner."

"Okay. We're thirsty."

"One sec." He finished the kiss.

By the time he'd washed his hands, filled a cup with water and ice, she'd formed four perfect patties.

"How'd you do that? Mine are more manly, meaning misshapen."

"I guess I have a more delicate, feminine touch."

"You've got something." He looked around the room. "This is nice. Usually kitchen time is a chore for me. Figuring out what to toss in the oven, or the mic or on the grill. Cleaning it all up until I do it again.

"This is nice."

"I like kitchen time. But if I'm not up at Grammie's, or I don't have family or friends over, it's just me. So yeah, this is nice. You need to stir up those carrots."

"I can do that. Stirring up's one of my skills."

Wasn't it just, she thought. He'd stirred her up with no effort at all.

She doctored up the fries, slid them into the oven while he started the grill. Then sliced up one of the tomatoes, fanned it on a small plate.

They sat together at the picnic table, with Ty spooning the peas and carrots onto Bray's plate.

"Why do they look like that?"

"Because they're fresh."

"I don't like fresh."

"You don't know yet. And that's your carrot right there. The one you pulled out of the ground."

Dubious, and Thea saw tears ready, Bray got some on his spoon. "Okay." He took the tiniest bite possible, then another. "It's yum, Daddy. I like fresh."

Ty breathed out. "Crisis averted."

"And Daddy knows how to make them fresh now."

"Thanks." Shooting Thea a look, Ty cut a burger in half, then half again. Added the two quarters and some fries to his son's plate.

"I like fries. These are more yum than yours, Daddy. Bunk's hungry, too."

Thea's mouth dropped open when Ty tossed the dog one of the spare quarters of burger. Bray gave out a gut laugh, then ate more peas and carrots.

"His limit's half." Ty shrugged. "And Bunk's hungry."

"Don't—"

But he'd already tossed the dog the second quarter.

"Bunk likes burgers. I like burgers. It's more yum, Daddy."

Ty sampled his own. "Yeah, it is. Beat an egg with it?"

"And rosemary. Or you can use other herbs. Bray, I bet you can play farmer with your daddy and help weed the herb patch."

"Okay. More." Turning to Ty, Bray opened his mouth.

And when Ty spooned more peas and carrots into that waiting mouth, it plucked every string in Thea's heart.

"More than that?"

"Okay."

Ty added another serving to his plate. "Now look what you've done," he said to Thea. "You're going to put Birds Eye out of business. We used to swear by them."

"Buy some actual potatoes, and I'll show you how to make hand cut fries."

"So, you're after Ore-Ida, too? What's next? Chef Boyardee, Tombstone?"

"One step at a time."

Once Bray cleaned his plate and played chase with Bunk, she helped Ty deal with the dishes.

"He ate three servings of vegetables. That's a record."

"Grammie has more in the garden, and so do I. He's welcome to whatever he'll eat. Listen, I shouldn't've given you a hard time about the frozen and the boxes. It sounded so critical when I—"

"I didn't take it that way." Taking her by the hips, Ty turned her. "And he ate three helpings. Plus, I had someone lifting the heavy weight. I'll weed the damn herb patch."

"Good, that's—"

When he kissed her this time, everything stopped. And everything started. Not so light now, not with the heat rising. His hands slid up her sides, lingered there for five galloping beats of her heart before gliding to her back to draw her closer.

As the kiss went deeper.

She gave herself to it, to the rush of being touched, tasted, wanted. Oh yes, wanted, because beneath the skill of a long, slow, deep kiss, she felt that wanting, and the quickening urgency behind it.

What slept inside her wakened, and answered.

He'd thought of her, too often, too often since that first day she'd rushed down the road toward him behind her mountain of a dog.

But he hadn't meant to do more than think. Complications, so many complications, and risks. But she'd pulled him in by doing no more than being.

And she smelled so damn good.

It had been so long since he'd had a woman's body pressed against his. A woman who not only stirred his needs to life but intrigued him, one he could just talk to. One who at least seemed to understand him.

When she pressed a hand to his shoulder, he made himself ease back. Then she looked at him, those gorgeous blue eyes drowsy and dazed.

"I—"

"Just give me one more minute."

Just one more, he thought as he took her mouth again. One more minute to feel what she could do to him. Hot blood flowing, the sweet aches of need, the rush of images in his mind of how she'd look under him.

He eased back again, but didn't let go.

"I've wanted to do that for a while."

"That's clear. Yeah, that came through." She nudged him, stepped back. "I have to go. I really have to go now or I'll be in trouble. I have to go feed my chickens."

The laugh just rolled out of him. "That's not something a guy usually hears when a woman backs off."

"It's true, and I'm not backing off. Well, I am, right now. Right now, I'm— God." Waving a hand in the air, she took another step back. "Just really . . . I'm usually better at this. I've been better at this."

"If you were any better, I might actually beg. And there's a kid outside."

"Yes, a kid outside. Exactly. I have to go. Um." Dragging a hand through her hair, she looked around. "There. That way." She made it to the door, stopped. "Thanks for dinner."

"You did most of it."

"Right. Good for me." She took a careful breath, then met his eyes. "I'm backing off temporarily and due to circumstances. Just to be clear."

"I got that. I'm saying the same to you."

"All right then, good night. Come on, Bunk."

"Bunk stay."

She lifted Bray up, then nuzzled into the hug he gave her. "Bunk needs his supper, but I'll send him down tomorrow to play."

"Okay." But he wiggled down to throw himself over the dog. "Bye, bye, bye."

As she climbed the lane, her system still sparking, she let her mind flow back to where she saw Ty, his son on his hip, watching her walk home.

And into that tiny opening, Riggs slithered.

"All hot and bothered because the pussy-man stuck his tongue down your throat."

Because she could see him, sitting on his bunk in his cell, the sneer on his face, the hateful gleam in his eyes, she fisted her hands.

"Get out. Get out."

"Always knew you were a whore."

Not trying to get in so much as pull her in, she realized. Pull her into the cage with him.

"I'll take you back there, Riggs, back to that island. Just to hear you scream."

"Fuck you. I'm here. All that was bullshit."

"Was it?" To steady herself, she laid a hand on Bunk's head. "Maybe you'll die there next time, and they'll find you in your cell. Your body broken to pieces, your skin still smoking from the burns.

"Try me, you bastard. Just try me."

"Fuck you," he said again, but she saw and she felt his fear before she closed him out again.

"Try me," she whispered to herself. "Because if I can't stop this from happening, one of us won't make it."

PART III

The Gift

To believe only possibilities is not faith, but mere philosophy.
—Sir Thomas Browne

He either fears his fate too much,
Or his deserts are small,
That puts it not unto the touch,
To win or lose it all.
—James Graham

Chapter Twenty-one

He'd put it off as long as possible, but if they stayed—more and more likely—he had to register Braydon for preschool.

His boy needed that structure, more friends, and, like it or not, that separation.

Telling himself he'd have the glory of a few hours without interruption, to work, to shower in peace, even to scratch his own balls, didn't help a lot.

But since his job meant doing what was best for Bray, he'd do his job.

He still had a month before the bus—he didn't know if there'd be a bus—would pick his baby up, swallow his baby up, take his baby away.

"Jesus, Tyler, be a man."

He had a preview of what was to come, as Bray had a playdate with Lucas and Rolan at Rolan's house. He had two hours in an empty house, and couldn't figure out what to do with it.

He could work—and should. Or finish his now half-completed library with office. Or do the laundry he'd put off.

The problem? Too many ors. Times like these, he admitted to wondering how he'd thought he could pull off a summer here, much less for good. Or, his current fallback, till Christmas.

He'd been decisive once, he thought as he wandered the too-quiet, too-empty house. Then came Braydon. Now everything he did or didn't do had to factor in a little boy.

He wouldn't change that, not for a second, not for the world, for the damn multiverse. But dear Christ, he wished he could find that decisiveness again.

Not just Bray, he admitted. But the way Bray came to be. Add his family, who always looked as if—in their eyes—he was about to make another major mistake.

Hadn't part of his coming here, for the summer at least, been partially because they'd insisted he'd be making a major mistake?

"Maybe," he muttered. "Maybe. But it wasn't a mistake."

He picked up a photo he'd framed, one he'd taken of Bray coming down the slide, Bunk the Giant Dog waiting at the bottom.

"No, not a mistake."

So why was he so damn restless?

Maybe too much thinking about the woman up the lane, who could equal a major mistake.

He wanted her—no surprise there. He was a straight, single man and she was beautiful, smart, interesting, and kind with it. She had real affection for his son. Not the put-on sort. He'd learned quick how to spot that sort.

And goddamn, he missed sex.

She wanted him back, and that came in handy.

But what if they moved in that direction and it didn't work out? Did they just go back to: *Hi, neighbor?* Did they ignore each other?

Would she ignore Bray and hurt his feelings, as he had real affection for her, for her family?

Factor in all that.

When his phone rang, he yanked it out of his pocket, and when he saw his manager's name, answered as if he'd been tossed a lifeline in a choppy sea.

"Talk to me. I'm going crazy talking to myself."

He paced, listened, responded. And felt Tyler Brennan, the musician, the songwriter, take a solid hold again.

"Yeah, yeah, I'm good with all that. Like I said, I've got two more I'm fine-tuning, and another I'm just starting to work on. I think so, too. Being here this summer's given me space."

He stopped, looked at his overcrowded, makeshift studio. "Well, it's given me something. Yeah, I'm sure I don't want to record any of them myself. Do that, sure. Thanks. Later."

When he set the phone down, he thought the hell with the laundry, the hell with setting up books or anything else.

He sat down at the piano, and got to work.

Thea never watched when Rem beta tested one of her works in progress. First, he never shut up when playing, and his constant commentary unnerved her. And last, making herself scarce gave them both space.

Instead, she put on hiking boots, clipped on a water bottle, and packed a can of bear spray as a precaution.

"I'll be back in an hour," she called out.

"Yeah, yeah, yeah. What the . . . Frigging snakes? You know I hate frigging snakes."

Because she did, she smiled as she went out the back door with Bunk.

"Gotta face your fears, right, Bunk? And if he gets out of the snake pit, he'll gain a power boost." She pulled her braid through the back of her ball cap, snugged it on. "He's going to need it."

The howl, the spate of curses that followed her out the door turned her smile to a grin.

Snakebite, she thought. Better find that antivenom.

As she walked by the coop, the girls clucked at her, their heads tipping, turning. A downy woodpecker pecked greedily at the suet in the feeder. The wings of a spotted yellow butterfly spread as it drank from one of her flood of purple coneflowers.

"Look what we've got," she said to Bunk as she turned.

Her not-so-little cottage with its windows open to the day, the porch swing ready whenever she was. Flowers just everywhere, exactly as she'd always wanted.

The thriving vegetable garden meant she'd need to harvest some, do some canning over the weekend. Cook up some red sauce, too, for fall and winter.

She'd take baskets in to Maddy at the clinic to share the bounty. And to Ty.

Maybe she'd see if Braydon wanted to help her harvest. She'd always loved filling a basket from Grammie's garden as a child.

He was young for it, but she could make it fun.

She heard him having fun often enough the way his laugh carried up on the air. Sometimes a mix of laughs that told her he had his friends over.

She'd heard Ty's music, the piano, charging notes or drifting ones. Or the undeniably sexy slash and clash of an electric guitar.

In the steaming early days of August, she'd walked with them twice, when the timing meshed, to her grandmother's. And once, in the blazing sun near where they'd first met, shared another long, lovely kiss.

But between his work and her own, with little boys and obligations, they remained, primarily, neighbors.

Probably for the best, she decided, as she climbed the beaten trail. He had complications, she had complications. And while his brought joy, hers cast long shadows.

While she knew she could tell her grandmother anything, she held back on the subject of Ray Riggs.

Why spread those shadows over people she loved?

He couldn't touch her, not really. However many times, in however many ways, he planned escapes, dreamed of finding her and doing to her what he'd done to her parents, and worse, she didn't believe he could or would travel beyond those prison walls with anything but his mind.

He'd never walk out of these woods as he had in her dream.

He could only taunt her, make her afraid. He could only spread shadows like a shadow himself.

"Head games," she muttered to herself. "That's all he has. And I'm better at games."

But she couldn't deny she had nights where she dragged herself out of sleep because he walked into her dreams.

She turned into the clearing and the house where her grandmother had once brought soap and balm for a baby with ringworm. She remembered the little boy playing in the dirt—about Bray's age then.

About twenty now, she calculated, and a corporal in the Marine Corps. His little sister, in high school, worked summers in the town bakery. And the baby—before twin boys had come along—an A student, a track star, hoped for a scholarship to make him the first in his family to go to college.

The mother, Katie, stood outside, humming to herself as she hung clothes on a line. She had a battered straw hat on her head, and an apron around her waist with pockets to hold the clothespins.

The little house had a fresh coat of paint, and Thea knew there'd be some money in the jar since her husband had joined Knobby's crew a few years past.

The yard boasted a tidy vegetable patch boxed in with marigolds.

Katie lifted a pillowcase from her laundry basket and spotted Thea and Bunk.

"Hey there, Thea, hey there, Bunk. Y'all chose a hot one for a hike."

"We did, but it's been a pretty one. Still some mountain laurel blooming."

"Bunk, you go have a drink from Rufus's bowl. The boys took the dog with them. They're off fishing, and I hope they bring supper home with them. Let me get you something cold."

"No, I'm fine." Thea held up her water bottle. "The house looks so nice, Katie."

"Billy and the boys painted it last month. Every day, I swear, I'm grateful he's out of the mines and on Knobby's crew. In my heart, I know it saved his life."

And maybe yours, Thea thought. Katie couldn't have hit forty yet, and though the years showed, Thea saw they sat lighter on her than they had a decade before.

"I'm nearly done here if you can sit a spell."

"I would, but Rem'll be waiting for me. I should've started back already, but I got hypnotized."

Katie laughed. "The hills do that. No place on earth like them."

"Not for me. It's good to see you, Katie."

"I'm glad you walked this way. You give your brother my best, and the same and more to Miss Lucy."

"I will." And because they'd known each other for those fifteen years, Thea shot her a smile. "Fish coming for supper." And held up six fingers.

On a hoot, Katie clapped her hands together. "I better get this wash hung, shuck some butter beans, and go make us some cornbread."

Pleased with the walk, the quick visit—and thinking cornbread sounded like a fine idea—she started back.

She might've picked a hot one, but spotting a stubbornly blooming wild rhododendron, the swish of a tail of a red fox driving into the brush, listening to the forest birds' call and response made it more than worthwhile.

Then she heard something else besides birds and chittering squirrels.

"I ride!"

Her hike took on a little more glow as she walked to a fork in the trail. Heading east, looking sweaty, Ty carried Bray on his back.

"I see a couple of explorers."

"Hi, hi, hi!" One hand fisted in Ty's hair like a rein, Bray waved the other. "We're taking a hike!"

"One of us is."

"We saw a deer and he had . . ."

"Antlers," Ty supplied.

"On his head! And a brown rabbit and a red bird, and Daddy thinks bear poop!"

"You will have that in the woods."

And I see two sweaty males, she thought, and the bigger one looks a little cranky.

She nodded toward the water bottle hooked to Ty's belt. "You're out of water."

"Somebody bogarted the bottle."

"I see." She unhooked her own, offered it.

"Thanks." A glug cleared most of the irritation vibrating from him.

"One for each person next time."

"Yeah. Last time we headed up here, one was plenty."

"Bet it wasn't as hot."

"Wasn't, and we walked farther than before." He held up the bottle. "Bray."

"Okay." Water dribbled down his chin, and Ty's neck. "Ice water's more yum."

"Lemonade's more yum, too, and I've got some." She turned her back. "Pass him over."

"He's heavy. I've got him."

She glanced over her shoulder. "Do I look weak?"

"No, but—"

"I ride Thea."

"For a minute," Ty said, and made the transfer, stretched his back. "What's up that way?"

"Some houses, some cabins, more hills, and a gorgeous wild rhodo that's still blooming. A friend of ours lives a little ways up."

She glanced at his high-tops as they started down the trail. "No hiking boots?"

"These hold up."

"City boy."

"Guilty. What is it about a long-legged woman wearing boots with shorts?"

"Good traction and comfort on a summer hike?"

"No. No, that's not it. It is nice to get out like this when you're not dying of thirst and carrying thirty pounds on your back. Tell me if he gets too heavy."

"He's fine. You've been busy. I hear you playing."

"Hit a stride. Sent a couple off to my manager to see if I hit it right. How's your stride, work-wise?"

"Rem's down at my place beta testing the one I'm working on. He'll tell me where I hit it right, and where I didn't. He's the worst critic, which makes him the best."

"Can I play with Bunk? See the chickens? Please!"

"I've got time if you do."

"I could use that lemonade and a few minutes in a chair."

"I happen to have both." She paused, pointed when they made the turn that brought both houses into view.

"It's nice, isn't it? The way the land rolls, how the houses sit on it."

"Yeah. Bray's registered for preschool."

"I'm going to school with Rolan and Lucas. My teacher's name is . . . I forgot, Daddy."

"Miss Mansfield."

"That. And I get a backpack with a lunch box and new shoes."

"This is exciting! I don't suppose you'd like an *Adventures in Endon* backpack."

Enthusiasm bounced on her back. "Okay!"

"I can make that happen. Stop," Thea warned before Ty told her she didn't have to do that.

"I run with Bunk."

"It's still a little steep, pal. Give it another minute."

"How many days till school?"

"Sixteen. No, fifteen now. Jesus."

"Jesus," Bray echoed.

"Don't say that in school. Okay, you can run now."

Bray wiggled down and took off with the dog loping beside him.

"I'd say he's looking forward to school more than you are."

"I am, and I'm not. He needs it. I need it. But."

"It's the next big step." A giant one she remembered very well. "I worked myself into a panic at the idea of being the new kid in school. Bray doesn't have that problem."

"He can't wait."

"So." She glanced over. "Longer than the summer now."

"At least until Christmas. I want to see how he does, how school works."

"Eastern Kentucky's beautiful in the fall."

"Looks like we'll see for ourselves."

He took her hand as they walked. Then stopped as they came to the end of the trail. "It's good to see you, Thea."

"It's good to see you, Tyler."

Still holding her hand, he brought his mouth to hers.

Till Christmas, she thought as they continued on.

It felt like another gift.

Rem stepped out of the back door. "Hey, Bullet Train," he called to Bray. "Hey, Ty, want a beer?"

"Oh God, yes."

"Got you covered. Macaroni salad in the fridge, too, and some of that brown bread she makes 'cause she thinks it's healthier. It's pretty good."

To prove it, he took a bite out of the slice he held in his hand.

"I pay him in food for beta testing."

"I could beta test."

"No. But I'll feed you." By the time they reached the house, Rem had already carried out the salad bowl. He unhooked one of the beers caught in his fingers, passed it to Ty.

"Didn't know you guys were meeting up on the hike."

"Neither did we." Ty took a long pull. "Jesus, this is the best beer in the long history of beer."

As Thea went inside to get the rest, Rem turned to Ty. "You got ideas about my sister?"

Ty took a second, more cautious pull of his beer. "I don't know that I'd call them ideas."

"Friend, I know ideas when I see ideas. Thea can take care of herself and all that, but she's got some tender spots that don't show."

"Noted."

"Okay, cool. That's it. Other topic advice? Hiking boots. Ankle support, traction, and snakes."

"Snakes? We didn't see any snakes."

Darkly, Rem looked at the back screen door. "Sometimes you don't. But they see you."

When they all sat at the picnic table, Rem turned to Thea. "I left you copious notes."

"I expected no less."

"It's a little squishy on the third-level fight-or-flight play."

She huffed out a breath. "It is."

"The snake pit's too dark."

"It's supposed to be dark. You need to earn the torch."

"You can't earn what you can't see. Now, say if the snakes glowed before they strike? You'd have that quick flash of light, even if it killed you. They got me half a dozen times, by the way, and I'm good at this. You keep getting killed, you get bored."

"Glowing snakes." Oh, damn, she could see it. "Different colors depending on what kind, how venomous."

"There you go. It's a damn good game, Thea."

"Damn good game," Bray repeated, chomping on generously buttered brown bread.

"Sorry."

Ty shook his head. "Happens. Happens a lot in our house. Why do they glow? Snakes don't usually glow."

"Good question." Rem toasted him.

"Because they've ingested irradiated mice over many generations."

"She's always got an answer."

"How'd the mice get irradiated?"

"From secret experiments in the secret underground lab run by the villainous Arkol Group that seeks world domination."

"Okay, that explains it. So not a fantasy game like *Endon*."

"I get an *Endon* backpack for school."

"No way!" Rem met Bray's statement with mad surprise. "I want one."

"Are you going to school with me?"

"I wish. Some fantasy elements because evil secret lab," Rem explained to Ty. "But heavy on the adventure and problem-solving. The chapter puzzles are a bi . . ." He caught himself. "A bit challenging."

"Nice save," Thea told him. "I'll read over your copious notes, and make the snakes glow."

"Great, and you should make Rowena a little more . . ." When he cupped his hands, palms up, jiggled them, Ty's laugh nearly had him choking on his beer.

"Oh, really?"

"Yeah. Not like—" He widened his fingers. "Just, you know, a little more . . . personality, considering present company."

"Spoken like a teenage boy."

Rem's eyebrows lifted. "And what's the most active demographic for video games?"

A breath hissed between her teeth. "Boys, eighteen and under. But the average demo overall is male, age thirty-four, and you'd think by that time a guy would . . . What am I saying, that obsession never fades."

"You're just jealous because you don't have a big personality."

"Get off my land."

"I've got to do that. Meeting in town coming up. I'm taking some of those chocolate chip cookies on my way out." Leaning over, he gave her cheek a noisy kiss. "Love you."

"The reason often escapes me, but I love you, too."

"It's 'cause I'm so charming. Charm's what landed me a date tonight with a hot blonde with a big personality."

"What— Who?"

He only grinned and slid off the bench. "See y'all later."

He jogged into the house, slamming the screen door behind him.

"Bye, bye! Time to play chase with Bunk."

"What blonde?"

"If I could interject?"

Frowning, Thea turned back to Ty.

"I know a little about personalities. Yours is lovely."

She rolled her eyes, but she laughed. "Thank you. But damn it, he's probably right about Rowena. I can beat him, name the game, nine times out of ten. And the ten is only when I give him a break. But he's got an eye for details at beta level, for little hitches and glitches I might miss, at least initially, because I'm too deep in it."

"It helps to have someone you can trust with your work."

"It does, a lot."

"I've got that with Mac. With Blaze and Scott, too, but especially Mac."

"You've written some great songs together."

"We have, and will. I ran the new ones by him before my manager. And I've got to get back to it. I guess you do, too."

"I should."

"Appreciate the post-hike fuel. Listen, I'll have some clear time Wednesday. I'm going to make another attempt doing chicken on the grill. The last failed, but I think I know where I went wrong. Willing to risk it?"

"I am." She laid a hand over his. "Marinade, one hour, liquid margarita mix with a glug of soy sauce."

"That doesn't sound like it could possibly be right."

She gave his hand a friendly pat. "You'll thank me."

"Maybe, but if not, it'll be your fault. We've got to go, Bray."

"Bunk can come. Please!"

"I'll whistle for him in an hour."

Ty nodded. "Yeah, he'll walk us home. I'm going to kiss Thea goodbye."

"Okay!"

He cupped her face with the kiss again, the way he had in his kitchen. The way that made her muscles go weak.

"I'd take you out, like an actual date, but—"

"You're not ready to find and trust someone to stay with Bray. I like home. And, you might as well hear it. It's sexy."

"Home's sexy?"

"Well, it can be. I meant the devoted father. That's sexy."

"Good to know, as I've got that one down."

Bray climbed onto the bench, hugged Thea, kissed her, so easy, so spontaneous that her heart spilled over.

"Cookie?"

She bagged half a dozen, then as Ty often watched her, watched them walk, hands linked, down the lane with the dog beside them.

"Time to suck it up, Thea. You're in love with both of them."

When they moved out of sight, she went inside. She'd been taught, and she strongly believed, giving or receiving love was a gift.

She'd accept the gift of giving love.

Chapter Twenty-two

She baked a pie. To Thea's way of thinking, if Ty failed with the chicken, she might find a way to save it. If not, they'd still have cherry pie.

Halfway down the lane, Bunk spotted Bray running through a wave of bubbles belching out of the mouth of a big plastic frog. One joyful bark and Bunk raced the rest of the way.

She saw smoke rising from the fancy grill, and the man with tongs in one hand, a beer in the other who looked her way and smiled.

Music poured out of the house through open windows, and overhead the sky held its hazy, summer blue.

To her eye, it all made a perfect August evening.

"Bunk bites the bubbles," Bray told her, and laughed like a lunatic.

"Maybe I should get him a bubble frog."

"Daddy knows how. Ask Daddy."

"I'll do that."

Bray wore Spider-Man sneakers, a Grave Digger fielder's cap, and a T-shirt sporting a Bernese mountain dog. If wardrobe depicted a kid's interests and passions, Bray's did the job.

Or his father did, she thought. The man knew his boy.

She stepped up to the porch, examined the chicken on the grill. "It looks like you've conquered this skill."

"Maybe. What's in the basket?"

"Cherry pie."

"The men in this house are fond of cherry pie. We get them individually wrapped."

"We'll see if the men in this house like a pie you have to slice. I'll just go put it on the counter."

When she went inside, she caught a familiar scent.

"I smell Grammie's roasted potatoes."

"Let's hope so. I bought actual potatoes, then wondered what the hell to do with them, so I called Lucy. She walked me through."

Curious, Thea peeked in the oven. "I'm impressed."

"They're another maybe yet. There's wine in the fridge if you want to pour yourself a glass."

"And I do. Do you want another beer?"

"I'm good."

She stepped out with her wine, looked at the boy, the dog, the fields, and the hills.

"This is the kind of evening where it feels like summer won't end. Or you wish it wouldn't."

"When I was a kid, summer was full of thrills and misery."

"Why?"

"Thrills? No school. A month later, still no school. Then misery, because it was coming."

"I liked the anticipation of going back. Fresh new notebooks, sharpened pencils."

"Droning lectures, homework. Bray's all about it, and I'm playing into that. But I couldn't wait to finish that part of my life. The idea of college, then med school or law school or grad school? Years and years more in classrooms? Misery. Music saved me."

"You found your path and you followed it. I think I told you, my first day of school here, after my parents died? I was terrified. New girl. I'd wear my hair wrong, or have the wrong shoes."

"I've observed girls worry about shoes, a lot."

"Of course we do. They're the foundation. But I had Maddy, and then Gracie. It's funny, and sweet, that part of them will be with Bray on his first day with Rolan and Lucas."

"He has no fear."

"Did you?"

"No. I had boredom." He glanced over to where Bray tried to chomp at bubbles along with the dog. "He's never bored."

The oven timer sounded.

"That could be the buzzer of doom."

"We'll find out."

She went inside to take the potatoes out of the oven.

When Bray declared dinner yum, Ty nodded. "It worked pretty good. But we're not giving up the tots."

"Next thing you know you'll be exchanging recipes when you're in line at the grocery store, and googling busy-day meals."

"Kill me now. Anyway, we have our busy-day meal. It's called frozen pizza. Before the invention thereof, I wonder why women—because it was mostly women—didn't just run screaming. Shopping for food, figuring out what to do with the food, cooking the food, cleaning up after, then doing it all again."

"You left out laundry, housecleaning, children bathing, diaper changing—"

"Not anymore. Though we're past the last, and thank you, Jesus."

"You could hire some help, with the housecleaning part anyway."

"Then somebody's in the house. How am I supposed to work when somebody's in the house?" He shrugged. "I went there before. Before," he said again, tipping his head toward Bray. "They ended up cashing in."

Sincerely horrified, she gaped at him. "They *stole* from you?"

"My privacy, yeah. Took pictures, did a couple tabloid interviews."

"Well, that's horrible. What did you do?"

"Besides fire their ass? Nothing. You sue, it keeps the ball rolling. And after, my family helped some. And there was Scott's sister's daughter. I knew her, could trust her with some babysitting when I really needed it."

He gestured toward her with his beer.

"You don't have a cleaning service."

"Then somebody would be in my house? How would I get any work done?"

He laughed, tapped his beer bottle to her wineglass.

"How's the game going?"

"Rem's copious notes were insightful. I both hate and appreciate that."

"So, glowing snakes?"

"Glowing snakes," she affirmed. "They cost me a lot of time and sweat to get right, but they seriously work."

"We saw snakes at the zoo. Giant snakes! But I wasn't scared. Bunk wants to play bubbles."

"Okay. Let me fill it up again."

"The frog," Bray explained while Ty got the bubble liquid, "drinks the bubbles. Then he burps bubbles!"

"That's amazing."

"We can't drink it or we get sick. But the frog can. You can watch."

She watched, had a second glass of wine.

"You know, I'm not sure who's happier with that bubbling frog, Bray or Bunk. I might just have to get him one."

They had pie while the sun set, then lingered while the boy chased fireflies.

When he sprawled on the grass with his head on the dog, Ty rose. "He's done."

"I think he wore Bunk out. Thanks for dinner, and the entertainment." Before she could rise, Ty laid a hand on her shoulder.

"Stay. It won't take long for me to put him to bed."

"I should—"

"Stay," he said again.

He walked over to pick up his son.

"More bubbles."

"Mmm-hmm."

As he carried Bray in, he sang softly.

How could she resist him, this, all of it? Why should she?

Why not embrace this perfect summer evening that had fallen so beautifully into a perfect summer night? Moonlight beamed, stars sparkled, and the lightest breeze carried the first hints of the fall to come.

She heard Ty's voice, soft as a wish, flowing out of the window as he put his son to bed.

When the fates handed you a gift, who but a fool would refuse it?

Rising, she carried in the dessert dishes, busied herself with the simple task to calm her nerves. While she did, Bunk circled, then sprawled on the kitchen floor, snoozing, and very much at home.

When she heard Ty coming back, she turned. "He went down easy."

"When I call bedtime, it takes longer than if I just let him drop. Tonight was a let-him-drop deal. He won't get many of those once school starts."

"On a night like this, it seems fair to go until you can't."

"That was my thinking."

He slid his arms around her. "And if you're not four, it's still early."

She rose up to meet his mouth and thought, no. For her, it was way too late.

Old needs, new needs waked inside her. All roused by a kiss in the kitchen with the summer night fluttering through the windows. And the heat of his body pressed to hers.

"Come upstairs with me, Thea. Come to bed with me."

"I want to." Why deny it? "I just—"

"He's out. And we'll be quiet."

Undone, she pressed her face to his shoulder. "I can be quiet."

"Come upstairs, and we'll test that."

He took her hand. It seemed so natural, and again so easy, to walk through the house with him, up the stairs. As if everything had been leading to this since she'd seen him on the side of the road holding his son.

As they passed Bray's room, she saw him sleeping, a stuffed dog and a dump truck clutched in one arm.

"He sleeps with a truck."

"Doesn't everybody?"

He drew her into the room across the hall, quietly shut the door.

She'd only been in the room once, the night Miss Leona died, but saw he'd changed things.

A different bed, sleeker lines, black wood, a bureau with a flat-screen over it rather than a mirror, shades rather than curtains on the window.

"It looks like you."

"Simplified it, I guess. Needs paint, but . . ."

He turned her into his arms.

"Some things can wait. Some? Just can't anymore."

With his mouth on hers, he circled her toward the bed. She felt his heartbeat against her own, his hand skimming down her hair.

No, the waiting time was over.

"I've sort of waited to see some guy walk or drive up the lane to your place. But not once, all summer."

"Longer."

"I'm going to ask why. Feel free to tell me to mind my own business."

"Considering where we're standing it falls under yours, at least some. Nobody's made me want to stand here like this in longer. Until you."

He cupped her face. "Nobody's made me want to take a chance on standing here like this in longer. Until you."

That made her smile. "I guess another test will be seeing if we both remember how it's done."

"I've got that part. It starts like this."

Mouths meeting, tongues sliding, hands gliding.

"I'm going to miss summer," he murmured. "When you stop wearing dresses like this."

He eased the zipper down, and when the dress fell at her feet, lifted her out of the pool of it. And stood, hands on her hips, looking at her.

"I've seen you in sunlight, imagined you in moonlight. Imagined you like this. I can say you're beautiful, but it's not enough."

"It's more than enough for me."

She drew his shirt up, off. Then pressed a hand to his chest. "And here you are. Your heart's under my hand."

She took his hand, pressed it to hers. "And mine's under yours."

So easy, she thought again, so natural when they moved together again. Skin to skin, heart to heart. Her hands didn't hesitate as she unbuttoned his jeans, because she'd never been more sure of anything than being with him.

They lay on the bed, turned to each other. When their eyes met, held, she saw everything she wanted in his.

Slowly, as if every moment begged to be savored, they moved together.

He hadn't looked for her. No, he'd stopped looking for anyone like her. But she'd slipped into his life, and she'd brought him what he'd needed. She filled a space he'd kept empty, deliberately empty.

And given him the one thing missing in his life. A woman to want and take, and trust.

He ran his hands down her arms, long, graceful arms he'd seen wielding a sword like a warrior. He saw her eyes, so deep and blue in the moonlight, look into his as if she knew him as no one else did.

When he kissed her, she gave back with so much warmth it filled, she filled, all those empty places.

Her scent aroused him; it clouded his mind until he thought of nothing but her. When her heartbeat quickened under his hand, when her breath caught on a sigh, he let himself take more.

His mouth, his hands took her on a slow climb up, and up, held her trembling at the peak before the breathless fall.

She arched to him, her fingers clutched in his hair to bring his mouth down to hers again.

He touched her in so many ways, body, heart, mind, she opened it all to him without a qualm. Her hands explored him, smooth skin over sharp planes, long limbs and lean muscles.

The little scar on his left hip from a broken chain-link fence he'd crawled under as a boy of eight. As her fingers brushed over it, she thought of the boy he'd been, the man he'd become.

His fingertips, calloused from guitar strings, thrilled her as they skimmed over her.

As his need merged with hers, she arched again, a welcome. And met his eyes as they joined.

She rose with him, fell with him, beat by slow beat.

She held him in those eyes, held him with her as they took each other in the moonlight with the faint summer breeze cooling heated skin.

He watched her go over the edge again, and surrendering, followed.

Blissfully limp, she lay under him.

Her world had changed, and would never be quite the same again. She knew love, the truth and power of it. She knew how it felt when it lived inside her.

Whatever happened, she'd have that.

When he turned his head, pressed his lips to the side of her neck, she thought love was like finally bursting into bloom after a long winter's wait.

After bracing on his elbows, he looked down at her. Once again, he brushed his lips lightly over hers. "Stay."

"Oh, but—"

"He's four, Thea. Well, almost five, but still. We'll just say you were tired, so you slept over."

"I was tired?"

"You're going to be." He kissed her brow, her cheeks, her lips. "Eventually."

"He'll be all right with that?"

Wrapped around her, he rolled over, reversed their positions.

"Let's find out."

The squeal shot Thea out of silky dreams. Heart pounding, she'd nearly launched herself out of bed when laughter followed the squeal.

Beside her, eyes still closed, Ty muttered, "Brace yourself. Here it comes."

Rushing footsteps followed the laughter before Bray pushed open the door. Dog and boy rushed in.

"Daddy! Time to wake up! Bunk's here! Bunk was in my room. Here's Bunk."

Bray, hair as wild as the joy in his eyes, climbed onto the bed in his Spider-Man boxers. "Hi," he said to Thea, and bounced his way between her and his father. "That's Daddy's shirt."

"He . . . let me borrow it."

"Okay. Bunk was sleeping in *my* room." Climbing onto Ty's back, he bounced some more, and patted Ty's head. "Time to wake up!"

"Got it."

"You slept in Daddy's bed."

"Yes, I—"

"Bunk slept on the floor in my room. I'm gonna play trucks with Bunk."

"Good idea," Ty said. "Go do that."

"Okay." After climbing off the bed, he raced off again with Bunk following.

"I guess he's all right with it."

"Thea, he woke up with a dog in his room. He'd've been all right if I'd had five women in bed with me."

"Really?"

Ty opened one green eye. "As an example not drawn from experience. Although, this one time on tour? I think it was Chicago—"

"Let's just table that while all your bones remain intact, and I ask if you have a spare toothbrush."

"Got spare brush heads for the electric deal." He sat up, and with his hair as wild as his boy's, scrubbed his hands over his face. "God. Coffee."

He waved vaguely at the door, then rolled out of bed. She got up more cautiously as he walked out, then checked to make sure the borrowed T-shirt covered all it needed to cover.

He stepped back in the doorway. "Bathroom. Toothbrush, fresh brush head, toothpaste. Coffee."

"Okay, thanks."

Then he smiled. "You look good." And walked away.

While Bray crashed trucks in the room across the hall, she went into the bathroom. A stool stood in front of the little vanity where two toothbrushes and toothpaste sat.

The smaller one had Spider-Man shooting out a web. She picked up Ty's, and got an instant flash of him with Bray on the stool beside him, brushing their teeth.

Though she admitted she wanted to linger in that flash, she blocked it out. Intrusive, she reminded herself.

She looked at herself in the mirror. Good was subjective, she thought, and wished she had a hairbrush.

Bray pushed open the door. "I gotta pee," he announced as she stood with a mouthful of toothpaste.

And proceeded to do so.

He flushed, then turned to study her. "Daddy says you gotta wash your hands after."

Nodding, she managed to rinse out her mouth and ease aside so he could climb onto the stool. He batted at the water.

"How about some of this?" She pumped liquid soap onto his hands.

"That's Daddy's toothbrush."

"He let me borrow it, since I don't have mine."

"I got Spider-Man."

"Do you want to use it?"

"Okay."

Since she was there, she supervised the procedure, the messy procedure, and made him laugh when she used a washcloth to rub the foam off his face.

"How about breakfast?"

"Is it Saturday?"

"No, it's Thursday."

"Aw. I can have Froot Loops on Saturday."

"I could make pancakes."

His dimple flashed on with his smile. "I like pancakes. You pour syrup on pancakes."

"Then I'll go get dressed and make pancakes."

"I'll tell Daddy!"

She put on her dress, and out of habit, made the bed. Smoothing the sheets brought on images of what she and Ty had done on them.

Not intrusive, she decided, and plumped the pillows. A memory that belonged to her.

Downstairs she found father and son, both still in their boxers, in the kitchen.

"I let the dog out. He seemed to appreciate it. Don't know how you take your coffee. I heard a rumor about pancakes. I have this."

He held up a box mix. Thea spared it one pitying look, then opened the fridge.

She found one lonely egg, a nearly empty carton of milk, half a stick of butter. And closed the fridge.

"I've got an idea. Why don't we have breakfast at my house? You could help me feed the chickens, Bray. And Bunk's gonna want his breakfast, too."

"Okay!" Bray headed for the door.

"Maybe you could put some pants on first. Is that all right with you?" she asked Ty.

"If it includes pancakes, I'm for it. Let's get dressed, pal. I've got a grocery list," he added as he went out of the kitchen.

Minutes later, they were back, dressed, hair somewhat tamed. It made her wonder how men managed it all so quickly.

"We'll drive up, so I can run to the store after."

So they piled in the car, Bunk included, for the short drive up the lane.

"Chickens!"

"They'll be happy to see you. Go on and say hi, and I'll be right there."

"You haven't even had coffee," Ty observed as they went in the front. "How do you form coherent sentences before you've had coffee?"

"One of my many superpowers. I'll get some after I feed the animals." She picked up her egg basket, got a container out of the fridge. "Help yourself if you want more."

"I'm coming out."

He watched her scoop dog food from a bag inside a wood chest on the porch before she crossed to where Bray talked to the chickens.

And would've sworn they talked right back to him.

It made a picture, he thought when she went inside the coop. Her in that breezy summer dress, chickens swarming all around her.

And his kid, thrilled when she let him add some sort of pellets to a trough. Which the chickens instantly attacked.

Out of the container she took scraps—lettuce, maybe, some bread she handed to Bray to tear up and toss around.

"Just some little treats," she told Ty. "They like finding them."

"Are those egg shells in that bowl over there?"

"Yeah, for calcium. They lose some when they lay."

"Isn't that kind of . . . cannibalistic?"

"Just shells, Ty, and we don't have a rooster to make fertile eggs. Let's see what they've got for us today."

She took Bray's hand, led him back to the nesting boxes. Then lifted him up.

"You have to be really careful, really gentle so you don't break the egg when you pick it up."

"It's big!"

"That's Zippy. She lays whoppers. Let's hunt in this one. Sometimes they like me to play hide-and-seek."

They made their way through the nesting boxes.

"Wow, we've got five today. You brought us good luck."

"One, two, three, four, five. Five eggs, Daddy!"

"I'm going to put these in a carton. You get to take them home."

"Okay." Bray hugged her legs. Then ran to tell his father the news, though Ty was two feet away.

Thea closed the coop. "Let's go make pancakes."

She let the kid help, something Ty knew from experience meant whatever you did took twice as long and made five times the mess.

But her patience appeared to have no bottom, even when Bray took one look at the milk and said: *Yuck*.

"That's not like Daddy's milk."

"It's buttermilk."

"Why?"

"Because it makes delicious pancakes."

She'd put bacon on some sort of paper on a cookie sheet, and stuck it in the oven. This interested him, as it seemed like less cleanup.

By the time she poured batter onto a hot griddle, he'd had a second cup of coffee and felt human.

And somehow she made a pancake in the unmistakable shape of a monster truck.

"Look! It's a monster truck!"

"I see that." Impressed, he lifted his eyebrows at Thea. "Another superpower?"

"Revealed only to good friends."

When they sat at the table, crisp bacon, summer berries, syrup in a crock warmed in the oven, he cut Bray's pancake truck into sections.

"I'm eating a tire! It's yum. Buttermilk makes delicious pancakes."

"You're not kidding. Thanks for this."

"It's nice to have breakfast company."

"If I tossed something else on the grill on Saturday, would you be interested?"

"I would."

"Can Bunk sleep in my room again?"

She smiled at the boy, looked at the father. "He'd like that. Should be a nice evening, too. We'll get a storm late tonight."

"How do you know that?"

She shrugged. "Farm girl."

After breakfast, she stood on the porch in that breezy summer dress, waving them off.

In the back seat, Bray clutched a dump truck. "I wish Thea made breakfast every day."

Ty flicked a glance at his son in the rearview, then looked back to where Thea turned to go inside.

"She makes good ones."

Chapter Twenty-three

She dreamed of a storm, and Riggs lurked in the rush of wind. She saw his eyes in the flash of lightning, heard his voice in the crackling roll of thunder.

And made a choice.

She pushed aside the curtain of the storm, opened the window, and stepped into his cell.

He sat on the bunk, grinning at her.

"Been waiting for you. Foxy Loxy."

Had he dug that out of her brain? That long-ago nickname her father sometimes called her or Rem?

He'd gone deeper than she'd realized.

But it cost him. She noted the dark circles that haunted his eyes and the lines cut deep around them. Lines bracketing his mouth like a marionette's.

Gray threaded through his hair, and that hair was thinning.

At thirty-three, he had the face of a man heading toward fifty who'd lived hard.

"You don't look so good, Ray. Not sleeping well?"

"I sleep like a fucking baby."

Deliberately, she laughed. "Babies tend to wake up crying every few hours."

"I'm doing fine, I sleep fine. I got you here, didn't I?"

"Yeah, I'm here." In control, she reminded herself. She'd stay in control.

"I thought, why not pay Ray a visit. It's been a while, but nothing much has changed. What's it been now?" She wandered to the door, put her hands on it. "Fifteen years. How about that, Ray, nearly half your life's been spent behind this." She gave the door a quick knock. "How's that feel?"

"I get out. I get out plenty."

"It's not the same, is it? Using the gift you corrupted to walk outside these walls, watch people go along as they please. Eating ice cream sundaes, having a drink at the neighborhood bar. Can you smell the air stirring up spring or the grass freshly mowed on a summer morning?"

She turned back to him. "Does that give you some relief from the stench in here, that smell of isolation and despair? I don't think it does. I think it eats at you, it eats away because you know you'll never really exist outside these locks, these walls again."

"You put me here."

"I did. I was only twelve, and I put you here. And, Ray, that's the biggest, shiniest personal achievement of my entire life."

"I'll get out, and I'll come for you."

"So you always say, but here you are."

He grinned again. "You, too."

When he lunged, she pivoted instinctively to block the knife in his hand. She felt the edge of the blade score along her shoulder, felt the shock of pain, and the impact of the door as her back struck it.

"You're here," he said again. As he lifted the knife to plunge, she pulled herself out, away.

In her bed she heard him shout:

"You'll die here before I do!"

Someone yelled, "Shut the fuck up, Riggs."

But he laughed, and as his laughter faded, as she came back to her own room, to the mutter of thunder from the passing storm, she pressed her hand to her shoulder.

And stared at the blood smeared on her palm.

Just past dawn, she sat at her grandmother's kitchen table. She'd held back too much, she had to admit that now. As she described the encounter,

Rem shoved up, paced the kitchen, stared out the back door, paced back again.

But Lucy stayed still, stayed quiet until the end.

"Let me see your shoulder."

Thea pushed up the sleeve of her T-shirt. She'd butterflied the shallow cut.

"It's hardly more than a scratch," she said, "but . . . Have you ever heard of something like this?"

"No. You cleaned it good?"

"Yes, and used your ointment. It's not deep, and—"

"Jesus Christ, Thea!" Exploding, Rem threw up his hands. "The son of a bitch cut you. He made you bleed. He could've killed you."

"I don't know if that's true. I just don't know. Grammie?"

"This is beyond me. I don't know how he could do this. I don't know how he knew he could."

"I think I know the answer to the last part." After staring down into her coffee, she pushed it aside. "He got into a dream I had. It happened right after Ty and Bray moved here. And, Rem, I'd appreciate it if you'd keep any smart-ass comments to yourself."

"I'm not feeling especially smart-ass at the moment."

"I dreamed about sitting on the back porch on a pretty night, and Ty sitting with me, playing the guitar. It was nice, innocent, just a pretty, harmless dream. Then Riggs walked out of the woods. He had a gun, and he shot Ty."

She closed her eyes for a moment. "It felt so real, all so real. And Ty . . . I could feel his blood on my hands, and Ty said it was my fault."

She pressed her hands to her face, dragged them through her hair.

"It upset me, it scared me, it infuriated me. So . . . I decided to pay him back. I thought, if I scared him, made him feel pain, really feel all that, he'd back the hell off. He'd leave me alone. Because he hasn't, Grammie. More times than I've told you about."

"We'll get back to that. What did you do?"

"I built a dream. A game I'd pulled out of my one-of-these-days file. I built the game, practiced. Then I built it into a dream, and I pulled him into it."

As she told them, Rem sat again, shook his head. "That's the game you designed, the one I beta tested. *Perilous Island*, snake pit and all."

"More or less, yeah. Actually, the one I made him play was a lot more violent—limited to two players—and more simplified."

She lifted her hands. "I kept it straightforward. And I liked making him play, seeing him fail, hearing him scream. I used my gift for that, even knowing it's given to help, not to hurt."

"I wish I'd heard him scream." Reaching over, Rem took her hand. "You fought back, that's how I see it."

"It did scare him, and he backed off for a while. He left me alone for a while, but . . ."

Because Rem couldn't understand in the same way as her grandmother, Thea looked to Lucy.

"You won't get blame from me either. He came after you, and you stood up to him. But you took a terrible risk, Thea. More, you didn't tell your family."

"I just didn't want to bring it here anymore, Grammie. I just didn't want that goddamn cloud always hanging over us. I wanted, just wanted to deal with it."

"Just you?" Lucy countered. "By yourself?"

The hurt in her grandmother's voice cut deeper than Riggs's mind knife. "I believed, I honestly believed I could handle it. I thought I was."

"No more holding things back from us. Let's make that clear."

"I won't, and I'm sorry I did."

She looked to Rem now. "I'm sorry because both of you had a right to know. What he did, he did to all of us. What he's doing now may be aimed at me, because he can, but it's still about all of us."

"Don't forget that. And the next time you come up with a way to hit back at him, we talk about it first."

"All right. I think what I did with the game scared him, hurt him. But I'm afraid it also gave him another way in, a way that lets him see more of me. He called me Foxy Loxy."

"Like Dad used to sometimes."

"He knows more about me now than I realized. He probably knows . . ." She paused, sighed, gave up. "I spent the night with Ty."

"This calls for a movie quote," Rem decided. "We'll go with 'There's a fuckin' surprise.'"

Lucy just cast her gaze to the ceiling.

"Hey, look, I found my smart-ass again. Hell, Thea, anybody who didn't see that coming wasn't looking."

"Does Ty know any of this?" Lucy asked.

"No. I'm not—we're not . . . No. Aren't I entitled to start a relationship, see where it goes, without dragging all of this into it?"

"You are, and that's your choice. But, Thea"—Lucy gave her hand a squeeze—"it's hard to build a real relationship when you close off part of what you are."

"The one time I opened that part up to someone I cared about, it didn't go well."

"You shouldn't judge Tyler or anyone else by someone else's failings. But take what you need, and you'll know when it's time. But on one thing, I'm putting my foot down. I don't put it down often, but you know when I do, I put it down hard."

"Yes, ma'am."

"You're not to go back in that cell."

"I can promise you I won't. It's costing him to pull me in, and it's cost him to do what he did." She touched a hand to her shoulder. "He looks sick. I told him it was eating at him, and that's just what it's doing, to his body and his mind. He gets nosebleeds, bleeds from the ear. Pushing so hard and long, it's doing something to him."

"Then let it, and leave him be."

"That's all I want, to let him be where he is. He's planned a dozen ways to get out—probably more I haven't seen. He looks into the minds of other inmates, guards, doctors, anyone he can, digging for something he can use to escape. That's costing him, too."

Though it had gone cold, she picked up her coffee. "I should've told you both all of this, instead of just the bits I did. And I'm sorry."

"You don't protect us," Rem told her. "We protect each other."

"That's why I keep this boy around." Leaning over, Lucy tugged him to her, kissed his cheek. "He may be a smart-ass, but the smart in him usually outweighs the ass. Now we've got animals to tend."

"I'll help. I already gave Bunk and my ladies breakfast before I came."

"I'll take it. You come on with me, Thea, and we'll bring Rosie in from pasture."

As they walked together, Lucy glanced back where Rem headed for the coop.

"I waited to say, as I know how brothers can be. You're in love with Ty. I can't help but see it all over you."

"I am. Completely. I know it's ridiculous, but—"

"Why? Love's not ridiculous, even though it can make us feel ridiculous. He's a fine man. That's clear as freshly shined glass, and he's raising a bright and happy boy."

"Who I'm also completely in love with. And you wonder why, when that's true, I'm not being completely honest with him. I want that time," she said as she opened the gate to the pasture. "And more, he may not stay. He hasn't decided, not all the way. I guess I want him to do that before I really think about telling him what I have."

"That seems fair."

She took the time, and enjoyed the flow of it. Evenings on his porch or hers, a Sunday at the farm with food on the picnic table and Bray racing with the dogs.

As August dripped away, she kept Riggs locked out.

She built her own dreams, as she had since childhood. He had no place in them.

If it cost her—a sudden headache, a restless night, a bubble of panic in her throat—she considered it a small price to pay for locking him out.

On the night before the first day of school, she walked down just far enough to see the lights shining in Ty's house.

She imagined a little boy wound up about what was to come, and a man a bit frantic. Standing, the air still summer warm, she stroked her hand over Bunk's head.

"They'll be fine. There's a dad who won't get a lot of sleep tonight, but they'll be fine."

*　*　*

Before dawn, Bray bounced on his father's back.

"Time to wake up! Time for school!"

"Oh God, Bray. We've got another hour before we have to get up. Go back to sleep."

Ty reached around, flipped Bray onto the bed, tucked him. "You can sleep here, but go back to sleep."

"I'm hungry! You said I could have bacon like Thea makes and Eggos."

"It's still dark."

"But I'm really, really hungry." He patted Ty's cheek. "Really hungry, and I have to brush my teeth and I have to get dressed and you have to tie my new shoes 'cause I still can't do it. And you have to take pictures, you said."

"You're killing me, Bray. Killing me."

Unconcerned by that, Bray wiggled, and babbled on while Ty clung to the illusion of sleep.

As he'd clung to it at two in the morning when he'd stared at the ceiling imagining the school bus as a toothy yellow shark and Bray as the clown fish—thanks, Nemo—it swallowed.

Or at three in the morning, when he nearly drifted off before he imagined Bray in a dark, empty school, crying for his daddy.

Had he really thought it would get easier as Bray grew? When he'd rocked and walked and tried to soothe a wailing, teething toddler, he'd convinced himself it would get easier.

When he'd struggled through the frustrations and complexities and general insanity of potty training, he'd sworn it had to get easier.

When he'd fought not to panic when Bray spiked a fever of 102.3, he'd promised them both it would get easier.

Mostly, it had. But there were times. Good God, there were times.

"Go down and make me coffee."

"Daddy!" Giggling, Bray patted Ty's cheek again.

"The minute you're tall enough, your primary job's going to be making my coffee."

"Okay."

Ty opened his eyes, looked at the face nose to nose with his, the utter sweetness of it surrounded by wild bed hair.

"I love you, Bray. You monster."

"Grr, grr, chomp! I love you, Daddy. I'm really, really, really hungry!"

"Yeah, yeah, yeah. Eat this!" And tickled the boy into delirium.

But he got up, lumbered his way downstairs. He gulped down coffee while Bray raced around the house like a maniac on speed.

He lined a cookie sheet with parchment paper—a product he hadn't known existed before he'd googled "bacon in the oven."

He shoved bacon in the oven, then, because the coffee hadn't finished the job, had to google "bacon in the oven" again for the next steps.

"Twenty minutes, pal. Let's go brush the green off your teeth."

"Not green!"

"They would be if I didn't make you brush them."

In twenty minutes, Ty had his second cup of coffee with bacon and Eggos. He decided Bray had meant the hungry, as he ate four pieces of bacon and two Eggos.

Which made Ty worry he'd puke up breakfast on the bus and start his school career in humiliation.

He helped his boy dress, added another shoe-tying lesson. Getting closer there. He packed the prized *Endon* lunch box that went into the prized *Endon* backpack.

Thank you, Thea.

He checked the contents twice.

Spill-proof water bottle, a juice box, the spare set of clothes, including boxers—in case—a nap mat, the chosen monster truck, a box of crayons, glue sticks, sunscreen.

Everything labeled, as advised.

As the clock ticked down, his nerves rose up.

"Hey, Bray, I could drive you into school, go in with you just to—"

"No, Daddy! I ride the bus. I ride with Lucas and Rolan!"

If a not-quite-five-year-old could look genuinely appalled, Bray pulled it off masterly.

"Right. Just an option. Now, you remember what we talked about. You listen to your teacher, share with the other kids. And don't say any daddy words."

"Okay."

"Okay. Okay. It's almost time for the bus, so let's put on your backpack."

As he helped Bray put on the backpack, as he smoothed his little boy's hair, the love almost flattened him.

Why couldn't he just keep him, keep him right here, close, safe?

Not the job, he reminded himself. Not the way it needed to work. And that was the bitch of it.

"You're going to have fun."

"So much fun."

"Right. Okay. Go stand by the door so I can take your picture."

He took one there, one on the porch. Then heard the bus rumbling up the road.

"Remember to wait until it stops."

"I *know*, Daddy!"

He held Bray's hand as they walked toward the road, and those doors opened into the maw of the bus.

"Hi there!" The driver, a woman with a bowl of steel-gray hair, beamed out. "I'm Miss Sally. And you must be Braydon."

"I'm going to school."

"You sure are. Come on aboard."

Ty struggled not to clutch, made himself keep the kiss light and easy. "Off you go, pal. Turn around once, yeah, right there."

He took a picture of Bray, face just glowing, on the steps of the yellow bus.

"Bye, Daddy, bye!"

"He sure is ready," Miss Sally said when Bray walked right on.

"Yeah, he's ready."

Guess I'm not, Ty thought as the driver gave a wave and the doors shut.

He stood, listening to it rumble away with the biggest piece of his heart inside. Then stood a little longer in the absolute quiet of the morning.

He told himself he could go back to bed, catch up on some sleep. But knew that for bullshit.

He walked into the house, where the quiet screamed like sirens. He went upstairs, made the beds because why not. He cleaned up the mess in the bathroom Bray inevitably made when he brushed his teeth.

He tossed some laundry in, wandered, actively thought about vacuuming.

And checking the clock, realized the bus hadn't even gotten to school yet.

"For fuck's sake, Ty, he hasn't gone off to war. Get a grip."

He had lyrics for a song, but hadn't nailed down the melody, much less orchestration.

Do that, he told himself, and settled into his studio.

His mind circled a few times, then landed on the work.

He worked out the bones of the melody on the piano, switched to guitar, added bass, his voice. Overdubbed with some harmony. He listened to the playback, made some changes. Listened again.

He needed another ear, he decided, and FaceTimed Blaze.

Blaze, man bun, scarred left eyebrow from a bar fight back in the day, hooded brown eyes, flashed a grin. "Hey, man, you caught me. I'm sitting by the pool drinking my beverage of choice. Iced freaking tea. Living clean."

"You look good."

"Damn right. And look here." He waved a blue-bound packet at the screen. "I'm reading a script. I'm a goddamn tee-vee star."

"Life is strange."

"I do like the strange. Where's my man?"

It put a twist in Ty's guts to say it out loud. "First day of school."

Blaze tossed the script aside, sat up from his reclining position. "Get the fuck out of here."

"I put him on the bus . . . Jesus, three hours ago. I'm sending you a picture. He got right on, basically, *See you later, Dad.* He's so happy here."

"You gonna be a Kentucky boy now, brother?"

"It looks like it. He's got friends, the neighbor's dog, room to run, which he does constantly. I'm thinking about building on a studio. You need to come down here, you and Mac and Scott. I could use some input there."

"We'll get there."

"Meanwhile, I've been working on one. It feels pretty solid."

"You run it by Mac?"

"He's touring, I think he's in California, so too early."

"I'm the default." Blaze shrugged, then settled back. "Lay it on me."

Ty hit playback, nodded at the opening notes, the first lyrics.

I see her in sunlight, and she shines. All day I wonder when she'll be mine. I see her in moonlight, and she glows. In my heart, the longing grows. I see her.

Simple, Ty thought. Slow, simple. No tricky key changes, nothing overorchestrated.

On-screen, Blaze sat, eyes closed. After the last note, he opened them. "Dreamy."

"That was the goal."

"Goal met. You know, that's going to be played at about ten million weddings."

"A handy by-product. Does it work?"

"Shit yeah. Makes me want to grab my lady and give her a nice, slow spin. You in love, brother?"

"No." On a laugh, Ty shook his head. Then stopped, shrugged. "Maybe got a thing."

"Don't tell me. The sexy, long-legged, blue-eyed neighbor with the big-ass dog."

"She hits some notes."

"Now I've gotta get down there, check out the one who got past Ty's guard. How about my man? What's he think?"

"Bray's crazy about her. Her big-ass dog doesn't hurt. The other day she had him helping her feed her chickens, get eggs, let him help her make pancakes. She's . . . different. Not like anybody else I know. But, you know, normal. No *How about signing this Code Red CD so I can cash in on eBay* or going online with how Tyler Brennan made her chicken on the grill."

On-screen, Blaze shot up a hand. "Hold on. You made chicken?"

"I'm developing untapped skills. Closest takeout's twelve miles away."

"You're in the freaking wilderness, man."

"Compared to Philadelphia, yeah. And here's a kick in the balls. I like it. It feels right here. It feels right for Bray here."

"We're coming down there, give you the Code Red seal of approval. We'll work that out. I miss you, man."

"I miss you."

"I'm signing off before I get sloppy. One thing first. You oughta record that song yourself. Don't start," he said before Ty could speak. "You don't have to do an album, just the single. No performances, no tour. Think about it. Check you later."

He signed off, leaving Ty frowning at the screen.

Maybe. Maybe he'd think about it.

And maybe he'd build a serious recording studio. If and when he wanted to record, he could do it right there.

Pull in people he knew and trusted.

Maybe, maybe. Maybe think about it.

But right now he had to deal with the laundry he'd forgotten he'd tossed in the washer.

When the bus pulled up that afternoon, Ty stood outside waiting. Bray scrambled off.

"Daddy! I'm home from school!"

He rushed over so Ty could lift him up.

"How'd it go?"

"I got *two* stickers!"

"Get out of town."

"I did, because I knew the whole alphabet and I can count all the way to a hundred and know all the colors. I know yellow and blue make green like Grave Digger, and . . ."

Ty listened as he carted Bray into the house.

"I have so many friends."

"I bet you do."

Like every boy in the history of boys, in Ty's estimation, Bray dumped his backpack on the floor.

"And when Joey didn't know the alphabet, Kevin laughed at him and pointed, and I said that was mean, and he pushed me."

"Wait. What?"

"And Miss Hanna said that wasn't 'lowed, and Kevin had to say sorry to me and to Joey, and I got to help Joey with the alphabet and got another sticker."

Ty crouched down. "You're a good man, Braydon."

"Okay. And we got to play trucks or build with blocks, and Miss Hanna read a book to us about dinosaurs, and we drew pictures of our first day of school. I'm hungry."

Because he'd done his research, Ty had a snack ready. As he set it out, he thought: We survived day one.

At the end of the first week, he felt like a vet. He had a routine, a loose one, but loose worked. Get the kid dressed—he never had to worry about getting Bray up, wondered if he ever would—get a decent breakfast into him. Pack up a lunch. Wait for the bus.

When it dawned on him he could hit the grocery store alone, he did that. Then decided he missed the company. He cleaned the house his way—in bits and pieces. Worked his way, which meant diving in until he surfaced.

And he started to make plans—vague ones, but plans—on expanding the house, painting the house, maybe remodeling enough that he could have an actual main suite and a shower where he didn't continually bang his head or elbows.

On the last day of that first week, it occurred to him he wasn't making a life here. He'd actually made one.

He decided to take a walk up the lane because it seemed to him Thea Fox was part of the life he'd made.

The dog came running, but he'd gotten used to that.

"Just me," he told Bunk. "He's not home yet."

After a long, hopeful look down the lane, the dog settled for him. They walked together.

She stood on the front porch, her hair braided back, watering pots of flowers.

He thought, yes, in sunlight, she shined.

"I wondered why I didn't hear music today. You've been busy with your music this week."

"Yeah." He stopped at the base of the porch steps. "A lot of quiet time on my hands this week."

"I liked hearing what he'd been doing in school when you walked him up a couple days ago. And you'll like hearing his teacher, my friend, says he's just delightful."

"He got three stickers yesterday and was pretty full of himself about it."

"Three stickers is something to brag about." She angled her head. "You look like a man who'd like to come in."

"I'm a man who'd like to come in. I'm hoping you're not working."

"Rem finished the last round of beta testing an hour ago."

"How'd that go?"

"Well enough I sent the files off to my boss. Now I'm anxious." Setting down the watering can, she pressed a hand to her stomach. "I put a lot into this one. I try to put a lot into every project, but this one . . ."

"Glowing snakes," he said, and walked up the steps.

"Glowing snakes and wild boars and sucking bogs and volcanos."

"Sounds dangerous." He ran a hand down her braid.

"It's not called *Perilous Island* for nothing. I don't expect to hear anything from New York until next week soonest, so I'm anxious."

"Maybe I can do something to help with your anxiety."

She tipped her face up to his. "Maybe you can."

He swept her up, made her breath catch.

"Well, that's a very promising start."

"I got more," he assured her, and carried her into the house.

Chapter Twenty-four

After *Perilous Island* got the go-ahead, Thea decided to take two weeks off before she got back to the parallel universe concept she'd put on the back burner.

Days where she'd take time to walk in the hills, for a good fall cleaning, for harvesting, for spending time with friends and family.

Time to read books, watch movies, bake, maybe to draw some for fun instead of work. And time to spend with Ty when his son was at school, and his own work allowed.

For her, it equaled a more perfect vacation than a trip to Paris, and was marred only by the occasional headache or mild nausea when she felt Riggs jiggling at her window locks.

But her confidence there grew. She'd win that battle.

As fall teased the air, she did as she pleased.

And it pleased her to go back to work after a break when she felt fresh and renewed.

If she wondered how long her life could drift this way—the battle of wills with Riggs, the house that seemed, for the first time, too empty, the man and boy down the lane that weren't really hers—she reminded herself how lucky she was to have her gift, to have her home, to have the man and boy down the lane.

Then Maddy said yes.

"What happened to six months?"

"He's sneaky." Maddy tossed her hair and curled her legs under herself on Thea's couch. "Arlo's a sneaky bastard," she said, and gulped down some wine.

"Let me see that ring again." She snatched Maddy's left hand. "A sneaky man," she agreed, admiring the princess-cut diamond, "of excellent taste."

"It is pretty, isn't it?"

"It's beautiful. I'm so happy." She threw her arms around Maddy and rocked side to side. "Happy for you, for sneaky Arlo, for me."

"Why for you?"

"Because my best friend's getting married to a sneaky but really great guy who loves her like crazy. And she's going to ask me to stand up for her. You better damn sight ask me to stand up for you."

"I didn't think I had to ask. Will you?"

"You know I will. Oh my God." She jumped up from the couch, danced in a circle. "When? When's the wedding?"

"Next spring. Probably May. He tried to sneak in right after Christmas so we could start off the new year married. Like I'd fall for that!"

Maddy *pfft!* that away.

"Not that I'm going to have some big, fancy deal. I want a great dress, but—"

"We're going shopping!" Thea sang it. "For a wedding dress for Madrigal!"

Moaning, Maddy covered her face with her hands. "Shut up. And you can pick your own dress. Style, color, whatever. I'm not going to dictate that. Except you'd look really good in blue, a soft spring blue. But"—she held up a hand—"your choice. I'm not going to be one of those . . . Oh God, Thea."

Eyes wide and desperate, Maddy clutched her hands together in prayer. "Please don't let me be one of those."

"Those what?"

"Brides."

"You're going to be a bride." Because it thrilled her, Thea did a nice, fluid pirouette. "A spring bride." Then another. "A beautiful bride." And with the third, took a bow.

"But not a crazy bride. Not one of those, Thea. If I start doing the crazy bride thing, you have to stop me. That's your job as my person. Not maid of honor because I refuse. You're not a damn maid, I'm not a damn maid. You're my person."

"I'll always be your person, and I'll wear a blue dress because I do look good in blue. You're allowed to get a little bit crazy, but I won't let you go over the edge into full-out crazy."

"Promise."

"Solemnly. You need to pick your second color. Not pink. Pink's not your color. It should be green."

"Done. That was easy."

"And you have to pick your flowers, the kind of bouquet you'll carry, and the music—"

"Thea. Are you going to be a crazy person?"

She didn't even think about it. "Absolutely. But I won't go over the edge either. I know what my best friend likes. And she's not going to want the traditional wedding march or procession."

"Oh, so much hell no."

"See? I'm going to help, as your person. We'll find the perfect music, what suits you and the sneaky bastard you're marrying."

"Yes." Relieved, a little, Maddy sipped more wine. "This is good."

"I bet your family's thrilled."

"If Mama was capable of handsprings, she'd have done them. Daddy hugged me so hard, he might've cracked a rib."

"They love Arlo."

"They do. Me, too. I love that sneaky bastard."

"Let's get more wine and go get my tablet and look up wedding dresses. Do it for me!"

"Well, if it's for you. I want a white dress." Maddy managed to look pained and resigned simultaneously. "It annoys me how much I want a white dress. Not white-white. I look better in ivory, like a warmer white.

"What is it?" Maddy demanded when Thea pressed a hand to her temple.

"Nothing."

Taking her arm, Maddy looked into Thea's eyes. "A headache. I see it. And it came on fast. Tell Dr. McKinnon."

"It's nothing, really. It's . . . Riggs. He comes at me sometimes. It gives me a little headache. It doesn't last."

"How often?"

"Maddy—"

The doctor left the bride in the dust. "How often, Thea?"

"A couple times a week, sometimes three."

"A headache, sudden onset, two or three times a week? What else?"

"Some queasiness. Not always, and it doesn't last either. Just a few minutes."

"Vomiting? Blurred vision?"

"No, and no. Honestly, it's—"

"I'm getting my bag out of the car and giving you a looking over," the doctor interrupted. "And scheduling you for a workup, including an MRI."

"Maddy."

"We rule out everything else. You do that for me, I look at wedding dresses for you."

"It's Riggs."

"We rule out everything else."

Since she'd have better luck fighting a phantom ninja than Maddy, Thea submitted.

Two days later, she let herself be poked, prodded, needle stuck, and learned during the MRI she had a touch of claustrophobia.

When she sat in the exam room, once again fully dressed, Arlo stepped in.

"Maddy had to handle an emergency walk-in. We didn't want to keep you waiting."

"Oh."

"Nothing major." He sat, lab coat over jeans, a stethoscope poking out of his pocket. "But a patient who gets a little anxious if it's anyone but Maddy. You can wait for her if you'd rather."

"No. I hardly ever see you in doctor mode. So how am I doing, doc?"

"It'll take a couple days for the lab tests, and a conclusion on the MRI. But I looked over the scan, and what I saw was a healthy brain. Nothing else."

"Good news."

328 | NORA ROBERTS

"You're a healthy weight for your height and build—barely, but you make it." He smiled at her. "I can go over point by point, but I'm going to tell you, you're fine physically."

Thea narrowed her eyes. "But?"

"The headaches, the queasiness. I know your history, Thea, and if the cause is what you say, it's out of my wheelhouse."

"It's Riggs, Arlo."

"I believe you. I know you, and I believe you. But that doesn't eliminate stress." Eyes gentle, he took her hand. "It brings stress. I can prescribe something to help with the symptoms."

"I don't want meds. I don't want to risk taking something that could loosen the locks."

"What locks?"

"I have to keep him locked out. Out of my head, block that connection we have. I don't know how else to explain it."

"That works. I'm not opposed to alternative medicine. Maddy knows more than I do in that area. Miss Lucy knows more than both of us combined, and I expect you have better than a working knowledge."

"And I'd go there if I needed. The headaches don't last. Four or five minutes, maybe. It's just a quick, sudden pain."

"The queasiness?"

"A little longer, but not as often."

He asked more questions, then took her hand again.

"This point here." He pressed a thumb on the back of her hand between her thumb and index finger. "It's called a Hegu. When the headache comes on, press your thumb there, keep it pressed, and move it in a circle."

"Acupressure, Doctor?"

"Acupressure, Psychic Girl." He sent her a reassuring smile. "It can't hurt. For the nausea, try here, inside of the wrist, between these two tendons. Fresh air, regulate your breathing, use the pressure point."

"Okay, I'll try those. I thought Maddy knew more in this area."

"I'm a quarter Chinese, so I guess I picked up something. If it persists? I want you to tell me or tell Maddy. We'll try something else."

"All right. Is the exam officially over?"

"It is."

She rose, hugged him hard. "I'm so happy you and Maddy are getting married."

His grin spread like sunlight. "I knew I'd wear her down eventually. That woman's crazy about me."

"That's true."

"I'll make her happy."

"You already do."

"We'll let you know when the test results come in, but I don't see anything to worry about. I wish he'd leave you be, Thea."

"I keep hoping he'll give up." She thought of the cut on her shoulder, then pushed that aside.

She wouldn't let it happen again.

"I'm going to take my healthy self back home. Tell Maddy that to pay for making me do all this, she's going to have to tolerate the outrageous wedding shower I'm throwing her. We're going to play games."

"She'll hate that."

Grinning, Thea picked up her purse. "I know."

She dreamed of a storm again, of slashing wind and crashing thunder. In the dream, Bunk whined as rain pounded the roof like fists. She rose, murmuring to the dog to soothe him as she walked to the window she'd left open to the night air.

And saw her garden in tatters, all the neat rows now a mire, the thriving plants, the carefully trained vines beaten into muddy ground by the fists of rain.

In the coop lay the bloody remains of her chickens. The eyes of the fox who ravaged them gleamed against the dark.

Though too late, far too late, she ran to her closet to take the shotgun down from the high shelf. She yanked open a drawer for shells loaded with rock salt.

With Bunk beside her, she rushed downstairs and straight to the back door. She yanked open the door.

Riggs walked over the muddied ruin of her garden. Not a knife in his hand, not this time. He held a gun, the same gun he'd used to kill her parents.

The same gun he'd used in the dream to shoot Ty.

"Told you I'd find a way."

As lightning split the sky, Bunk charged. Riggs lifted the gun.

Thea fired first.

And woke not in her bed, but standing at the open kitchen door on a calm, clear night. She held on to relief that her hands were empty, and her garden was undamaged. No fox in the coop, no blood on the ground.

She stood, rubbing her thumb on the acupressure point to counter the headache. Because her breath whistled in and out, she continued to stand until she could control it again.

"We're all right." She laid a hand on Bunk's head. "We're okay. He wanted to see what I'd do, that's what this was. But he doesn't really know, does he? He can get inside my head, but he doesn't really know me, and can't understand there's nothing, just nothing, I wouldn't do."

She stepped back, and though she rarely did so, locked the door. Then went through her home to lock all the others.

Work helped. Though she wasn't ready to dig deep into her new concept, she worked with teams on other projects. Her garden provided a bounty that filled her pantry with colorful jars, allowed her to share the rest.

She had visits with a little boy who whisked away shadows, and time with a man who could make her forget there'd ever been shadows.

With summer behind her, she prepared for fall and winter. She stocked and stacked wood for the fires she'd burn on those cool nights. She planted garlic, more carrots, scallions, and a host of vegetables she'd harvest through late fall and into winter.

She dug in pansies and violas to give her cheer and color when her summer blooms faded away.

Because she knew he'd enjoy it, she took pansies down the lane for Bray to plant. Ty stood on the porch watching as Bray dug in the dirt.

"Isn't it a little late to plant flowers?"

"Not pansies," Thea told him. "They like it cool. They can bloom right through winter if they're happy enough."

"They're smiling."

"They are." She ran a hand over Bray's hair. "Now whenever you leave for school or come back home, they'll be here smiling at you."

"We did shapes today. Square, rectangle, triangle, circle—I like circles best 'cause they go round and round. Hexagon, octagon, pentagon, pyramid. I got a sticker. Can I put the flower in now?"

"Almost, just a little deeper. You want the roots to take hold and spread."

"Can you move them in the spring?" Ty asked her. "If we widened the porch?"

He'd said spring, not Christmas, and Thea kept her eyes on Bray's hand.

"Pansies go leggy in the summer. They don't like the heat. You can plant new ones in early spring. You made a fine home for this one, Bray. Let's put it in."

"We're going to fly on a plane next week," he told her as he pushed and patted dirt.

"You are?" Now she looked up at Ty.

"Professional day at school next Friday. I have some business in Philadelphia, so we're taking off Thursday after school. We'll be back Sunday afternoon."

"That's exciting."

"I'm going to see Nana and Pop, and I get my birthday present."

"Even more exciting."

"And when we get back, in . . . how much?"

"A couple weeks."

"A couple weeks, I'm having a birthday party. You can come, and Grammie and Rem. Rem's funny."

"He really is," Thea agreed.

"And all my friends can come."

"I wouldn't miss it for anything."

"He means *all*. He's decreed his entire preschool class is invited. Fifteen four- and five-year-olds. Fifteen."

"We get to play games, and have cake and ice cream, and I get presents."

"Fifteen," Ty said again, and made Thea laugh.

"It'll be fun. I'll help."

With the planting and watering done, Bray raced off with the dog. Thea put her gardening gloves in her bag.

"Get a piñata."

"A piñata?"

"Everybody loves a piñata. They're five, so you can go old-school with things like Pin the Tail on the Donkey, or Musical Chairs. You can set up a beanbag game. You'll have balloons, party favors, and they'll be all over that play set out back."

He looked up at the sky. "Pray it doesn't rain."

"I'll do that, but if prayers aren't answered, you bring all that inside—except for the play set. You pull out your guitar and play. It's a dance party."

"I should take notes," Ty muttered. "How do you know all this?"

"I have nieces and nephews, Ty, and friends with children. At this age, it's a couple hours. Play games, open presents, cake and ice cream, hand out party favors. Then clean up the considerable debris."

"And the party favors are?"

She pointed at him. "Google's your friend."

"Yeah, it is. Okay, we're still praying it doesn't rain, but okay. So, I'm thinking of making grilled cheese sandwiches, maybe nuking a can of soup for dinner. Interested?"

She tossed her braid over her shoulder. "You're saying that so I'll cook dinner."

The little dimple came out to play.

"Maybe, but that was the plan before you brought those flowers. And added to my workday because now I have to remember to water them. So, it's the least you can do."

"When you put it that way. I'll go see what you've got."

"If you do that," he said as she stepped onto the porch, "it seems like the least I could do is offer you a place to stay for the night."

"That seems like a good bargain."

She never dreamed a Riggs dream when she slept beside him.

But too often, when alone, she woke with the echoes of a storm in her head.

She took a day when the hills began to shine with autumn to walk with Lucy, delivering soaps and medicinals.

"You look tired, honeypot."

"I am a little. It feels good to get out like this."

She loved how the light looked when fall came, that tint of gold, warmer than the white summer light. And the colors autumn painted, so russet and orange, bold yellow and red mixed with the blue-green of the pines.

"And I never get tired of this," she added. "Every season, when I'm in it, is my favorite."

"Every one has its time, and its wonder. Darling, I know all those tests came back clear, just like I know you're still getting headaches."

"The pressure points help there. They really do. I thought he'd give up, Grammie, because I know it hurts him more than it does me. I can feel that. But . . . I think he's feeding on the pain now."

Reaching over, Lucy touched Thea's shoulder. "He hurt you."

"Did he? I think I did that."

"What do you mean?"

"I think he sucked me in good that time. I was angry, and he sucked me in so for a minute, it was real. It was real to me, the way I made the game real when I sucked him in. So I felt the knife, and I bled. I know I'm stronger than he is, and the more I think about it . . . I don't think he could've done it.

"It's not the first mistake I've made with him."

Lucy read Thea as if the words had been spoken.

"You were a child, Thea. A grieving child."

"I was, and I'm not going to blame that child. But I should never have opened that way, gone into his cell that way, let him know I could. If I'd blocked him out all those years ago, who knows? But I didn't, and I tangled us up again instead of hacking off the root."

She linked fingers with Lucy's. "But here I am, walking in the hills, and he never will. If I'm not sleeping well, neither is he. I've got a new game coming this spring I'm really, really proud of. I'm going shopping with my best friend for her wedding dress. I'm going to a birthday party for a little boy I'm just crazy over."

"They're coming home tomorrow?"

"Tomorrow."

"Knobby tells me Ty's talking about taking down some walls, and adding on. Adding on big."

"Really?"

"Sounds like a man who's fixing on staying. We're going to stop up here. Bob Parker's arthritis. And one of his grandchildren just over the way has pink eye."

Thea wrapped an arm around Lucy's shoulders. "I used to love taking these hikes, making these visits when I was a kid. I still do."

"These hills are in our blood. You, me, Rem, and all the rest of the family."

The hound that had sired Tweedle and Dee got up from his snooze on the porch and let out a howl.

Lucy just grinned. "I do love a coonhound." She gave Bunk's head a rub. "And you, too, big boy."

On the morning of the day of what he thought of as Birthday Insanity, the forecast called for clear skies. Ty thanked all the gods.

Since Birthday Insanities required—he was firmly told—a theme, he'd ordered a Spider-Man birthday cake. He'd bought Spider-Man plates, cups, napkins.

Then because his long-legged neighbor informed him—again firmly—that the two picnic tables—his and the one from her place that Rem helped him haul down—required tablecloths, he'd sweated out the overnight delivery of Spider-Man tablecloths.

Rather than a donkey, Thea created a Pin the Web on Spider-Man board because, to Ty's mind, she fully embraced the insanity.

But he couldn't deny it was pretty damn cool.

As he hung the Green Goblin piñata he'd found through relentless internet searching, he considered the fact that just two short weeks earlier, he'd been in Philadelphia, in a recording studio.

Two of his bandmates had joined him there, and through the magic of technology, Mac's guitar and harmonic vocals would be mixed in.

It had felt good, he couldn't deny it, to be there, to do what he loved, to take back some of what he'd lost when the too much, just too much, had dimmed the light of it.

Now he was hanging a supervillain piñata in the backyard.

And he couldn't deny that felt good, too.

Across the yard, Rem showed Bray tricks with the beanbag game.

Lucy arranged chairs—most of them borrowed—in two back-to-back lines. Thea hung balloons.

Like family, he thought. Over the past months, they'd become his family.

His parents had given Bray a nice birthday party in Philadelphia. Scott and Blaze had come, with their ladies. His sister and brother, their families.

No games—but Bray had been fine with that, because presents. And cake.

But he couldn't deny either that had been a visit, because it simply wasn't home anymore, not for either of them.

He was kidding himself when he talked about maybe until Christmas or until spring.

They weren't going anywhere. Not when he looked over, watched Rem holding Bray under his arm and pretending he'd toss him like a beanbag, and Bray screaming with excitement.

Not when he watched Thea tie the famous theme balloons together.

He glanced back at the house. "You're going to take a lot of work."

And it was time to take Knobby's advice and hire an architect.

He was going to build himself a recording studio.

One day back in the studio had shown him he hadn't finished with that part of his life. The touring, yeah, that was done, that was dusted. Performing—depended, and depended first on Bray, his needs, his schedule. But he wanted to make music again. To write it and to make it.

No reason in the world he couldn't do that right here, where his kid had planted smiling pansies.

Job done, he walked over to Thea. "Is that right?"

She turned, one hand fisted on her hip. "He's ghoulish. So perfect, and just the right height. And in good time. You've got about twenty minutes before kids start arriving."

"He's ready. And he's already having a great birthday. Hell of a backdrop for it."

She looked to the hills as he did, and their sweep of color. "Nothing like fall. It paints a picture."

He cupped her chin, frowned a little. "You look tired."

"What woman doesn't love hearing that?"

"I mean it, you look tired."

"I guess birthday excitement kept me awake." At his long, quiet look, she shrugged. "Just had one of those nights where my mind wouldn't shut off, so I worked late."

"And you're working now."

"This isn't work. It's a party. I'm thinking about having another one."

"Next year, when he's six."

"A dinner party. Maddy and Arlo, Rem. Did you know he's started half dating Hanna Mansfield?"

"Bray's teacher? I did not know that."

"It's not serious. But they're seeing each other. So a party of six, if you'd come."

"That's an adult dinner party."

"It would be. Grammie would love to keep Bray, if that's okay with you."

"You're sure about that?"

"You should know the answer to that by now."

He glanced over at Lucy.

"She would. An adult dinner party where I don't have to cut up anybody's food, or wash off their face and hands after?"

"Rem can get pretty messy."

"He's on his own. I'm in. When?"

"I'll need to check with Maddy, and the rest."

"When you say Lucy would keep him, are you talking overnight?"

"I was, if that works for you."

"I'm definitely in."

Bray raced over. "When will my friends get here? When?"

"Any minute now." Thea hauled him up. "Happy birthday."

He hugged her neck. "I'm five years old! That's a whole hand old."

When she laughed, hugged his son, Ty wrapped his arms around both of them.

No, he wasn't going anywhere.

Chapter Twenty-five

He survived his first horde-of-kids birthday party.

As he cleaned up the—as predicted, considerable—debris scattered by two and a half hours of noise, small bodies in constant motion, and crazed excitement, he put the entire interlude in the success column.

And one he wouldn't have to deal with for another year.

He filled a trash bag while Thea and Rem broke down the game area and Lucy boxed up the remains of the Spider-Man cake.

The birthday boy, in a cake, ice cream, overload of fun coma, lay sprawled on the grass with the dog, like a drunk on a barroom floor.

While Ty stuffed paper plates smeared with red icing and melted ice cream in the trash bag, Lucy came out.

"How're you holding up?" she asked him.

"Better than him." He nodded toward Bray. "My ears are still ringing, and that may be a permanent condition, but like Elton, I'm still standing."

"You did good."

"No blood spilled, no broken bones. I couldn't have pulled it off without you, Rem, Thea pitching in the way you did."

"I think you'd have done just fine, but we'd've missed out on the fun."

He turned to her and, unable to resist, ran a hand down her braid. "It really was fun for you."

"Why is that surprising? I'm a grammie."

"My mom loves Bray—she loves all her grandchildren, and it shows. But this? This wouldn't have been her idea of fun."

"Well, like another song says, different strokes for different folks."

"And so on," he added, "and so on."

On a laugh, she sang, "And scooby dooby dooby. All right, daddy of the birthday boy, it looks like you're about cleared up here."

"Close enough. I'm going to break out the adult beverages."

"I wouldn't mind one before I have Rem take me home."

When they all sat on the porch, Lucy raised her glass. "To the birthday boy, and his very good daddy."

"I'll add friends to that," Ty said, "who know how to throw a hell of a kid bash."

"Here's to all of us." Rem took a pull of his beer. "Good times. Halloween's just around the corner. You could throw a spook party."

"Don't make me hurt you."

Undeterred, Rem shifted to Thea. "Remember how Mom and Dad went all out for it? Weird lights, really wild jack-o'-lanterns, spooky music. They even got a fog machine—big hit. They'd dress up, too."

"Gomez and Morticia—that was my favorite. They'd have candy, of course, but they'd set up a buffet table. Eyeballs, severed fingers, fresh blood punch."

"Good times," he said again. "They do a trick-or-treat night in town, all along Front Street."

"I could handle that." Ty looked over as Bray sat up, stared blindly. "We could handle that. We could do that."

Bray staggered over, very much like that barroom drunk, and crawled into Ty's lap.

"I'm hungry."

"How is that possible?"

"I'm five!" He held up a hand, studied it as he snuggled in. "Can we have pizza? Grammie stays, and Thea and Rem, too. And more cake."

"Sounds like a plan. If you're all in, I'll go order some."

"Since it's somebody's birthday, we can do even better. How about I make pizza?"

Bray smiled at Lucy. "You take it out of the box and put it in the oven."

"Even better than that. Rem, why don't you run on down to the house. You know what I need."

"I've got everything, Grammie. I'll go get it." Thea rose. "My place is closer."

"Take my truck, keys are in it." Rem winked at Bray. "You're in for a major treat now. Grammie's pizza's the best. And I've got time for a couple slices before I take off."

"Like an airplane?"

"Like a man who's got a hot date."

"What's a hot date?"

"Keep digging," Ty murmured.

"It's when I take a pretty woman to the movies."

"Why's it hot?"

"You can't have a movie without popcorn, and you can't melt butter on popcorn unless you get it hot."

"Prime save."

Rem shrugged. "It's a skill."

Good times, Ty thought.

That night when his boy slept, when Thea slept beside him, Ty lay awake.

His life, he realized, had taken a major turn. His great-grandmother hadn't just left him a house and five acres in eastern Kentucky. She'd given him the opportunity to make that turn, build another kind of life.

He hadn't expected it to be like this, to find himself rooting here, and making plans to spread those roots. To see his little boy thriving in this new place.

He hadn't expected people who'd been strangers only months before to become such an integral part of that life. To become not just friends, but a family he never really understood he wanted.

He sure as hell hadn't expected the woman sleeping warm and soft beside him. A woman he'd started falling for almost from the first minute of the first day.

He'd put even the idea of a real relationship aside, locked it away. Too many betrayals, small and large, to risk another now that he had Bray.

Then Thea changed everything.

She'd opened her own life to him and his son in such an easy, loving way. No demands, no slyness, no hidden agendas.

She'd given him something he'd missed, something maybe his early, rushing success had tainted.

She'd given him someone who cared about who, not what, he was. And who understood and accepted who he was now. Someone he could trust in a way he'd been unable, or unwilling, to trust in a very, very long time.

He had to find the right time, the right place to play her the song he'd written for and about her. The right time to tell her what she'd come to mean to him.

For the first time he wanted someone not just to be in his life but to make a life with him.

She was the one, he thought as he drifted to sleep. The only one.

It became a kind of routine. Ty grilling on a Friday or Saturday night, often both, with Thea joining them.

She never dreamed of storms when she shared Ty's bed.

If Ty came to her door during the week, during the school day, she found she could block out Riggs.

Maybe happiness served as her lock.

Though the headaches lingered, she worked, and found her focus there helped keep him at bay.

They broke routine on Halloween when she stepped out of the house in snug black, with knee-high boots, and with a sword at her side. Bunk, with a pair of red wings on his massive back, trotted down beside her.

When she opened the car door, Ty gave her a long look.

"First, wow. Second, you have a sword."

"It's rubber, until the ninja needs its keen blade. This is Bunk, the flying dog, the protector of the innocent."

As he jumped in the back, Thea looked in, feigned shock. "Spider-Man! Ty, Spider-Man came to Redbud Hollow!"

"It's me!" Bouncing, Bray laughed like a maniac. "It's really me, Bray!"

"No! Wow, you sure fooled me." Sliding into the car, she studied Ty's T-shirt, jeans, high-tops, hoodie. "And who are you supposed to be?"

"Peter Parker."

"That's one way to get out of it. But how can Spidey and Peter be in the same car?"

"I'm from the multiverse."

"That explains it." She shifted to talk to Bray. "How was the Halloween party at school?"

"So much fun! We got cupcakes, and Miss Hanna was a witch! And Lucas was Blaze."

"From *PAW Patrol*," Ty explained.

"Rolan was Iron Man and Jenny was Princess Peach."

"You asked for it," Ty murmured as Bray recounted costumes.

She had, Thea thought, and it delighted her.

So did the ghouls, goblins, fairy princesses, and superheroes walking down Front Street. Kids swarmed the shops where costumed staff handed out candy, and the houses where towners handed out more.

It surprised her a little, and delighted her even more, when she realized how many people who walked their kids or who handed out those treats Ty knew.

It shouldn't have surprised, she thought. He did business here, banking and shopping and marketing. His little boy went to school here. He'd built a foundation here.

Nearly half a year now, she thought as she shifted Bunk's leash to her other hand, and took Ty's.

He hadn't said absolutely he'd stay, but he'd talked to an architect, and he talked about adding on a studio.

She didn't look for promises, but she'd take hope.

She felt that hope when they took a sleepy boy home, and with his head on his father's shoulder, he asked for four books.

"Two."

"Thea reads one. Bunk sleeps in my room. Daddy reads, Thea reads, Bunk sleeps in my room. Please?"

"Okay with you?"

She went upstairs with them, watched Ty strip off the costume. "Hey, it was Peter Parker under there all along."

"Daddy."

"Into pj's, Pete."

"I'm Bray!"

"Are you sure?" He flipped Bray upside down, then right side up before tossing him on the bed.

"I'm Braydon Seth Brennan, and I'm five."

"Huh. Well, you do look familiar."

"Thea reads first. *Picklebottom*!"

Ty glanced at her. "We like saying *Picklebottom*."

"Who wouldn't?" Thea agreed when Ty took a book from the shelf. She sat on the bed so Bray could see the pictures and follow along.

Less than ten pages in, Ty reached over. "He's out." He tucked the covers, skimmed a hand over Bray's hair. "He had a big day."

After taking the book, setting it aside, he took her hand. "Let's go downstairs. I'll start a fire. I'm getting pretty good at it. We can have some wine, raid Bray's candy stash. Maybe a little later, you'll show me some ninja moves."

"I do have some."

"Yeah, I saw that once already, with a real sword. Time for an encore."

She didn't dream of a storm that night, but of standing at her window—closed tight, locked tight—and watching one build over the hills she loved.

Lightning flashed in the distance, and the mutter of thunder followed.

In the dream, she shivered.

She woke with a mild headache, and rose to let Bunk out, to step out herself to let the brisk autumn air clear it away. She'd promised Bray another round of pancakes, and had stocked Ty's house with what she needed.

At home in his kitchen now, she put the coffee on, lined a cookie sheet with parchment paper for the bacon. With the headache gone, she hummed to herself.

She wondered if she could talk Ty into taking Bray on a Saturday morning hike. The fall morning just called out for one.

They could circle around, come down the trail behind her grandmother's, pay a visit there.

Too pretty to spend a Saturday inside, to her mind. She could go up, feed the chickens, get her boots, then—

The arms that came around her from behind made her jump, then laugh.

"Who doesn't love coming into the kitchen on a Saturday morning and finding a beautiful woman making breakfast, and the coffee waiting?"

"I promised pancakes."

"Yeah, you did." After kissing the side of her neck, Ty went straight for the coffee. "And since the first time you did, Bray says the boxed mix is yuck."

"I wouldn't say yuck, but compared?"

Ty gulped coffee. "He hasn't yet refused frozen pizza, but I fear that day may come. Thankfully tots are still on the approved list."

"I bet I can make them from scratch."

He looked sincerely aggrieved. "Please don't. Seriously. I've got to have some fallback here."

He leaned back against the counter. "I know you're doing that dinner party thing, coming up on that. But how about an adult dinner neither of us have to cook? If Lucy would take Bray again. We're going on six months without a single traditional date."

"We're not really traditional people."

"Aren't you, Thea?"

She glanced over. "I guess, in some ways."

"I guess in some ways, so am I. And in that traditional way, I'd like to take you out to dinner."

"Daddy."

"Hey, pal," he said, but his eyes stayed on Thea's.

"I can't find Grave Digger."

"Which one?"

"The one that does the tricks. Somebody stole it."

Ty topped off his coffee. "Right, forgot. We were supposed to look yesterday. Nobody stole it, Bray. It's around here somewhere."

"They did! Somebody stole it so I can't find it. I need it. Get it back, Daddy!"

"We'll look for it after breakfast. Pancakes—Thea's kind—remember?"

"I need it. If somebody stole it, I can't take it to school for show-and-tell. And I said I was."

"We'll find it. Maybe it's in your toy chest."

"It's not, 'cause I looked and looked."

While Thea laid bacon on the cookie sheet, she heard tears threaten. "This time I'll look and look."

"Somebody came in my room and took it." Devastated, Bray knuckled his eyes. "I'll never ever see it again."

"Bray, take a breath. Who'd do that?"

"Monsters. Bad guys."

"Come on, man." Ty set down the coffee, picked up the boy. "We don't have any monsters or bad guys around here."

"I think Grave Digger's playing hide-and-seek."

At Thea's words, Bray sniffled back another whine, and frowned at her. "He is?"

"I bet he is, and hoping you'll come find him. Did you look in the library your dad's making, in the box of books he hasn't unpacked yet? The box that came a few days ago?"

"No."

"Maybe you should."

"I'll look now!" Bray wiggled down, raced off.

Moments later, he shouted.

"I found him, I found him. He was playing hide-and-seek in the box. His 'mote was on the floor!"

"Pretty sneaky." Thea finished laying the bacon, reached for a dish-cloth.

"Bray, take Grave Digger upstairs, play with him in your room awhile."

"Okay." Clutching it like a lover, he ran.

"How did you know where that toy was?"

"What?" She picked up the cookie sheet, and turning, saw Ty's face. Everything inside her began to shake. "I just . . ."

"He said something about it a couple days ago, and I forgot. Then yesterday, and I got busy. I haven't been in that room since I put that box in there, opened it. Monday. Since Monday. But obviously you have."

"No, I—"

"Why would you go into a box of books? What else have you gone into?"

"I didn't." Her lungs felt hot. Hot and tight. "It's complicated. I can—"

"It's not complicated. It's really so fucking simple. You've still got a key? How many times have you been in here, going through our things when I was out?"

The words, as harsh as a blow to the face, took her back a step.

"I never did that. I wouldn't. I gave your father the key I had at the funeral. Ty—"

"Then you made a copy. I trusted you. I trusted you with my son."

"Oh my God, Ty. I'd never do anything to hurt him, to hurt you. Please listen."

"You really played me." In visible disgust, he dragged a hand through his hair. "Jesus Christ, I should've known better. You need to leave. You need to get out, now. Stay away from my boy. If I find out you've sold pictures of him, I swear to God there'll be a reckoning."

"I swear I didn't—"

"I want you out." He yanked open the back door. "Get out of my house. Don't come back here. Don't send your dog down here. Keep your family away. We're done."

He wouldn't listen. He wouldn't hear. He wouldn't believe. Everything that pumped out from him now was disgust, was rage barely held in check.

As she walked by him, the headache spiked so hard and fast it took her breath. But she kept walking. She called for her dog and kept walking.

One moment of carelessness, she thought, one moment brought on by a child's tears, and she'd lost what she wanted most.

Halfway up the lane, she stopped because her knees buckled, and the nausea roiled a storm in her belly.

She couldn't hold him off, couldn't with her head pounding, her stomach churning. In her head, Riggs laughed.

Kicked your sorry ass out! He just wanted an easy fuck, and you sure gave him that. Crawl on home, bitch. I'm not the only one in a cell. He's done with you. Nobody wants you, freak. Nobody ever will.

Bent over, her hands braced on her knees, she fought to breathe as Bunk licked her cheek and whined.

"I'll be all right. We'll be all right."

No, you won't. Not now, not ever. You fucked it up. You always will.

Because the sickness was worse than the pain, she used the pressure point at her wrist. She straightened up, kept walking.

Just kill yourself. Riggs whispered in her head now. *What've you got to live for? Never gonna have anybody, always gonna be alone. That guy in college, he had it right. Freak. Fucking freak. Never gonna have what dead mommy and daddy had. Never gonna have that till-death bullshit.*

You'll die alone, so get it over with. Slit your wrists, and be done. Pay him back, too, right? He'll feel like the shit he is.

Do it. Do it.

In a battle, she reminded herself, use any weapon. She used the flood of emotion streaming inside her, and drowned Riggs out.

She wasn't alone. She had family, she had friends. She had life.

She had to feed Bunk, tend the chickens. She had to take one step, then take the next.

Her house, she thought when she reached it. Her home. Not a cell. She walked straight through it, picking up her egg basket. Fresh food and water for Bunk, then out to the coop; she took one step, then the next.

No tears—she wouldn't shed them. A man didn't want her, love her, trust her. He wasn't the first, but Thea promised herself he'd be the last.

She'd never put herself through this again.

Then she turned to see her grandmother running toward her, and nearly broke the promise seconds after she made it.

"Oh, my baby!" Lucy wrapped her arms around Thea, held tight. "I felt your heart break. What happened?"

"I ruined it. I ruined it."

"No. Here, give me that." Keeping an arm around Thea, Lucy took the egg basket. "You'll sit down, come on with me, and we'll sit down. You'll tell me. We'll fix it."

"We can't. I'll be all right. I just need to . . . I don't know."

"You had a fight with Ty."

"It wasn't like that."

"If you don't want to tell me, I won't look. We'll just sit and be awhile."

"I wanted too much. I started to want too much. I should know better."

When they reached the porch, Thea just sat on the steps. She'd taken all the steps she could. She'd take more later.

"Everything seemed so right, Grammie. I didn't think or look beyond that. I didn't want to. I was making breakfast. I was going to make Bray a Spider-Man pancake. I was thinking of that, and how good I felt. How happy."

She had to breathe, in and out. She just had to breathe.

"Ty's drinking coffee, and it all felt so good and right and easy. Bray comes in, and he's upset. He can't find his truck. Grave Digger, the one that does tricks. And he and Ty are talking. Bray said somebody stole it, and Ty said we'll look for it after breakfast, and how it's gone missing for a few days.

"He's such a happy boy, Grammie, and he was so upset, starting to cry, and I just didn't think. I was careless. I told him where to find it."

Because her eyes ached, Thea pressed her fingers to them.

"I looked and I saw him playing with it in the library Ty's setting up, and how he heard Bunk coming, and dropped it in this box of books that Ty hadn't unpacked."

On a sigh, she laid her head—no longer throbbing—on Lucy's shoulder. "Bray was so happy when he found it, and Ty told him to take it up to his room and play. Then I turned around, and saw Ty's face, and knew I'd made a mistake. Everything that was good and right and easy died away. He was so angry, so cold with it.

"How could I know where to find that toy unless I'd been in the house when I shouldn't? I hadn't been there since he opened that box of books."

"Did you explain?"

"I couldn't. He wouldn't hear me. He thinks I broke his trust." She squeezed her eyes tight. "And maybe I did. But he thinks I used his little boy, I used his feelings, so he wouldn't hear me."

"You'd never do that, never." Tears thickened her voice as Lucy held Thea close. "He'll come to realize that."

"He told me to get out, to stay away from Bray, from him, to keep y'all away."

"We'll give him a little time to simmer down, then I'll talk to him."

"No, Grammie." Shaking her head, she breathed in and out, she looked up at the hills.

"No, it's not a misunderstanding, it's not a . . . spat. It's who we are. Both of us.

"Both of us," she repeated. "He thought that of me, thought of me sneaking into his house, going through his things, using that sweet little boy. Using sex. That he could think that of me, it's worse, so much worse than understanding what I have and thinking I'm a freak. I know what that feels like, and this is worse."

She reached for Lucy's hand. "And for him? He's been betrayed before, so he doesn't give that trust easily. He gave it to me, and I betrayed him. Worse, I betrayed the most precious thing in his life. Braydon."

"But you didn't, darling."

"Didn't I?"

The facts lined up in front of her, and she wouldn't deny them.

"We've been together awhile now, since summer. But I never told him what I have. I didn't want to look ahead, so I didn't. I didn't want to tell him and have him look at me like something was twisted inside me.

"He trusted me, but I didn't trust him. Not enough. Which is worse?"

"Thea, you were protecting yourself."

"Yes, yes, I was. And he's protecting his son."

On a shake of her head, Lucy let out a long, frustrated breath. "And you don't see that boils down to what you said it wasn't? A misunderstanding?"

Thea shifted, looked into Lucy's eyes. "When did you tell Grandpa you had a gift?"

"Now, that's different."

"Why?"

"We both grew up here, and people knew about my granny, my mama, me. And back before that."

"You never told him directly?"

"I suppose I did, but it wasn't something that came as a surprise. You'd've told Ty when you were ready. It just got away from you."

"And how would knowing what I have let him trust me again? It's trust, Grammie, that's so important to him."

"If he can't trust and respect what you have, who you are, well, darling, he's not worth what I thought he was."

"I wanted too much," Thea repeated, "so I wasn't honest with him. I didn't and I don't deserve what he said to me, what he thinks of me, but I wasn't honest. I didn't respect myself enough, I didn't respect what I have, so I held back because I wanted him, I wanted Bray, I wanted that pretty picture too much to risk it.

"Now I've lost it."

"Listen now." Lucy laid her hands on Thea's shoulders. "You'll take time, and give him time. Then you'll risk it, Thea. You're not a coward. God knows you've taken more risks in your life than I'd like. Love takes risks. You'll make him listen. You'll make him hear you. The rest is up to him."

"I was a coward about this. I didn't think of it that way, but that's the truth. So I won't be. I'll give us both time. There's really nothing to risk now anyway."

"Why don't you come on home with me?"

"I'm going to work. I can lose myself in my work. I'll be all right, Grammie. I'm glad you came. You're what I needed. You steadied me up."

Now Lucy laid her hands on Thea's cheeks. "If that steady starts to wobble, you come to me."

"I will. Can you tell Rem? Just tell him to give Ty some space?"

"Don't worry about that." With a murmur, Lucy pressed a kiss to Thea's forehead. "He's going to want to go over there and give Tyler the what for. I'll hold him off."

"Good, thanks."

When Lucy left, Thea sat a bit longer, one arm around Bunk. The last gusts of October had stripped trees bare. Now all but the pines stood stark and ready for the coming winter.

The sky had gone gray—not storm gray, just dull. Sheetrock dull, with the sun closed behind.

"That's how I feel, Bunk. Sheetrock dull. Let's go inside, light the fires."

She rose, walked onto the porch. Not a cell, no, her home wasn't her prison.

It was her sanctuary.

Chapter Twenty-six

For three days Ty dealt with Bray's questions about the dog, about Thea, and made excuses. He tolerated the whining, hoping the kid would eventually lose interest.

Since he knew his son, he understood that was a doomed hope, but he held on to it for sanity's sake.

He knew what he had to do. Pack up and move back to Philadelphia. Easier, by far, if he hadn't sold the damn house. Buy a new house, new start? Sounded fine.

Something with a good-sized yard, a quiet, kid-friendly neighborhood. He'd contacted his Realtor, put her on the hunt, so they'd see there.

He wouldn't uproot Bray until he had the house, and even then not until the end of the school term.

Packing up wouldn't be that hard. He'd sell the house furnished. What the hell did he care?

But they couldn't stay here. This was her place, full of her people.

The woman who'd broken his goddamn heart.

He needed to have the locks changed, another pain in his ass. But he couldn't risk going out for a damn quart of milk without wondering if she'd let herself in.

How could he have been so wrong about her? That single question hounded him.

She had pictures of his son. God, she'd taken pictures at the birthday party, when Bray had first climbed all over his play set. Pictures of Bray with her dog.

How stupid had he been to let her take pictures, pictures she could sell?

Maybe that didn't sound like her. Maybe there was a place deep in his gut that didn't believe it of her. He had to ignore that, because facts were facts.

He'd fallen for her, and so had Bray. And he'd thought . . .

Didn't matter. Couldn't matter what he'd thought.

And right now he had a kid home from school—just sick enough for staying home with a fever of 100.2 that morning. But not sick enough by midmorning—down to 98.9—to stay in bed and sleep, or eat some canned soup and watch TV.

"I want Bunk to come."

Ty looked down at his son, his heart, the center of his world, and wished he'd just shut the hell up.

"He can't."

"Why?"

"You're sick, remember? You've got germs."

"I feel better, and dogs don't care 'bout germs."

"I care. Go play with the racetrack I set up for you."

"I don't wanna. I wanna see Bunk. I'm hungry. I want Thea to make me pancakes. She promised!"

Around and around, Ty thought, went this particular, irritating loop. "She can't. She's working."

"I wanna go to her house. I wanna go see Grammie. I wanna see the chickens."

Ty dragged more books off the shelves it seemed he'd just put on them. "To quote a classic, pal, you can't always get what you want."

"Why? I want pancakes. Thea's pancakes."

"Well, you're not getting them. I'll make you a jelly sandwich."

"No, Daddy!"

When the tears started, Ty wondered if beating his head against the wall would work.

"Braydon, I said she's busy."

"We can call her."

Enough, he thought as his temper snapped. Just enough.

"No, we can't." He looked down at the tearful, angry face and decided it was time to lay it out.

"We're not going to see her anymore. We're going home for Christmas and we're staying there. Got it?"

"This is home."

"No, it's not. We're going back to Philadelphia."

"No!" New tears, furious ones, spurted. "No! No! No! This is home. We're staying home. You promised!"

"No, I didn't." He knew that truth, as he was damn careful with promises. "I said we'll see, and we've seen."

"No, no! I go to school. I have friends."

"You'll go to school back home, and make friends."

It seemed to Ty fire spurted from his son's eyes along with the tears.

"I don't want that school, I don't want those friends. I'm not going there."

"Pal, you go where I go, that's how it works."

Since he'd counted to ten a half a dozen times in his head, he judged himself calm enough to use reason.

And bribes.

"We'll get a new house. You can help me pick it out. And we'll get you a puppy. You can have your own dog."

"I don't want that stupid, ugly dog. I want Bunk! I don't want that stupid house. I want this house. I'm not going. You can't make me."

And fuck reason, Ty thought. Time for discipline. "Can and will."

"No packing!" Bray yanked books from the box, threw them down.

"Stop that." When Ty picked him up, Bray pushed and struggled with enough furious strength, he nearly popped out of Ty's arms. "I said knock it off!"

"You're mean. You're mean, Daddy."

"And about to get meaner. You go up to your room. You've earned a major time-out."

"I don't want you. I want Thea."

"You're not getting her. Go to your room." He set Bray down. "If I have to carry you up, double time-out."

"Don't want you to carry. Don't want you." Bray stood, little hands in fists at his sides, body vibrating with fury, face red with it. "I don't like you anymore."

"Yeah? I'm not real fond of you at the moment," Ty called out when his little boy stomped out of the room.

He listened to Bray stomp up the stairs, then sat on the floor with the scattered books.

Jesus, sometimes parenting sucked right out loud.

Full-blown tantrum, he thought, waiting for his own temper to cool. It had been a while, and this one sure as hell topped all the other meltdowns along the way.

"Shouldn't have told him that way. Fuck, fuck, fuck." After pressing his fingers to his eyes, he started picking up books. "As much my fault as his. More."

If he hadn't gotten tangled up with the woman, hadn't opened himself and his boy up to her the way he had . . .

"Done, just done."

He tossed books in the box, thought the hell with it.

He got up, went into his studio. He chose a guitar, plugged it in. And played loud, pissed-off rock to take the edge off.

The music made Bray even madder. Daddy didn't care what he wanted. He didn't care about his friends, about Bunk, about anybody.

He wanted Bunk. He wanted Thea and his friends and Grammie and Rem and Miss Hanna.

Still wearing his Mario pajamas, he put on his shoes. He could tie them now. He was a big boy, and he could tie his shoes. He could walk to Thea's all by himself, and she'd let him play with Bunk and make him pancakes and he'd live in her house because his daddy was mean.

Choosing his blue monster truck, he went downstairs while the music rang out. He went out the front door.

Deep in the work, Thea nearly didn't hear the knock on the front door. Bunk did, and ran for it.

"All right, damn it."

Annoyed by the interruption at a critical point in her coding, she pushed up to answer.

When she opened the door, Bunk rubbed himself all over the little boy with teary eyes and a runny nose.

"I'm cold," he said, and sobbing, threw himself on the dog.

"Oh my goodness, Braydon." She shrugged out of her cardigan, wrapped it around him. "Is Daddy all right?"

"Daddy doesn't like me anymore. I want to stay with Bunk. I don't want to go back to 'delphia. Can I live in your house?"

"Oh, baby." She picked him up and dug in the pocket of the sweater for a tissue. "Of course your daddy likes you. He loves you more than anything in the whole world. Did you walk up here all by yourself?"

"I'm a big boy." He sobbed it. "I tied my shoes."

"You are, such a big boy." She swayed, she stroked, she soothed. "Your daddy's going to be worried."

"No. He says we have to go and I can't have my school and my friends and Bunk, and you're too busy."

He wrapped his arms around her neck. "I don't want to go away. I want my daddy. I want my daddy to like me. I want to stay here with my daddy."

"Okay. It'll be all right. Everything's going to be all right. Let's get you home. Your daddy's going to be scared if he doesn't find you."

"I said I didn't like him anymore."

"He knows you didn't mean that. It's all right." Crooning, Thea carried him to the car.

"Tell him we have to stay."

"Don't worry about that." After she set him in the car, she buttoned up the cardigan. "Don't worry."

With Bunk in the back, she drove down the lane.

When she pulled up, rushed around to lift Bray out of the passenger seat, Ty bolted out of the back door.

"Braydon."

She set the boy down, then stepped back as Ty sprinted over to grab him. "I couldn't find you, I couldn't find you. Don't ever do that. I couldn't find you. You scared me."

He pressed his face to his son's hair, breathed him in. "I love you so much. I'm sorry I yelled at you. I'm sorry."

"I'm sorry, Daddy. Don't be mad at me again."

"No, no, I'm not mad. I won't be mad."

He glanced over to thank Thea, but she was already driving back up the lane.

"We're okay. We're going to be okay. Nobody's more important to me than you," he said as he carried Bray into the house. "We're going to take care of each other, right? You and me."

He let Bray sleep in his bed that night as much to comfort himself as his son. Nothing had ever scared him as much as the shattering fear in that few minutes after he'd taken Bray a jelly sandwich and found an empty room.

Searching the house, calling—pissed at first that the kid had defied the time-out rule. Then realizing his boy wasn't there. Wasn't anywhere.

His heart, his soul. His son.

And his fault, Ty thought when he checked Bray's temperature in the morning. Normal. When he got him ready for school, when he watched him get on the bus.

His fault.

He'd brought Bray to this place, and he'd made it home. He honestly hadn't realized how much of a home until he'd searched the house and couldn't find his little boy anywhere in it.

So, his fault, because he hadn't listened. Because he hadn't wanted to admit he broke his child's heart because someone had broken his.

He'd have to find a way to stay. He'd have to work out boundaries with Thea. Get the locks changed, get Bray a puppy. Hell, he'd get chickens if that's what it took.

He'd build his studio, and put up a fence for privacy.

He'd do whatever he had to do.

Because he never wanted to see that abject misery on his son's face again.

He picked up the cardigan he'd tossed over the back of the sofa.

He had to return it, and he had to thank Thea for bringing his boy back to him. And holding on to his temper, he'd make certain she understood to keep her distance.

To give that temper time to stay cool, he grabbed a jacket and walked up the lane.

He hadn't wanted to move either, but still thought it the wiser choice. Unwise or not, they'd make this work.

Locks, a privacy fence, a security system. But she'd damn well give him that key.

And he'd be as calm and reasonable as possible when he told her to delete any photos she'd taken of Bray.

The dog trotted across the yard when he spotted Ty.

"You're going to keep your distance, too."

Maybe he'd fallen for the damn dog, too, but he had his priorities.

He knocked on the front door.

She looked tired, he thought when she opened the door. Pale with it. And, he realized, wary.

"I wanted to return this."

"Oh. Yes." She took the sweater. "Could I ask how Bray is?"

"He's fine. I appreciate you bringing him home yesterday."

"Of course. You . . . must've been frantic."

"That's a word for it. I'd like to talk to you if you have a minute."

"Yes, sure. Come in. Stay out for a while, Bunk." She closed the door. "Do you want to sit down?"

"No." He'd make this quick, and he'd make this clean. "I know Bray told you why he was upset."

"Yes. I understand why you're leaving, but I . . . I wish you wouldn't because of what you think of me. You told me to stay away, and I have. I will."

"I need the key back, and I want you to delete any pictures you took of Braydon off your phone."

She just stared at him, then something flashed in her eyes as she turned, gestured. He followed her into her studio where she snatched a framed photo of Bray and Bunk from her workstation.

"Here, take it. I printed out one of my grandmother and Bray and gave it to her. I'll get it back."

Her movements fast and fluid, she opened a closet. "I've done a little Christmas shopping." Turning back, she pushed another framed photo at him. One of Bray coming down the slide and Ty standing at the base, grinning.

"I was going to give this to you then, so take it now. Those are the only ones I printed out."

She grabbed her phone from the workstation charger, swiped up her photo roll, then shoved it at him.

"Delete away. Hey, while you're at it, go ahead and search through, see if you find where I've communicated with whoever-the-fuck for selling them. That's what you think of me."

She'd ditched the wary, he noted, and now stood in full righteous fury mode.

"I'm not going through your phone. I'm asking you to delete the photos."

"No. Do it yourself. After, you can go through my computer—not that one, that's strictly work-related and you're not touching it. But my others, my tablets—I have two. And you can search the goddamn house for the key I don't have because I gave it to your father after the funeral.

"If you think you have to protect that child from me, you're a complete dick."

When she stalked out, he put her phone down and followed her back to the living room.

"I lock the house, Thea. I don't leave the house unlocked, ever. I'm going to change the locks, but I want that key. Those books, that box, they weren't there when you were. That damn truck wasn't in there the last time you were in the house with us. It's just that simple."

"No, it's not. You actually think I've snuck around inside your house, that I'd sell pictures of your son." Fury burning, she lifted a hand. "Oh, hey, maybe I put a camera in your bedroom—you better check. I could sell sex videos because I'm so obviously someone who craves the spotlight, and money, let's not forget the money."

She threw out her arms, circled like a cat in a cage.

"I've gotta rake that in even though I inherited a substantial trust fund when my parents were murdered, and I make a damn good living. I make it with my own time, effort, and talent, but I need to cash in on you and your little boy, because, wow, I just can't get enough."

Tears flowed now, but hot ones as she stood rubbing her right thumb under her left.

"You can get out now. You can stay away from me. I don't want someone in my life who'd think so low of me. I love Bray, but you can't see that? I love you, but that doesn't matter?"

Spinning around to pace, she pressed the heels of her hands to her eyes. "Damn it, damn it, damn it! I'm not wasting tears on you. I'll get over you. You're making it easy. Change the locks, put up a goddamn force field, run back to Philadelphia, or go to hell. I haven't done anything to deserve being treated like a thief, like a user, and I don't need your brand of cynicism in my life."

"You're not going to turn this around on me." Every bit as enraged as she now, he snapped back. "You didn't come in the house, use a key? How the hell did you know where to find that fucking truck? What, are you psychic?"

She gave him a long, cool look. "It's a gift that runs through the women in my family."

He'd have laughed if it hadn't been so damn insulting.

"Are you serious? For Christ's sake. So you just"—he flicked his free hand at his head—"poof, used your internal crystal ball to find freaking Grave Digger in a box of freaking books? All I want is the goddamn key, Thea."

"I don't have a key to your house. I don't have a secret way into your house. I've never stepped foot in your house since you moved in without an invitation. You should leave now, because I'm done being insulted."

"You're insulted? That's rich. You're psychic, the psychic finder of kids' toys? Great, prove it. What number am I thinking of?"

"Oh, how typical." Rubbing hard on her hand, she turned away from him again. "How utterly childish and typical."

"That's what I thought."

She didn't turn as he started for the door, just clasped her hands together.

"G minor seventh isn't a number, it's a musical chord. But clever."

When he stopped dead, she turned again. She didn't look furious now. She looked tired, just tired.

"You want more? That little scar on your hip?" She tapped her fingers on her own hip, then started rubbing her hand again. "You got it crawling under a chain-link fence, a broken one, and one of the—what is it, spokes? Whatever, it caught you there. You could've used a couple stitches, but you couldn't tell your mother because you and Scott and . . . Henry weren't supposed to poke around the old, abandoned house. You were nine, and you've still never told her that one."

It took him several shocked seconds to find his voice. "How the hell did you know that?"

"I touched you there, the first time we were together, and I was so open, so unguarded, I saw you, I saw the little boy. I don't look, I don't. It's rude and I was raised better, but I just . . . my defenses were down, and I saw."

Tears came again, faster now. "It's a gift, and I respect it, value it. It doesn't make me a freak or—or some demon seed. I don't use it to hurt people, or to pry or for my own gain. I didn't mean to use it that day, but Bray wanted that truck so much. He was so upset, and he's such a good boy, and I got careless. I just didn't think, and then you said those things to me, about me, and you wouldn't listen. I didn't know how to explain, not then, and you wouldn't have listened or believed me, not then."

After scrubbing her hands over her face, she left them covering it. "Go. Just go. I don't want to know what you think. I don't want to know."

"I think you should sit down."

"Don't tell me what I should do."

"Okay, but I need to sit down."

"Sit, stand, stay, go. I don't care. I'm not some sideshow here for your amazement and amusement. I have a gift, one that runs through the women in my family. Tall, rangy builds run in my family. Neither of those make me evil."

Setting the photos down, he sat because he needed to catch his breath. "Who said anything about evil?"

"That would be a boy in college—my first time, as I got a late start in that area. I told him because I had feelings for him, and I'd slept with him, and I thought . . .

"He didn't react well. The people he told ran the usual gamut from *You're a freak* to *How about telling me the questions on the test coming up.*"

"Listen, I—"

She rolled right over him.

"It was painful, and demoralizing. I nearly ran home after that, but I stuck. Kept to myself more, was a lot more careful. It's my gift, it's my business. I don't have to share it."

"How long have you been able to . . . know stuff?"

"Always. What difference does it make?"

"What's wrong with your hand?"

"Nothing." She stopped rubbing under her thumb, and crossed her arms.

"If you'd told me or—"

"What?" She lashed out the word. "Everything would've been fine? You, such a trusting individual, would've trusted me not to walk into your private thoughts like you assumed I'd walked into your locked house? Because I said I wouldn't?"

He started to speak, stopped. Then lifted his hands, let them fall. "I don't know. I'm trying to get my head around it. I don't know."

"You hurt me." Her breath shuddered out as she tried to steady it. "You hurt me more than anyone ever has."

"I know it. I can see it. I'm sorry for it. And goddamn it, you hurt me right back. Look, this is a little—this is a lot. I'm trying to . . . process."

"Well, you do that, Ty, you take your sweet time and process. It doesn't change a thing. I'm the same person I was five minutes ago, five hours ago, five days ago. I'm not ashamed of that. Being careful doesn't mean I'm ashamed."

He saw the pain even before she sucked in her breath, and rubbed at her hand.

"What the hell's wrong with your hand?" He pushed up, reached for it, but she snatched it away.

"Nothing. Nothing. It's not my hand, it's my head. He's pushing, pushing. It hurts. It's harder to keep him out when I'm upset, and it hurts."

"Who?"

"Riggs! Ray Riggs, the bastard who murdered my parents. He can get into my head; I can get into his. I don't know why. God, he's loving this. He loves to see me suffer. I sent him to prison, and he needs me to pay. I saw him. I was there when he killed them."

Not just pale now, he thought, but almost translucent. And breathing too fast. "Sit down. Let's sit down. You said you were here when it happened, with Lucy."

"I was here, I was there." She tried to resist, but he pulled her over to the couch. "It was a dream, it wasn't a dream. I was there, but I couldn't stop him. I couldn't do anything but watch. Watch him break into the house by the back sliders. He hated them for having a big house. Should've been his, everything should be his. He'd take it. The watch, he wanted her watch."

"Slow down."

But she couldn't.

"He'd seen her, dressed for a meeting. Professional Woman, she called it. Dressed so nice, wearing the watch Dad gave her for their anniversary. I knew because he knew, because he thought it. The gallery wall. My picture. He knew something when he saw my picture. He wanted to kill me. Rem, too, but me more than anything."

"Slow down, Thea. Come on now, slow your breathing down. Look at me."

But she couldn't, not when she was back in the house, seeing it all again. He could almost see it himself, in eyes brilliantly blue.

"He has a gun, and I can't stop him. Upstairs, looking at everything, hating them just for being, for having. He doesn't even know them, but hates them. They're sleeping, and he takes one of the pillows, the pretty pillows Mom likes to put on the bed. He puts it over my father's face and he—he—he shoots him through it.

"I'm screaming, screaming, but it's only in my head." Clamping her hands on her head, she rocked. "Mom wakes up, and calls for Dad. *John, John.* But Riggs puts the gun to her head. *Shut the fuck up, bitch.* But she can't stop. Crying, calling, and he hits her, he makes her tell him where to find the safe, the combination. She's holding my father's hand, crying, and he puts a pillow over her face and shoots her."

Somewhere in the story, he'd actually felt his own color drain. "You saw that?"

"I saw, I saw. He takes Dad's good watch and the earrings and more from the safe. And I see, I see when he goes to the dresser for Mom's watch. I see his face in the mirror. I see him, and he feels me, looks behind him, but he can't see me. Not then. But part of him knows, and when he goes downstairs, he takes my picture off the wall. He takes it with him. One day he'll kill me, too.

"He's killing me now. I can't breathe."

"Yes, you can. Look at me now. Damn it, look at me. Slow it down, slow it all down. Long, slow, easy now. That's the way."

"It hurts."

"I know. It's going to be better in a minute. Long, slow, easy breaths. I'm going to get you some water. Tell me why you're rubbing your hand that way."

"Acupressure. Headache. Helps."

"Keep that up then." Her color seeped back; her breathing slowed. "Scott, back at the beginning, had panic attacks before a gig."

"I don't have panic attacks."

"You just did. I'm going to get you some water."

When he left, she, mortified, exhausted, let her head fall back. She'd fallen apart. What good did it do to fall apart? She'd let Riggs break her to pieces because she'd let herself fall apart.

When Ty came back, she took the glass. "Thank you. I'm fine now. I'd like you to go."

"Not a chance." He sat, and though she stiffened, took her hand to rub where she had. "Has this been going on all this time?"

"On and off, but not like this. Not this bad. I can handle it."

"Can you?"

"I handled it before you got here, and I'll handle it after you leave."

"You overloaded, and I'm part of the reason. So let me get this out of the way. We're not leaving. I was going to change the locks, put up a fence, security cameras because I thought you'd screwed with us. I don't know what else I was supposed to think—but we'll get back to that.

"I was going to leave. Bray comes first. And you hurt me, okay? What I thought you'd done hurt. I've got a history with this we can get into later. I was going to leave," he continued, "and stuck with that when I thought Bray was just pissed at me for it. If you don't piss off your kid now and then, you're probably not doing a good job as a parent."

He put a hand on the glass to nudge it back up. "Drink a little more. You're still pale."

"I don't need anyone to take care of me."

"Right. Still pissed. Accepted. But after yesterday, after we had our mutual detonation, then I couldn't find him . . ."

The memory of it had him rising, circling the room. "What if he'd headed to Lucy's, walking along that road, no sidewalks, barely a shoulder? What if someone . . . Can't think about it. I've never been so scared, and I hope to Christ I never have a reason to be that scared again. My fault. Mine, because I wouldn't listen to him. Father knows fucking best, so I wouldn't listen to him."

He stopped, looked at her. "Then you brought him home, wrapped in your sweater. Safe. He wasn't just pissed at me. I broke his heart, I pulled everything out from under him because you hurt me. Because I was pissed at you. Because I have a history. I'm not taking him away from his home, from his friends, from a place that makes him so god-damn happy. I was going to change the locks and all the rest, but I'm not going to do that, because I believe you. I might've been a dick, but I'm not a complete dick, and I believe you."

"All right." She set the glass down. "All right."

It wasn't, he thought, but he hoped she would be.

He sat beside her again. "I'm sorry. I'm not going to dump my history, that baggage on you right now. You've had enough. I could take on some of yours. Does Lucy have this?" he asked before she could protest.

She sighed instead. "That night when I woke up, I ran to her room. She was sitting on the side of the bed, crying. She knew, she'd seen—not like I did. She wasn't there like I was, but she knew. It comes down through the women in the family."

"Okay. Can you tell me what happened next?"

Chapter Twenty-seven

What could she say? What could she think? He'd said *Okay* as if she'd told him black hair came down through her family.

Her headache had dwindled to just that. An ache rather than a stabbing pain. When she looked down, she watched his thumb rubbing circles over hers.

Not ready to feel again, she drew her hand free.

"Rem was only ten. We didn't wake him. She called Sheriff McKinnon. Maddy's father. He knew Grammie, and he believed her. Everyone knows Grammie has a gift."

"Everyone?"

"She grew up here, her mother grew up here, and her mother's mother. The sheriff called the police in Virginia. When they went to the house, they found where he'd used the glass cutter on the sliders. They went in, and found them. In bed, holding hands. They loved each other so much."

She shuddered a breath in and out.

"It had to come out how we knew to call the police. The detectives didn't like that much as it turned out, but they sent down a police artist, and I could describe him. I saw him in that mirror as clear as I see you. I could see where he was, sleeping in that motel room bed, with my picture on the table beside him. My mother's watch. I could tell them where he left the car he'd followed my mother home in. A car he'd taken from someone else he'd killed."

"They found him, where you said."

"They found him. He had their things, my picture, the gun, all of it. But the detectives, they came down. He'd confessed, but . . . They still had the death penalty in Virginia then, and he confessed, so they gave him life—two life terms—instead. But the detectives came down.

"The one, Detective Musk, he thought the gift was bullshit, and maybe we'd planned it, or Grammie had, for the money. There was money. Or I had told Riggs to do it out of some sort of ugly rebellion. I just knew too much for it to make sense to him. Grammie got so mad. I've never seen her so mad. Not even when she talked to my father's mother, to say how sorry she was, and my dad's mother said how they were going to bring Dad out there to California, just him, and how they were going to bring us out, Rem and me, for boarding school."

"Well, Jesus," Ty murmured.

"Grammie let her have it good. Our parents made Grammie our guardian in their wills for a reason. That reason. Mom, Rem, me? We were never good enough. We were a mistake, just hicks from Kentucky.

"They didn't even come to the funeral. Not one of them."

She shook her head. "Doesn't matter. Never did. Grammie loved my father like a son, and he always knew it. But the detectives didn't know that, Musk didn't believe that. So I proved it. Like G minor seventh. I told them things, about themselves, their families. Things I could pick up easy enough by looking. It's rude, invasive, but I had to. I had to protect my family. And they believed me, they had to."

"You protected your family."

"I had to. I did. But I made a mistake. Rem said something to the deputy about wishing they'd killed Riggs like he did our parents. And the deputy said prison was worse. Knowing you'd never get out, never be free again. I wanted to see, to be sure of that, so I went there."

"To the prison?"

"Yes, but . . . in my head. I wanted to see, and I let him see me. It was bad, like a cage. Not bars, a door, but a cage, and he was scared, and angry. I was glad of it. But I took that opening to satisfy myself, and I think that gave him one, too. It made more of a connection. I made a mistake."

"You were, what, twelve? And grieving."

"But I went back again, more than once. I shouldn't have used what I've been given for that. I did."

"He killed your parents."

"He killed my parents, and others before them. He corrupted what he had long ago. And he used it. Used it to kill people, to steal, to hurt. He uses it to hurt me when he can. He always will."

"There has to be a way to stop it."

Weary, she just shook her head.

"It's going on sixteen years now. It's hurting him more. Physically. He gets nosebleeds, bleeds from the ears. Gets vicious headaches, but he won't stop. I don't think he can. I'm handling it."

At his long, quiet look, her spine stiffened.

"Today—you called it overloaded, and that's accurate. If that was a panic attack, it was my last. I know how to control things, how to block. My mother didn't like it. It all made her anxious and unhappy. Grammie shut it down when Mom was here. I learned to do the same as a child. Grammie taught me more, a lot more. And after I made the mistake with the boy in college, I taught myself more. Riggs barely got in for years. Then . . ."

She got up. "I need some caffeine, something."

"I'll get it."

"I need to move." She walked back to the kitchen, got out a Coke, chugged some down. "You can have one if you want."

"I do. And then what, Thea?"

"Musk and Howard, the detectives. It was the same day my professor called me in to talk about the game I'd designed for my final. The day I was beyond happy because he was going to send it to his cousin at Milken. I wanted that so much. I was going back to the dorm, get the rest of my things to head home on break. And they were waiting for me."

"About Riggs?"

"No. They wanted my help, and I couldn't say no. I wanted to—I kept all that away since I'd told that boy who turned out not to be worth it. But I couldn't say no. A girl, abducted, the last of a series of them. Just fifteen. He'd hold them for four days, then kill them, dump their bodies, and she was running out of time."

She drank more Coke. "They had her earrings, a pair of her earrings, so I took them, and I opened to her, and I saw her, so scared, so cold.

And I saw him because she had, then the outside of the house and the house number because he had, his car, the plate."

"You saved her life."

"That's what they said when they told me they'd gotten her out, and they'd arrested him. Opening so wide like that, it gave Riggs a bigger crack. But I can't regret it. I don't regret it."

"Have you done anything like that again?"

"A few times, but . . . I wanted this place, not just for Grammie and Rem, though they're the biggest part of it. The people around here, they know about my family, and it's a natural sort of thing to them. I needed that. I wanted a life here, a quiet life here, a place I could do my work.

"I slipped, Tyler, with that damn truck, I just slipped. I wanted him to have what he wanted, and it was such a little thing. Just like Rem swearing because he can't find his wallet—and he's always misplacing it. I'll say, or Grammie will, where he'd left it this time. Just a little thing. And with your scar, all the barriers were down. The only other time, and that was deliberate, way back in the summer, I was starting up the lane from your house and I wanted to see if you watched me. So I looked without turning around. Silly, indulgent, but I swear that's it."

"Was I?"

She gave a little nod. "Boosted my ego, that's all. But I'm careful, and controlled. I don't pry."

"Understood. How's the headache?"

"It's gone. I was too emotional, too upset. I just lost the wheel for a while."

"I'm going to be honest and tell you I wouldn't have believed any of this, not without proof."

She looked away from him, shrugged. "You're hardly alone there."

"I do believe it, all of it. I don't think you're a freak, Thea. I think you're a miracle. Oh Christ, please, please, don't cry again. I don't think I can take it."

"I hardly ever cry, not this way. The happy tears, they're easy."

"I want to know where we stand now. If you'll give what we started another chance."

"You scare me. I don't scare easy, but you scare me because I love you. Who you are here and now, and that scares me."

"I wasn't leaving just because I thought you'd betrayed my trust. I was leaving because I thought the woman I'd fallen for—really fallen for—had betrayed my trust. You're going to have to forgive me for that."

"I've already done that. I'm still scared of you."

He didn't touch her, didn't move closer. He just looked at her.

"I'm probably supposed to say I won't hurt you again, but that's bullshit. People screw up and hurt each other."

"They do. I'm a little tender yet, Ty."

"I can wait. I'm not going anywhere. I'm never pulling that crap on Bray again, or you, or myself. This is home, and I can wait."

"I'm not being—what would it be?—coy about it."

"*Coy* isn't a word that springs to mind when I think of you. I think we both screwed up. I'm willing to take the lion's share of the screw-up and wait. Don't delete the pictures, Thea."

"No, I won't."

"Maybe you could send the dog down this afternoon. Bray really misses him."

"It's mutual. I'll send him."

"Anytime you decide to come down with him . . . Anytime."

When she only nodded, he set down the Coke, stepped back. "He came to you. When I pulled the rug out from under him, he came to you. He loves you. Don't stay away from him because of me. I'll give you space."

When he went out the back, walked across to the lane, Thea got the framed photos from the table where Ty left them. She put them both on her workstation.

She needed time—she understood herself well enough to know that. But it didn't mean she couldn't have those small pieces while she took that time.

That afternoon, much to Bray's delight, she sent Bunk down the lane. Alone, she went into her home gym and worked up a sweat. She'd get stronger, physically, mentally, emotionally. After choosing a sword, she executed a complex kata—then did it again, as she didn't feel sharp enough.

She'd get keener, and cagier.

She ended her time with yoga—more mobility, flexibility, discipline.

If she'd fallen apart, she'd damn well put herself back together again.

As she lay on her mat in Shavasana, she felt her body hum with fatigue. Muscle fatigue, a kind of reward to her mind.

She'd wallowed long enough.

In the bathroom she switched on the fireplace—an indulgence she'd never regretted—lit candles, and took a steam shower. Clean out the pores, soothe aches, let the hard-worked muscles relax again.

Then rinsed off in cool water that woke her back up again.

She dressed, took time to braid her damp hair before walking through her house. Her house, her home, her place. Riggs could only come into it through her mind. He'd battered at her, taunted her when she'd let her emotions rule.

She wouldn't blame herself for it; she was entitled to feel. But she wouldn't be weak, never again weak enough to let him tear at her the way he had.

He knows you're a freak now. He just wants to bang the freak, tell all his friends.

She knew better. She needed time, but she knew better.

You'll never have anyone. Nobody sticks to freaks. You'll always be alone.

She had her family, her friends. Alone? A choice. She would choose.

You're locked in, bitch. And when I come for you, nobody's gonna care. Take yourself out first, get it over with. Get yourself some pills, go to sleep. Leave it to me? I'll make you scream.

"Not in a million years," Thea muttered as she stepped outside to whistle Bunk back home.

But she did need to find a way to end this, to sever this terrible intimacy. Until she found that way, she had to do everything she could to block him out. Find some peace.

While she waited for Bunk, she went to the coop, stroked soft feathers, tended to her ladies.

She'd feed her dog, have a glass of wine, feed herself. Maybe go back to work for an hour or two, make up the time she'd missed that morning.

She needed to dig into the new game, focus on that new project.

She'd sleep on it.

When Bunk bounded up, she bent to greet him. He had an envelope, with a hole punched in the corner, a ribbon threaded through it and tied to his collar.

"All right, whatcha got here?"

She untied the ribbon, absently sticking it in her pocket before opening the envelope.

She found a construction paper card with a red heart drawn over a blue field. She wondered if Ty had guided the little hand to help print the sweet and shaky:

TO THEA

She studied the photo tucked inside first. Bray wearing a zip-up hoodie and mile-wide grin had his arms around Bunk's neck. Bunk looked straight at the camera, his grin just as wide and love lights in his eyes.

Bray had drawn his version of the photo on the inside of the card in many Crayola colors. He'd signed it:

LOVE BRAY

"I do," she said, and sighing, rubbed Bunk. "A picture's worth a thousand words, right? This is the right picture and the right thousand words."

The next afternoon, Bunk came home with a bright yellow dessert plate decorated like a smiling sun. She hung it by its bright blue yarn on the board in her office.

Need time, she thought, but felt her heart slipping. Time she put to good use with daily workouts—get stronger—walks that fed her spirit, and the beginnings of a new game that kept her mind sharp.

When Lucy turned in the lane, she spotted Bray and Bunk in the yard. She debated driving on to Thea's, then stopped. Damned if she would.

When she got out of the car, Bray shouted, "Grammie! Grammie!"

And that was why, she thought as he ran to her, as she had her arms full of boy and dog.

"Got roses in your cheeks," she said, and kissed them.

"I got two stickers in school today, and I can spell dog. D-O-G! And Bunk is B-U-N-K. And . . ."

While he regaled her, and she looked suitably impressed, Ty stepped out.

"Watch, watch what I can do. Watch, Grammie," he shouted as he ran for the play set.

"I'm watching."

She wandered over as Ty walked down.

"It's good to see you, Lucy."

"Good to see both of you." She threw up her hands in amazement as Bray came down the slide backward.

"I owe you an apology, too."

"You don't, but I'll take it. It's between you and Thea."

"I tossed you and Rem in there."

"Well, we do seem to be one big ball of wax." Then she cheered as Bray came down the slide headfirst. "Lord, but that boy is thriving."

"Lucy." Ty put a hand on her arm. "You'd have talked to her. Is she all right? She looked— I know part of it's on me, but since I know the rest now. She didn't look well. Like she's not sleeping, and then the headaches."

"I'm going to go see for myself, but I have talked to her." She lifted her eyebrows at him. "And I have other ways of seeing and knowing."

"Right."

"She's better, by far, than she was. And doing what she needs to do to stay that way."

"This Riggs." He shifted his gaze to make sure Bray remained out of earshot. "I hit the internet, looked up more about the case. More about him. He's a monster."

"He is. I question why such a thing as him was given a gift, but I don't have any answer."

"He killed more people, several more people, and he was only eighteen when he went to prison."

"Thea, still just a child, saw that, saw what he'd done to others. She contacted the detectives, did that on her own, and told them what she saw."

"I should've known," Ty murmured. "There were a couple stories, more sensational sorts, that claimed he could read minds, but there's no mention I found of Thea in any of them. I mean, as the daughter of two of his victims, yeah, but not as a witness."

She looked back at Ty as Bray climbed onto a swing. "Detectives Howard and Musk never brought her name into it. We owe them for that. I'm grateful for that."

"She helped them again—like with that girl who was abducted."

"She told you about that." A good sign, to Lucy's mind. "Yes, she helped them. With or without the gift, but maybe more with it, when someone needs help, you help. A witness—that's the right word for it. When you see, you witness, someone needing help, you give it."

"Not everyone does."

"Those who don't have to live with the choice of turning away. It can be as big as stopping a monster, or as small as telling a little boy where to find his toy."

He shoved his hands in his pockets. "I screwed up there."

She nodded, but patted his arm with it. "Well, you did, darling, but you had a reason. He's playing on that swing over there. I know what it is to protect a child, and to be the only one who can."

"I . . . Thea told me about her dad's family. I just can't understand how . . ."

"They're not his family." Lucy snapped it out. "We're his family. I didn't carry John in my womb, but he was my son the same as the children I bore."

"It made me think about my family. We're not that big ball of wax. When Bray walked into my life, they were shocked. But they were there, right there. They didn't turn away, they embraced. They love him. They helped me when I really needed it—and boy, did I need it. I started off the dad thing on the ground floor, and they were there for us."

"That's family. Are you going up north for Thanksgiving?"

"We're scattered for that. Not that big ball of wax," he repeated. "A resort for my sister, in-laws' for my brother, my aunt in Maine for my parents."

"Well then, if you're not joining any of that, there'll be places at my table for you and your boy."

"That's . . ." He looked up the lane. "I'm not sure Thea would be comfortable."

"She'd say the same as I just did. We'll be a houseful, and kids among that. If you're not traveling, you come to my table. Braydon Brennan, come kiss me goodbye."

"Can I go with you? Can I go see the chickens and the goat and the cow and the dogs?"

"I'm not going home right now." She added a fierce hug. "But I'll be home all day Saturday, so maybe your daddy can bring you to see me and the rest."

"Okay."

She turned, kissed Ty's cheek. "You come see me," she said, and walked back to her car.

She drove up the lane, hefted the box out of the passenger seat. Knowing Thea, she carried it straight into the house.

"Special delivery!"

"Grammie." Thea hurried out of the kitchen. "Let me take that."

"I got muscle to spare. Got your milk and some samples. I'm trying a couple new scents. Thinking spring, as I'm tired to death of holiday scent right now."

She set the box on the kitchen island.

"Did I time it right?"

"Perfect. I just shut down. I needed a head break. I've already got the kettle on."

Thea put the milk in the fridge, started pulling out soaps, candles, lotions.

"You've been busy."

"Just the way I like it. You needed a head break, I needed a scent break."

Thea picked up one of the soaps. "Lemon, but not only."

"Pickled lemon. I was preserving some the other day, and thought: Why haven't I done this? That needs to cure yet. But you've got the liquid, the lotion, the candle. And a pickled lemon salt scrub. It passes muster, I figure it'll go on sale the middle of March."

"Oh, it passes." Thea squeezed some lotion on her hands, rubbed, sniffed. "I say sensational. Sit down, Grammie, I'll make us some tea."

"I could sure sit. I stopped down the lane."

"Oh." Thea turned to choose a teapot, and thinking of Ty, took down Miss Leona's.

"Ty asked about you, if you were doing all right. And I have to say, Thea, it's a relief to me to see you're looking more yourself."

"I'm feeling more myself. A lot more. I lost my grip, but I've got a good, strong hold now. It wasn't just what happened with Ty, though that broke me. But there were cracks already."

"How about the headaches?"

"Clear for the last few days. I've got that grip, and I'm in control again." Pushing up the sleeves of her red sweater, she measured out tea. "He pushes—I don't think he can stop now. But I've shored up those cracks. He's sick, in his mind, in his body, and I honestly think he was pushing that into me. So I'm taking better care of myself."

"I can see you are. Now I can tell Rem just that so he'll stop muttering about giving Ty the what for."

"I should've told him once we got involved the way we did, so I'll take that share of the blame. And telling him, all of it, cleared me out more than I knew I needed to be. So I'm taking better care of myself, and I'll be better prepared for whatever happens. With Ty, with Riggs, with my life."

The last weight on Lucy's heart lifted. "You don't just look like my Thea again, you sound like her."

"Because I am your Thea."

"All right, my Thea, I invited Ty and Bray to Thanksgiving dinner."

"Oh. Wouldn't they go to his family?"

"He says they're scattered, going different places. I couldn't have that man and that little boy alone like that."

"Of course not. So they'll come?"

"He was worried you'd be uncomfortable."

"That's just silly. I— Wait, I need to whistle for Bunk."

She went out and around to the corner of the porch, let out a long, loud, three-note whistle.

Sipping her tea, Lucy smiled when she came back in. "Remember the summer I taught you and Rem how to whistle like that?"

"It took him longer to get it."

"He's younger. Lord, it's nice to sit. I'm going to be running around all day tomorrow. Got a list of errands as long as my left leg."

"Do you need help?"

"No, no." She waved that away. "We all have our work. Now, when are you and Maddy getting that wedding dress?"

"She's got her eye on one online, but I'm dragging her out Monday, she's taking the day off, and we'll see if we find something like it, or she likes better. If we do, we're Zooming with her mother and sister. Do you want to Zoom?"

"I absolutely do. Leeanne wants to see Maddy's dress, and yours, too, before she starts hunting for hers. Though I've already seen a dozen mother-of-the-bride dresses she showed me. Leeanne, Abby, and I are going to make a day of it when she's ready. Fancy ladies' lunch included. I can't think of the last time I went to a fancy ladies' lunch."

"We should do that." When she heard Bunk's let-me-in woof, she rose. "Why don't we ever do that?"

"I guess we're not fancy ladies."

"That's true, but it doesn't mean we can't put on the fancy now and again."

She opened the door, and Bunk wagged his way in. "What is it today?" She untied the ribbon on his collar and held up a flower cut from construction paper, its misshapen petals in every color of the rainbow pasted on a thick green stem.

"Isn't that the sweetest thing?"

"It is," Thea agreed. "Bunk's been bringing home sweet things all week. The card and photo there on the fridge, a smiling sun out of a paper plate. Now this. Bunk gets to play, and I get a thank-you for it."

Lucy just laughed. Her Thea was as sharp as they came—about most things. "Honeypot, that's not a thank-you. Those boys are courting you."

"Grammie." Thea laughed it off. "With construction paper flowers?"

"You'll think of them every time you see it, or that card—or the sun I want to see before I go. That's some very clever courting."

"I'm not—" Flustered, Thea looked down at the flower. "Nobody courts anymore."

"You're holding that sweet flower in your hand right now. He's a patient man, and I wondered if he'd be too patient. Now I see he's just subtle. I like his style. And I'm glad I was right about him all along. Haven't lost my touch."

Saying nothing, Thea put the flower on the refrigerator.

"Made you smile," Lucy pointed out. "And I bet your heart fluttered with it."

"Maybe." Sitting again, Thea picked up her tea. "Maybe a little. Don't look so smug."

"I look smug because I am smug because you look happy."

"Maybe." Thea drank some tea. "Maybe a little. If I let him back in, Grammie, open up to that again, he'll hurt me again."

"Bound to. Hurt you, make you mad as hellfire, make you happy. And you'll do the very same to him. That's love, darling. That's life with love in it. Now, I've got to get home, so show me that sun."

When they walked into the studio, Lucy put her hands on her hips and laughed. "Just look at that face! A card with a heart on it, along with a picture of your dog, his son, a smiling sun, now a paper flower. Darling, you're too smart not to know when you're being courted."

"I'm just . . . confused."

"Love can do that, too." Lucy gave her a hug, a kiss. "Enjoy it."

Enjoy it, Thea thought when Lucy left and she walked back to the kitchen. She ran a fingertip over the paper petals.

"Maybe," she murmured. "Maybe a little."

Chapter Twenty-eight

Thea pushed away from her workstation. She needed to move awhile, decompress. She'd been at it since seven that morning, as she'd waked with a fresh solution to a hitch in her new project.

Now, over three hours later, she needed to let it sit while she didn't.

She'd get a workout in, she decided. Stick to that self-care, since, for now at least, it worked.

Upstairs, she changed out of her pajamas—a side benefit to working at home. Neither Bunk nor the chickens cared if she wore ancient and sloppy pj's when she fed them, as long as she fed them.

Bunk watched her as she put on a sports bra, tank, workout tights.

"I'll let you out first. You take an hour, I'll take an hour. Then we'll settle right back in. It's going to start rolling again once I do," she told him. "Parallel universes are fun stuff. I just need to—not think about it right now," she reminded herself.

She started down again, and Bunk let out a trio of barks and charged ahead to the door.

"Really ready, are you? Why didn't you say so before?"

When she opened the door, he rubbed himself on Ty's legs as Ty stood with an arrangement of rust and pumpkin and gold fall flowers in his hands.

"I was going to leave them on the porch. I was in town, and I happened to . . . Anyway, I was going to leave them on the porch."

He looked off-balance, the vase now tucked in the curve of his arm, his other hand on Bunk's head.

"I figured you'd be working."

"I was just taking a break, letting Bunk out for a while." She reached for the flowers. "Thank you." And making the decision, stepped back. "Come in."

Bunk plodded down the porch steps; Ty stepped inside.

"Men think flowers are a gateway."

"Well . . ."

"They're usually right. And you're lucky I haven't had a chance to replace my kitchen flowers. You can come back. I'm going to make some tea. Do you want some tea?"

"I wouldn't mind. You look good."

She glanced at him as they walked to the kitchen.

"I'm a lot better than I was when you saw me last."

"I'm glad to hear it, to see it." He smiled at the card and the paper flower on the fridge. "Bray'll be happy you put those up."

"Pretty clever, using Bunk as a carrier." After setting the flowers on the island, she turned to make the tea—and her hands reached for Leona's pot. "Whose idea?"

"The first round's on me. But the others, stuff he made in school? He wanted to send them. I'm trying to talk him down to one a week so you're not buried in preschool art. I cop to it being a little sneaky."

"Grammie said subtle."

"I'll take subtle." He slid his hands into his pockets. "Bray misses you. That's a fact, not a ploy. I miss you. I miss the hell out of you, and that's a fact."

Other decisions coming, Thea thought as she set the pot on the counter. "I miss him, and I miss hearing your music, since I'm not outside as much, and have the windows closed."

"When you're ready . . . Maybe we can't pick up where we left off, but I'd like to. Or at whatever point works. Or you could come down with Bunk sometime, and I can make myself scarce, so you see Bray."

"You'd make yourself scarce?"

"If that's what you need, sure. He's just five. He doesn't get it." Then he shrugged. "He's five. He shouldn't have to get it."

"No, he shouldn't. Let's sit down a minute." Taking the initiative, she sat at the kitchen counter. A casual spot, and friendly enough.

She kept her hands busy pouring out tea.

"I didn't trust you with a vital part of who I am. I had reasons, but that part's on me. I'm going to tell you why. I didn't have a need to tell anyone before my parents were killed, and that's mostly because it made my mother uneasy. I'll never know exactly why, but it did. After, being here, it just was. I'm Lucy Lannigan's granddaughter, and that's that. But when I went to college, I decided I'd just be . . . ordinary. Nobody knew me there, I'd study and make new friends, and just be."

She picked up her own tea, then set it down again. "Then there was a boy, freshman year. I told you, late start for me. I told him, and he said awful things to me. Breaking it off wasn't enough, but he said awful things. And he told someone else who said awful things, and someone else who wanted me to perform like some sideshow."

"I'm sorry. Betrayals are tough."

"They are," she agreed. "So I closed off, and kept to myself until that died down. Anyone else I cared enough to be with, I didn't tell. I remember what it felt like to have someone I cared about enough to share myself with turn on me, and I never wanted to feel that again."

She picked up her tea again. "That's on me."

"Private's private. I understand that."

She nodded. "The other part's on you. You never gave me a chance to explain, or to tell you, or try to."

He kept his eyes level with hers. "And I said awful things."

"You did. You said you had a history, and that's why. I'd like to hear it."

"All right." He shifted as if he'd prepared to do exactly that. "I told you about Bray's mother."

"You did."

"It goes back before that. Before finding an underage girl naked in my hotel room bed, and other incidents. You had a boy, I had a girl. We were together through most of high school. She was my first, I was hers."

He smiled a little. "I didn't get a late start there. I loved her, figured it was forever the way you do at sixteen, seventeen. She liked the music. Maybe she thought it was more a hobby, but she liked it. Liked when we had a gig and she could come and watch."

"*I'm with the band,*" Thea murmured.

"Yeah, like that. She didn't like it as much when we started getting more gigs, and she couldn't always come. But we stuck." He shrugged. "Until we didn't. She went off to college, I didn't, but not a lot of drama there."

For a moment, he frowned down at his tea, but didn't drink.

Seeing her, Thea thought, the girl, his first. Seeing himself.

"The way I figure, looking back, we both believed the other would change their mind, right? But instead, we drifted into our own worlds. Then Code Red hit. Recording contract, 'Ever Yours' blasting its way up the charts. I don't know how ready we were for it, but man, we were in it.

"And in the middle of that first rush, the touring, Grammy nominations, she did some interviews. My high school sweetheart, complete with photos of us from back then. And how I broke her heart, dumped her when I got a taste of success. How I hated my family."

"Oh."

"Yeah, oh. I said shit to her when I was battling my parents about college or music. Shit you'd say to someone you loved, you trusted when you're seventeen and feel pressured and misunderstood. You know what I mean. Sorry," he corrected quickly, "you don't."

"I had my moments with and about Grammie as a teenager."

"Impossible. She's perfect." He sat back. "After, she contacted me, telling me they'd twisted her words, took things out of context, but the fact was, she told them things, private things, things that hurt my family. For money, for a little reflected shine. That was the first, not the last. The last, Bray's mother. It's not just me now, Thea. I have to look out for him."

"All right."

"All right?"

"I know what it's like to feel betrayed and sliced open. I know the shields you put up so it won't happen again. I guess we have to figure out what we want to do about it. Lowering those shields, trusting someone not to do that to you again, it's a lot."

"This is a start. Sitting here, having tea. Maybe you could come down and see Bray. I really screwed up his happy when I locked you out."

"I will. I've missed him." Looking at him, she lowered a shield. "I've missed you."

"Thea." He reached across the table; she reached back.

Outside, Bunk barked.

"That's the someone's-coming signal." Sliding her hand from his, she rose. "I need to go see."

Since the signal came from the front of the house, she walked through. And took the time to remind herself she'd be wise to take this slow. Lowering shields, yes, but opening herself again, really opening to him, to her own feelings?

Best to take it slow.

When she opened the door, she saw Bunk greeting Nadine, who walked with her youngest on her hip, another in her growing baby belly, and a diaper bag on her shoulder.

And with fear all over her. A fear so deep, so wide, no shield would have blocked it.

"Nadine." Alarmed, Thea rushed down the steps, ran to meet her. "What is it? What happened?"

"I can't find Adalaide. I can't find her." Tears rolled down cheeks already splotched by them. "I went to Miss Lucy, but she's not there. Help me. Please help me, Thea."

"Come in. Here, let me take him. Come in, sit down. You've walked a long way."

"I looked everywhere. I called and called for her. It's been more'n an hour now, and I don't know how much before . . . I don't know. Help me, please."

"Of course I'll help you." She juggled the baby on her hip as she reached the open front door where Ty stood.

"I'll call the sheriff."

"No, no, please!" Fresh fear leaped into Nadine's swimming eyes. "They could take her away from me. What if they take her away? Thea, please."

"We won't call Will just yet. Don't worry. Sit now, by the fire. Your hands are freezing. Ty, get Nadine some tea, would you? Sit, Nadine. Think of the baby inside you and sit. Sit, and tell me what happened."

"She's mad at me. She's awful mad at me." Sobbing now, Nadine covered her face with her hands. "She wants to go to school, with the other kids, and her daddy says no. She's too young to go off like that, and how I can teach her at home just as well. She won't be five till next week.

"She's just a baby, and I can't find her. She was so mad at me, and I snapped at her. I was tired because Curtis Lee was fussing half the night, and I still feel poorly some mornings, like I did when I was carrying her and Curtis Lee."

"Take that tea from Tyler, and drink some."

"Please, I can't. I just—"

"Nadine, I need you to calm a little before I can help you, so you drink some tea, and trust I will help you. Ty, can you . . ."

"Sure." He took Curtis Lee. "Hey, big guy." He fished his keys out of his pocket, handed them over before sitting on the floor with the little boy and Bunk.

"She was upset," Thea said.

"So mad at me. She wants to go to school, but her daddy—I didn't stand up for her. And her cousin Marlie showed her this paper flower she made in class, and it set her off. This morning she said how she'd walk to school, and how she was gonna go live at her granny's, and I was too stupid to teach her, and I snapped at her how she wasn't walking anywhere, and how she lived here and should be grateful, and should be ashamed saying her mama was stupid. So I wasn't teaching her anything today, and she could go mope and whine in her room."

"Drink some more tea, Nadine."

"I heard her banging around in there for a while. And oh, Thea, I was so mad at her for sassing me that way. I got busy with Curtis Lee and my housework, and when he finally went down for a nap, I lay down with him for just a little bit. I was so tired."

"It's all right."

"But no. No. When I woke up, the house was so quiet, and I felt a draft because the front door was open. She wasn't in her room, or in the house. I went out looking for her, but I couldn't find her. She took her coat, and the little backpack I got her so she'd feel like it was school when we had our lessons."

Her hand shook as she set the cup aside. "Please help me. Please find her for me. She's lost, and maybe she's hurt. I called and called all the way down to Miss Lucy's, but she never answered."

Nadine rummaged in the diaper bag and pulled out a worn pink stuffed bear. "Her granny made this for her right after she was born. She still sleeps with it every night."

"This is fine. This is good." As she took the bear, Thea blocked out the sound of the baby babbling, the keys rattling.

"Nadine, you can help me by staying calm, showing you trust me."

"I do trust you. I do, I do. But—"

"Calm, and you just close your eyes and picture Adalaide back home. Safe and warm, your arms around her. You picture that, and that'll help me make it true."

"I'll try."

Thea stroked the pink bear, felt the little girl cuddling it, soothing herself, talking to it, telling it her secrets. Holding it close, Thea opened.

So angry. Mama sleeping with Curtis Lee because she loved him more.

So defiant. She *would* walk to school. She *would* live with Granny and Paw. She'd make paper flowers and play with friends and have a real teacher.

She walked, and she walked. Along the road at first, but then turned off, onto a trail.

"The road seems too long," Thea murmured. "Mama walks on the trail going down and down, and once we saw a bear, but it didn't bother us any. Tired, though. Stop and rest, then walk. Tired now. Thirsty. Wants Mama now.

"Shh," Thea cautioned when Nadine began to cry again.

"Tired, and sad and hungry, too. Mama has to come. She got a scratch from the brambles, and Mama has to come fix it, kiss it better.

"Rest again. Curl up. Cold."

Thea rubbed the bear, rubbed her hand, then breathed out.

"There you are. I know where you are."

"Where is she? Oh, Thea, where's my little girl?"

"She's just a couple hundred yards from Katie Roster's house, sleeping under an oak tree. You sit!" Thea snapped as Nadine started to leap to her feet. "Do you have Katie's number?"

"No, I—"

"I do, in my office. I'm going to call her, and she'll go get Adalaide, get her inside and warm a lot quicker."

When Thea walked away, Nadine hurried after her. And Curtis Lee toddled behind her calling, "Mama, Mama, Mama."

Nadine scooped him up as Thea made the call. And Rem walked in the front door.

As he gave Ty a long, hard look, Ty lifted a hand. "If you want to punch me, save it for later. We're in the middle of a crisis. A missing kid. Thea found her. She just . . . found her."

"Whose kid? Nadine?" He rushed back. "Adalaide? Sit down, Nadine."

"I've been sitting. Please, Thea. Did she find my baby? Did Katie find her?"

"Katie's girl's home, and she's already going out to get her."

"Katie is easy a mile from our place. She walked so far. She's just a little girl. When I think of what could've happened . . . Do they have her yet?"

Thea held up a finger. "Thank you. I don't doubt it. Katie has her. Rem's going to drive Nadine up right now," she said to Katie as Nadine turned into Rem's arms to sob. "I'll tell her. Yes, I will. Thank you, Katie. Bye.

"She's fine," Thea told Nadine as she hung up. "She told Katie she was hungry because she didn't pack a lunch for school. They're going to give her some hot chocolate and some soup. Rem, you'll drive Nadine up to Katie's, won't you?"

"Sure. We'll talk later," he said to Thea, then looked at Ty. "We'll talk later. I've got this one. Whoa! You eat bricks for breakfast?" he asked Curtis Lee.

Nadine turned from Rem to embrace Thea. "Thank you." She stepped back and swiped her hands over her face. "Adalaide's going to school. Her daddy's just going to have to get used to it."

"Let's go get the future scholar." Rem put an arm around Nadine and led her out.

"With Bray it was minutes," Ty murmured. "I've never been so scared. She's been looking more than an hour. Pregnant, hauling a toddler, scared out of her mind. And you found that little girl. You just . . . found her."

"And she's fine. A few scratches, one tumble where she banged her knee. But she's fine."

"What you did? Thea—it was amazing. And you look a little pale now, so you should sit down."

"It can take a little out of you, depending." But she did sit, back in the kitchen, and drank the tea that had gone cold to soothe her dry throat. "Between Nadine and Adalaide, a lot of emotion."

"You're rubbing your hand again. It gave you a headache."

"Opening like that . . ."

"It's Riggs," Ty realized.

"It'll pass. I just need to settle, and it'll pass."

"You knew this would happen, but you did it anyway."

"Of course I did. When you can help, you help."

"Just like that."

She nodded, closed her eyes as Bunk laid his head on her knee. "It's what I have and who I am. I wouldn't change it, not for anyone. Even you."

A lick of temper burned in his voice. "Who's asking you to change it? I said it before, and I'll say it now. You're a goddamn miracle."

Her hand shook a little when she set the tea down again, and Ty paced.

"I wanted to call the sheriff, and was trying to figure out how I could do that while you were getting her calmed down. They'd've found her, eventually. But meanwhile that woman's going out of her mind. I'd've been going out of mine. And all she had to do was ask for your help, and in minutes, just minutes really, the kid's safe and drinking hot chocolate.

"And you? You're sitting here fighting off that son of a bitch who'll do everything he can to hurt you."

"It's already passing." Faster than she'd expected. It felt as if Ty's anger sucked the pain right out of her.

"That's not the point." He stopped, turned on his heel to stare at her. "It's not the damn point. You took this on knowing he'd find a way in to hurt you."

"What would you have done?"

"It's not about me. No, hold on, it is. It's going to be about me right now."

He paced the kitchen again. "Yeah, it's about me because I saw you do this. I saw you hold on to a handmade pink bear and find a child lost up there somewhere. I saw you reach in and know where she was, and how she felt. And if that isn't enough of a kick in the balls, I see the price you paid for it, the price you knew you'd pay. So I know who you are now, what you have. I don't know how you have it, but I know why."

He shoved his hands into his pockets. "And I'm done. Finished." He yanked them out again. "The whole idea of taking this, with you, step-by-step, slow and easy, seeing how that works? That's bullshit."

"Then you need to—"

"Don't interrupt a man in the middle of a watershed moment. If the only way I can get you is that step-by-step, slow-and-easy, seeing-how-it-works bullshit, I'll give it my best shot. Because I'm not letting go. Goddamn it, Thea, I'm not letting go."

He took a beat, and with it, the anger seemed to drain out of him.

"But since this is about me right now, you need to understand the slow and easy's not what I want. I want you. I want you in my life starting right now. And I'm going to tell you what I, very deliberately, haven't said to another woman since I was seventeen. I'm in love with you. I'm in love with every part of you."

Because she'd stopped rubbing her hand, he sat and took it in his. "You said you loved me. If that's still on the table—"

"You don't clear love off the table like an empty serving dish."

"Then give me a chance. Give us a chance, Thea. If it won't hurt you, dive in. See what I'm thinking, feeling."

When she just shook her head, he took her other hand.

"Then I'll tell you, and I'll hope you believe me. I've never felt about anyone the way I do about you. Because there's no one else like you. I don't want to pick up where we left off. I sure as hell don't want to go backward to see if we can get it rolling again. I want to start right now."

She looked into his eyes, and didn't need to go deeper than that to believe him. "Now's good for me."

"Just like that," he said softly, and brought her hands to his lips.

"I could find a way to live without you, but I don't see why I should. I want someone who understands who I am, and loves me anyway. And here you are."

With their hands still linked, she leaned toward him. With the kiss, that first meeting of lips, everything inside her settled into place. Then she rose, drawing him up so her arms could wrap around him, and his around hers.

"*Now*'s currently my favorite word." She sighed against him. "*Now*'s everything tied up in a bow. Come upstairs with me now. I've missed being with you."

When her phone signaled, she sighed again, glanced down to read the display. "It's Rem. If I don't answer, he'll just come back."

"He wants to kick my ass." Accepting, Ty stepped back. "I don't hold it against him."

She picked up the phone. "How are they? Oh, that's good. That's good. I know you mopped up your share of tears today, but you couldn't have come at a better time. Yes."

She flicked up a glance at Ty. "Ty's still here. No, I don't, and we can talk about all that tomorrow. I'm more than okay, Rem. You've done your good deed today, and I'll let you know when I need you to do one for me. Now stay away. You really want to know why? Because I'm about to take Ty to bed. You asked. Bye."

After ending the call, she put the phone down. "Everyone's fine, and Rem wanted to make sure you didn't need your ass kicked.

"Now," she said, and boosted herself up to wrap her legs around his waist.

"Now's also good for me."

She drove him crazy as he carried her out of the kitchen, turned to walk upstairs. Quick, hot kisses along his jawline, fingers streaming through his hair. A light nip at his throat before her lips came back to his to savor long and deep.

"Something else comes down through my family," she told him. "You should know. When we love, really love, we don't stop. It's . . . for all time."

"I'll take that." He turned into her bedroom. "And I'll give it back to you."

He lay with her on the bed, looked down at her. "Thea in sunlight," he said, "and she shines. I see you."

Because he wanted it loose, he tugged the band out of her hair.

"I've told you, but now let me show you."

As she had his, he savored her mouth. Let time spin out, for both of them. The sounds of pleasure that hummed in her throat urged him to take more. But his hands didn't rush, not yet, as they roamed over her.

He'd missed the feel of her under him, the length of her, the shape of her, the scent that always seemed to cling to her skin. He took time to savor those as well even as she busily unbuttoned his shirt, when he felt her hands run over his chest, then his shoulders to tug it away.

"I want your skin against mine," she murmured. "I've had to not want that. Now I can. I do."

He drew the tank up and away. "You were dressed like this when I saw you dancing with a sword. That was a moment."

He trailed a finger just above the sports bra. Then lowered his head so his lips took the same route.

"I couldn't let myself want you then, too much, because Bray was with me. Now I can. I do."

He peeled the bra away. "More than I knew I could."

She drew him back down to her, let the sensations and the pleasure that wound with them saturate her. This was hers now, the love, the trust, the knowing she'd always dreamed of.

With him she could float on that pleasure, then flash when her nerve endings sparked. Heat came alive under her skin, then a dreamy spread of warmth followed as those artist's hands glided over her.

A laugh bubbled up when he started to tug her pants down.

"They're called tights for a reason."

"That's what I like about them." He exposed an inch, then another. "This may take a while."

Then his mouth glided down her throat, over her breasts, lingering, lingering before roaming down her torso. And down.

No floating now, but flying, catapulted into the sudden storm of pleasure. Her hands gripped the bedding, then released as she gave herself over.

Alive. She'd never felt more alive than in the spinning, whirling now.

And she could take more, she could give more. Desperate to do both, she rolled with him in the sunlight, his heart beating out the moments against hers. It seemed the planes of his body had been made to fit the curves of hers.

She stripped off his jeans and reveled in the feel of him over her, under her as they tangled together.

Love and lust and life surged through her as she straddled him, as she looked into his eyes and saw the same in them.

Here was a dream she didn't have to build.

"Now," she said, and took him in.

He gripped her hips as she drove him toward more, and still more. Above him, her body rose, every line of it somehow perfect. The air went thick as he struggled for some slippery hold on control, enough to let her ride. And ride she did, body arched, arms lifted.

With every rise and fall she drove him closer to the edge.

Then her body shuddered, her hands slid down as if embracing the heat.

He reared up, wrapped around her, and took that final, glorious leap.

Love. She loved, and was loved. And the world changed. The sun didn't really shine brighter, the air didn't really smell sweeter. But it seemed so.

Everything seemed brighter and sweeter when she lay with the man who loved her.

Half dreaming, she opened her eyes, found his looking into them. And his hand covered hers, nudging her circling thumb away so his could take its place.

"It'll pass," she told him.

"There has to be something else, something more. Some way to stop it. Stop him."

She didn't want to think about it now, not now when her world had changed, had opened. But wasn't that exactly why Riggs pried so hard at the block?

"I think there might be. I need to think it through a little more." Because thinking it through terrified her.

"Tell me."

"I haven't worked it all out. And Bray'll be home from school soon."

"You're stalling."

"Yeah, yeah, I am. But I really do need to work it out. I need a game plan, and when I have one, I'll tell you. You love me?"

"I do."

"That's the first step in the plan. I won't do anything without telling you. It's gone. He's gone." For now.

Thea laid her hand on his cheek. "When I have that game plan, I'll tell you. I think I'm going to need your help."

"You'll have it."

Chapter Twenty-nine

She'd approach it as she would any game concept.

When Ty left, taking a joyful Bunk with him, she gave it an hour. If she thought of it as a game, it calmed her.

Because the risk wasn't just losing, having your avatar destroyed. There'd be no rematch, no restart.

All or nothing this time.

But she laid out the concept as any other. She drew herself, she drew Riggs. Then drew others.

While she'd build the game for only two players, others would take key parts.

She imagined the worlds they'd inhabit and started her basic research.

Then she set it aside. Riggs wouldn't dominate her life. And if she succeeded, he'd never come into it again.

Rather than pin her notes and images to her board, she put them in a file. Just hers for now. There would be no beta testing, no consultations.

All or nothing, she thought again, and grabbed a jacket.

As she walked down the lane, she imagined absolute freedom, the kind she hadn't felt since the night Riggs murdered her parents.

Despite him, she'd found happiness, contentment, fulfillment. But what would it be like to have that freedom?

She intended to find out.

Bunk spotted her first, and galloped up the lane. With a cheer, Bray scrambled after.

When he launched himself at her, she swung him up and around.

"I'm sorry I've been so busy."

"No more so busy."

She pressed her face to the sweet curve of his neck. "No more so busy."

As she held the boy, Ty stepped out onto the porch.

This was hers now. It could be hers tomorrow, and the next day and the next. That was worth the risk.

She worked through the week, rejecting scenarios, refining others. Every time Riggs pushed, she pushed harder. Did she worry him? she wondered. Did he have some whiff she planned something?

Let him sniff, she thought as she paced her studio. Let him sweat.

She didn't intend this game to be fair or equitable. She just intended to win.

She studied every pitfall, every obstacle, every move and counter-move. Some, she knew, she'd have to deal with on the spot. Her opponent had a surplus of guile and viciousness.

But he'd fight to kill while she fought to live. She firmly believed that gave her the advantage.

At last, she sat back, admitted she could refine and polish and antic-ipate for months. But when it came down to it, it would be her mind against his.

It had always come down to that.

Time, she thought, for the next step in the process. She called a family meeting.

In her kitchen, Lucy dished up some apple cobbler.

"We haven't had a family meeting in a while," she said. "Let's start off with some good news."

"Sales were up for Mountain Magic in October. And look to be up another five percent in November."

"That's good news, Rem, but I'm not talking business." Lucy scrubbed at his hair before she set down the cobbler.

"It's not just business, though, is it?"

"It's not. I heard Adalaide started school."

"She did," Thea confirmed. "Bray told me, and Nadine came by to see me. She said Jed was so shaken by Adalaide taking off like that, getting lost, he drove her in her first day himself."

"Time something knocked some sense in his head. I was hoping you'd called the meeting to give us some happy news about you and Ty, but that's not the look I see on your face."

"Ty and I are fine, Grammie. More than fine."

"Teenage dream realized."

"Maybe." Thea looked at Rem and didn't mind the smirk. "And the possibility of that's part of why I asked us to meet. I can see that possibility, and if it doesn't fully realize, then it wasn't meant to. But I can see it. Because I can, I can see having a life free and clear. One without Riggs clawing his fingers into my head."

"I thought things were better there."

"They were, now they're not. It doesn't last, Rem, the better doesn't last. It never has. And maybe I have some part in that by taunting him the way I did right after he went to prison. And more than a few times after. But if I helped open the door, it's way past time I not only shut it, but eradicate it."

"How?"

"I'm going to Virginia, to the prison, to see him, face-to-face."

"No, absolutely no. Are you crazy?" Rem's chair scraped the floor as he turned it toward her. "You'll just give him more power. For fuck's sake, Thea, if going there through some mind meld deal started this, how much worse is this?"

Lucy reached out to pat Rem's fisted hand. "I have to agree with Rem on this, darling. The more distance between you, the better. I've often wondered if the fact the prison's only about an hour from here plays into this."

"It didn't stop him when I was at college, or when I've been in New York. He just worms his way in, and it's getting worse. I can't go on this way, I can't keep living this way, just waiting until he finds another chink. Whatever connects us, I have to break it. Finish it."

"How's being in the same room with him going to do that?" Rem demanded. "Even if they'd let you."

"He's allowed four hours' visitation a month. I only need one. If I can't do what I'm set on doing in an hour, I can't do it at all. I'd never be free of him, and I've got to be. So I will do it."

"Do what, exactly?"

"We'll play a game. My game. A head game."

"This is bullshit. Grammie."

"Thea, this isn't something you play with. You don't risk yourself, your mind, your gift like this."

"If not for this, then what?" Frustrated, Thea lifted her hands, palms up. "Do I spend my life this way, waiting, fighting, hounded? I have a chance, a real chance. Ty loves me, and—"

"This isn't about Ty," Rem snapped.

"No, it's about me. About the possibility of that life, one I want, of being free to have it. How can I have it this way?"

She took a moment, then said what had lurked in her mind for years.

"What if I have children? I want children. What if I have a daughter? Do I pass this to her, and does he hound her? How would I protect her from him? He's young, he could live for decades yet. How could I even think about having a daughter he'd torment?"

"Wouldn't you risk it, Grammie? Wouldn't you risk anything to pro-tect a child you want so much?"

Lucy covered her mouth with her hand, then dropped it. "Yes. Yes, I would."

"Grammie."

"Rem. Do you think if I could've saved your mama and daddy, I wouldn't have fought that bastard with my bare hands? If you could've spared Thea from what she'd dealt with all these years, wouldn't you? It's who we are."

She reached across the table for Thea's hand. "I don't want you to do this, but I understand why you would."

"I want a clearer picture. A hell of a lot clearer. Or I swear I'll find a way to stop you."

He couldn't, she thought, but she had to appreciate a brother who'd try.

"I've built a game. It's rudimentary, as it has to form as we go. I can't anticipate his every move or choice. We played before, and I hurt him. I scared him, and, hurt and scared, he backed off for some time. But if I win—when I win this," she corrected, "he won't come back from it."

"That's not a clear picture. And it doesn't explain why you have to go see him."

"Because, Rem, I'll be in charge. I'm free to walk out at any time. He isn't. And he knows it. Because he does, that weighs on my side of the scale.

"I put him there. And I know him. I know his mind much better than he knows mine. Being there shows I'm not afraid of him, and he wants me to be. Needs me to be, but I'm not. He'll be afraid of me before it's done. I have the advantage."

She shook back her hair. "I haven't designed a game with a level playing field. I'll have considerable advantage."

"Maybe I like the sound of that part. Spell it out."

"It's his life. His wasted, miserable life."

They'd get behind her. That's what they did for each other, Thea knew. And they'd worry. Family did plenty of that, but she'd have them with her in mind and heart and spirit.

Another advantage, perhaps the most vital. And one Ray Riggs would never match.

When she turned onto the lane, Bunk began to rumble and wag at the idea of another visit. She hadn't intended to stop now, when Ty would likely be working.

More of an excuse than a reason, she admitted. The idea of going over it all again with someone who loved her exhausted her.

But she had a game plan, and she'd promised to tell him when she did.

So she stopped, and told herself if she heard music, she'd get back in the car and wait until later.

The minute she stepped out of the car, even before Bunk leaped out behind her, she heard it.

The long, loud, defiant guitar riff blasted against the windows of the little house, shot out into the air, and vibrated straight into her body.

What followed was charged, as electric as the instrument he played, and as fast as lightning.

Unable to resist, she followed that rage of sound around to the back of the house.

She saw him through the window, and lost her breath.

He stood outside his studio, worn jeans slung low, a flannel shirt loose and open over a gray tee. And fingers flying over a slick black guitar.

He moved with it, slicing the neck down, swinging it back. His eyes almost burning green as his hair flew.

This, she thought, exactly this, had done her in at sixteen. Not just the look of him—though God, wasn't that enough—but what he could create, what he had inside him that he could send soaring out into the world.

Ready or not.

She had to admit, it sure as hell hadn't lost its power.

Then abruptly, he stopped. She clearly saw him mouth: *Fuck, no. Again.*

He set and ripped out that wild opening riff again.

Sheer admiration made her want to stay, a silent audience of one, but she started to back away.

He caught the movement; his fingers stilled. And he smiled. Guitar still strapped on, he walked to the door and opened it.

"I'm sorry. I'm so sorry to interrupt. I heard the music and . . ."

"I guess it was pretty loud."

"It's meant to be."

"Yeah." He took her hand to draw her in, his fingers still hot from the strings. "And pissed off. Haven't quite hit that."

"It sounded pissed off."

"Not enough."

"No, don't stop." She eased back when he started to take off the guitar. "I was just on my way home."

"I could use a break, let that simmer till it boils. The boil's what I'm after." He set the guitar aside, then scooped his fingers through his hair the way she wanted to. "And I could use some cold caffeine. You want?"

"Actually . . . Yes. I could use some to cool off after that. I was six-teen again for a minute."

He shot a finger at her as he walked to the refrigerator. "Then I'm getting there. Pissed-off rock makes teenagers of us all."

"I don't suppose you're writing it for the longed-for Code Red re-union."

"Maybe."

"Oh, Ty, really?" And laughing, laid a hand on her heart. "There's the teenager again."

"Just some talk about maybe doing a one-shot deal, live streaming it. Maybe next year, maybe in Philadelphia because that's where we started. *Maybe*'s the key word."

"I'm there."

"A lot of logistics to work out. I've got a kid, Scott's about to have his second, Mac would be coming off tour, Blaze has that TV thing going. It's more than just walking onstage and cutting loose. There's those logistics, and rehearsals and production. Anyway."

He handed her a glass, while he settled for a bottle. "Maybe."

And he'd told her about the maybe. That was trust, she realized. She lifted her glass. "Here's to pissed-off rock."

"It made me what I am." He watched her as he drank. "You've got more than that on your mind."

"Yes." She set down her glass, linked her fingers together. "I called a family meeting. I was just coming back from it."

"A family meeting about?"

"My game plan. I said I'd tell you when I had one. I have one."

"Okay, what is it?"

"I'm going to Virginia, to Red Onion State Prison, to meet with Riggs face-to-face."

He started to speak, stopped himself. Walking to the window over the sink, he took a long pull from the bottle. "My first instinct is to say *Don't even think about it. You shouldn't get anywhere near him.*"

He turned back. "Only you can't do that, can you?"

"No."

"But how would this help you? How would giving him the gift of you going to him like this—and it would be for him—help you?"

"That's the right question." Because it was, she sat, breathed away the tension she'd held tight inside. "He'll think it's a gift, enough to excite him at first, let him feel like he's gained the advantage. But it's the opposite. He won't know I'm coming until I'm there. He won't have time to plot and plan. I have. I've thought about this a long time, even made notes, drawn images. I kept a folder, but I kept tucking it away, thinking later, maybe later. Later's now."

"What folder?"

"The game plan. Literally. He's back in seg—segregation. Solitary. It's a room with a cot and a toilet. A steel door with a little window in it, another little window up in the back wall—frosted glass. He can't even see outside. When they put him in general population, he screws up. He can't and won't follow the rules. He's violent—he's made of violence.

"He's spent more than twelve of the last nearly sixteen years in one of those rooms. Twenty-three hours a day. His meals come through a slot in the door. One hour a day, he's cuffed, shackled, and led down to a mesh cage so he can exercise. He doesn't. He paces sometimes, or he broods, or he tries to climb the mesh, screams obscenities."

"You've watched him."

"Yes. Keeping to the edges of things, but yes. I know he reads other inmates as much as he can, and guards, medical personnel. Once he was in population for over six months—and managed to score some opioids. He'd trade what he read for favors, for drugs, for whatever he could get. He even qualified for one of the prison programs, and used that privilege to attack the instructor."

"So back in segregation."

"Yes."

Not exhausting after all, she realized. Telling him, feeling the way he listened, invigorated. It helped her believe she could do it.

"In all the years he's been in there, he hasn't had a single visitor, a single letter. He has no friends, no family who care about him on the outside, no friends or community inside. He's alone."

"He has you."

She closed her eyes and thanked whatever power had placed this man in her life. The man who understood, really understood.

"Yes, and that's his obsession, his lifeline, really. No one else knows him, no one understands what he has, except me. I took away what he wanted most. Not things, but the ability to kill and take things."

"You've got a reason for telling me all this."

"I want you to have a clear picture. Maybe he was born broken, maybe circumstances broke him. I don't care. He became a monster, and he remains one. But his focus has narrowed and narrowed. He can't read others the way he once did because it's so narrowed on me, and so much in him is broken."

"Because it's all on you, it's worse on you. It's hurting you more."

"It is, and I've had enough. Physically he's healthy enough. He could live a very long time, focused on me, hurting me, shadowing my life. I've fought back, Ty, but it's always temporary before the cycle starts again. It's like . . . Nadine's husband hits her."

"Christ."

"Not every day, not every week, but she never knows when something's going to set him off and the fist is coming. She's carrying her third child with him. She doesn't leave. Maybe she fights back, I don't know. But it's temporary. I won't be like that. I'm going to break the connection, break the cycle. I'm going to break him."

"Good. When do we leave?"

The heart that clogged her throat made her eyes sting. "I—"

"Don't say you're going alone. That's not a possibility."

"I already had this with Rem. I can't have him or Grammie with me. My mother came from Grammie, Rem came from our mother. I don't know if Riggs could use that somehow. I don't know if that's part of what ties me to Riggs or not."

"We're not blood, you and me, so that reason's out. And if I know Rem, if he didn't go with you, he'd be right behind you."

"We went around there, too. I said I'd ask you. But I didn't have to ask. They won't let you in to see him. I don't know if they'd let you into the prison at all."

"Then I'll wait outside. But I'll be there. When?"

"I called Detective—no, it's Captain Musk now. Detective Howard retired last year. I asked him to pave the way. It can take a while to get permission to visit an inmate at a supermax. Applications and background checks and paperwork and so on. I asked him to push this through. I'm waiting to hear back."

"Okay. When you do, we'll go. But you haven't told me what this could cost you. I want to know."

"I'm afraid if I lose, he'll get stronger. But I'm more afraid, if I win, using my gift this way, I'll lose it. It's part of me, and the price could be taking it back. I know that's why I kept tucking that folder away, but I'll risk even that to finally be free of him."

"Did you ever consider one of the reasons you have this was because of what you're going to do? You're not going to lose anything." He came around the counter, lifted her off the stool and into his arms. "Start by believing that."

She almost could, standing here where everything was safe and warm and normal.

But better, she thought, to understand the risks, to accept them before entering the field of play.

"It helps me that you're going, and it'll go a long way to easing Grammie and Rem's minds. I want this over before Thanksgiving, when the family's all here. I don't know if that's possible. It could take weeks."

Even as she spoke, the phone in her jacket pocket signaled.

And she knew.

"It's Captain Musk."

"Answer it, Thea," Ty said when she stared at the pocket of the jacket she'd draped over a chair.

Take the next step, she told herself, and pulled out the phone.

"Captain Musk." As she spoke, she rubbed a hand at her throat. "No, I haven't. No, no, I don't. Captain—all right, Phil—yes, I'm absolutely sure."

Her gaze shifted to Ty, and she nodded slowly.

"Yes, I can. I will." As she listened, she reached for Ty's hand, squeezed it hard before she released it. "I understand," she began as she opened the door to let Bunk out when he wagged in front of it. "I didn't expect you to . . ." Her laugh came even as she rubbed her fingers between her eyebrows. "Well, I didn't look, did I?"

Closing her eyes, she listened, nodded. "I will. I'm grateful. It'll be good to see you again. No, not my family, and they're very well, thanks. But someone's coming with me, just for the drive there and back. All right, yes. Oh, and tell your daughter to break a leg with her ballet recital Friday night. It's on your mind, and I always feel I have to prove my bona fides with you, at least a little. Thank you again."

She ended the call, turned to Ty. "Monday morning at eleven. I should be there by ten-thirty, as there are protocols and procedures."

"Monday."

"Visiting hours are Saturdays and Sundays, but they're not treating this like that. Captain Musk and Detective Howard are going to meet me there, guide me through, and they'll be in an observation room while I'm with Riggs. It's so kind of them. Riggs—he'll be cuffed and shackled the whole time in a kind of room where inmates can talk to their lawyers. But there'll be a guard in there with us. I'll have an hour unless either he or I want to break it off.

"I won't let him. I won't let him until I'm done."

"He doesn't know who you are."

"No, but he thinks he does. I don't know what strings Phil pulled, but I'm glad I don't have to wait. I'd drive myself crazy thinking I've waited too long, or haven't waited long enough. It's another now, or now comes on Monday."

Ty took her face in his hands. "You'll kick his ass."

For the moment at least, she believed it. "That's definitely part of the game plan."

She used every skill she had to block Riggs out through the rest of the week, over the weekend. She wanted him frustrated, angry, itchy.

On Monday morning, she dressed carefully and deliberately. The Professional Woman look, her mother would have called it. A pretty, clean-lined sheath in deep blue she'd bought in New York and navy pumps that added a couple inches to her height. She dressed her hair in a sleek, sophisticated twist.

It amazed her just how much the image in the mirror looked like her mother.

"Still miss you," she murmured as she put on the pink diamond studs, strapped on her mother's anniversary watch.

"He'll remember you, both of you. I'll make sure of it."

When she went downstairs, Rem stopped pacing, pulled his hands out of his pockets to stare at her. Lucy stopped playing tug-the-rope with Bunk and put a hand to her throat.

"I forget sometimes how smart you are." Rem shoved at his hair. "You look so much like her."

"Part of the plan. I don't have a pink dress, but I don't think it matters."

Rem took her shoulders. "Don't screw this up. You screw it up, I'll lord it over you forever."

"If that's not incentive, what is?"

When he grabbed her into a fierce hug, she felt it all. The love, the anger, the worry.

"I've got Bunk." Lucy moved into the hug. "And if you're not back before, I'll be waiting for the school bus, and take Bray home with me."

"I promise I'll contact you the minute it's done. I have to leave my phone, everything but my ID, in the car."

"I know." When their eyes met, the flash came that was strength and connection.

"And I know you have my blood, and the blood of all the women who came before me. We are formidable, darling. Don't forget it."

"I won't." She turned when the door flew open, expecting Ty. But Maddy rushed in.

"I tried to get here earlier, but I got hung up."

"Maddy."

"I'm not here to argue with you. Did I argue with you when you told me what you're up to?"

"No."

"And look at you! Duded up right. Your mama's earrings, her watch. I got one more." Reaching up, she unhooked the chain she wore. "Remember when you gave this to me, Miss Lucy?"

"Your sixteenth birthday."

"And what you said when you put it on me?"

"You have the key to unlock your own future."

"That's right, that's just right. You wear this today. Crouch down, Legs. Some of us aren't built like flamingos."

"Thank you, Maddy."

"You have the key." Maddy gripped her, gave her a little shake, then a kiss. "Remember that."

"I will. There's Ty now. Be a good boy for Grammie." She kissed Bunk's nose. "Try to send strong vibes, not worried ones."

They stepped out with her and stood on the porch together as Ty got out of the car.

"That's a look a guy has to open the door for."

He kissed her lightly before she slid into the car. After closing the door, he looked up at the porch. "She's got this. And I've got her."

Lucy took Rem's hand on one side, Maddy's on the other. "That's just what she meant by strong vibes. Let's follow his lead."

In the car, Ty paused at the foot of the lane. "That's a new look for you."

"It'll remind him of my mother. This." She tapped her wrist. "This is the watch he killed them for."

He closed his hand briefly over hers, then made the turn.

"What do you need?"

"To finish this."

"Until then, from me. Small talk, pep talk, silence, tunes?"

"Before that, I want to say this is more than a little surreal. I haven't set foot in Virginia since I was twelve. Now you're driving me there, someone up until about six months ago I only knew as . . . don't let it be weird, but as an icon."

"I can go with surreal. A lot of firsts right here. The first time I've seen you look like you could run a board meeting without breaking a sweat. The first time we've been together in this car without a kid in the car seat. The first time I've driven you or anyone to the big house."

That made her smile a little. "It's funny they call it a house. It's so not. When I looked in the mirror before I left, I saw my mother."

And she's with me now, Thea thought. She'll be with me, as Grammie will, as all the others who came before will.

"This is her professional look. Her 'I'm strong and smart and put together' look. This is what he saw in the grocery store that day and hated because she was strong and smart and put together and wore an expensive watch."

"And that's what he'll see when he looks at you."

"That's the plan. An in-your-face move. That's how I want to begin. And you begin as you mean to go on."

"You don't need a pep talk."

"I'm ready. I'm nervous, but I'd be stupid not to be. I left three people back there who'll worry about me. Grammie will light candles, then keep herself busy. Rem will take his meetings and pace. Maddy'll go to work and check the time between patients. And you."

She turned to him. "You'll worry, and you'll wait. But the worry doesn't mean y'all don't believe in me.

"He doesn't have that, Tyler. He'll be alone, and I won't."

Saying it, saying just that helped settle some of those nerves. "Let's try some not-so-small talk. How's the pissed-off rock going?"

Chapter Thirty

No, it looked nothing like a house, and certainly nowhere life might thrive. The prison consisted of a series of unadorned, low-slung white buildings surrounded by a high, sheer wall.

She'd studied images of it online, had dozens of them in her file. More, she'd seen and felt and smelled what Riggs had seen and felt and smelled. The catcalls and cries, the wild laughter and wilder weeping from inside the blue doors of segregation that echoed constantly. The bright, bright lights through the narrow window in those blue doors.

The hopeless sounds of doors, or bars, sliding shut and the final thunk of locks.

But she'd walk inside there now, and needed to block everything out but Riggs.

"That's Phil, Captain Musk, oh, and Detective Howard. I have my ID, it's all I can take. My purse stays here with you."

"I got it."

Before Thea could open the door, Musk reached it and did it for her.

"Right on time." He held out a hand for hers.

Though he still had a head full of hair, the gray had taken over. She thought it made him look like a captain.

The hug surprised her a little, and warmed her a lot. Then Howard moved in for his own.

"It's good to see you." He drew her back. "I was against this, but now that I look at you? I should've known better."

"How's retirement?" she asked, and Musk snorted.

"So I'm doing a little consulting," Howard said, and flipped off his former partner. "I tried golf, even tried pickleball, and my wife said I was driving her crazy."

"You're too good a cop not to use your skills and experience."

"See that?" Howard pointed at Musk, then turned to extend a hand to Ty. "Chuck Howard— Whoa! Get out of town." Gripping Ty's hand, he shook enthusiastically. "Tyler freaking Brennan. I embarrassed my kids belting out 'Where We Run' in the car back when that one hit."

"You embarrassed everybody," Musk claimed. "Here's a curveball." Musk extended a hand. "I'd like to hear about the windup and delivery, but we have to get started. You're waiting here?"

"I'm waiting." Ty turned Thea to him. "Right here." He kissed her. "See you in a few hours."

Howard took her arm, guided her away. "Now I really want to hear how that happened."

"We're neighbors."

"Is that so? Well, the rest can wait. Got your ID?"

"Yes, in my pocket. Nothing else."

Inside the walls, the world outside vanished. Not an illusion, Thea realized. The purpose.

And worse, so much worse when with Musk and Howard and their uniformed escort they were cleared through the first security door and into a building.

Sudden claustrophobia clogged the air in her lungs.

"It's normal, what you're feeling," Howard told her. "I don't have to be a mind reader, Thea, to know what you're feeling. It's normal."

"Okay." She had to resist the need to rub the cold chill from her arms. "It's okay."

"If at any time you want to call this off—"

"I won't." She shook her head at Musk.

She submitted to the scans, answered the questions, signed the paperwork. She listened to instructions.

No physical contact. Remain seated. Do not approach the inmate.

More doors, more cameras, more hallways.

"Here's your stop." Howard took her hands. "He's already secured inside. Cuffed, leg shackles. They're bolted to the floor. He can't get up. He can't touch you."

Not physically, she thought. But he had other ways.

They both had other ways.

"I understand."

"There'll be a guard inside the entire time. There are cameras, and Phil and I will be watching, also the entire time. We won't be far away."

"I know. I'm fine." More than she'd expected to be. She felt she'd already run a gauntlet, and survived.

"Do what you've gotta do then."

The guard opened the door, and she stepped inside.

She felt it, felt his first stab of shock when he looked up, when their eyes met. Confusion followed it, then slowly, very slowly came the almost giddy delight.

His mouth twisted into a smile.

"There you are! In the fucking flesh."

"That's right, Ray. Here I am."

She walked to the single chair across from the steel table, sat, crossed her legs.

"I'd give you a hug and a big, sloppy kiss, but . . ."

He lifted his cuffed hands to the end of the steel wires that secured him.

"You got all slicked up for me. I'm touched."

"Obviously you couldn't do the same."

The prison blues made his eyes look only more faded. His hair had continued to thin and straggled its way to his shoulders. Pale as a ghost and saggy with it, his face bore scores of deep lines.

He seemed smaller, somehow smaller here, in the room, in the flesh. As if he'd been whittled away by the jagged knife of his own rage.

"Remember this, Ray?" She held up her arm, wrist turned to him, and tapped the watch.

She saw the way his eyes lingered on it. He still had that lust, that toxic envy.

"Bitch got what she deserved. So'd your old man."

"They weren't old." As she spoke, she began to slide in, slowly, like smoke through a crack in the window. "Barely thirty-two when you killed them. Only a few years older than I am now."

"You'll be lucky to make it that long. But you'll do yourself. Put on some weepy girl music, light some candles, fill the tub. Drink some wine. Slash your wrists."

"Now, why would I do that, Ray?"

"Because your life is shit. Everybody knows you're a freak, a fucking freak of nature. I know what you want. A man to bang you, stick kids inside you. Big house with pictures of snot-nosed kids on the wall. Pool in the yard, fancy cars in the driveway."

A little deeper now, just a little, and he didn't know she'd put that image—her family home in Virginia—in his head.

"Is that what I want, Ray? You know me so well. What do you want?"

Those faded blue eyes chilled, like ice over a dying lake.

"To watch you die. Maybe I can't do it myself, but I can watch."

"I think you want that big house, Ray, and the pool, the fancy cars. Fancy watches like this." She drew his eyes and attention back to it, turning it so the stones glittered.

"You never had that. Just an ordinary house, an ordinary life, nothing special. But you were special. You knew you were so very special. Your parents were afraid of you, weren't they? Not so much because you knew things, though they'd've prayed that away if they could have. But it was the things you did. The awful things. To stray cats, to birds, to other kids, especially the ones smaller than you."

"You don't know shit about my life."

"But I do, Ray. I've read your life like a book. One I can't wait to toss in the trash heap, but I read it, Ray. Start to finish."

"There ain't no book." He shrugged his shoulders as if trying to dislodge a weight. And his fingers began to drum on the steel table.

"But there is. It's a sad, ugly book, but I've read it through. Why don't I pick a chapter now? Remember this?"

She pushed, and hard. He actually jerked back in his chair as if she'd used her hands.

He was eight on a hot, sticky day, sitting in the stupid, half-assed tree house his father had built for him.

But it wasn't so stupid because his mother never came up here. Afraid of heights, afraid of him.

Afraid of everything.

She always called him down when she wanted him for something. Mostly something he didn't want to do.

Chores, church, visiting his decrepit old grandparents.

Up here, he did what he wanted.

He liked smashing flies, and ants. He'd learned if you dropped some sugar or honey on the floor, those ants came marching. Then you could stomp the shit out of them.

He caught lightning bugs at night and peeled the wings right off them. Lights out!

And butterflies would tear like paper if you did it right.

He'd hidden an air rifle up here. He'd stolen it because he was good at stealing and he'd *wanted* it.

He should have what he wanted.

If you were quiet enough, got close enough, that air rifle would do a number on a bird.

The neighbor's cat liked to roam the neighborhood like he owned it. He'd been easy to catch and lure into the sack with raw hamburger. Maybe he'd gotten pretty mad about that, but a good whomp against a tree—not too hard, just hard enough—quieted him right down.

Now, up in the tree house, he opened the sack. Some blood, and that excited him, but old Tom was breathing. Insects died so easy. He wanted something that took more, lasted longer.

He had his father's hammer and one of the penknives he'd stolen, since his parents wouldn't buy him one. He couldn't decide which to use first, then the cat started to stir.

He lifted the hammer. He'd break one of its front legs. Let it try to roam around and climb trees like he owned the place then!

As he lifted it, Thea spoke.

"Don't do that, Ray."

The hammer slipped out of his hand as he jumped to his feet. A little boy with a killer already alive in his eyes.

"Who are you? How'd you get here?"

"You know who I am, Ray." She wore workout tights now for easy movement, a snug tank top, her hair in a braid.

She'd kept the watch and earrings, the key. She wanted him to see them.

"Don't hide inside a kid. And don't think I won't kick your ass if you do. Because I know who you are."

It was the man who reached down for the hammer, and the man she kicked straight out of the tree house door. As the man in her mind hit the ground with a bone-snapping thud, the one across from her in the room jolted.

"First round, you lose." She climbed down. "And it's your leg that's broken. Bet it hurts. And look, Tom's a little dazed, but he'll be fine. Heading for home."

"This didn't happen. It didn't happen."

She leaned down close. "I'm making it happen. Time for another chapter, Ray. Better get up. I'm getting away, too."

In the prison room, he tried to choke out words, but she dragged him under again.

Sixteen now, pale, rail thin. He'd already left home. Goodbye and fuck you. One day he'd go back, burn the house down with them in it. Try to send him to a shrink? Talking about military school or church camp and all that bullshit?

He knew what they thought. He always knew. He was better than them, than anybody. And he could have whatever he wanted. Take whatever he wanted.

Like this girl he'd found on the street. Give her a bed for the night—in a dump, but he had to stretch the money for now. All she had to do was put out.

She hadn't argued.

Now he had her naked and he pumped and pumped and pumped himself into her. She made all those noises like they did in porn videos.

But he couldn't, just couldn't. And he heard her thinking how he couldn't, felt her rolling her eyes, smirking, faking the noises because she needed a place to sleep.

As he went limp, his hand slid up toward her throat.

He'd kill her. Time to graduate. He wanted her dead so he'd make her dead. Strangle her, beat her bloody. Stuff her in the closet and take off. Paid for two nights, he'd be smoke before anyone found her.

And no one would care.

"I care, Ray."

Breath fast and short, he scrambled up. "You're not here."

"Right here, right inside that sick head of yours. Let's get you dressed because I really don't want to look at that pitiful thing."

She put him back in prison blues because that's all she'd give him.

Then she bolted out the door. "Come on, Ray, put some life in the game!"

She felt the wind, cold, icy, against her face as she ran. She heard her feet pound on the pavement as she ran for the street.

"I knew you'd be slow." Timing it, timing it. "Such a loser."

She dashed across the street. Screaming, he charged after her. The car hit him head-on, sending his body flying up before it hit the ground.

As the cars she'd built in faded away, she crossed back. She walked back to where he lay in a heap, trying to suck in air from lungs collapsed by broken ribs.

"You should look both ways, but you're so goddamn stupid."

"This isn't real."

Because she needed him to feel rage—helpless rage—as much as the pain, she leaned down close.

"I bet the pain feels real. You're dying, Ray, right here in front of me. But I'm going to save you because we're not done. You get another chance."

She felt him trying to push back, push her out. She wouldn't have it. "My game, my rules," she said, and changed the level.

"They're sitting there, staring at each other."

Howard shook his head. "I don't think so, Phil. Something's going on. We just can't see it. Except . . . he looks shaken."

"He keeps jerking. I don't get it. But she's following the rules. She's got the rest of the hour."

* * *

The big house had an alarm system, but Riggs plucked the code right out of slutty trophy wife's head when she pulled up. She kept saying it over and over—because they'd changed it, and she kept forgetting.

On this moonless night, after he cut through the glass on the atrium doors beyond the pool and outdoor kitchen—like they cooked—and into the big kitchen with its vaulted ceilings, he walked straight to the control panel and coded in.

He thought what he always thought as he walked through the house. How he deserved all this, and they didn't. How they needed to die so he could have what he deserved.

He walked up the wide, curving stairs, ran his gloved hand over the shining banister, looked up at a big chandelier.

He bet that shined, too, when they turned it on.

He could see it if he wanted, see it shining and sparkling.

But he couldn't shake the feeling something was off. Just off. How did he know how everything looked before he saw everything?

Because he was special, he reminded himself. He had something no one else had, so he could do whatever he wanted, take whatever he wanted. Kill whoever he wanted.

He walked straight to the main bedroom because he knew, just knew exactly where it was.

Like he knew the old man would be snoring away, and the woman wore a silk sleep mask. Roses on the table where they had chairs. Long curtains over all the windows.

He'd just slit the old man's snoring throat and get that out of the way. Then give the slut wife a couple of good pops to wake her up until she told him where to find the safe, the combination.

But he already knew. He knew there were two safes, his and hers. Like they had two dressing rooms. He knew she'd beg for her life, tell him everything, and beg him not to hurt her.

His vision blurred; the room faded in and out.

"Having some déjà vu, Ray?"

For this level she wore leather, black pants, a leather vest, a sword at her hip.

"You're not here. You weren't here. I killed them, and I took what I wanted."

"You did. So much blood, right? That was exciting, but it made too much of a mess, even for you. But I am here, and you won't kill them now because this is my world."

At the ripple of pain over his face, she smiled. "Got a headache, Ray? They're a real bitch, aren't they?"

"I'll kill you."

He lunged with the knife.

She sidestepped, pivoted, then plunged the sword through him.

"Little knife, big sword. I win!"

Blood dripped through his fingers as he groped at his midsection. "No. No. This didn't happen." But he stumbled, dropped to his knees.

In the prison room, a blood vessel burst in his left eye, threading the white with red.

"It's happening now. It hurts, doesn't it? Dying can hurt. You're running out of lives, Ray."

"I'll get out. I'll get out, and make you sorry."

"Here's the thing, Ray. I'm never going to let you out."

"You can't keep me here."

"Who's going to stop me?"

He had to believe it, for her to win the game, she had to make him believe it.

"Every time you try to get out, I'll just kill you again. Every time. It's your life, and you're stuck in it, mind and body now, so get used to it. I'm going to skip a few levels, because I'm getting bored. And to be honest, you're starting to look ragged."

She felt ragged with the effort of maintaining the grip on him, and on her own emotions. A line of sweat, cold, so cold, slid down her back.

She'd use even that, she determined. She had to be cold. Cold, controlled. Merciless.

The last level, the final push, required all she had. She slid a hand up to close it over the key around her neck. She held the key to unlock her own future, she reminded herself.

And took them both into their mutual past.

* * *

He'd stopped for some road snacks. Gonna head to the beach in his fine new car, get himself some sun. But there she was. Rich bitch with her fancy watch. Thought she was special in her fancy pink dress.

Blue dress? Pink dress? How did the color keep changing?

His vision wavered for a second, brought on a sudden, spiking pain behind his eyes. Something told him to walk away, but he wanted that fucking watch. More, he wanted to kill that rich, better-than-you bitch.

He walked away, but he waited, waited in his fine new car, then he followed. Everything so familiar . . . it gave him the heebies. Familiar because he knew what he was doing. As he sat and watched the big, fancy house, he beat a fist on the steering wheel.

He knew what the fuck he was doing. He'd done it all before, he'd do it all again.

Get some eats, bide his time. He could just head south, but he wanted that watch and the money, the shiny things inside that big house. He wanted the rush of the kill.

And that face, the bitch's face. He knew that face, wanted to smash it, obliterate it. Had to.

The toothy, zit-faced boy who handed him his food said, "Have a miserable day, asshole."

"What the fuck did you say?"

But the boy was gone, the food was gone. Riggs stood in the dark, glass cutter in hand. The hand shook.

Then he remembered why he was here.

His back itched the way it did when someone watched him. But when he looked around, he stood alone in the night. No one could stop him from taking what he wanted.

He went inside, put the glass cutter in the duffle, pulled out the gun. The gun he'd taken from a rich bitch he'd killed who'd lived in a big house. Even bigger than this one.

Hate, already rooted, sprouted its thorny stems, opened its poisonous blooms as he wandered through.

The pictures stopped him. He would have sneered, but that face, the girl, stopped him. She looked right at him, looked into him.

The girl. The woman. The girl.

The spike of pain struck again. Something warm trickled out of his left ear. He balled a fist, and barely stopped himself from smashing it into that face.

Have to be quiet, Ray, someone whispered inside his head. *Don't want to wake them up.*

"Don't want to wake them up," he muttered, and continued up the steps.

And there they were, the rich assholes who had what he wanted. What he'd have.

"You're wrong, Ray. You'll never have what they had."

Thea walked to the foot of the bed.

"Look at them, Ray. Really look. They never hurt anyone. They had such good in their lives. They loved each other. You never had that, did you? Someone to love, to love you back. And you never will."

"This is bullshit. You're bullshit. They're already dead because I made them dead."

"That's right, Ray. You took their lives. Congratulations. I wonder, though—please tell me what you think—would you have done it, would you have done all this if you'd known it would cost you your life?"

Turning toward him, she put him in his cell, just for a moment, just to make him feel that isolation.

To make him know it as a little blood dribbled from his nose.

"If you'd looked ahead and seen yourself sitting in that little room, hours and hours, days and days, years and years? Would it be worth it to you knowing a little girl would see to it that you never walked down a city street or country road again? Never ordered another pizza or bought an ice cream cone? Never went to a baseball game or drove a car? If you'd known I'd make sure your life was four walls inside more walls?"

"I'm not going back. I'm out. I told you I'd get out. I'm standing here, and they're dead."

In the bed, her parents lay, pillows over their faces, hands linked. And it tore at her heart.

And it made her stronger.

"No, I can't change the past. I can't bring them back. There's no remorse at all inside you, is there?"

"Fuck remorse. I'm out, staying out. And you're dead."

He lifted the gun; she lifted her sword. And as he swayed, eyes jittering, she sliced his hand at the wrist.

In the game, he screamed, and his screams echoed off the walls of segregation as he threw himself against the blue door with the narrow window.

In the prison room, Thea let out one shaky breath. "All those choices, all along the way. You always made the wrong one."

Because they wanted to shake, she gripped her hands together in her lap as she watched his face sag, watched blood trickle from his nose, his ears.

She watched his eyes, those pale eyes, go blank.

"But you made the choices. Now you're locked down, locked in, mind and body."

When that body began to convulse, she spoke as calmly as she could. "Guard, I think he's having a stroke."

She sat as the guard rushed to Riggs, as he called for medical. She could see Riggs slumped in the bolted chair, and she could see him screaming in his cell.

When they escorted her out, she didn't look back.

Howard put an arm around her waist. "Let's get you out of here."

"Yes, please."

Musk didn't speak until they stood outside the walls.

"What the hell happened?"

"He made bad choices."

"The two of you sat there staring at each other for a solid half hour."

"Is that all it was? It felt longer. He was given a gift, one he abused, corrupted, defiled. I took it away."

"Are you okay?" Howard asked her. "You're white as a sheet."

"I will be. Thank you for being there. It helped me knowing that. I just want to go home now."

"Okay, honey."

Musk started to speak again, but Howard sent him a sharp look, shook his head, and guided her to where Ty moved quickly toward them.

"We're going to turn you over. You stay in touch."

"I will. If you ever need my help . . . anytime you need my help."

"We'll both hold you to that. You have a good life, Thea. You deserve one." He gestured his former partner away.

"Jesus Christ, Chuck."

"Put it away, Phil. It's way above our pay grade. Just put it away."

Ty rubbed her hands between his. "You're cold. Your hands are cold."

"I need to get away from here."

"Okay. I've got you."

He didn't speak again until they drove away, until the prison walls receded.

"Water bottle there. Drink some."

"In a minute. I have to text home."

"I texted Rem and Lucy the minute I saw you come out. Kick back. Close your eyes."

She did just that while he gave her the quiet.

"You haven't asked what happened."

"You'll tell me when you're ready."

"I . . . I broke his mind. I pushed and pushed until—"

"Thea." He reached for her hand, held on to it. "His mind was already broken."

"I smashed what was left of it. I knew he'd make all the wrong choices, all the wrong moves. I took him through points in his life where he could've chosen differently, but he didn't. I knew he wouldn't. And each time I hurt him, made him feel the pain, made him face the consequences until his mind couldn't cope."

Laying her hand over the watch—*For All Time*—she opened her eyes.

"He had a stroke, and I locked what's left of his mind inside that cell, behind that blue door. He won't come back from it, escape from it. Wherever they take him, his mind's trapped there inside that cell, with no gift to lift it out because I stripped it away."

"Good."

"Ty."

"Stop. I'll give you two minutes to feel guilty, and I'm saying you've used those up already. So no more, Thea. He's an evil son of a bitch, a sick, evil son of a bitch. You helped put him in prison, where he belongs, but that didn't stop him from coming after you. So you did. You stopped him. Now his mind's in prison, where it fucking belongs."

He let out a breath, shook his head in wonder. "I admire the living hell out of you."

"Oh God."

"What number am I thinking of?"

"Ty—"

"Come on. Show me your stuff."

She feared to, feared to find herself empty. But he took her hand again. Took her hand, and smiled at her.

Her quick sob ended on a laugh. "Trick question. C major diminished seventh isn't a number."

"Just can't fool you. What you have helped you protect yourself. Your spine did the rest."

He glanced over. "Better."

"Yeah, or starting to get there."

"Good. I hope I have a way to help you cross the finish line. We're going to take a little detour."

"Oh, but—"

"Do me a favor. I had a lot of time to think about this detour, find a place. I texted Lucy earlier, let her know we'd take the long way home."

He pulled off the highway, took some back roads. When he pulled up, she stared straight ahead.

"A playground?"

"Hey, got the mountains, a nice water view over that way. Pretty quiet, too, this time of day. And a picnic table, since you're not dressed to go hiking around. Let's go."

"It's pretty," she agreed as she got out of the car. "And quiet. But it's pretty and quiet at home, too."

"Couldn't wait. There's something I want you to hear. Have a seat."

He pulled out his phone. "I've been trying to decide the best time to play this for you, and realized when I was waiting, it had to be now."

He cued up the song, hit play.

She smiled at the opening chords. She'd heard them flowing in the air.

I see her in sunlight, and she shines.

When she heard the words, his voice, she knew. When her eyes met his, everything else faded away. As her heart filled, the tears came. From gratitude.

"I called it 'I See Her,'" he said when the last chord drifted away. "I see you, Thea, and I love everything I see. It's the first song I've recorded in a long time. I recorded it when I went to Philadelphia right before Bray's birthday. Maybe that's why I reacted the way I did when I thought you didn't have real feelings for me. Because I was already in love with you."

"I've loved you for years. I think the reason I fell so hard at sixteen, the reason I could never feel quite that way about anyone else is part of me knew. Part of me always knew I was yours. I was yours, Ty."

"I want to be yours." He reached for her hands. "I come as a set."

"I love him."

"I know."

"Maybe you could hold on to me now. It's been a hell of a day."

Rising, he drew her to her feet and held on.

"It's a beautiful song, Ty. You couldn't have picked a better time to play it for me."

She lifted her face, met his mouth with hers in the sunlight, with the autumn breeze whispering through the pines.

"How do you feel?"

"Loved, free, grateful."

"Sounds like a good time to bring up this other thing. I'm going to record more, when the mood strikes."

"That's wonderful."

"But Redbud Hollow doesn't run to music studios. I can change that. I'm going to change that," he corrected, "and build one."

"Did I say wonderful?" Laughing, she hugged him hard. "What's several levels up from wonderful?"

"I like stupendous," he decided. "So I'm going for that. But then if I want to pull in other artists here and there, I need a place to put them."

"There's the inn right in town, and—"

"Yeah, a couple places, but I'm thinking Knobby could work some magic with the house. Add on, fix up. Plenty of land for it. It could be an option for artists to bunk where they work."

"That would be—I'll go with stupendous, too—but I can't imagine you'd want all those people basically living in your home, even for short periods."

"No, I wouldn't want that. That's why we'd need to move in with you."

"I . . ." After she blinked, her mind went blank. "Oh."

"Need a ring first?"

"A . . . I have to sit down again."

"No, you don't. I've got you. Take us on, Thea." He touched his lips to hers. "Take us in. We love you. Let's make a family."

Speechless, she cupped his face in her hands.

"Read my mind if you need to," he told her.

"No. No, I just need a minute. You've turned one of the hardest days of my life into one of the most beautiful. This is what I want, everything I want, and now, now I can have it. If Bray's okay with it."

"That's exactly what he said when I talked to him about it last night."

"You talked to him about it?"

"We come as a set," he reminded her. "He said okay. And wanted to know if Bunk could sleep in his new room. There was mention of moving the play set. And pancakes."

"How could I say no to any of that?"

Her life, she thought. She had her life, and she'd unlocked her future.

"I love you both." Looking into his eyes, she let the happy tears come. "I'll take you on, I'll take you in. We'll make a family. But."

"Uh-oh."

"We have to have two more children."

"Two more."

"When I wrote in my journal about you, and how we'd meet someday, somehow, and you, of course, would fall completely in love with me. We'd get married and have three children."

"Where's this journal?"

Laughing, she lifted her face to the sun. "You'll never find it."

He kissed her forehead. "Two more. We'll be good at it. And Bray? He'll make a damn good big brother."

He lifted her off her feet, swung her around. "Let's go home and get started."

But they held on to each other for another moment in that gold-tinged sunlight. And holding him, she didn't need to look to know she hadn't just unlocked her future.

They'd unlocked theirs.

It waited for them in the hills and forests of home.

About the Author

Bruce Wilder

NORA ROBERTS is the #1 *New York Times* bestselling author of more than 230 novels, including *Inheritance, Identity, Nightwork, Legacy, Hideaway,* The Chronicles of The One trilogy, The Dragon Heart Legacy trilogy, and many more. She is also the author of the bestselling In Death series written under the pen name J. D. Robb. There are more than 500 million copies of her books in print.